RENDEZVOUS

AT

LOCK 6

HELEN VAN ROOIJEN

DEDICATION

For Martin.

ACKNOWLEDGMENTS

Cover design and original painting by Martin van Rooijen,
cover assist by Matthew van Rooijen.
Edit assist by Rowena Holloway, Matthew van Rooijen, Christine
Houweling, Margaret Vivian, Martin van Rooijen and Eyre Writers.
Mary Gudzenovs for preparation of book.

Chapter 1

Officially the camp didn't exist.

The young soldier flipped his killing knife. The blade he'd called, with a naive soldier's wit, his Toy. It spun and quivered into the stained wooden plank set between two empty oil drums near the perimeter wire fence. He grinned and glanced down to the overseas welfare fruit that somehow, most days, got past the road blocks and the rebel guns to the refugee camp.

As the youngest private in the guard squad he was responsible for the distribution of this fruit to the camp children. This was fine by him he liked children, even these wretched kids. Already his steel had ripped the tough skins off hands of under-ripe green bananas; peeled the pitted skins from two dozen green apples, and quartered one of two ripe pears. The other pear he left untouched.

'OK, then,' he said. 'Who's ready?'

At his signal the waiting children surged forward jostling each other for position. Somehow they could still laugh and shout though, like extra sets of lashes, iridescent flies clung to their eyes. Crawled up their noses. Most ignored the insects as shoulders nudged shoulders and the children's shouts changed to entreaties aimed at the young soldier. Their eyes stayed fixed between the piles of cut fruit or darted up to the soldier's face.

'Give me! Me mister! Me!' They yelled. 'Give me… please!'

The words were flung at him; their total soldier vocabulary spent. The last word was drawn out as they had learned that this soldier liked the word 'please'.

As the children moved dust swirled about their thin knees to lodge on the filthy scraps of rags they wore. They licked pale lips in anticipation as the dust settled on the colourful fruit. It began to resemble the refugee camp. Dry, dirty and worn out.

All the children moved, except two.

The girls were a smidgen cleaner than the rest. The elder girl, ten or eleven years old, pushed back her long dark hair. She had a white streak, as if someone had dragged a finger full of paint along her forehead scalp and the swatch of pale hair fell forward to frame her face. Maybe she'd been wounded in the conflicts or maybe it was genetic, but it marked her as different.

Her bearing gave her a further presence.

She stood still and quiet, a metre or so off to one side, shielding her fairer sister behind her. They were a demarcation point away from the jostle of the other noisy children. Her dark eyes switched from the soldier's face to the large green pear.

'Get on with it boy,' the sergeant growled, 'we haven't got all day for you to muck about.'

The soldier's blade finally cut into the last pear. It bared the white flesh to expose the black seeds at the core. The girl's brown eyes stared at his face. She waited while he gave out the pieces of apple, other bits of the pear, oranges and darkening banana to the pushing throng of other children.

Finally part of the pear remained. Held back.

The others had grabbed, gobbled the fruit into their mouths, and then they stood back. Waiting.

Hoping for more fruit, a piece of the remaining pear, but aware that there was yet a small drama to be played out.

They waited. Watching him.

Turning to watch the two orphan girls.

The soldier glanced back at the relaxed soldiers behind him. This was the highlight of the day until the beer ration was given out at dinner in the military mess tent.

'Hey girl! Yer want this?' the young soldier said. There was a smile in his voice and he raised an eyebrow to the girl as he held four pieces of the pear within the precincts of his knife blade.

Only then she pushed forward and thrust out her hands to take the fruit from the bench plank. With care she separated two pieces for her younger sister then turned back to the soldier. She tossed her hair in apparent thanks and her eyes now returned to his as she bit through the crisp skin into the warm flesh of the pear. A small dribble of juice escaped her mouth and her tongue flicked pink to catch it.

The soldier's gaze travelled from her face down her thin frame to where buds of breasts were beginning to push against the fabric of her blue shift. She noticed, with the innate knowledge of emerging womanhood, and slowly pulled her shoulders back. Without taking her eyes off his she shooed the green flies that sought to settle on the juice around her lips. She growled a warning in her throat and elbowed away a boy who tried to snatch a remaining morsel of fruit from her sister's hands. The boy retreated and the fair girl gulped down her pear un-chewed.

Slowly the older child swallowed the last bite and spat away a seed. Aware that she was being watched by this soldier and the men standing behind him, she licked her hands clean in a slow glide from each wrist and across each palm to the tips of her fingers.

He watched and his stance shifted as his body, unbidden, responded and stiffened to her actions.

She saw the tense movement and her mouth curved in a slight smile of power. She had seen before that this movement, initially innocent on her part, could affect the fair haired guard. Her challenge, enacted each day, could get the fruit she wanted for her sister and herself. The small figure shrugged a shoulder then, hustling the other girl before her, she turned back into the dirty shuffle of the homeless behind the wires.

As before the youngest private soldier was ritually vanquished.

He smiled in rueful acknowledgment as his soldier friends jeered and clapped. The sergeant echoed his men's attitude; but his eyes were hard towards the girl, calculating.

At that moment the attack came from within the camp.

An attack spawned by fighters who watched the daily ritual of the fruit, and the clump of diverted soldiers with their dogs. Rebels with smuggled arms. There was a warning shout, perhaps directed to the children, and some dropped down to the dirt.

Machine gun bullets shuddered in an indiscriminate barrage through the huddling children and cut down the scattering soldiers. Cut down the men with slower reaction times.

The novice soldier should have died, but didn't.

Shock and pain tore through his body above his umbilicus as one bullet unzipped his flesh from left to right. For a moment his wrecked shirt held in his glistening small intestines before they spilled out over his belt buckle. There was little blood.

His own knife took life in his frantic grip. It sliced off the whole of his little finger of his left hand with the ease that it had cut through the flesh of the pear. He doubled over grabbing his guts.

Cursing, screaming, what was left of the soldier squad returned fire.

The two girls should have died, but didn't.

The younger was hit. A bullet tore through her developing womb to exit beside her spine; she heaved and twisted as her blood dribbled into the dust. A slow puddle of red that pushed out boundaries of brown dirt. A fade-out of unconsciousness tunnelled her pain away.

The other child shrieked as lump of steel spun in below her right breast. Another fragment ricocheted into her thigh. After her first startled sharp scream she did not cry again and she lay awake. Tears escaped from her eyes but those same eyes followed every movement around her until the sharp engagement was over. Her eyes would follow the flight of crows disturbed by the guns until she too lost awareness to shock and numbing pain.

The sergeant and the corporal survived; injured with minor wounds but each man had been able to fight back. Later they tended to their injured men, and in vengeful rage, they worked out a sequence of events to report in official military communiqués and to the damning enquiry that would follow.

Many of the wounded children had died before the military medivac helicopters arrived two hours later.

As the wounded soldiers were loaded shells thudded around them, whistling in from hills kilometres away. The unarmed choppers attracted fire like dragonfly magnets.

In haste, and against orders, a young medic bundled the fair girl up with the soldiers. He was raw to the arena of civilian refugee deaths and he refused to leave the bloodied rag doll to die alone. In time he would mature to the everyday carnage and leave the civilians. A man of compassion and love; his family would raise this first child he had saved.

The other girl he triaged as dead and left her with the abandoned refugee corpses.

The few adults, women who did not matter in the realms of civil war, screamed abuse at the soldiers as the helicopters departed. The women had sworn the same curses at their own fleeing fighters. They wailed their grief and waited, huddled until dusk, when Medicines sans Frontier's contingent came in trucks to tend to the camp wounded and to bury the dead.

The doctors were surprised to find the dark haired girl still alive. They took her but held little hope that she would survive her injuries.

Or the night.

As darkness spread shadows from the western hills, to tuck an enclosing shroud about the camp, a pair of hawks circled overhead searching for prey.

Nothing human moved below.

The camp was deserted as the few people left after the fire-fight had fled once again out across the plains to the hills and into hiding. Camp dogs scuffled in the darkened blood and gore until the stains were one with the sand and dirt.

By midnight the stars shone bright as a discarded diamond bracelet flung across the sky.

The moon stayed away, and a chilling wind alone keened for the dead.

Chapter 2

PRESENT TIME

The day had started deliciously.

Ana Foster had heard the alarm clock 'ping' and then Peter, knowing very well how to stroke and push all her buttons, had nuzzled up. He'd trailed flickering fingers from her gold anklet, lingered a moment, before tracing her breasts to her neck. At her sleepy smile he'd slipped inside her and they'd begun slow easy movements together. It was the occasional wakeup bout that started any day beautifully.

Then he'd fouled up the mood.

Mucked it up.

They'd basked in the warm aftermath legs and arms still entwined until Peter said, 'Maybe my lovemaking will make you pregnant this time.'

That rankled.

His love making! Not their lovemaking just to begin with!

She pushed herself out of his embrace, flung herself out of bed, and stomped into the hottest shower she could bear before she was tempted to snap a terse comment back at him. So it was going to be the usual. Another niggle, niggle quarrel with Peter before she left for work.

Next week she was scheduled for a much needed and longed for two week's holiday. This argument was the last thing she wanted today. When she was ready for work she passed his study door. He was sitting, un-showered and still naked, tapping a ruler in irritation at his computer.

'Can't you at least get some pants on?' she said. 'Going to sit around all day like that?'

He grunted. Why men grunt when they're sulking and feeling incommunicado, she thought. He was supposed to be already on holidays, so why was he antsy.

'Leila wants more changes. Bloody more! Why won't the woman make up her mind?'

'Still?'

She felt an element of empathy in the frustration he was experiencing. The fractious, but very wealthy, woman couldn't make up her mind where she wanted her walk in wardrobe placed. Each change made complicated modifications to Peter's architectural designs.

'I'm going to have to alter whole parts of the interior plans yet again and yet again when the silly cow changes them back again.' Peter said. 'Why can't you women make up your minds?'

The 'you women' did it. Ana's empathy disappeared.

She took a deep pained breath and briefly closed her eyes. Elements of their ongoing quarrel about a baby were locked in his grumbles. She shook herself free from the guilt he implied. Anyway, as to Leila, she thought, with architectural computer programs altering plans wasn't the hassle of Peter's earlier days. But he had to moan about it. Prima Donna stuff. All part of owning a business, she thought. Of being a designer of up market and expensive homes.

'Well, are you going to sit there and complain or get on with it?' she snapped. 'And it's Mrs Williams' day today. She'll be here soon.'

A mistake. Peter didn't like it that a strange woman, as he put it, came in to clean the house once a fortnight. It was Ana's responsibility to do the housework.

Ana's thoughts went to curse her splendid mother in law whose only vice, in an otherwise excellent relationship with her, was to have brought her son up to believe that his wife would be happy to do all the housework. Ana didn't. Damned if it was on her list of fun things to do at all. She paid for the service, and she liked Mrs Williams, so she wasn't about to make any domestic changes. Still she set about at least tidying up an already tidy kitchen by putting her breakfast dishes into the dishwasher.

'Well, will you be finished soon?' she called to change the subject. 'So that we can spend some time in the garden together this evening.' Peter liked gardening it suited his artistic temperament well. 'You promised too that you'd be finished so that we can go to Dutton Bay fishing for a day next week.'

He'd put up with her fishing while he hiked for kilometres if she packed a decent picnic lunch. Decent meant chicken, salad, wine and maybe home baked scones with jam and cream. Great but not the best for his health or waistline. After the first week of her holidays, at and near home, they'd plans made for the following week away. She'd checked the internet and booked a road trip visiting Clare Valley and Barossa wineries staying at Bed and Breakfasts.

But, a baby.

Peter wanted a child, and soon.

Ana bit her lip in annoyance. Ana wasn't ready to have a baby yet. She huffed an unamused goodbye at Peter and left for work.

Chapter 3

'Wait for me' Kelsey shouted.

Silhouetted against the sun that glinted off the sea, Emma ran laughing from their car parked just off the gravel track in the Lincoln National Park.

He paused a moment more to let his new bride run ahead of him. The chase started the fun. He took a deep breath, and breathed in the scents of autumn, the trees and the earth that smelled of last night's rain. A hint of eucalyptus mixed with a tang of salt.

'Catch me if you can...' she sang. Her hair was a tangling dark red thatch against the blaze of golden wattle and blue native bush wisteria. 'Catch me...' her laughing face shone with love and excitement.

His quick footsteps were approaching. 'Just you wait! You'll be sorry you ran...'

They had been married for less than a week. After being friends for years a flash had ignited their relationship and the passion had taken them by surprise. They were immediate lovers and they couldn't take their hands off each other. They married barefoot, like gypsies, on Snapper Rock on the Boston Bay shore and their family and friends flew over from Adelaide to share their joy. Their honeymoon cabin by a sunlit beach was perfect, and the rising moon made a golden wavy web across the dark waters most nights creating glorious isolation from everything.

'Catch me then...' Emma called.

As Kelsey chased her with delicious intent, a scrap of silly ditty ran through his head. 'Catch me, catch me if you can, I can run faster than anyone can! Catch me...'

Emma squealed and ran further into the bush.

Their ideas of bush lovemaking in the fragrant grasses began to dissipate as a sweet cloying stench carried towards them on the cool afternoon breeze.

Something stank.

They slowed their heady rush.

For just over a week she lay there. Life's dreams gone. Gone with the love of the earth and sky. Gone with the love of her family, her friends and the quiet humour she was known for. Gone...

She lay sprawled face up in a patch of scrub, not far out of Port Lincoln but close enough for the coastal city to have been her likely home.

Above her the gum trees shivered in the winds as if the branches whispered in revulsion at what she had become. At what was dumped below them. As the days passed it seemed that nature attempted to cover her stark female nakedness with fallen leaves. The parrots, as they fed, bit off the first autumn gum blossoms and dropped the spent flower heads and petals onto the body. Tall straggles of grass had stuck to the blackened dried blood as decomposition drew the stems and leaves into the gaping wounds and into the rotting flesh of her torso and breast. Blowfly maggots had time to breed and breed again; and the features of her face had fallen away from the white teeth and bones beneath.

A dark mat of long hair clung about her head in an untainted cap of midnight although a few forehead hairs were bleached white and looked as though she had grown suddenly old and grey as she lay there. Thin strands of hair clumped into the black blood crevice of her neck folds. Some curled out in abject flirtation as the tiniest of breezes flicked the ends.

Nothing else moved.

After attacks by vermin, rats and feral cats, her damaged hands clawed upwards as the tendons dried and shrunk. The hands seemed to beg the sky above for help.

The inherent dignity of the young woman's body had descended into the nightmare pit of horror.

'Wait,' Emma said. 'Phew! What a pong! This's not a not much of a place after all. Let's find somewhere else.' Her laugh quietened. She slowed, as she innately became aware, and then suspicious.

'Wait…' she said again as he caught up to her.

But Kelsey was keen to tug her along the track to delay curiosity and to pursue his immediate sexual gratification.

'Come on back to the car,' he coaxed. His hand went to her neck to that delicious spot at her hairline where he could make her shiver. He loved those dark red tresses, loved the renewed ardour that their marriage ceremony had brought. He loved these moments.

'Wait…'' she said again touching his hand, pulling the caress into her neck. His other hand reached for her breast under her halter top and cupped the full warmness there. 'We should see what smells…'

Still distracted and playful, he grudgingly agreed.

They followed the smell and looked.

What was left of their arousal lapsed into gagging. They backed away from the face, from the body, and stumbled back to their car. Kelsey grabbed his mobile phone, taken as a precaution on their honeymoon and, until now, turned off. He thumbed the mobile to action and dialled 000.

The wait seemed eternal.

'Police, Fire or Ambulance,' the quiet official voice enquired.

'Get me the Police,' Kelsey's voice was unsteady. He gulped at the saliva forming in his mouth, copper penny tasting, and unknown to him the body's timeless reaction to the smell of decaying human flesh. 'Hurry...'

Hurry wasn't necessary.

What they had found was going nowhere.

Chapter 4

Detective Mark Llewellyn took a last long drag of his cigarette, dropped the butt and, with the heel of his Doc Martens, stamped it into the dirt. By habit he picked up the butt and put it into his pocket. Better not to contaminate a crime scene's evidence. His lips twitched. Police Detection 101, he thought. Do it right especially as a very young motor bike copper, waiting for the first senior policeman to arrive at the scene, was watching him closely.

Perspiration plastered the patrolman's hair against his forehead. His skull was patterned with helmet markings except for a tuft that stuck like an upright fair feather. He was packing the weight of responsibility.

Mark identified himself. He locked his car and pushed the keys into the back pocket of his black jeans.

Just looking at the young man, almost quivering in his excitement, made Mark feel older than his thirty four years. He remembered what it was like to be first at a scene that all the cadet training had been about. It was always more overwhelming than expected. An eyebrow flickered as Mark strove to keep his smile to himself.

The motor patrolman lifted the yellow crime scene tapes to let the senior man pass. Mark noted that he'd wound the tapes around the acacia and eucalyptus trees to fence off as enormous area. Probably used most of his of tapes, he thought.

Dry scrub litter of leaves and sticks crunched under Mark's

feet and he glanced back to where he'd stopped for his smoke. He defended the nicotine; a cigarette helped in his calming process as he readied himself for a potential crime scene. That was his story and he was sticking to it. One day soon he would try the nicotine patches, but not today.

Especially if this was as bad as reported.

It could make body number two.

He looked a question at the patrolman. 'You are?'

'Constable Brian James, Sir. Sorry I didn't introduce myself, Sir. ' He straightened in apology and for one brief moment Mark thought he was going to snap a salute.

'OK, Brian,' he said. 'You got here smartish?'

Usually the first coppers on a scene were in patrol cars; not roaring around national parks on traffic motor bikes. Alone. Always check the first there, they weren't always what they seemed, he mused. Another 101. He checked himself and looked again at the patrolman who was tugging at the top button of his uniform shirt. This one was OK. Nervous as all hell. Working in Major Crime made Mark suspicious of just about everyone and everything that moved. And wary of some things that didn't.

'I was called out by the National Park Rangers. They've had young idiots doing wheelies in the scrub yesterday. Mucking up their fences.'

Mark waited. The younger man would continue.

'Been some grass...marijuana, Sir,' he corrected, 'found out here too. A big crop a year or two back...and they reckoned that maybe there's more...'

'Sounds fair. So the call came to you as a police officer already out here.

Yes, Sir.'

What the hell was Control thinking? Mark frowned. One body already...and yet they'd sent someone, so very wet behind the ears, to respond to a triple zero out in the bush. Lack of man power maybe... but still. Could have been anything. He glanced at the police issue gun buttoned down on the patrolman's hip. That gun had never been drawn in anger...

A waft of smell assaulted his nostrils.

Mark could feel the horror radiating in the other policeman's rigid stance and swallowed... There was no way that he'd ever get used to the stench of a corpse, he thought.

'You're sure that what's here is human. Not a kangaroo?'

'No, Sir, I got close enough to have a look. It's no roo. Looks like a woman's body to me.'

Mark glanced towards the other man to gauge if his own discomfort to the smell was evident. The patrolman gulped and grimaced an agreement before Mark passed over a set of rubber foot protectors to the patrolman, and put his own over his shoes.

'OK, then.' Mark had no trouble following the trampled path that led to the body. Regardless of that he said. 'Don't tread on anything that could be evidence. Take it slow and step around anything that looks out of place. And touch nothing with your hands... OK.'

'Yes, Sir. I don't know if I did right but I let the young couple go. Them... who found the body and called it in. They've gone back to their motel... the Blue Horizons in town. The woman was vomiting and they were very distressed.'

Distracted Mark frowned and tucked a long strand of curly dark hair back behind his ear. He pulled a pair of rubber gloves from a pocket of his jacket and eased his hands into them. He wasn't planning to touch anything, before the arrival of the technical boys, but being prepared never did any harm.

The officer continued, his voice earnest, 'I got their names and addresses and told them that they weren't to leave town before we spoke to them. Honeymooners looking for a bit of bush nooky,' he managed a short laugh cut short as another chunk of breeze sent a stronger wave of the almost solid smell towards them. He made swallowed noises. 'This changed their mind.'

'It would,' Mark said.

Brian tore a page out of the back of his notebook and handed it to Mark. His sweaty hand shook slightly. The couple's name, address, phone numbers, occupations and the local motel were listed. Also his time of arrival and what he'd done to secure the scene.

'This's a cleaner copy for you. I've got the original as I wrote it still in my book in case it's needed in the future in court,' Brian said.

Mark grunted. This was a young cop eager to show he'd listened to the academy lectures, he thought. At least the constable's writing was legible and he'd got all the information needed. Letting the couple go was probably the best thing to do. 'Good work. We'll get their statements later.'

They were closer now to the body and ahead they could see the darker patch that was human remains on the leaf littered bush floor. 'Wait – stay here,' Mark said.

'Yes, Sir.'

Mark paused and grimaced. Damn, he should have left his black leather jacket in the car. Somehow leather took in foul smells and he didn't want to replace his jacket. Again. He shrugged out of his jacket. 'Chuck that into my car, will you, then come back and wait here,' he said. His keys followed the jacket. At three metres distance he stopped and spoke as the younger man set off to the car. 'Hang on. Has my boss called in yet?'

'Senior Sergeant Charlton? I sent him a text message via my boss, but nah... Haven't heard from him at all.' A hint of reverence came into the younger man's voice. Rick was already making himself known to all ranks.

Mark flexed his knees impatient now to be left alone to view the body. To just let the scene tell him what it could, and to start his investigation. It was rare that he was the first detective on any scene and he wanted a quiet undisturbed look before anyone else arrived. He moved forward to stand beside the remains. He pushed his dark glasses up. He needed a clear view and the glasses held back his hair. This hair, gave evidence of the Danes invading Wales in centuries past, had reddish tints in the unruly curls and brown colour. His blue eyes dissected the crime scene.

Within five minutes the patrolman returned. 'I've got the school crossings to check for speeders now. Do I need to wait?'

'Yes, definitely you'll have to stay.' A hint of impatience crept into Mark's voice. 'As first police officer on the scene you remain, you should know that. Someone else can do your school patrol. That's not your concern now.'

The slight reprimand was tempered by an accepting glance. Part of the changing job of the patrolman was to become an effective police officer. Mark reasoned that he'd have to lead the junior man a bit more and pointed back down the track through the bush where they all had walked. 'Set up a car park area back there for a command position. Don't want the local mob coming in to mess up the scene any more than it is already before Rick and the forensics team get here,' he said.

'Sure, there's plenty of space where the young couple parked their car, sir.'

With reluctance he turned back to the young patrolman. 'No...cordon off that car area as well. Maybe another car was parked there and maybe that young couple aren't all they seem. Never trust anything, anyone at first glance. Check everything even the most unlikely. OK?'

'Sir?'

'It wouldn't be the first time that the persons reporting a

crime are the perpetrators. Part of a profile on some of them...'
Mark gave a half smile; the young couple didn't seem to fit any
Quantico training he'd done, 'not that I really think it this time but
it's happened in the past.'

'Yes Sir. I'll put the parking area further back along the track
then.'

'It won't hurt everyone to walk a bit.'

'Yes Sir.'

'Look, Sir's not necessary. I'm only a detective sergeant. I
answer to Mark. Keep the Sir's for the Senior Sergeant. He doesn't
mind them at all.'

'Thanks... Mark.' The young officer still put an implied 'sir' in
the response.

The detective let it stand.

'Anyway there probably won't be much in the way of
evidence left but we'd better do it right.' Another brief smile. 'The
Sarg'll want to have a look as well before the forensic boys arrive
from Adelaide. But there's little doubt that this body's been here
for a few days.'

Mark looked up. A few clouds had gathered as though
summonsed by the drama developing. It was always strange,
silent at first, as though even the birds were disturbed by the
shock below. He grimaced at his own whimsy as overhead the
birds started their late afternoon territory calls and chirpy
warnings. It reminded him that the daylight would be fading soon.

'Could you also get some big lights organised. We'll need a
generator too. Speak to your own boss; he'll know the drill. It's
going to be a long night.'

'Not a problem, Mark. I'll phone it in... You're with Major
Crime Squad aren't you?' the patrolman said. 'Came over for the
first body?'

Mark nodded.

The uniformed man was almost shouting as if Mark were a long distance away, 'This'll be a homicide won't it? First one I've seen...'

The detective brought his thoughts back. 'Oh yes, it's definitely a homicide from what I can see here already.' Certainly not my first one though... he thought.

Mark squatted beside the body.

There was resignation in his tone, but it covered the building excitement he felt every time he was faced with a new crime-scene. Every person had the right to be found and laid to rest properly. If there was a crime involved then again that person had the need to be, revenge wasn't a necessity, but there should always be an accounting. He was young enough to still believe that credo.

The professional detachment never could succeed completely especially a crime-scene like this that wrapped a malodorous blanket about everything.

Chapter 5

Ana thumped down hard on the accelerator. She crossed the highway tarmac too fast and her car's back wheels skidded as they met the gravel of the unpaved road leading to the Port Lincoln Prison. Lifting her foot she slowed to control the potential skid.

Shit she was tense...

It was the other problem according to Peter. One he brought up time, and time, again.

Why on earth had she chosen to work in a bloody, to quote him, state prison environment when she could run a private psychology practice? That option was certainly more profitable and she could have a baby and work part time. Ana's voiced reasons for choosing to work at the prison always sounded feeble when she tried to explain them.

Her real reasons were less so.

But now everything for the annual holiday was planned. She'd got departmental approval and a replacement counsellor was coming. There was never a problem with getting replacements to Port Lincoln Prison. Many people wanted to work where the country prison was much more relaxed in comparison to the tough clamped down city establishments. Off duty time in the coastal environment was worth it. A few minutes' drive back in the evening with an amazing view over the Boston Bay and far flung islands as the car topped Winter Hill before the sweep down into the town. A small city really; with pubs, beaches, national parks, and tourist opportunities if a person was adventurous.

Only this last week to go, she thought as she approached the prison. One week to placate Peter, yet again, and to wonder why she put up with his bouts of temper.

'Shrink heal thyself,' she muttered and felt a grin tickle the corners of her mouth. It wasn't that bad. As she loved and teased Peter, a baby would come in time and practicing for it was pretty good. More practice on holidays. That soothed the beast in the man. So far...

Her little car rattled over the cattle grid as she passed through the prison's steel gates and on down the avenue of tall gum trees to the staff parking area. She pulled her car into the shade. The garden was busy with prisoners hoeing rows of what looked like cabbages and potatoes. In the glass house shadows moved and, attached to the main building, the workshops hummed with the bark of men's voices and the rattle of machinery.

Ana had parked beside a blue flowering garden bush. She carefully locked her car and stopped in delight as a froth of butterflies rose in a white cloud. She'd disturbed their sipping the flowers' nectar. It was a mood altering moment. She needed something like that after the altercation with Peter and often she found find it in the prison gardens. They were a delight and seeing them began the work day well.

As she walked towards the buildings there was a flicker of movement above a departmental car parked nearby as a grey shrike thrush took off. Already this morning the bird had perched on the bonnet to sing territorial songs to its reflection in the glass and leave a signature poop of its excitement. Her own mirrors would be decorated with the same droppings, she knew, by the time she returned after work. A pesky mess, but the bird's glorious melodies could often be heard inside removing a snippet of menace from the prison. She doubted anyone other than herself noticed the singing birds, except for the droppings. The trustees grumbled about cleaning the official staff cars.

Her eyes scanned the sky seeking any other movement in the sky or trees. Birds, any birds, were a passion and had been all her life. A source of interest and solace.

Ana knocked at the toughened steel barricade and grinned up at the security camera overhead. There was a rattle of keys, and her friend Gus McMahon opened the huge metal door for her.

'G'day,' the huge bulk of a man in uniform greeted her. 'Lovely day.'

His attempt at the Australian slang phrases didn't work. They never did. Never would. His burr, as soft as a breeze over purple heather valleys, was still there despite his long ago migration as a young man. It elicited a smile from Ana and that was exactly what the older man wanted.

The huge door thumped shut behind her as he closed the latches, locked it and went back into his domain. She handed over her handbag and he glanced into it as she passed through the metal security detection.

A bell pinged loudly.

'Oops! Sorry, I forgot to take off my ankle bracelet,' she said as she lifted the leg of her dark green trouser suit a trifle to show the slim gold jewellery above her high heel pump. 'I must be thinking too much about my holidays.' Or after this morning with Peter I forgot, she thought. 'It's almost too nice to have to come here today,' she smiled as he gave back her bag.

She leant through the archway into the large room that was his control area. Gus's barrel belly pushed against his shirt front and he made any room look smaller. But on more than one occasion prisoners had been surprised when they took on the hard core underneath Gus's soft looking exterior. He was a kind man who did a hard job well.

A female officer, working at a viewing security screen, raised a hand in greeting.

'Hi Sally,' Ana called. 'How's it going?'

'Good,' Sally's return grin was red lipstick bright and wide. Her attention returned to her duty screens.

'Anything new? Anything I should know about?' Ana asked.

'The transit van came in this morning. Otherwise everything's as usual.'

'So what've we got?'

'Two new prisoners. Both on rotations from Adelaide.'

'Two only?'

'The place's full to bursting. Two's enough. One's in for a double murder. Medium high security.' Gus flipped open the blue travel file. 'Twenty years and he's done about eight. Nasty bit of work, they reckon, but he's never had a rotation and been cooped up in Yatala for his entire sentence so far. Been in with a tough group.'

'Probably time for a change then.'

'The rotation was recommended and the Parole Board approved it. Unusual process, I reckon, but that's what they are starting to do with some of the long term lags. The counsellors haven't seen much of him, but they think a change of scenery might loosen him up. I'm not sure how it will help him here when he's still confined inside all the time.'

'That's all on the official network, is it? He's been sent over by the counsellors...?'

He raised his eyes to the ceiling in a smiling gesture. 'You know counsellors,' he teased, 'sometimes they think they know it all...never listen to us old timers.'

Ana grinned back at him. 'So he could be trouble? But maybe the change of air will do him some good.' Gus raised an eyebrow and shrugged his doubts. 'What about the other one?' she asked.

He swapped over the files. 'A protectee. Paedophile.'

She grunted. Here we go again, she thought. More possible trouble.

'As if we need more of them here,' he echoed her thoughts.

Ana shrugged in agreement.

These men could cause chaos with other prisoners in the rigid hierarchy of criminals. Regardless of the security of the personal records the, so called, ordinary prisoners usually found out the reason for most other inmate's imprisonment given the availability of TV and newspapers. The men had long, but not always accurate, memories and the treatment of paedophiles, the 'rock spiders', and could be brutal from fellow prisoners.

The action was covertly condoned by some of the wardens.

As far as Ana was concerned, the court ordered imprisonment was the prisoner's punishment, not being subjected to additional cell abuse and tough yard violence. Psychological treatment and rehabilitation towards an inmate's eventual release was another matter entirely and that concerned her.

'What's he like?' she asked.

Sometimes it was obvious what these men were in prison for. Sometimes they masqueraded as ordinary men.

'I saw him when he came in. You wouldn't know he's a spider looking at him so maybe he'll be OK here,' Gus said. 'Could work out in the farm or yards. It's not up to me – I'm not paid the big bucks to make those decisions,' another dig at her counsellor role in the management and placement of prisoners, 'but the other one will be easy. He can only work inside in the kitchens or the carpentry workshop. That's providing he behaves himself.'

Ana had to see all new men on the day of their arrival for placement assessment. These early interviews were often a start of the rehabilitation processes that could make for positive changes in the prisoner's lives. Prevention of repeat offending depended on so much; the prisoners' attitudes and even the short staffing of prisons that politicians saw as an easy way to save money meant that all the counselling, training, education and the like, would sometimes achieve little positive results.

'The lifer might do better in the system here. It's happened before,' she said.

Port Lincoln Prison was a protectee establishment housing some prisoners who couldn't survive in the general community of an ordinary prison. Ana liked working less with the sexual and child abusers who offered all the excuses in the world as to why they did what they did. None of these were remotely acceptable to her, and getting them to change the psychological pattern of their thinking was one of her most difficult tasks. They were often great manipulators. They'd try to convince her, and others, that they would do anything required of them while they did, and changed, nothing.

'Both men are in their forties.' Gus continued. 'Should be tough enough to survive the system.'

'That's something. Set the interviews up for me, please, after lunch. I'd need to read their on-line files first, and maybe have a chat with the boss regarding his take on the medium high security man.'

'Not a problem,' Gus smiled.

She changed the subject. 'What's for lunch?'

One thing with working at the farm prison was that she could buy lunch in the Officer's Mess. It was always good with home grown vegetables, meats and chicken. Often, in the summer season, the fruit trees would provide apricots, plums and peaches to die for.

'I know they killed last week so it's probably roast lamb,' the older man smiled. They shared this question and answer session every day.

'Yum,' Ana said unprofessionally and for his ears only. 'I'm going to get fat one day with all these lunches.

'Not likely, Lassie, Gus stated with an appreciation of her trim figure. Ana laughed as she passed through the next security door and down the passage to her small office.

Chapter 6

The steel fishing trawler wreck lay beneath 30 metres of water.

An immovable hulk; it had been sunk there as an artificial reef to attract fish ten, or more, years before. The seas moved in regular rhythms around it and soft weed had long since garlanded every part of the structure with weaving and waving multi-coloured fronds. Pink and white corals covered the wooden planks with lace bony structures and the metals of the wheelhouse hung with rust ribbons. Fish darted into and around their refuge and fed on any new morsels left for them by the tides.

There was a swarm of fish darting there now.

Although the naked body had been there for less than a week, it had long since swelled and split from the decomposition gases trapped within. It should have risen to the surface, to dance a macabre waltz in the waves and tides but instead it wallowed, bumped and softly thumped against the underside of the wheelhouse roof.

Trapped. Waiting.

Caught and yet it appeared trying to escape to freedom as it rolled with every water movement.

The grey-white, and now bloodless, body had been ripped and torn so that bones of the rib cage hung exposed. Most of the soft body parts were gone and the sea had neutered the corpse.

But it was female as they all were.

Long scalp hair, which was somehow still attached, had

garnered weed embellishments, and the corpse hung face down gazing through the dark web through empty eye sockets. What was left of the arms and hands swung as though beseeching the fish to leave it be.

But fate said its rest would not begin, then.

Nor there.

The wreck was a favourite spot for the local dive instructors to take their successful dive students intent on gaining employment in the local million dollar fishing industry at the end of the professional dive course. The tuna fish rings, oyster beds, mussel ropes and tourist ventures of diving with great white sharks or tuna, all needed convoys of divers to work the twenty-four hour, six and seven days a week, shifts. Most of the diving courses were conducted in the deep end of a heated swimming pool, or in the marina waterways, but this last dive was always done in the open sea regardless of weather conditions.

A testing reward.

The depths were manageable, and the wreck added interest because of the variety of fish that always swam there. After experiencing this dive in deep water most students eagerly sought a return trip to the reef or booked into the advanced dive classes. The canny instructors liked to initiate the purchase of personal equipment as the dive boat made its way home in the evening after this special ocean excursion. There was extra money to be made.

Hence the instructors were smiling, relaxed and confident.

The students, of both sexes and mostly young as diving required fit younger bodies, clustered on the aft deck in their new wet suits. The suits were in all colours; most personalised already by their owners.

'OK line up, now. In your working pairs,' Ollie the chief

instructor said.

'There'll be fish today, you reckon?' from a red suited student.

'Sure. There always is. Plenty of small stuff and often snapper. Good sized ones too. That's why the old fishing boat was sunk to make a reef in the first place.'

One student, ever the group clown, bent his elbow above his head to imitate a shark fin and hummed the dirge from 'Jaws'. Other swimmers obligingly pretended fear. A fear not quite imagined as the sharks inhabited the area, and there was a history of a swimmer being taken by a Great White from a nearby bay.

Abalone divers were at greatest risk. Two of the class, destined to be abalone fishermen, locked eyes. Shrugged. They were young and invincible.

'C'mon Mike, stop fooling,' the instructor said, as he checked their apparatus for the final time. With a grin at the enthusiastic divers he ticked the names off his list pad as they leapt feet first overboard to fin in quiet circles waiting. He passed the pad to the deck hand, and then joined them in the water ready to shepherd the class as a group down to the wreck. The clarity of the water, and the fish evident below them, would make this day most satisfactory.

'Ready? Stay clear of anything that looks sharp,' the second instructor yelled as they trod water prior to diving.

'Yeah! ' the responses were shouted around snorkel mouth pieces.

'And despite Mike's jokes to keep an eye out for sharks. Remember this isn't the pool.'

'Yeah!' 'Yeah!'

They'd heard it all before but eyes scanned the sea around them.

As crew on the aft deck young deckhand Jake, left minding the ship, sat watching a sea eagle hover over a shallow reef where a breaking wave wove a boa of white foam feathers on the dark blue waters. As the bird wheeled away he closed his eyes against the warm sun and settled back for a bit of a snooze.

He'd had a good time the night before in the pub with the students, drinking while ensuring that they kept to the 'no alcohol for twenty four hours before a dive' rule. He wasn't diving today so he'd had a few quiet ales.

Minutes later, the two instructors and the teenager deckhand, found themselves performing rescue and resuscitation on the two leading students who had gulped water past their mouth pieces.

They had ventured first into the wreck's wheelhouse - and looked up.

Chapter 7

Ana glanced at her watch and then swore under her breath.

Peter could have done the banking. It was his architecture business after all and he was closer in the city. But no, he'd rung to say he had a lunch time meeting with the troublesome Leila. Might have to talk to his builders later so he didn't have time to do it. She'd gobbled her roast lamb lunch, nipped home to pick up his bank papers, and then headed back into town to park on Tasman Terrace.

A relic, an escapee blast of the summer north wind, buffeted her. It chuffed a plastic bag along the foreshore lawns to come to rest against the statue of the three time Melbourne Cup winner, Makybe Diva. The big black bronzed horse seemed to stomp the plastic aside and the bag cart-wheeled on towards the Port Lincoln Yacht Club.

Gulls whimpered and hunched low on the foreshore lawns. Waves, unusual in the sheltered harbour, fronted up to the town beach sands. Under red and green parachute shapes a couple of kite-surfers were skimming the white-caps and launching their bodies high above the surf.

That looked fun.

'Have you got a minute for a quick word for the "Port Lincoln Times"?' The short woman had a big demanding voice for her size. 'A photo and a comment. We've got two topics today,' she said with a note of enticement in her voice. 'There's the need for a swimming pool or on the recent murders?'

Ana stopped. 'No! I'll be late back to work,' she said and

thought, and no I don't want to be featured in the newspaper.

The woman raised her camera. Spoke from behind it. 'Hold it.'

'No. Please don't take my photograph,' Ana insisted, 'and I don't want to comment thank you.'

'But you must have a comment about the murders. There's a rumour that the victims are all young with dark long hair. You look like that. You could be next...aren't you afraid?' There was a gleam of "this'll get her" from behind the reporter's owlish glasses.

It didn't.

'No!' Ana was insistent. She frowned at the sleek blonde woman and noted her pony tail hair was drawn back tight enough to look as though she'd had a face lift. It was department policy that they never commented to the media about any criminal case that they could ever be connected to in the future. She paused, curiosity aroused, and almost asked about the victims.

The reporter's spider thin hand touched her arm. 'Come on, it'll only take a minute.'

'I said no! Don't you listen?' Ana shook her arm free and, hair tangling in the wind; she crossed the road to her car. She backed out almost side swiping the reporter who'd followed her. Ana raised her voice. 'For goodness sake...go away!'

She thrust the car into forward gear, pulled the wheel sharply, accelerated too hard and the car lurched down the street before she turned right before the Tasman Hotel. She unclenched her hands on the wheel. I have to relax, she thought. The way I'm driving today I'll be having an accident. God, I need this holiday...

But did she look like the recent murder victims? They were random, she'd read, but all dark haired and about her age. The possibility sent a cold tightening of the muscles at the back of her neck.

It was a long time since she'd felt in danger.

Senior Sergeant Rick Charlton shuffled through the pile of papers and reports on his desk. He found the buff coloured file, and flicked through the pages looking for the particular note he was seeking. His chair protested as he eased his large frame back and balanced on the back legs. He turned to the last page to see who had written the report. The chair protested again as he reverted it to its normal position.

Rick grunted and looked towards Mark. 'You're sure about this?' His pen tapped the stapled papers.

Mark looked away from his computer screen and swung his chair to face Rick. 'What boss?'

'This initial report from the pathologist. The knife wounds...' The pencil tapped again.

'On which victim, boss?'

'The bush body,' Rick's exasperation was never far from the surface. 'Never mind, I'll find the later report myself. Don't know why I bother to ask...'

Now, two days after the discovery of the boat victim's body, the detectives and uniformed police personnel arrived for the mornings briefing in the conference room. The tension was broken as a young local detective was congratulated, and teased, when he announced his long overdue engagement to one of the station's researchers.

Rick stood back and raised his eyes skyward. 'You'll be sorry,' he said a smile on his face. 'Police marriages never last. Doomed from the get go. Long bloody hours. Away all the time. You wait. She'll have you wrapped around her little finger so you won't even notice when she'll get sick of it and finds someone else. Sorry to say this, son, but it happens.' He moved forward and slapped the groom to be on the back. 'O well. Congratulations but take Mark here,' he continued, 'he's engaged too. Erica, gorgeous piece. A defence lawyer of all things. He hasn't seen her in weeks. God knows what she's getting up to in Adelaide ...'

Mark grinned self-consciously noting that his boss's smile didn't quite stay in the man's tired eyes. He knew Rick's marital history. 'OK. 'Congratulations, Ray, but let's keep this for the pub later. Back to work now please.'

In the large room, where glass blocks diffused the light, there was a general shuffling of chairs as the group sorted themselves into chairs and regained the seriousness of the investigation.

Again Mark had led the briefing.

This was unusual as Rick, the senior Major Crime detective, was responsible for it and he usually revelled in the process. He had an easy way with the men under him and he ranged his report from the serious to banter as the moment and content decreed, but with this case he had passed the duty to Mark.

'Time you did this,' Rick commented dryly and moved to sit at the back of the room. He only took part when he was asked a direct question or had a comment to make.

Mark noted that his boss either fiddled with his pens, or leaned back in his chair with his hands behind his number two barbered head. His usual big man image, but still, Mark decided, his boss was showing respect for his competence and appreciated the confidence shown in him. He was very glad that Rick still did all the media work. Rick suited up better and he looked impressive in front of the cameras. There was going to be much more media and it was already getting nasty. So far the killings had been off the main city radar with election and political scandals taking precedence. It couldn't last.

'So...have you got the final autopsy report, for the last bush one, from the coroner yet?' Rick's blue biro pen described a double ended whirling arc between his first and second fingers.

'Yeah Sarg. We've got that one and the pathologist's initial report on the boat case. He's worked a miracle getting it done so quickly.'

'These last two bodies, the bush and boat bodies, they're like the first one? The one we came over from Adelaide for. That and the unusual number of missing women?' Rick had a way of making a statement of something he knew into a question. His way of clarification. Not that he needed it. He was usually a jump ahead of everyone else in putting crimes, and the criminals responsible, together.

'All the victims are young, small women. The local coroner's reports noted this specifically. Both bodies were child-like even though the women are in their early twenties, or older,' Mark said.

'That was pretty obvious,' Rick commented. 'We could see that at the crime scenes. Even the boat woman when she was brought ashore in the body bag. We all sensed she was a small and slender, ergo probably a young woman. What else?'

Mark went to the white board that ran the length of the room. He pointed. 'This first victim, we know, is Tara Henson,' he said. She led the multiple crime scene photographs that Mark had neatly arranged. The horror of the scene was emphasised by the studio like pre- death portrait of the lovely young woman she had been.

Using magnets he put up the two latest series of photographs; of the body found in the National Park, and the boat victim. They were without any identifying portraits.

Yet.

On a side table a small heap of missing person files and photographs waited for their moment to be identified and called forward, as though to take a theatrical bow, above the death grotesqueness displayed in the crime scenes board.

'There are marked similarities in the crimes,' Mark said. 'All were killed in knife attacks.'

'Tell me something new.' Rick's abrupt comment showed signs of his frustration.

'The pathologist thinks that they were struck first by a single knife strike across the throat, from behind, left to right. This indicates that the killer is right handed. That one blow killed them. Then they were viciously knifed multiple times in the chest and abdomen from the front after they'd hit the ground.'

'He could tell that even with the boat woman?'

'Yeah, he could. Without any doubt at all.'

The worst part of Mark's job, other than the Death Knock, was standing beside an autopsy table. Earlier, summoned by a text from the pathologist Dr James Myers, he had set out for the Port Lincoln Hospital basement morgue for the post mortem examination of the boat woman.

Just my luck, Mark had thought as he pulled into a reserved parking space. He went inside and picked up a scrubs suit to cover his tall lanky body from the possible contamination he might acquire in the morgue.

Attending 'posts' was part of a detective's job and Mark was never comfortable. Rick had assigned these jobs to him saying he'd seen his share but he was ready to attend when it was necessary. Rank had its privileges and most times it wasn't necessary.

Morgues always had a cloying smell, Mark thought, no matter how much water and disinfectant was pressure gushed down the floor channels. Blood and body bits had filled the gutters just as they did those on the stainless steel tables.

Further Mark could never understand the need for quietness.

The dead didn't hear so why were there huge soft rubber wheels on the gurneys, when the wheels squeaked in protest anyway when they were moved sideways? The bank of cold store doors too had rubber seals but they were always closed softly, as though death and bodies could be hidden away if you did it like that.

Morgue staff were as abstract as morgues, he'd found. They either, could cheerfully read a newspaper and eat their lunch in the glass panelled room next door to the pathology tables, one would hope after they'd shed gloves and scrubbed up, or they acted as if the place was a sacred shrine. Some were so dead-eyed they could move into one of the freezer trays and no-one would notice them gone, except perhaps at the daily count, or when a new body was registered.

Doc Myers was different.

Maybe it was just from being a country general practitioner placed in the pathologist situation. Warm, yet troubled eyes met Mark's as he fronted up to the table. Things were well under way. In fact the doctor had halted proceedings especially to show him what he was so concerned about.

Mark inhaled through his mask. Thank the gods of these places, he thought, feeling relieved as today the smells usually involved with the dreaded witnessing of autopsies were not present. The sea had washed away the odours. Now the body, or what remained of it, lay exposed on the steel table. The pale flesh and white bones were held together by sinew and had been arranged in their natural anatomical position by the staff and doctor. The ribs were spread, with the pathologist's Y incision, and the abdominal cavity was laid open back to the spine.

'I want to show you these terrible wounds,' Dr Myers said. 'I've never seen anything like them before.'

Mark looked into the indignity of the wrecked body before them and, and, as he listened to the doctor, he felt his jaw tighten.

Chapter 8

'Mark?'

The detective's thoughts were dragged back from the vision of the post mortem he had witnessed.

Rick raised an eyebrow at him. He'd put his pen into his top pocket and was now mangling a paperclip into a submissive straight line.

'Sorry, boss.' Mark looked around at the assembled officers. 'I saw the post. The pathologist wanted me to see just how violent the attack had been. The victim's throat wound was so deep the knife slashed through to the spine. It left a deep gouge on the internal vertebrae. Cut went right through the lower skull processes and through the top of the cord. That one vicious blow had to have killed the woman outright. It just about took her head off.'

Rick grunted as there was an uncomfortable shuffling of position from the assembled officers.

'It had to be very bloody. To slice through the main arteries and veins would've sprayed blood everywhere.'

Rick nodded a 'go on'.'

'Like the others too. The doctor showed me that while the first fatal slash was always from behind, the killer then pounded the knife into the women's bodies after they were on the ground. He'd turned them face up and struck again and again.'

Mark stopped. He realised he was raising a clenched hand and imitating the blows as he spoke. There were almost perceptible flinches from the men and women before him. He waited a beat before he went on.

'Every time the knife penetrated right through the bodies, leaving more cuts and puncture wounds on the bony processes of the spine.' Mark let his gaze travel to the sky filled window blocks a moment. 'It was almost as if the killer was inflicting punishment'

'That's a bit far-fetched, isn't it?' Rick's comment was dry. His hands rubbed through the dark greying stubble of his hair. Questioning. Looking for an explanation from his junior detective. Again his way of getting opinions.

'Well, what I think from what I saw, and the written medical description of the wounds in the pathologist's reports, confirm it. My instinct is of revenge, anger and punishment. I'll stand by it too.'

'Profiling again, Mark? That's OK,' he said as the younger detective flushed in protest, 'It's is a valid assumption. We've seen it before in DV cases.'

Mark waited as a movement of agreement went through the assembled men and women. They'd seen vicious domestic violence case wounds all too often.

'This woman had long dark hair, just like all the others, too,' he continued. 'All had good overall health. None of the vics appeared to have anything of drug or toxicological interest that the coroner's been able to establish, given the condition and time elements.'

'That's a welcome change in this day and age,' said Rick. 'Maybe it's country living...'

'But all had missing body parts. Most of this was due to animal or fish attack. But there's one interesting point the pathologist's noted. All three women have lost fingers and in every case the whole of the little finger of the left hand was gone.'

'That's hardly surprising, is it? Look at the photos. There's damage to all their hands...most likely coincidental.' Rick shrugged. 'The other stuff...the likeness of the victims, the knife attacks. Yes! That tells me that we could have a serial perp doing this, but one similar missing finger on all of them when so much other damage's done? It hasn't convinced me yet he's a trophy hunter.' He half grinned towards Mark. 'You'd like there to be a collection aspect wouldn't you? Been reading your profiling books again?'

Rick's comment had no sting, just his brand of friendly banter, and the other officers in the room shuffled, grinned with, or for, Mark.

'That's my job isn't it? My speciality. They sent me to the FBI course.' The younger detective shrugged. 'Well, everything's here,' he indicated the board, 'but it doesn't give us much. All the bodies were too decomposed to really indicate from post mortem hypostasis that they'd been moved but they must have been.'

'So they'd been killed elsewhere? Surely somewhere there'll be blood evidence?' an officer questioned.

'Yes, especially the boat woman,' Mark said.

'We just have to find the where...'

'Again yes, but there's not much other evidence.'

'By the time they're found, too many factors have come into it to help us much. That's a bugger!' Rick stretched, His chair squeaked in complaint. He'd given up on the twist of paperclips and his retrieved pen did its flying loops again.

'We're still waiting on the blow fly and bug analysis at the bush scenes but the killer's been careful.' Mark summed up. 'I think we're dealing with – I think you've heard the term before - an organised killer, rather than a disorganised one. He, and I'm sure it's a he, is clever enough not to leave the knife. He chooses to place the bodies where he wants to. I suggest they're left where they'll be found but not too soon. He's crafty, knows a bit...'

'Reads books like you do maybe? Watches CSI crime shows.' As usual Rick listened but had to have a jab. 'Bloody TV. Tells the crims too much,' Rick's last words were a mumbled aside. 'And the coppers solve everything in an hour!' A wave of chuckles went around the room.

'...so I think he's male, mid-thirties to fifty.' Mark stated when he could be heard again.

'That's a hell of an age range. Doesn't help a lot. He's strong, and someone who's got a grudge on women. Maybe he's been convicted of assault, rape even...OK so there's no real indication of rape or sexual assault. Anything else that can help us in your learned opinion?'

'I also think that this man's intelligent...'

Rick interrupted. 'Bloody hell! This perp's clever all right. But he's...' Rick pushed his chair back, hard enough to bang against the wall behind him. 'Shit! Whatever you think about intelligence start looking at any local perps, especially as there's a prison here. Sometimes the buggers stay where they're released, even if they're supposed to go back to where they were arrested and convicted.'

'That's under way already. We're liaising with the parole people. They don't like it much but they've got in line because it's multiple murders.'

'Bloody parole system. They get out too soon...' This was another of Rick's beefs. 'So we wait for something to turn up as evidence. God I hate that! Or the next body! That'd be worse...we've got enough bodies already...too many.'

There was a shuffle of agreement from the assembled ranks.

'OK today's assignments.' Mark looked around the room. 'No one, other than a couple of local cranks, has reported anything useful. So it's back to basic police procedure. First the National Park. I want every park ranger checked. How long they've been on the job here, any criminal records. Anything – parking fines, financial records. The lot. Know how many work out there?' he asked looking about the room.

'Six permanent and a couple of others. And there's a volunteer group that work out there too. Tree planting, clearing beaches and such,' the local Sergeant said. His tanned face said that he was possibly one of the volunteers of the park or somewhere out of doors.

'Check them all.' There were clicks as pens were readied to take notes.

The sergeant said, 'I can give the names and addresses.'

'Good. Thanks. I understand that people sign in when they go into the park...OK I don't think our killer signed in but check the car registrations for the past two weeks. Then check the locals using the park and tally the visitors. Did they stay in the camping area? For how long? Get any names you can and get onto computers and see if anything interesting comes to light.'

'The same goes for the boat woman then?' the local sergeant's question led Mark on.

'Sure does. Get local boat owners checked like the park rangers then ask them to inspect their boats to see if they've been used illegally. Everything at the marina and maybe a local call on the radio.'

'Some dinghies are left at beaches for a long time, unused.'

'Could have done the job.' Mark raised his eyebrows, 'He'd need oars or a motor, wouldn't he? Do a visual and check each one. Probably take two to turn the dinghies over and look properly.'

'It's a big area...?'

'Then check first the ones closest to the reef,' a note of

43

annoyance crept into Mark's usual quiet delivery. 'I know it's a huge ask but it's got to be done. We're after a multiple killer. Then, once you've done that, tally with the group contacting the caravan parks regarding caravans with boats over the same period. With a little bit of luck this leg work will turn up something.'

Obviously Rick had enough of the briefing. 'Use your heads. Get out there and do your stuff.'

'OK – thanks. You know the locals and they know their area. Check them and then see what they can tell you. That's all for now.' Mark concluded. He flexed his shoulders before he dragged together the files.

Rick touched the board before returning to his desk. 'No physical evidence of the perp? Get the State Emergency boys to comb the scenes again. Something must have been missed.'

'Maybe another look could help.'

Rick rattled two empty cups as he swept a folder towards Mark. 'Well, get them onto it. And the pathologists. There's got to be something tangible to go on. Some nice fat DNA would be useful...some evidence!'

'Evidence? There's been nothing under the victims' fingernails, or on the bodies. The poor women didn't have a chance to struggle to get physical contact evidence. There isn't really anything other than they were killed in knife attacks. Not that we'd get much from the boat woman.'

'Yeah...probably been in the water too long.'

Mark shook a plastic tray of potential evidence that had been retrieved from the wheelhouse floor of the sunken boat. It should have been in specific bags but sometimes Rick liked items found at scenes, random items that were clean and could not have interest to the 'forensic mob', as Rick called them. They added to the older detective's tying mentally in with a case.

He grinned as he found a couple of shells that were beginning to smell as the tiny molluscs inside started to rot. Soon the boss would be complaining about the stink in the room. There were bits of multi coloured plastic swept in by the sea, and a small stainless steel nut that had dropped from a diver's equipment. He picked up a ring there that should not have been there. A man's ring, cheap probably low carat gold and metal but hardly tarnished by the salt water. He looked inside but could not make out any markings.

'Boss, this should be bagged,' Mark offered the ring.

'Thought it just looked old. Dropped by a Sunday diver,' Rick replied. 'But on second thoughts you'd better put it with the official stuff...I didn't think it was significant.'

'I'll get someone to follow up on the initials with the dive course. Maybe something...' Mark put the ring in an evidence bag, made a 'to do' note and tossed them onto another detective's in tray. He turned back to Rick. 'I was talking to the uniforms. If there's a floater they eventually find the body on a beach over on Boston Island. That's over ten clicks away.'

'Did they search on the island for any of the other missing women?'

'Yes, of course they have. More than once. But I think that the perp, going on my profiling, has been leaving the bodies where they can be found after a short time. Within a week or so of the killings.'

'That's quite a statement. Why?'

'It's a feeling really. He doesn't want to be caught. He just wants to show that he's clever.'

'Humph...?' Rick's doubt showed in spades. 'You said that before. Not sure I agree. I think the perp's already been done for assault or a sexual crime in the past. And he's local, or he's been here before. He knows the area. That's who we should be looking for.'

Mark asked. 'Do you reckon it would've taken quite an experienced diver to put the boat woman out there?'

'What's the depth over the boat reef?'

'Twenty plus metres at low tide. That's what the dive instructor's statements said after the boat woman was found. Thirty plus at a really high tide.'

'Nah! Any reasonable diver could have done it - so you'd better check again with the dive people and see who's taken their course. See if any of them have records.' Rick stretched. 'Especially the instructors. Check too if any of the women were divers. Maybe they met someone on a dive course … Shit!' Rick bumped a pile of paperwork and just managed to stop it sliding onto the floor.

'That's under way.'

'Rick's grunt was his usual approval response to a positive action.

Chapter 9

An hour later, Rick Charlton, Mark and the local station CEO attended the Adelaide Major Crime briefing via video link. This daily session was designed to keep all detectives up to date with the serious crimes under investigation state-wide. It was a forum where knowledge of individual criminals, various gangs, their methods and trends could be discussed, collated and acted upon. With the Major Crime section of the police force small the hierarchy could transfer officers, as needed, to different areas.

Mark had turned their crime scene board towards the cameras. After the two high ranking officers had gone through the Adelaide list of current cases, Inspector Gilles turned his attention to the Port Lincoln investigation. Rick quickly outlined the days proposed activities.

'Good. That's about all you can do until something turns up.' Gilles said. The string bean officer leaned forward in his impeccable suit. 'Anything yet on the victim IDs.'

Rick motioned to Mark to answer.

'There's three possibles, Sir. A Naomi Simpson.' Mark produced a photograph. He turned the print towards the camera and tapped it twice gently. 'She's twenty two. Apparently she was going to check on an adult university course and hasn't contacted her family in two weeks. There's no record of her at the uni so she may never have left town.'

'You've checked both Adelaide and Whyalla campuses?'

'Yes. Nothing.'

'Interstate uni's. Checking them?'

'It's under way, Sir. And the PM report says that the boat woman's body may have been in the water for about a week. They're doing rush DNA comparisons hopefully ready if we need them.'

'For the boat woman? There's enough left?'

'Yes and the others. Another possible victim is...' He checked his notes then moved down the table to touch another print. 'Elizabeth Woods. She had a fight with her father and drove off in a blue Honda. Again a couple of weeks ago. There's no sign of her. Or the car.'

Rick reached over and took the slim file from Mark. He nodded and the junior detective continued.

'Then there's Petra Cullen. This missing person case's older. She booked a flight almost six months ago but didn't show. It's unusual as she flies over to Adelaide on business regularly. Always confirms her flights and she generally arrives early. There's been no movement on any of her bank or credit cards and that's the clincher to the family fearing something's happened to her. Apparently she was quite a spender. She's got a medical problem but everything else adds her to the missing list.' He again passed the file over to his superior. 'That's her...' he pointed to the photo in the file.

'This's all on the computer as well as in all this paper?' Rick interjected. He disliked the regime of conferences unless they produced something. Today looked like just reporting. His superiors on the Adelaide link exchanged knowing smiles as Rick continued on his hobby horse. 'Double... triple, work! We're swamped as usual with paper.' He stopped, shrugged, and he got back to the business in hand. 'Anyway a few of the files and photos answer the description of the bodies we've got. Young,

Caucasian, small boned and had long dark hair.'

'Petra Cullen's fairer but otherwise fits the general MO of the killings so far,' Mark noted.

Inspector Gilles took a file from the silent man beside him. 'So two bush bodies. Tara Henderson identified; the one you came over for originally; then this latest bush victim. Now the woman in the boat who could be any of the ones listed as missing. See if you can hurry the ID process will you. The usual, teeth with local dentists and all the rest. DNA testing is fine but it takes too long. The old methods are often sufficient and they cost less. Always consider costs. But we all need to get on with this. Get a name for this boat woman. Narrow it down. Dig deeper into these women's lives. Start checks on any associates. We might not be dealing with a serial killer, it could just be coincidences.'

'Unlikely, Sir,' Rick said, 'and we are doing all you suggest. The local boys started many of these Missing Person questions before the bodies started turning up.

'Well, try to keep the lid down tight. Otherwise the media scrum will start and we'll be caught up in that.' Gilles signed off and the Port Lincoln CEO turned off the link and left the room.

'Well that's done. Interested as usual in the media. And costs. Not much help. It's really up to us here.' Rick turned to Mark as the two men gathered papers together, his impatience and exasperation showing. 'Get something happening!'

Standing back from the board, Mark said. 'My gut tells me that our victims are the women we've mentioned. They fit the time frame best, except perhaps Petra Cullen. She's been gone for six months. I hope at least some of the other missing women turn up.' I'm going to put all their photographs up. That OK with you?'

'Can't see a problem.'

Mark blue tacked the three prints down the side of the board. 'Cripes Boss, the town's getting paranoid. The local paper's screaming for all women to stay at home. Old and young. So far they haven't commented on all the links as to the type of women.'

'Our CEO had a chat to the editor to keep the missing women reports minimal,' Rick said.

'Good move, boss, but it won't be long before someone starts making comparisons and that'd send them ballistic!'

'Yeah, gotta happen soon.' Rick briskly stood up and reached for his jacket. 'Are these the best photos of the three missing women you think are the probable victims?'

Mark nodded. 'Yes, the latest.' Already they had been enlarged on the printers.

Rick ran his fingers over the photographs. 'Lovely looking girls,' he said. 'All ordinary though. No-one with an obvious past. No-one with anything remarkable other than their size and colouring. Maybe worth another deeper look into their backgrounds...' He stretched again. 'That's it for now. I'm going down to have a chat with the local Mayor. He's asked for a briefing. Bit of a pain, but maybe he can help us keep a lid on things. I'll walk there, got to keep in shape.'

Mark stayed working in the new police headquarters office, stayed long enough to receive an email from the Coroner's Office.

The knife used was definitely similar in all the killings. Although given the varying state of the bodies he was examining, Dr James Myers could still rule out one factor. The knife didn't have a serrated edged blade. A large heavy knife was all he could suggest at this stage.

Not surprising, the knife. Mark thought.

Port Lincoln had a large fishing population. Knives were associated with that type of work and he'd have to find out if the local abattoir was still in operation. The country farming area had large knives everywhere too. There was a headquarters of army reservists, weekend soldiers, in the town. They had already been called upon to help the SES with the general searches and had cooperated with everything they were asked to do. The wharfs, he mused, ships came and went hauling grain overseas. Could a killer come and go from Port Lincoln by sea? Probably nothing there, but a fuel tanker delivered petrol and diesel almost fortnightly. The shipping schedules - they needed checking. Lots of possibilities were being followed up. No problem. The country police were organised and keen to assist, better than the city officers who prevaricated. Too busy, too many cases, unless they could smell personal advancement in it for themselves. Or overtime dollars.

Mark pulled his thoughts back to the last notation on the email.

Dr Myers wrote that he had requested that Adelaide send another forensic pathologist to assist. Mark suspected that, although he had years of general experience, Myers wasn't used to multiple murder cases. Mark already recognised the pathologist's reluctance to make strong recommendations in written reports. In conversation, over the phone, he'd give an opinion but there was that hint of indecision in writing. Yes, but by a man who would seek assistance but not feel threatened when he asked for help.

Mark picked up the phone to call him to say thank you for his excellent work. It never hurt to give credit where it was due and the reports, verbal and written, were so far detailed and extremely insightful.

James Myers' voice was fatherly yet firm yet Mark remembered the tired grey eyes above the mask. The eyes of a man shocked and distressed at what he was seeing.

'Young women my daughter's age! Thank goodness she's studying away from home and I speak to her every few days.

Lately the city seems a safer place,' he said.

'The city, the country, murder is horrific wherever it occurs. Nothing else you suspect?' Mark asked.

'No, not right now.' The older man's voice was hesitant. 'I did an extra examination of the oral cavity when I was x-raying the bush woman's teeth and I may have found one tiny hair that doesn't seem to belong to her. It may be hers but there's a slight possibility that it isn't. It could even be from an animal.'

Mark drew in a breath. 'You're telling me that there's maybe something....?'

'No, not yet. I'm waiting on expert examination and an ID of the hair. It could be good. The hair has a follicle that looks human to me but I'm not qualified to identify it.'

'But a hair! How soon can they do DNA tests?'

'Hang on young man. If it proves human then they'll do the tests as a matter of urgency. I've already asked for that.' There was suppressed excitement in the restraining words. 'There's toxicology reports that had to go to Adelaide too. You'll have everything as soon as I get them through.' The older man sighed and Mark could hear the tiredness in his voice.

Thank you again...' Mark started to say.

Dr Myers continued. 'Oh, and they're sending over Tim Hayden to assist while this terrible business is going on. He's a good man, young but experienced in murder cases.'

'I know Tim,' Mark said. 'I've worked with him before.'

'Good. Dr Hayden will go over all these murder cases with me as a revision and he's an expert on knives. I can do the local work and there's always accidents and sudden deaths that keep me more than occupied.'

New eyes might add even more new information, Mark thought. 'Call me any time...' he said.

Chapter 10

Mark put his head around Rick's assigned office door in the Port Lincoln Police station and adjoining Courthouse.

'Two bits of news,' he said.

'OK the most promising first.'

'Doc Myers has found a hair…'

'Where…?' Rick cut in.

'Give me a go, Boss!' Mark said. 'In the mouth of the bush victim. He can't say it's human, it doesn't look like hers but it may be.'

'Tell me it's gone off to forensics!'

'Yes it has. Packed up and sent with an escort on the next commercial plane. He'll be met at Adelaide airport and taken to the lab. They'll look at it immediately.'

'Got the procedure of line of evidence right. Should be OK with court when, or if, it gets to that.'

It was always satisfying to tell Rick potentially good news. As he stood up his fist hit the desk with a resounding thump. 'Now at last we're getting somewhere. Tell the coroner well done!'

'Done that already.'

'And…' Rick invited the next news. He rocked back and forth from heel to toe.

'I'm just about to put up Elizabeth Woods' photo. The DNA supplied by her father was a match,' Mark said. 'That report came through at the same time as her dentist's report. Both concur.

Elizabeth Woods was the boat victim.'

'She's the one who had a fight with her father and left home?'

'Yes.'

'Following up any possibilities that the old man killed her, are you?'

'Yes, course we have, but it doesn't add up. He's a frail old bloke, invalid pensioner. Early to mid stages of dementia. Forgetful, argumentative and pernickety.'

'Doesn't sound like him then?' Rick stopped rocking. He abruptly sat down again.

Mark eyes returned to written report he held. 'No. He often quarrelled with Elizabeth and she'd go off in a huff. That's what he said, but she'd be back after a grizzle with friends at the pub.'

'So … where was she last seen alive?'

'After the old man was cleared I contacted a teacher friend of hers. She'd got a text to meet Elizabeth at the Wheatsheaf pub after work and drove out there. It's about ten, fifteen, clicks out of Lincoln.'

'I know the place. Had a meal there one time. Good pub food.' Rick broke in.

'Anyway Elizabeth didn't show up. Didn't come into the pub at all. The barman said she was seen speaking to a man in the car park and she followed him in her car.'

'The barman knew her well enough to recognise Elizabeth's car?'

'Yes. But he was busy and has no idea of who the man was or what he was driving. Did say it was possibly a white sedan though. Most of the population drives white sedans. Either that or four by fours.' He laughed, 'Most government cars are white. Hell, I drive a white car! Not much of a lead there.'

'So no-one saw anything at the Wheatsheaf.'

'Nothing other than her leaving with a man.'

'Pity. What about someone taking her out to the reef? Going out to the reef would be easy from there.'

'There's a boat ramp by the North Shields jetty.'

'No-one reported anything unusual? A fisherman on the jetty?'

'No. We'll keep asking...'

'A probable dead end then...?'

Mark nodded. 'But there's one sad factor. Apparently Elizabeth was a champion swimmer and loved diving and fishing. Used to go out with her father before he got sick. If she was alive when she was dumped she could have swum up from that sunken boat. Didn't get the chance.'

'Don't get too close to the victims, Mark. It's damn easy to do that.'

'Sure Sarg, but who wouldn't feel something about these women. They all seem decent sorts, especially Elizabeth, looking after her old man. What a life! She'd know that he's only going to get worse and she just goes off to the pub when she's had enough of the arguments. Her friend said this happened once in a blue moon.'

'Yeah, but someone has to have seen something. The perp, or perps, has to be a local to know where to dump the bodies.' A pause. 'You've checked on this friend?' Rick said.

Mark leaned against Rick's desk. 'Yes, Sarg. The full interview. All the alibi checks. She couldn't be involved in Elizabeth's murder as she stayed at the Wheatsheaf all evening waiting for her. I've checked that alibi with the pub manager. He knew both women.'

'Check the pub staff. Alibis and any past history.'

'Done computer checks while you were away talking to the Mayor. Nothing other than a couple of speeding fines.'

'So another bloody dead end...' Rick's chin jutted.

Mark looked incredulously at his scowling boss. Things never moved fast enough for Rick. He needed evidence then his speciality was linking things. A master at that he'd earned the respect of all with his insight and drive.

'Well, find me something. Get that DNA evidence from the bush woman matched asap. Otherwise we're getting nowhere! ' Rick said.

Mark stood up from his own desk, stretched, and went downstairs and outside to have a smoke and a think. When that didn't help he went back inside to stare at the white board line-up of photos and notations.

There was one fact he'd been wondering on and he'd spoken again to Dr Myers with the question. Could the missing finger or fingers have been chopped off, rather than been bitten off by an animal or fish? Was it possible?

The pathologist had thought for a moment before replying. 'Yes. There were clean cuts on proximal joints of the little fingers of the left hand. All three phalanges were gone. I was puzzled by it and made the note, if you remember that either a knife, a fish even a shark probably severed that finger off completely.'

'You'd state that in a court? The whole little finger could have been cut off at the first joint?'

'Yes. At the metacarpal phalanges joint. Nothing's a hundred percent, but there's a good possibility that the finger was removed at that point. A knife I'd say. When Tim gets here he'll have a very close look at all the victim's hands. Knives and the cuts they make are his speciality. He may be able to confirm what I suspect, that other victims' hands have been mutilated in this way, and he'll make a better expert witness in court than me. Have you got a suspect?'

'No, nothing like it. Just wondering. Following hunches.'

Hunches alright.

Now that he knew the identity of the boat body, he was sure that Elizabeth Wood's body couldn't have ended up under the roof of the sunken reef boat on its own if it were dumped at sea. Someone had to kill her then take her body out to sea by boat. Then the perp would have to tuck it away underwater so that the roof structures would hold it against the tides. Mark made a note to check again the diving instructors. But why would they take a bunch of students to the wreck if one of them knew that she was there? Maybe the person thought that the sea and fish would have done their job. But surely there'd be scattered bones left. It didn't add up but perpetrators had motives that sometimes surprised.

Even to profilers.

Sometimes especially to profilers.

Who'd been in recent dive courses? Maybe done a course even before the first murder of Tara was committed? Was she the first victim? Were there other unfound victims, corpses of young women lying or buried still in the area. Or elsewhere? Why had the perp not buried the bodies? So far there seemed to be no beginning, no starting point, to the murders.

Why had they started? How many more?

Mark's eyes skimmed along the line of photograph of missing women. The questions were endless and Mark felt the Major Crime detectives' reputation resting, like a dragging weight, on his shoulders.

Not that Rick ever showed worry.

It was not his style.

Mark went back to the papers and the smelly remains of an old KFC pack on his desk. He shoved the yellow and red pack into the bin and refreshed his computer from the scrolling police emblem. He'd finish soon, he promised. Yes, sure, he thought; he'd go back to his lonely motel room, drink beer and eat more rubbish while he turned the murders over in his mind until the early hours. By staying in the station he knew it would still be a long night but there were the computers, and people around.

He'd hash over pathology, toxicology, odontology, police incident reports and witness statements. Information provided by family and friends. He'd re-read everything.

Even the minor flood of confessions and the many sightings. Most useless – some almost funny. Ridiculous.

All needing to be checked.

'I killed them for their kidneys!' on a completely traceable email to 'I saw her shopping in Kmart' or in 'Maggie T's in Adelaide' from an earnest and elegant older man. Old enough to be her father! He'd have to ask if 'Maggie T' made clothes that the victims could have worn just to cancel that one out. Somewhere in the back of his mind told him that 'Maggie T's' things were for larger women. Still it had to be followed up. It all took time. The local boys could have a little talk with the kidney email sender, just to warn him of the hampering the course of justice offence. It wouldn't be the first time either that a perp had contacted the police just to show off that he was clever. Detective school 101, Mark's face relaxed for a moment into a grin.

Something would be somewhere but all he really needed, maybe to make a breakthrough, he thought, was that hair that the pathologist had found.

The results of that one hair...

Otherwise there was little enough else yet despite all the hard work.

Chapter 11

Ana's office at the Port Lincoln Prison was small.

The Records Room was bigger but as she was the first female counsellor at the prison, she'd got what room was left over.

The room was painted pale green and had two windows. One fronted onto the farm paddocks and the other was a mere slit high above her desk that was a conduit to the internal prison parade ground. From there she was privy to things she usually didn't want to hear; snatches of pure lurid porn discussed knowing she was in her office, and sometimes swearing that inmates expected to embarrass her. She'd heard it all before and she could have surprised the voices if she'd responded in kind.

On two occasions she had been quietly told about knives hidden in the prison that the prisoners wanted out. They trusted her enough to get the information to her for their own safety. To protect the informants in these cases she'd waited a few hours and then informed John Fellows, the Manager, of the location. An area sweep was done and John triumphantly paraded the contraband before her.

Ana and John worked well together; but their one bone of contention was the placement of Ana's desk. John suggested that the desk should be a barrier between her and the inmates she was interviewing. This was totally contrary to Ana's mode of work. She felt that the desk position with the chairs adjacent to each other allowed her to interact better with each man. So far John had conceded to the arrangement of her room.

Lately, when she typed her reports into the prisoner computer files, she'd begun to play a bit of quiet modern jazz on her player. She'd been surprised to hear a 'thanks missus' from listening men outside as they waited to be called onto parade for the numbers count before their evening meal and lockdown.

The other window had a view out over the prison farm that spread for a thousand hectares across the hills and down towards a brackish lake locally called Big Swamp.

Today, a prison farm tractor was carving fire breaks around the knee-high late wheat crops that intersected with canola paddocks in gold and green gridded patterns. It created an effect like a striped t-shirt spread out to dry. Did the inmates, confined totally inside, know that the canola which looked golden and buttery but the plant smelled foul? Like rancid mustard. Or that, when the crops were reaped, Cape Barron Geese and swans followed, like gleaners, picking up the spilled grain? In a nearby paddock cattle grazed with sheep and, as she watched, a huge Murray Grey bull lifted its massive head to look around.

A look out of her office window sometimes altered a prisoner's mindset during a scheduled consultation.

Ana switched her attention back to her computer screen and the reports of the two new inmates. Both were hard cases and would require many interviews, and the view outside her window would have to do a great deal to help her.

The thought of her holiday kept the hint of a smile on her lips as she planned the series of interviews for the incoming relief counsellor and those she would need to do, after she got back from leave.

Rick Charlton took the police station stairs two at a time and bounded into the Squad Room. The detectives and police staff looked up from their tasks and screens.

Something was up.

Some breakthrough.

They stopped and waited.

Mark was excited and sat upright in his chair. He had news alright, faxed to him from Adelaide. In turn he'd texted Rick and asked him to return to the police station stat; immediately. He'd wanted to report to his boss first in person. Protocol, and the way they worked together.

'Mark!' Rick yelled. 'Where the hell are you?' There was no going to his office to make his report. This was an open door result announcement. 'Your text? What've you got?'

Mark grinned. He stretched back from his chair, aping a movement that Rick often used, and looked at his boss.

Rick charged to Mark's desk and stood over him. His clenched jaw, his fisted hands and it showed in every molecule of his impatient being.

This was Rick the hunter.

The best policeman Mark knew.

The greyness; the dragged down appearance, which had begun to hang about Rick's face from exhaustion and absolute frustration at the slowness of the investigation, was gone. Blood had returned to his face. Mark suspected that he looked better too.

'That hair that they took from Naomi Simpson got a hit! An immediate hit! I'm waiting for the more details, but the name connected with the DNA is Demetrius Quinn...' Mark said.

'Quinn! Bloody Demetrius Quinn! I know the mongrel!' Rick cut in. 'He was one of my first cases when I was a junior dee out of Port Adelaide. The bastard! I'll never forget him. Multiple rape and manslaughter of a young woman. It should've been a bloody murder conviction.'

'Well, he was released from Yatala Prison four months ago after a long stretch. It fits completely,' the younger man said as he put his password to cross the linked police and parole screens of his computer.

'You're right! He used a knife before too.' The excited flush on Rick's face lessened and he thrust his jaw forward. 'If Lee Thomson and I'd got him banged up for murder as he deserved then, we wouldn't have this mess now. We were livid! Ten years, that's all the bastard Quinn got! Got off too bloody lightly.'

Mark looked surprised at Rick's outburst. 'Sometimes these things happen, boss...'

'Well it should never have happened. These women vics would still be alive here...' Rick said. 'Quinn must be in this area.' He straightened. Thrust his hands on his hips. 'Shit he's here! In the Port Lincoln area.'

'He'd still be on parole so finding him shouldn't be too difficult. I've made a call to the Parole people in Adelaide asking them for his details. Told them not to act in any way on their own either. Not to frighten him off.'

Rick scowled. 'Bloody Parole Board... letting murderers out. The local office'll have to give us his whereabouts. No pussy footing either because of Quinn's so called charm.'

'Charm? What do you mean?' Mark had finally woven his way through the screens and got the Quinn file up on his computer. It was sometimes difficult getting current access to a suspect if he was either in prison or on parole. The police had to go through the Corrections system in a slow process that infuriated detectives like Rick, and Mark too for that matter.

'The bastard, if I remember correctly, had a certain charm for women.' Rick always remembered correctly. 'He had a female brief at his trial who thought the sun shone out of his arsehole. Had women picked on the jury doubting he could hurt a bloody fly. The bitch got him manslaughter when it should have been murder.'

'So him getting to Naomi and maybe the others too wouldn't have been too difficult?'

'Nah, not with that bastard's looks.' Rick started to take his coat off then changed his mind. He shrugged back into the sleeves. 'C'mon sign off...work to do.'

Mark complied. 'Coming...?'

'We'll have a little chat with the parole people ourselves.' Rick said. 'They've seen the papers, felt the town's panic, so let's see if they will be co-operative right now.' He looked towards the other officers. Felt the buzz. 'This is to stay in total confidence to this room. Nothing on the police radio. Nothing on phones anywhere. The bastard could have a scanner and we don't want him clearing out. Any peeps to the press or anywhere else and you'll have me to contend with...'

Rick and Mark started towards the door.

Mark grinned as Rick stopped, looked back into the room, and continued speaking to the men. 'You'll all be in on the bust if he's anywhere here. Do a check. Has Quinn come to any police notice in Port Lincoln? Or the West Coast. Got a speeding ticket? Does he fit in anything else that has happened here? Anything else that we could use as a parole violation if the murder arrest looks tricky.'

Rick aimed a playful punch at Mark's shoulder. 'Are you waiting for a personal invitation or do I have to do this on my own?' he said. They went down the corridor towards the CEO's office. 'We'd better see the station boss and put him in the picture before we go...'

'Yeah...we'd better.'

Rick thumped his big hand onto Mark's shoulder again. 'Bloody hell, Mark we're going to get him!'

Sometimes it was good being a cop, Mark thought.

Chapter 12

The weatherboard house was fifteen kilometres outside the Port Lincoln City limits, at the end of a rough twin tyre forged track that wound the one hundred metres from a main road.

It was the sort of the old farm house that unscrupulous landlords put up for rent to people who couldn't afford to complain. Many such houses exist near country towns. Especially in places like the outskirts of Port Lincoln; a town that attracted all types from fishing millionaires to the societal characters, the disenfranchised and those wanting to be just 'away' lived. Easier to live and pretend that you were doing well where the surroundings were beautiful. Even on government benefits.

Something had brought, and kept, Demetrius Quinn in Port Lincoln.

The two bedrooms at one end of the house were sheltered by a huge white ghost gum. Rain markings, like spilled brown-grey paint, flowed down the trunk, and when the western heat poured in on the late summer afternoons, the tree provided the only shade. The rest of the drab house slumped under a leaf littered roof. Thin cotton curtains hung at two windows looking like sleep sand in a grey unwashed face.

A TV blared from a sitting room in the middle of the house. A room where furniture was almost absent, having been pawned to buy the wide screen. Onions frying in the kitchen at the end of the building smelled enticing, until the odour of stale cooking fat seeped through to change the smell to rancid.

A boy, thin in stature. Pale. Small, in blue jeans, wearing a striped t-shirt in blues and yellow, swung from a car tyre strung on a rope below a hefty branch of the ghost gum. At the end of bony legs his sneakers were tatty and his blond hair straggled too long on his neck.

A little boy who rarely smiled or laughed.

Just swung on the tyre while the game shows played endlessly inside on TV. His pale blue eyes stared ahead robotically; his mental images and thoughts turned inward.

Suddenly a male voice erupted from the sitting room.

It drowned out the game show. 'Where's the boy?'

The boy winced.

He stopped his swinging then got off, stopped the movement of the tyre, and walked with furtive steps down to a hen coop behind the house. He crept between the warmth of the hens already roosting on an irregular shaped perch. They fluffed feathers, muttered hen noises, and then resettled as the boy sat totally still.

There was a mumbled reply from the kitchen.

'What muck are you making for dinner, you fucking cow?'

Another mumble.

'Feed him properly!' the male voice yelled. 'Do I have to tell you everything?'

'He'll only eat chips and sauce...' the woman's voice whined.

Quinn's woman glared towards the front room at Quinn's shout. She'd thought that things would be different once he got out of prison but the smiles, from the man in front of the TV, were only for the boy. She'd learned to keep out of the reach of his lightning fists and the hard fingers that pinched bruises into her arms. He'd pinched her even under the stern looks of the prison screws when she'd visited.

He gave her photographs of himself, looking handsome and fit from hours working out in the prison gym, to show to the boy.

In her long sleeved blouses she showed the photos to her friends; women who had similar hard men as partners or husbands. 'See how good looking he is?' she'd said. She'd raise an eyebrow. 'He's gorgeous. You can see why I visit him. Says he loves me and our boy.'

She remembered his promises of how they'd be together when he got out of prison. He'd be nicer, kinder. Fat chance of him being different, she knew it soon after he was out. He'd insisted they leave Adelaide; come to this god forsaken house and god forsaken place where she had no friends. No one to see his violent ways with her. No one to see her cry in pain.

He only wanted the boy.

He stayed with her only for the boy.

He threatened. If she left him she was dead.

Dead meat.

Three police cars pulled up on the main road, as dawn flared red a set of clouds strung along the eastern horizon.

Red clouds in the morning, shepherds warning; the words threaded through Rick's mind. Demetrius Quinn had better not have been warned or he'd have the person's responsible testicles strung around their necks. He hoped that everyone ahead was a late sleeper.

No sirens.

No lights to announce their presence.

Rick with Mark, the contingent of detectives who were promised a place at the kill, and a couple of uniformed men pulled up. He signalled and an officer unlatched the wooden and wire 'cow cocky' front gate and lifted it open. The motorcade procession inched forward. They pulled up before the ghost gum and got out of their cars in silence.

'Let's do it...' Rick whispered. He felt the heat of action rise in his chest; it was always this way, and he covered his excitement with a 'thumbs up' to the men.

'Keep it down,' Mark responded with unnecessary caution; his excitement at the chase evident. 'Keep it slow now.'

Gun drawn Rick was first through the broken down door... but he insisted that a local detective make the arrest.

Chapter 13

The prison had gone into lockdown. Immediate lockdown.

There was a scuffle in the corridor outside Ana's open office door. She was working on the case studies, including those of the two new prisoners, who she had met earlier in the week. There was nothing very unusual in a scuffle sound and she ignored it.

Curiosity and apprehension at every prison noise was something she'd learned wasn't her business. The place wasn't an open book; the prisoners had secrets they tried to hide from everyone, usually especially from the guards and the management. Even she had secrets, she admitted. The walls hid reasons why everyone was there. She grinned at her image reflection in the blue computer screen; she was reflective herself today. Maybe it was the promise of the holiday.

It was half an hour since lunch, she'd had her usual banter with Gus, and she hadn't had any inmates sent down yet for the afternoon interview sessions. There were always men on her lists. Men who wanted to see her for many reasons; sometimes just to get out of work or to see a woman in civvies when they were inside and away from their families. The latter was always apparent and they got a short abrupt visit only. The local men she saw regularly as she prepared them for re-entry into the town's society. There was the problem of job hunting and parole reports. For many others it was remedial and psychiatric counselling; long term and ongoing. Her case load was more than full and a general lockdown was an inconvenience because she couldn't get on with her work.

But if she couldn't see prisoners at least she'd the time to get some other conference reports done. The internal and probation reports were a continual catch up process. She clicked over to the appropriate screen of her current file and sat back in her chair to reread what she had already typed.

'Don't move, please.' The male voice in her doorway was quiet and full of authority.

She didn't move.

In a prison if someone said 'Stay' or 'Stop' she did just that.

Stopped. Without question.

Ana froze as a pair of German Shepherds flooded the room with their immense canine presence. She should be used to it, but these huge black, brindle and longhaired dogs appeared bigger to her than their adult structure warranted.

A thought thrust itself at the distant edges of her memory. A fear of dogs. She mentally drew herself into her shell as she brought her feet together under her desk and clamped her hands on her thighs.

Don't move, stay calm.

Stay looking relaxed. It's alright, she told herself.

The dogs sniffed around the room, then one paused and its nose pointed. It sniffed harder. A question and it abruptly sat looking up; still and rigid.

'I'll just have a look at that.' The voice of the tall uniformed police officer's voice was firm.

Ana looked up. 'They're only my daffodils bulbs...' She began. She stood from her chair to reach the pot plant from the barred window ledge that overlooked the prison farm outside.

'If you don't mind I'll get them,' the officer moved forward and lifted the pot of green spears down. He ran a hand along the window edge. The dog sniffed at the pot and turned away disinterested.

'Good boy Jazz,' the officer said. 'Thanks. Got to be sure.' He smiled at Ana. 'You never know what's hidden in flower pots, even those in innocent offices.'

She should be used to sudden raids by the Dog Squad, searching for drugs in the prison, but they still intimidated her. She'd seen a few in the three years she'd worked in the country facility.

'Yes,' Ana managed to smile back. '...and I've had offers from some of my clients for me to plant different seeds in the flower pots.' She flushed. That statement could be misinterpreted.

A smirk-less chuckle. 'I'll bet.'

'I tell them... no, thank you... but I'll just have my daffodils. Or my ferns.' She nodded, aware she was babbling. She forced her eyes to look at the man and not at the still forms of the sitting dogs. 'Sometimes I have ferns but I kill them with kindness by over-watering them.'

There was a silence as Ana fought for something more to say to the officer. I'm a counsellor, the thought raced through her brain. Talking and getting people to talk to me is my business. The dogs pushed every lucid thought away.

'I'm Ana Foster; prison counsellor,' she managed, flushing at her own verbal incompetence. 'Being around guard dogs isn't usually my scene.'

'Shaun Richardson.' He offered his hand and they shook. The dogs sat motionless although golden eyes flickered back and forth at every movement. 'You're not sure of the dogs are you?' Shaun said as another smile extended up to his dark brown eyes under a thatch of spiky black hair.

'Does it show that much?' she asked.

'Yes, the dogs sensed it. Always do, immediately. Especially Louis here…' He touched the darker dog. 'Jazz was more interested in the pots he's had special training for.' The smile again. 'They know about pot plants, but Louis knows when people are wary. His body language tells me immediately and very often I want to know why.'

Ana took a deep breath.

'I was attacked by a dog as a child. I ran and it attacked.' She paused, daring to glance down at the dogs. 'One like these, and as big, grabbed me from behind and shook me. I was terrified.' She repressed a shudder as she looked back at the handler. 'It tore a hole in my dress…a hole in me too… I still have the scar.'

'That must've been bad,' the officer said. 'Running, that'd set off a dog attack. They're natural predators and they'll give chase. These,' he ruffled the head of the nearest dog, 'these are my boys. Wouldn't hurt a fly when they're not on duty. My kids romp and climb all over them at home.'

The two dogs looked intently and intelligently at her before the officer moved. They sprang to heel and the trio left the room as a pack.

'He's admitting nothing. Full of protests that we've got the wrong man.' Mark and a uniformed officer came out of the interview room to report to the hovering Rick. It'd been a long interview. Mark stretched his shoulders and the packet of papers in his hand went wide. 'Thanks,' he said to the officer. 'You got the same impression of Quinn?'

'Yes, sir, he's a tight bastard.'

'Yeah, well, you'd expect that. Experienced.' Rick said.

'But his woman didn't appear too surprised when we arrested him for the murder of Naomi. She'll confirm whatever alibi Quinn wants but any prosecutor'll break her down in court.' Mark continued his muscle relaxing movements. Head forward and back. He hunched and shook his shoulders to loosen his neck.

'It's obvious. The poor bitch's under his thumb. Scared as all hell of him.' the uniformed man said.

'Even the DNA evidence didn't throw him. It wasn't him. Wasn't his. That's all he'll say. And that they can't take him away from his son. He knows he'll be sent to Adelaide and he's demanding that we get the woman and boy back there immediately.' Mark said.

'The cheek of it! Us to do that.' Rick stormed. He'd stayed away from the interview because he had been Quinn's arresting officer in the past. There was not to be any conflicting situation that an enterprising defence 'rat', as Rick put it, could use later in court.

'Well, we've got enough already for the local magistrate to send him to the Remand Centre to await trial. We'll get more evidence; most of it circumstantial, but that DNA is the clincher.'

'Let's see him get a woman brief this time to charm his way out of these murders,' Rick said.

'We've only got him on one yet, boss,' Mark insisted.

'The others will follow. Circumstantial evidence if necessary. He'll go down for the lot this time.'

'I'll get the paperwork started pronto...there's going to be a load of it,' Mark said referring to masses of evidence that the prosecutors needed to get a complicated case to the court processes.

'Yeah, let's get him out of here soon. The local population will be screaming for his carcass as soon as they hear we've made an arrest.'

Three hours later Rick was fuming.

The magistrate had confirmed the warrant for the detaining

of Demetrius Quinn on a charge of murder. He was to be transferred to Adelaide as soon as the police and Corrections van arrived. But a burst water main had flooded the cells in the new police building. Although Quinn was to be kept for probably one night only, he would now be sent to the local prison for that time, and then transferred to Adelaide. Rick hated the chink in the process. He questioned the prison's security until he was convinced that they had a High Security section and Quinn would be adequately housed there over night in a single cell.

Demetrius Quinn was fuming.

He'd been informed that the woman and his boy had left on a bus to Adelaide. The police had no immediate reason to keep her in Port Lincoln and she'd stated that she wanted to go to Adelaide.

Quinn knew that the bitch wouldn't stop there...

She'd be to hell and gone.

Taking his son away.

Chapter 14

Ana went down to the staff kitchen to make herself a coffee.

It would be awful muck, as usual, because the prisoners who cleaned the area on a regular roster stole the better staff coffee, and substituted coffee from their own mess area.

Her irritation grew as she looked over the kitchen. Dirty plates and cups lay all on the table and sink, over every surface. Discarded fast food packs, disapproved of by management when there was good food to be bought from the officer's canteen, littered and overflowed the bin.

Ana scowled.

She was not impressed.

Fast food evidence fostered resentment in the prisoner ranks and, as she trying to encourage the men to eat right for their health and pocket when they got out. She felt that the some of the staff were unsupportive. Others plain ignorant. The place was left a pigsty and the prisoners hadn't been able to clean up because of the lockdown. It was no wonder that some prisoners had such a low opinion of the officers when they were treated by them as servants. She cleared the bins and stacked the dishes before she made her coffee. It was a vicious circle. Often staff and prisoners abused each other as humans in a difficult situation, and she was meant to prepare the prisoners for eventual release. It was the stupid little things like this that caused societies demarcation lines, she thought.

Bother them, she grunted, but the poor coffee was better than nothing. Her nerves were still raw after the dogs. She'd have to drink the horrible stuff. Sometimes the manager, John Fellows, got his coffee machine going then and she could cadge a cup from him. He was not in his office right now but a cup would come later, he'd promised.

As the sound of barking erupted from the cell and prisoner areas, she carried her coffee back to Gus's area. There wasn't much she could do as far as interviews went until the sweep was over and chatting to him elicited information gathered over his long years as a warden. It all added to her knowledge and ability as a counsellor.

Gus stood, rocking back and forth on the soles of his feet, and chuckling at the noises that come through into the front offices.

'We got them this time! They didn't know the dogs were coming. Caught them before they could get word that the sweep was on its way,' he said.

'So their own network let them down?' Ana smiled at his satisfaction. The early 'family' telephone calls that warned them when something is up.

'Yeah,' his satisfaction was evident. 'They think they're so clever getting the word through. Sometimes they get wind of the dog van as it comes through Port Augusta Prison but this time we tricked them. It bypassed Port Augusta. Took the truckies ring route via Yorkey's Crossing.'

'Well, did it do any good? What did they get?'

'I haven't heard all the details yet but lots. It'll be the usual hard stuff, white powder, rollies, pills, steroids and plenty of grass,' he said.

Gus was a man who distrusted prison visitors. Prisoners harried their women and children to smuggle drugs in. Sometimes in baby toys or even nappies. Officials working in the prison from other agencies were sometimes coerced into bringing in banned goods. Often they had no idea what was banned or why.

Some innocents did too.

Gus looked at Ana with a smile lurking below his moustache.

Ana laughed. 'Yeah... Yeah... I remember when I picked up that tennis ball full of grass that'd rolled into the car park and I passed it into the front office. To be sent back to the prisoners! It'd had been thrown in from the boundary. I was so green...'

'Yeah! Green as the vegetable matter in it! Do you know what the latest is? The boss was talking about it yesterday. They're getting clever out in the outer farm grounds and gardens. Even the dogs can't always cover the large hectare area out there. Do you know what they're doing now?'

He waited for her to ask him. His pattern.

'What are they doing now?'

'Bloody ingenious! They're filling rock melons, those still on the vine, with sultanas. Pushing them in with sticks and waiting for it to ferment into alcohol. It's crude syrupy muck, but its grog. We caught on when they started fighting over the stuff last weekend! You heard about that...but it took us a few days to find out how they were getting so drunk. Drunk and mean.' The older man sighed. 'I'll be glad to retire. Drugs and knives now - not like the old days...'

The phone rang and Gus picked up. 'They've finished inside and the dogs'll be back here soon. Need to rest a bit and have a drink, before they go on out to the farm. I'll be able to call up the remand prisoner who's demanding an interview with you. OK?'

'Sure. Thanks Gus.'

Ana looked up as the sounds of heavy footsteps threaded down the long corridor outside her office. She did not recognise the voice that thrust mouthfuls of obscenities into the echoing space and through her open door.

Gus cautioned the obviously new prisoner.

'Settle down! Mind your manners or you won't be able to see the counsellor. '

'I demand to see the bloody counsellor! Someone's got to fix things so that the bitch doesn't take off any further with my son...' was the gist of the words spoken, excessive expletives deleted.

'Stop!' the officer ordered and the reluctant feet stomped to a loud standstill outside her door.

Ana sighed.

This was one interview that she wouldn't usually be required to do. It was the man who had been arrested this morning in Port Lincoln for murder. He had come in shouting his innocence, and asking about the whereabouts of his son. John Fellows had come to her office and, with a bribe of a good cup of coffee from his coffee maker, and had sought her assistance with the prisoner on remand. He needed to be quietened down so that he would go on the transfer van next evening as scheduled. He'd refused to see a local lawyer but demanded to see a counsellor. Right now!

With reluctance, she'd agreed to the interview.

It was a question of evidence.

If this man spoke about the murders then she could be called to court to report what he'd said. After the interview the police would ask her for a report, and she knew that they hated counsellors being involved before a trial. This court case was a long way off and interviewing him now made her position, and the creed of confidentiality, difficult. Ana was between a rock and a hard place and she didn't like it at all.

She tugged her rebellious dark hair back into the clip at the back of her head and checked that her desk was clear of anything that could be used as a weapon. Her usual practice. Her eyes flickered to the emergency security call button within reach at the side of her desk. It was OK, tested a week ago. A clear desk confirmed confidentiality of each prisoner she saw as well as complied with security. Just her computer, a pen and some papers lay exposed. She dropped the pen into a drawer, closed it shut, and pushed the computer back against the wall.

Ana stood as the remand prisoner was brought in.

Gus introduced him then said. 'He's going out on the transfer van so you'll have to attend to anything you can for him today. Maybe a tall order but...' He turned to the scowling man. 'You behave, Quinn, you've not long out of Yatala Prison so you know the drill. You talk properly to Mrs Foster. No nonsense. And cut the language, she doesn't have to listen to you swearing. She knows things, maybe what you want, and if you behave she may be able to help you.'

Gus looked towards Ana and gave a nod; an unspoken nod that said – 'be careful of this one and I won't be far away.'

The officer left the room.

The glass panelled door remained slightly ajar behind him.

Another hint to be careful.

Quinn's whole attitude was an angry sneer.

His tall, powerfully muscled frame spoke of hours and years spent in prison gyms. His presence seemed to take up more of her space than the man warranted.

Her room was being occupied by overwhelming presences today, she thought, first the dogs and now this man.

His anger filled the room.

He waited.

She waited.

Ana didn't usually look at prisoners as anything other than clients, but this man had probably one of the most handsome faces she had ever seen in her life. He had film star looks. A wide brow, high cheekbones and a strong jaw. Blond hair without a trace of grey though his age, she knew, was mid-forties. The hair was cut short but still allowed a hint of curl to inch over his forehead. Deep blue eyes. Moody bedroom eyes. Why this man had to kill to achieve anything in life flashed through her mind? With those looks life should have been handed to him on a platter.

A golden platter.

Her professional demeanour kicked in and she thrust aside the impact of his appearance.

She nodded towards the chair next to her desk.

Those eyes looked her up and down before he moved.

He strode, defiantly, further into the room then stopped, just as most men did when they got inside her office.

It was her window that stopped them. Especially the men who hadn't seen the outside world in a long while. This man had been outside, but a fleeting tensing of the mouth, of worry crossed his face.

A hesitation before the scowl returned.

In this case, she wondered if the man standing before her had time to understand that this scene, or any outside scene, could be gone from him now that he'd been arrested for murder. OK he was innocent until proven guilty but his conviction was more than on the cards.

There was little apparent reaction from the man other than that first flicker of hesitation.

He stared out then looked away from the window and down to his boots. The sun coming through the barred window left fingers of shadow on the leather. He turned to face her.

The pupils of his eyes had contracted against the outside brightness. It was like looking into twin dark pin points; hard tunnels in the cold flat plateau of his eyes.

Usually, Ana offered to shake hands with each prisoner when

she met them, especially for the first time. It was her way of recognising their humanity, whatever the circumstances. Often the man was surprised at her action. To come into an office with a window offering such a view, and then to have a woman offer her hand in a common act of greeting, was unexpected. It was also a way to begin to gain a prisoner's confidence.

But sometimes a sixth sense said: 'Not this time. Not this man.'

Today she obeyed it.

Her hand stayed at her side as she sat in her own chair and again motioned the man to take the interview chair.

He scowled at her, then sat down abruptly, drawing the chair away from the desk. He thrust one leg over the other, his irritation and anger showing in the agitated small up and down jiggle movement of his upper ankle and booted foot. He was at the edge of control and it showed.

'Do I call you Demetrius?' she asked. Again the gesture of common courtesy. 'Or would you prefer Mr Quinn?'

He was unshaven. Male musky. Obviously he hadn't showered before he was arrested earlier that morning. Now he hadn't been able to shower in the prison because of the lockdown and the dog sweep. Covertly she watched as his hands clenched in his lap and the prison inked tattoos of 'HATE' and 'LOVE' tightened on his knuckles. That and the foot movement made her wary.

Very wary.

There was a short pause before he spoke.

'I don't care what the shit you call me.' A pause. 'But no-one dares to call me Demetrius.' His voice was deep and harsh. Brutal. 'I'm only wanting you to stop that bitch taking my son and going off. Away from Adelaide...taking my son...' He stopped, perfect teeth biting into his lip. 'The scum said she'd already got on the bus. Left town.'

He looked away and she waited a beat before she asked. 'Does your partner have friends in Adelaide?'

'Nah, Sydney. Melbourne. The bitch was born in Katherine, but she hated the place...doubt she'd be going there.'

'She's a long way from home here if you have to go back to Adelaide.'

'Course the filth may have been baiting me. They're stitching me up, the bastards...'

Ana broke in. 'We're not here to discuss your case just...to see if there's anything else I can do.'

He looked hard at her and she smiled briefly, a small smile. She gave him time to speak again. Often her silence worked for the men, to help them regain their composure. He took his time as he continued to stare at her.

Perhaps it was her small intake of exasperated breath. A whisper of resigned thought. The woman and boy were free agents and had the right to go where they wanted and, to her knowledge, the police had no reason to detain them. Her face said nothing of his impossible request.

'I know your type!' he paused then sneered, 'Bet you're like all the whores. You won't help me get my son back. I've changed my mind. Bitch! I won't talk to you!'

Quinn banged his hands down on his knees in readiness to stand.

'Don't talk then,' she responded. Her tone quiet, flat. She leaned back in her chair. Ana wasn't going to be verbally abused and she knew she could report him already for his language. 'If you don't talk to me then there's nothing I can do for you ... or your son. You don't have any other options before you leave here and you may find that I can help you.' She paused, left the slightest gap. There was no response. 'Tell me about your son.

How old is he?' she asked.

There was a long moment before Quinn spoke. He appeared to relax a little into his chair. Then in a softer voice he said, 'Clinton's eight. I'd only just found him again before I got out. The stupid cow of his mother thought she could hide him away with me in prison but I found the bitch...now she's gone again. Taken off. Now I'll lose him for good with what I've got hanging over me.' Quinn took a deep breath. 'The bastard cops have got me. Framed me.' He looked hard at her. 'I didn't do any of these murders,' he repeated.

Ana checked her question about the boy's age. Mathematically she'd realised that Quinn was in prison when the baby was conceived.

Not the right question.

Not the time for that question.

'I've said before that my job is not to talk to you about the arrest or the murders. I can get you a lawyer for that, but if you give me your partner's name and previous address then I'll see what I can do about your son. His welfare is really his mother's concern and...'

Quinn cut in. 'Her name's Faye Bishop. Not that's going to help. The bitch's gone already. I had to force her to stay once I got her to Lincoln. I only want the boy. He's mine.' He stared hard at her.

She took her eyes off his face and turned to take a pen and paper from her desk drawer. 'Now...' she started. 'Tell me her...'

'You wouldn't understand,' he cut in. 'And of course you know where he is. But you're like them all...worse than them all...a whore...fucking whore!'

In that instant he lunged at her.

Chapter 15

Quinn grabbed a fistful of her buttoned blouse under her chin and wrenched it hard sideways. It tightened into her throat.

It cut off her air. Cut off her voice.

Ana struggled.

She tried to get her hands up to break the fabric choking her. Tried to get her fingers between the fabric and her throat.

With his other hand Quinn grabbed a hunk of her hair at the front and pulled her head forward, so hard that her chin was pushed down onto her chest, again blocking her airway. He kicked his chair away and crouched over her and started to rant, to chant, "Whore! You know where he is!' Fucking whore!' The words grated, pulsed into her ears, stung like molten sand. 'Tell me, whore!'

The chant was almost conversational and all the more frightening by the intense quietness of the insult. Neither of them was making enough noise that could alert the guards.

The emergency button under her desk!

She reached for it.

He sensed her movement and dragged her too far away to press it. He was using the wheels of her own chair to move her ever closer into his strong shouldered grip.

Away from the button and help!

Her vision was restricted now to just his hand gripping her shirt and his arm. Pain shot through her scalp as he wrenched her hair and held her head down. She tried to get her fingers between the strangling shirt and her neck. To get some air. Her other arm flailed as she attempted to get her balance to pull herself away. She registered strands of hair on her arms. Her own hair.

She forced herself to think. Not to just feel.

She kicked out wildly for his groin. His shins. He blocked the blow with his knees.

Quinn had stopped his incessant chant.

His heavy breathing.

His silence was all the more threatening.

She swung her elbow at his face, as she had been taught in defence classes. Aimed for the bridge of his nose. Her elbow struck the corner of his eye hard and he growled, 'Bitch!' She swung again lower at his belly. She didn't connect. His backward movement was too quick.

In the next moment he released his grip on her shirt then clamped both hands around her throat.

Again she tried to pry loose his choke hold. It didn't work. He was too strong.

She reached out wildly and blindly for his eyes with her clawed hands. Her fingernails slashed at one eye. Her hand grabbed at his mouth. She scratched him before his teeth clamped onto her hand.

He bit into her fingers. Bit down hard.

A lightning bold of pain shot up her arm.

He spat her blood out with another curse.

Ana was fighting for her life and she knew it.

Fighting in slow motion! Seconds were ticking away on the clock where her oxygen battery was fast running down.

She could smell his stinking sweated intensity. See the darkness of the expanded pupils of his eyes, tunnels of darkness in his rage.

'You know where he is... tell me... Whore... whore.... whore!' The chant started again.

In desperation she kicked out at him. Her bloodied hands grappled again ineffectively with his hands around her neck. The room spun and darkened. Her brain was being starved of life giving oxygen. The pain in her throat and head were like razor slices.

Light faded into a tunnel as she was crushed against his chest.

She could feel her knees hammering against him.

Her heels hammering against the floor. Her flailing arms bashed weakly against him. They hit her desk.

His words 'Whore! Whore! Fucking whore!' hammered into her ears until his voice too was dimming with the light.

She felt her body go limp.

She slipped unconscious into her chair with his hands still pressed downwards into her neck.

Chapter 16

Ana's office door was thrown wide open and the world erupted into noise.

The dogs were in first.

Their frenzied barking and snapping jaws were more than a warning.

The prisoner thrust her away and he threw up his arms to protect his face as one great beast hurled itself at his head. Its lunge flung man, the chair behind him, and beast against the wall.

Quinn screamed profanities as the dog Jazz's teeth drew blood.

The huge dog, Louis, wrenched Ana away. Its powerful jaws dragged at her clothing, pulled her free of her chair and thrust her down onto the floor.

With a whimper she rolled herself into a ball.

The dog stood over her, teeth barred. Its bulk protected her from the mêlée of shouting men who had followed the dogs into the small office.

Ana gulped huge lung-fulls of air down her burning throat.

From an indeterminable distance she heard 'Jazz! Heel!'

Four wardens bodily lifted the struggling Quinn away from Jazz. He punched out at the dog standing guard over Ana and kicked out at the officers. They delivered blows of their own and then, cursing still against Ana, Quinn was bundled out of the room.

The noise receded down the corridor, but the screams inside her head stayed.

The dog remained straddling her body.

'Louis! Heel!' was spoken in a softer tone and the huge dog obeyed, growls rumbling a protective warning in its throat. Then it moved clear of her and slowly Ana lifted her head. 'You're OK, Miss. Someone'll be here soon for you.'

Shaun Richardson snapped leads on the dogs' collars. Still on an adrenalin alert, they strained against the restrictions, towards the noise in the corridor. 'Steady boys,' she heard as they followed the contingent of officers and the prisoner out her door. Security first. They might be needed again if the prisoner broke free.

Ana reached up to her desk and used it's stability to drag herself to her feet. She could see blood on the floor.

On her desk. On her clothes.

Her blood and the prisoner's blood overlaid and mingled.

Someone moved into her field of vision and she looked up at the stricken face of Gus, her knees gave way and she sagged into his arms. He found he was supporting her limp unconscious body.

Peter's phone rang.

He grunted. Great, an interruption when he had almost done the computer changes that woman insisted upon to the house plans. Just what he didn't need. He wanted to finish and get out for a game of golf with a friend while the weather held. Holidays weren't supposed to be spent on work but that's what often happened. He picked up the new plans as they flowed in a long sheet out of the printer, located his mobile from under the avalanche of paper and leaned back into his chair.

'Peter Foster,' he announced.

He listened, tension lines building in his face and tightening across his shoulders. He sat up straight and his heart felt as if it had jolted in his chest.

'Where're they taking her, John? To the surgery or the hospital? She's that bad...?' He was on his feet as the spate of words continued into his ear. The adrenalin surged as his eyes sought his car keys hanging on the rack by the office door. 'All right...I'll meet the ambulance there.'

Peter beat both the ambulance and the Prison Manager to the hospital by more than ten minutes.

He cursed the prison for being so far out of town.

Why were they taking so long to get her here?

He paced in the waiting area of the Emergency Department, and then ran out the door to stand by as the ambulance arrived. He rushed to the side of the gurney carrying Ana as it was pulled out of the back.

'Ana...' he started.

'Give us room, Sir,' the ambulance officer said. 'Please.'

Peter stepped aside, still in the way Then he followed the gurney as the procession moved efficiently through the automatic glass doors, through the slide key locked section and on into the treatment area.

Relegated again to the waiting area, Peter could just see Ana through the glass windows.

She was pale, with an oxygen cannula in her nose and an IV drip in her arm. She seemed to be thrashing against it.

Just before a nurse pulled the curtains around the scene, blocking his view of his wife, Peter saw Dr Valerie Shaw arrive and to go to Ana's side. He breathed a sigh of small relief. Valerie was Ana's own doctor; a lucky break in the small town that raised its eyebrows at this young and forthright, female doctor with her no nonsense brand of medicine.

His wife liked and trusted her. One small consolation.

'Ana, you're safe! Lie still now,' Valerie commanded, firm yet gentle. She captured her patient's free hand and cupped her warm hands around the cold clenched fingers.

Tears glistened in Ana's eyes, leaked out the sides and down into the hair at her temples. Dark eyes with hollow terror etched in them.

'Hang on a minute, Ana. I need the ambulance report. You're OK.'

Screams were still in Ana's head. The voice that chanted 'Whore! You know where she is! Whore!' over and over. Dogs barking.

Now lights were above her. A blind of bright lights. Ana tried to concentrate on the report. She knew about reports. They told you things.

She heard her name. Her age. How does he know I'm 31, she thought? Why does he know?

She saw glasses and mousy hair. The ambulance officer's lumpy nose had lost a battle with something hard in the past.

She heard the words... 'a victim of an assault by a prisoner... attempted strangulation with temporary loss of consciousness... given oxygen by the prison staff and we've continued the treatment. She's been conscious but, at times, lapsing into incoherent mumblings. Shock symptoms. Massive bruising to her throat...'

Of course she had bruising to her throat! Couldn't they see? She was gasping still.

'A head and scalp injury... minor...some other scratches and bruises and she's been bitten on the hand. The punctures are deep and irregular.'

She tried to see her hand. There was a roaring in her head.

When did they bandage that? She wondered.

'Her BP and heart rates are elevated. We've also put in an IV with normal saline for shock.'

She suddenly remembered she'd been bitten.

By the dogs? Before the dogs? Not the dogs.

By the man? A flash of anger roared into her head.

Ana tried to look at her hand. There it was - bandaged. It wasn't good to be bitten by someone at the prison. She knew that but she couldn't remember why.

'She's refused pain relief.' The ambulance officer quiet voice completed his report and looked again at his patient.

Ana stilled her thoughts and attempted a smile up at him. She whispered 'Thank you.' She had to say that because he'd helped her, been kind, she remembered. 'Thank you,' she said again; through hoarse sandpaper the words trembled. But it was louder. It hurt to speak.

The ambulance officer's face came closer to hers. She flinched, pulled away. 'You'll be OK now,' he said and drew back.

The noises in her ears had diminished but the lights were still too bright. She raised her hand to shield her eyes and saw the bandage again. Her hand was hurt. Bitten. She had to remember.

'Thanks,' Valerie said to the attendant as he handed his written report to her. 'Will you assist me to lift her over onto the bed please?'

She turned now and shook her head as Ana struggled to try move herself across from the gurney to the bed. 'No, we'll do it. There was a bustle as the ambulance officers disconnected the oxygen from their cylinders and plugged it into the wall connections, gathered together equipment, their stretcher, and left the room.

'Thanks,' Ana heard Valerie say to them.

A mature looking nurse clipped a blood oxygen monitor onto

Ana's finger and took observations of blood pressure and pulse. Her movements were smooth, unhurried and her eyes, above the cotton mask echoed the wisps of grey hairs that had escaped her cap, were soothing.

Ana lay quieter; stopped the reactive thrashing as Valerie began her examination. 'You heard what the ambulance man reported, but have you got any other places that hurt?' she asked. She was watching her patient breathe carefully. 'That hurts still?' she asked.

Ana's panic was beginning to subside. Her professional self surfaced and she kicked it into place. The self was a mask she could hide behind. Somehow she knew she would need that mask. She would need it soon.

'It does …but…it's mainly my dignity that's taken a battering,' Ana croaked. Images began to flood into her head. Images from before the attack. The prisoner's stance, his cursing her; the myriad of warning signs of potential violence she was trained to recognise. 'I should never have let this happen,' she said her voice a rasp.

'We'll deal with all that later, but I don't think for one moment that you were at fault.' Valerie's fingers were careful as she felt about Ana's neck. Instinctively Ana pulled away. 'It's OK, that's a natural reaction, but do you remember how long you blacked out for? Was it moments?' she asked. 'Or longer?'

'No…it wasn't for very long… everything went dark when…it was happening. I can't tell. I can't remember.' Her head was clearing. 'I know I went … I sort of fainted when it was all over. There was blood on the floor.'

Valerie looked over to the blood oxygen monitor.

The nurse said, 'Blood gases at 90%, doctor. The other obs are stable. The same as the ambulance report.'

'Blood everywhere…' Ana repeated. She pulled at the tube

going into her nose. 'My blood and ...his blood.'

'The gases'll get better still if we keep the cannula on you a bit longer and you breathe slowly and deeply.' Valerie looked over to the nurse. 'I don't think there's permanent damage from the asphyxia, but I want to keep an eye on her carotid arteries and jugular veins for a while. They've been squeezed and there will be more swelling. We'll run some more tests if needed. Maybe an ultrasound.'

Valerie directed the next question to Ana. 'Was it just his hands around you throat?'

'He used my clothing, I think. Whatever it was...was pulled tight across my throat and he yanked my head... my hair down hard.' Ana lifted her hands attempting to demonstrate. 'I think he grabbed my throat too with his hands before I started to black out.'

'I thought it wasn't just a manual hand assault from the marks. You are in for some spectacular bruises over the next few days and weeks.' Valerie paused and turned to the nurse. 'Would you get the camera please? I'll need to take photographs of her neck and face. There's bruising on both. Also of her hair where there's damage and blood. They may be needed in any criminal action. And an assault pack, and a dressing tray. I'm going to have a look at the hand when I've done a quick physical to check to ensure there's no other injuries. Injuries Ana doesn't remember.'

The nurse went out of Ana's line of vision.

Valerie did the body examination. At least there were no signs of rape, that was a relief, but sexual assault hadn't been mentioned. She noted the scars she'd seen before and where bruises were forming, contusions and scrapes everywhere. On her arms and legs. One on her body where she'd been pulled against something hard. Ana had put up one hell of a fight. The doctor frowned as she slipped a few hairs that still clung to the blood on

Ana's scalp, into an evidence bag. With gentleness and care she scraped under Ana's fingernails to collect the blood and tissue there. She put these into a second evidence bag.

'These specimens say that you were attacked if and when it goes to court,' she commented as she shed her rubber gloves.

The nurse returned and the doctor took photographs.

'I must look a mess,' Ana attempted a joke. She thought, I hate looking messy.

Valerie smiled, 'I've seen worse,' and took the dressing tray from the nurse and slipped on new surgical gloves. 'Now, do you remember if the dogs bit you or was it the prisoner?'

'Him. Quinn.'

'Are you sure?'

'Yes, it wasn't the dogs.'

The doctor carefully removed the bandage to reveal the bloody and bitten fingers. Both semicircular wounds extended over the two exterior joints on three of the fingers of her left hand, extending to the knuckle. Valerie saw that the bites were deep, to the bones almost, and irregular as reported. She stood back as the nurse took more photographs as evidence.

Ana stretched her fingers and gave a sharp intake of breath. It hurt. She waggled them. 'I can move them,' she said. 'I don't think they're broken.'

Valerie was relieved.

Her patient was lucid and could reason. The threat of brain damage from the lack of blood lessened. 'Good. I don't think they're fractured either. But try curling your fingers in... Ahh! That hurt too didn't it?' Valerie pulled a sympathetic face. 'And I've got to take more scrapings from under your fingernails on this hand also for the police. Then I'm going to clean these wounds and flush them out with saline. We'll see after that. I think they'll need sutures but maybe not. I'll also give you a new tetanus shot if you haven't had one recently.'

Ana shook her head. She remembered that much.

'OK then we'll do that, and start antibiotics...you're not allergic are you? No. Then I'll do the blood tests...'

'Blood tests?' Ana repeated. The reason was surfacing more strongly. She pushed it away as she felt the panic noises in her head start again.

'Yes,' her doctor said, 'the blood tests are mandatory and essential.'

Valerie took a swab of the bitten area before she flushed the wounds again and again, sutured then taped and re-bandaged the hand. She checked again Ana's scalp, where blood was still oozing, and she instructed the nurse to place a soft bandage around her head. No need for sutures there. The pulled hair wounds would heal themselves when they had stopped bleeding.

'The nurse'll stay with you while I go out and have few words with Peter Then I'll be back. He can come in after that,' she said.

Ana lay on the bed and waited. Her thoughts went round and round and an undeniable fact surfaced. She turned her head away to the wall and covered her face with her hand.

The hand that was bandaged with such care.

Chapter 17

John Fellows joined Peter in the waiting room.

They had become friends over the years that Ana had worked at the prison. He touched Peter's arm. 'It's not as bad as it looks,' he said.

John was a big man, ex-army and combat experienced, but at that moment he was pale with shock. Or maybe it was anger, Peter couldn't tell. In agitation, John's tattooed arms, usually covered by his uniform shirt, were exposed as he'd thrust his sleeves up.

'So what happened?' Peter asked. He was in the post adrenalin state when a man can hit out at the nearest object, person, as the fear wavered. 'You said on the phone that there had been an incident and Ana was hurt. What bloody happened? She's not supposed to be in any danger. You bloody people are supposed to look after your support staff, she's not a screw. Her role's different. That's what they told me when she accepted the position out there.'

John attempted to cut in. 'Yes...but... sometimes things happen so fast...'

Peter's face was closed; he was not listening; incensed. 'You always said... So who wasn't doing his bloody job? What happened?' Peter demanded. His usually immaculate figure was tense, his dark blond hair mussed from his hands being thrust through it as he waited. 'They've got to let me see her, now! It's taking too bloody long.'

He was pushing against the Accident and Emergency door as Valerie came out into the waiting room.

'Come with me,' she instructed the two men, and led them to a small side office.

She held up her hand to stop Peter's urgent questions, sternly indicated for them to sit down, sighed and sat down herself at the desk.

The two men sat.

Valerie gave it to them fast and factual. 'Ana is going to be OK, from the attack, as far as I can see,' she said. 'The damage to her throat doesn't look serious in the long term. Minimal hopefully, except for very severe bruises. There will be others that'll appear too. I am concerned about the possibility of swelling in her neck area and I'm going to keep her in hospital overnight just to keep a check her airways and the blood vessels there. Her scalp wound is superficial just a hunk of hair was pulled out. She's in extreme shock, both physical and mental, and she'll need some counselling to help her psychologically.' She smiled, 'She may be a counsellor herself but like doctors being bad patients so counsellors usually, no always, give poor counsel to themselves.'

'She looks awful...' Peter said. 'You're sure she's going to be fine?'

'Yes...But...' Valerie looked at John. 'Ana's hand wound may be infected.'

'What do you mean, infected?' Peter demanded.

John looked uncomfortable. He shifted in his seat. He knew what was coming.

'Human bites are much like dog bites. Germs and infections can be transmitted in the saliva. Bad infections!' She turned to John and asked bluntly. 'She wasn't bitten by the dogs, but can you tell me if the man who attacked Ana is hepatitis or HIV positive?'

Peter's intake of breath was sharp. 'Oh hell, surely not? Not that...'

John looked distressed. 'I can't give you that information,' he said. 'It's confidential to any prisoner, you know that.'

'What?' Peter exploded. He leapt to his feet. 'The hell you can't. This's Ana we're talking about.'

'Don't you think that I know that? I can't tell you for confidential reasons and I can't tell you right now because I don't know. This man's currently a remand prisoner, not a convicted prisoner that we usually get here. I haven't looked at the man's past medical records from when he was in Yatala serving time before.' John's military shoulders slumped. 'I'll get the records as soon as possible but he's been on the outside for three months, things could have changed in that time.'

John was fazed. Peter's glare of accusation didn't help. He shifted again in his chair: like a naughty school boy caught out by his friend's obvious anger. Dammit – it wasn't fair. 'The prisoner arrived unexpectedly this morning and was to go out tonight or tomorrow. I'd never have got his medical records anyway in that time frame...' He didn't add that the dogs doing a sweep of the prison was more time consuming that day.

He was in an insidious position and they all knew it.

'Have you said anything to Ana?' Peter turned on Valerie.

'No, not yet. But I should tell her what the swab and blood tests are for. She's not stupid and she's worked with prisoners with positive status before. She'll know what the situation is...once she gets her head together after the shock of the assault. She'll remember and put two and two together. And I'm very definite about her working with a counsellor she knows and trusts, as soon as possible.'

The nurse knocked on the door. 'Can I take Mrs Foster up to

the wards now, doctor?'

John interrupted before Peter could speak. 'She's to have a private room if one's available. Especially as the police insist they need to question her. They were called before I left and they'll already be asking questions out at the prison.'

The nurse stood motionless.

Peter opened his mouth to protest about the police interrogation but both Valerie and John stopped him.

Again John got in first. 'It's a criminal matter, Peter. The police work is essential. The bastard's got to be charged and a prosecution case started. He's been arrested for other matters and will now be transferred back to Adelaide Remand Centre to await trial. My chaps are arranging the prison transfer as we speak. He's already in solitary and he can't stay for more than a day or so in this prison now.' the manager said wryly. 'Ana has the confidence and respect of most of the other prisoners and they would bash him if they got the chance. I've actually got to protect him...'

'Protect him! Bugger the law!' Peter voice was a gritted rasp. 'Let them have him...'

'Is there a private room available?' Valerie asked the nurse over the commotion of men's voices. She nodded affirmative. 'Good. Then take her up and please tell her that she'll have her husband and boss to see her when she is settled.' As the nurse left Valerie turned to the two men. 'Now treat her gently. She's been assaulted. She's in shock, remember that.'

The nurse returned to the doorway. 'The police are here and they want to talk to Mrs Foster now,' she said.

'I'll handle this. You go up with Ana.'

Valerie met Detective Senior Sergeant Rick Charlton, who had hiked up the stairs as the gurney went into the lift, and was already standing outside Ana's room. His whole body language screamed impatience. He hated hospitals and had started to pace up and down near the nurse's station. The nurse offended by his abrupt manner and demands to see Ana 'right now,' resolutely stared into her own computer screen and ignored him.

He stopped Valerie physically as she tried to pass him to enter the Ana's room.

'Wait a minute, Miss. I need to interview Ana Forster. I haven't time to hang about...' he said.

Valerie's back stiffened.

She eyed the alpha male type who barred the doorway with distain. She took in his dark hair greying slightly at the temples as he again raised a hand to block her path.

With a sharp turn of her head she faced him down until the man lowered his restraining hand.

This was her territory.

She felt his eyes flick up and down her person, frisking her. She was almost as tall as he was and had a firm, but voluptuous, body. She had changed from the scrubs she wore in A&E and her trim black skirt was topped with a white blouse and blue jacket. The effect coupled with her black mid heeled pumps was more reminiscent of a corporate executive except that her stethoscope broke the line of her clothing as it swung from of one pocket.

She tossed a head of honey hair; hair that often belied her toughness, but her eyes were stern as she forced him to meet her gaze.

'I'm Doctor Shaw; and you'll just have to wait a bit longer. My patient isn't ready to be interviewed by anyone yet.' She tried to temper his obvious impatience. 'Can't this be done tomorrow morning? The Prison Manager said that assailant is in custody ready to be shipped to Adelaide as soon as possible. There's no problem to the public. He's not going to hurt any other women.'

'Look…' Rick attempted bluster, 'I do need to speak to Mrs Foster today. I've spoken to the prison staff and they're doing written reports. Do you know those reports have to go through the Corrections in Adelaide before I can have them? It's ridiculous! I've talked to the crim and just got a mouthful of abuse for my trouble. He's trying to say that it's self-defence.' His face reflected a lack of belief. 'He reckons she slapped him…and then the dogs bit him! And then the screws thumped him! I have to have her side of the story to get additional criminal charges underway.'

'What rot!' Valerie retorted. A small tickle of a smile curled her lips. 'You'd believe that?'

'No, of course not! But Mrs Foster's a civilian. A bloody civilian! She's a contract worker for the department. This makes it worse for me as any prison assault against a civilian comes under Major Crime. It's a matter of paperwork. Bloody paperwork!' He pulled up in his tirade. 'You do know that this man's been arrested on more charges. Some lawyer could challenge them but this assault means that we've got him for sure.'

'I know that the prisoner is on remand. Why wasn't he in the police watch-house?'

'A problem with the plumbing at the station. We didn't want to but we had to put him out in the prison.'

'So this assault couldn't have happened if he'd been where he should have been? In police custody.'

'Yes maybe.' Rick's face suddenly looked smug. 'But we still need a load of time to gather further evidence for other matters. This'll help…'

Valerie glared at the affront of the police office now pacing before her. She'd almost felt a smidgen of sorry for him when he moaned about paperwork. These days governmental paperwork was endless but when he seemed gleeful that this assault firmed the position against the prisoner she wanted to lash out verbally herself.

Rick was continuing. '...and my offsider isn't here at the moment.'

The 'offsider' hurried down the corridor towards them.

'Sorry Sarg. Just got some more info on the latest murder victim. I wanted to talk to the officer before I came here. It's another thing we wanted.' He pulled up and acknowledged Valerie. 'Hello doctor. I'm Mark Llewellyn. I heard our bastard prisoner did over the woman counsellor at the prison today. Sorry about the language...' a flash of self reprimand crossed his face. 'Is she OK?'

Despite her annoyance at Rick Valerie warmed to the younger enthusiastic man who had, at least, asked after her patient. Then she smelled his tobacco breath and the rapport lessened. 'Mrs Foster will live, but she's very traumatised,' she said. 'I'm still not happy about you seeing her tonight. I repeat. Can't it wait?'

Mark looked towards his scowling boss. 'No, ma'am, it would be best straight away to make sure that the crim gets to stay in the Remand Centre. It's a very high security there and he'll get no favours. We need to charge him with the assault. Maybe for attempted murder. That charge will stick while we get the rest on the evidence we need on the murders.'

'So you've just confirmed that this man, who attacked Mrs Foster today, is the person I've heard was arrested today for murder?' Valerie demanded. 'How on earth did he get anywhere near a counsellor?'

'Well, it happened, but I promise we'll go easy on her. From reports I've heard she's lucky to be alive,' Mark said. He smiled a quite beguiling smile. 'The prison doc had to patch up the crim too. She hit him hard, busted his eye. You sure we can't see her tonight? Makes things easier to clear this up.

When it seemed inevitable Valerie relented. 'Five minutes and remember, be very careful you don't upset her,' she said. 'Her husband is with her and I'd like him to stay.'

Rick thrust one hand into a pocket and muttered as all three went into the hospital room.

Ana looked very small in the hospital be

d. There was an oxygen cannula threaded into her nose and a clear saline drip in place in one arm. She was pale under the forming bruising and agitated, her face and neck were already swelling. She pulled at the bedclothes with the bandaged restless hand. Another bandage circled her head where the hair had been pulled out and only tufts of dark hair showed around it.

Peter looked up from his chair by the bed and frowned.

Valerie put up a hand to contain his protest. She spoke to Ana. 'I'm sorry, but I think that you should try to get this interview over with...perhaps while it's fresh in your mind. These detectives are adamant that it's got to be tonight.' She went to the bed and laid her fingers on Ana's wrist. The pulse thumped. 'Five minutes. That's all, and Peter, you can time them,' she frowned at the detectives before she left the room.

Rick moved close to the bed head and formally introduced them both. He waved his Warrant Card near Ana's eyes. Mark stood back by the foot end.

'I've heard the prisoner's story,' Rick said bluntly. 'He said you hit him. What's your version...?'

'What!' Ana whispered in a voice that croaked. Her eyes went wide.

Peter jumped to his feet.

Mark looked incredulously at his boss. 'Sarg...?'

What was the matter with the man, Mark thought, he'd been blunt with women ever since he'd split up with his wife a couple of months ago. Gone into the tough guy mode; into sports and took time off for them despite everything else they had to handle since then.

Less bluntly, Rick continued as though no-one had reacted. 'In the scheme of things this isn't a big case. Open and shut as far as I'm concerned. I don't believe the bastard for one minute, but something must have set him off. I need to know if there's anything in his story. Even a grain of truth! Did he say anything about the murders? Anything - or we'll get done by the lawyers he'll get his hands on. I've seen it before.'

He paused as Ana's eyes brimmed with tears at the onslaught.

'Sorry, but I am a busy man and I want to get this done.' Suddenly the big man wanted out. 'Look, I have to go. I'll leave Mark here to complete the interview. Here's my card, phone and mobile number, if I can help in the future...' He thrust a card on the over-way table and started for the door. 'Hope that's OK with you,' he said over his shoulder to the younger detective. 'I need to get back to all the other matters.'

The door banged shut.

'You can go too. Look what he's done to my wife. Upset her again...' Peter was more than annoyed.

'I'm not going to apologise for the Sarg. Things are pretty hectic at the moment and he is a good bloke under all of that...' Mark was apologising. 'Can we at least get a statement started and maybe you can complete it in the morning? I'll come back then. I can see that you're still upset.'

'That would be better,' Ana whispered agreement. 'I'll have a bit of trouble writing now with one hand bandaged and a drip in the other. By morning I'll have at least one hand free... and that prisoner attacked me. I didn't provoke him. He wanted me to get his son away from a woman. I started to ask him who she was but then he just attacked. He said he knew me but I've never seen him before in my life! He just grabbed me...' her composure broke.

'And he kept whispering "whore ... whore" at me. I can hear him now. It was awful...'

Mark looked towards the door as though expecting the doctor or nurse to come back and order him out. 'Thank you for that. Never thought for a moment that you'd provoked him. And I think that you were lucky to have survived the assault. From what I've heard you fought him off well.' Mark paused looking at Ana's pale drawn face. 'I think my time's up. I'll go now. Take it easy and I hope that you're much better tomorrow.'

Mark smiled, and after shaking hands with Peter, he left the room.

'Some things will be better in the morning... but not everything,' Ana whispered. 'I think I want to try to sleep now. Do you mind, darling?'

She closed her eyes and Peter stretched back in his chair to wait beside her; his fingers touched her arm. He needed the contact for his own reassurance as she appeared to sleep.

Chapter 18

Ana had lain; mostly awake, in the hospital room all night with the town street lights throwing a white beam across her bed through the crack in the heavy curtains. She could hear pigeons shuffling on the wide window ledge outside the room and there were the continual noises of nurses as they moved about the corridors. A clock ticked every fifteen seconds and the wharf, just over a kilometre away, groaned noise into the night as a ship was loaded with grain for some destination far away. Every time the door to her room was opened she could see a green 'running man' EXIT sign. It pointed the way out and she wanted to escape and run far away herself.

On the hour, as the cardiac monitor whispered a drawn out jagged line above her head, the nurses entered the room to check her pulse and the swollen flesh of her throat. She knew her neck was enlarged because she could feel it like a bulging hot collar under her chin. In an effort to keep the internal voices at bay she had concentrated on everything external to her. Ana had refused the sleeping pill Valerie had ordered and by the end of the long night she'd wished she hadn't been so stubborn and had taken the chance of a night's oblivion.

Just as the beam across her bed yellowed with the rising sun, the nursing staff had come into her room when she felt she'd just managed to get to sleep. She watched, in passive resignation, as the nurse pulled back the curtains and let the cruel morning light flood the room.

Stark memories from yesterday swarmed back with the light.

The assault. The dogs.

The ambulance.

Then the HIV reality...that was the hardest part. Overnight the black implications had pressed down like a vice that tightened into her brain. There seemed no escape. Not until the blood tests came back. Six or seven weeks! No wonder I couldn't sleep, she thought. The early daylight start didn't help.

'How's the neck? The pain bad?' The nurse was too cheerful for the morning although her question was caring.

Ana turned her head towards the nurse. Oh hell! Her neck! Not only swollen it was rigid and so painful she could hardly move. It wasn't just her neck, her shoulders hurt and she ached all over. She felt that she had been in a concrete mixer. A rotating concrete mixer.

'You can have paracetamol for it if you need it, the doctor's ordered it,' the nurse said. 'I've got to look at your hand too.

'Perhaps something for my neck,' Ana agreed. Bloody hell, her thoughts raged. 'Valerie could have ordered something stronger, preferably mixed with brandy or whiskey,' she tried a feeble joke.

She shut her eyes again against the day as the nurse, chuckled then left the room to get the medication. Late last night they'd taken out the drip so her hands were free but she still wore an oxygen cannula.

The nurse came back. Ana looked in horror. The woman was gowned, gloved and masked just to look at her hand.

'I'm sorry,' the nurse said. 'I have to...'

'Of course, I understand...' Ana faltered. She took and swallowed the offered tablets hardly registering the pain of swallowing in her anguish at the reality suggested by the nurse's apparel.

The nurse first removed the bandage around Ana's head and tut tutted at the hairless wound just above her forehead.

'This won't show,' she said. 'Your other hair will cover it easily.' She didn't replace the dressing just dabbed disinfectant carefully, and then gently smoothed the hair over it. 'The red streaks suit you,' the nurse offered smiling, 'but they must be a semi. Most of the colour's come out with the disinfectant...'

Ana didn't bother to reply.

It was almost as if the nurse was hesitant to start on the other obvious treatment. Finally the woman undid the bandages over the two bite wounds. They were red and swollen and they looked infected. She deftly swabbed the area then applied new protective dressings. 'Your hand must look a sight to you now but actually doesn't look all that bad to me. It'll probably heal without too much scarring,' she said.

It's not the scarring, Ana wanted to shout at the soft brown eyes above the woman's mask. It's the muck inside... Instead she smiled back and played the patient role expected of her. 'Yes, I expect so. Valerie said as much last night... and she said I could go home this morning.'

Suddenly, getting out of there and going home was all that mattered.

Mark Llewellyn came into the hospital room next, and was slow, meticulous and gentle as he led her through yesterday's assault. Her voice was scratchy and she sipped water every few minutes.

After being reassured that the prisoner had said nothing relevant about his arrest, or the crimes he was accused of, Mark teased every moment of the assault out of her. He clarified details and helped her explain what she felt, saw and did. As he sat opposite her, the morning sun slanted across his face and she felt safe enough to let it out. He waited, without pressuring her, while she fought to control herself and he encouraged her professional telling of the incident.

Unlike others he made no adverse comments about the fact that she did not wear a prison warden uniform and listened while she told him her street clothing was more appropriate to her profession. Mark even raised a smile, as she did, when she explained that the day after she started working in the prison John Fellows had suggested she be fitted for a uniform.

'I told him I'd resign, right there and then. On the spot! A psychologist isn't a warden and I'd have better results working outside the obvious custodial aspects. We agreed on suitable clothing for the job and he'd only ever commented that I looked good.' Ana stopped before rasping. 'I was maybe wrong when I insisted on the configuration of my room. He might not have got to me if I was on the other side of a desk...'

'I doubt it would have made much difference.'

'But maybe I could have got to the call button sooner.'

'Maybe. But he still attacked you. I've seen your small office and it's impossible to conjecture if a desk would have stopped him. I think that you might have sustained different injuries, but he was probably so angry about the boy being taken away he would have lashed out at you anyway. At least you're still alive.'

Ana looked down and saw that, in his effort to reassure her, the detective had taken her free hand in his. He flushed red as he released her hand and she knew she would be secure in his working of the case.

At the end he thanked her, told her he'd get her statement typed up and give it back for her to read and make any changes that she felt were needed.

'That wasn't so bad, was it?' he allowed a grin to ease across his face. 'I'll need your signature on the statement documents and I'm quite sure that the courts will have more than enough to make a conviction. You may not even need to attend and I'll do my best to make it so.' He indicated his notes. 'From this statement he should get a decent sentence; maybe banged up for a very long time. I'll go for attempted murder and I think we'll get it.'

'I thought I was going to die,' Ana said, 'that he was going to kill me.'

'You won't have to worry about Demetrius Quinn again. He's been arrested for murder, now this attempted murder on you. He's a goner. We'll have him banged up for life when we get all the evidence before the courts.'

An hour later Peter arrived beside Ana's hospital bed.

By that time she was waiting for clean clothing. Her work clothes from the day before were now police evidence. Dammit, she liked that trouser suit and the blouse but on second thoughts she'd never wear it again without the reminder. If she got it back it was destined into the rag bag. Or straight into the bin. That was a good resolution, she thought.

Peter was all bustle as he pulled underclothes, fresh jeans, a shirt and jacket that didn't match from a shopping carry bag.

Going home. That was all that mattered to Ana. She pulled the curtain screen around her bed and struggled into her clothing. The bruises were beginning to develop on her arms and legs and the large patch on her ribs was red. She winced as she pulled the shirt over her head.

'You'd better show that to Valerie,' Peter said. 'Maybe you've got a cracked rib there – like you did when you fell water skiing last summer.'

'I'll be OK,' she said but no way was she going to be strapped up again. Besides she could tell from his preoccupied look that he was bursting with his own news instead.

Out it came.

'John wants to talk to you about immediate leave. I called Tom and Lauren last night. They've telephoned back this morning. They've hired a houseboat on the Murray out of Renmark. Our old friends the Liba group.'

Ana looked amazed at Peter. 'For us?'

'They'll come too. It'll be great fun on the river together. Like we did last year and it will be just the thing to get away.'

'What about our other plans...?'

Peter shrugged, 'What about them? This'll be better.'

So Peter had contacted their friends who had the money to hire a houseboat at any cost. Despite the generosity Ana wanted to shout, deny everything that had happened and creep away into the security of her own house. To hide into her own little shell.

She opened her mouth to protest.

'It's a great idea...' Valerie said from the doorway. 'Get away. Relax that's what you need and have some fun. I can get the doctor at Renmark to check on your hand if necessary.' She was definitely in on the plot for Ana to escape. A change of scenery was essential.

'Lauren was a nurse before she was married Tom,' Peter reminded Ana, and this holiday time off was planned already. 'We'll just stay away a bit longer. It's all arranged.'

'But the tests...' she countered.

'They'll still take six weeks whether you're here or there. I know you're aware of precautions necessary, so go. I'll get a dressing kit arranged for your nurse friend to change the dressings.' Valerie paused before she delivered what she knew would be a factor. 'If you stay here I'll order immediate extended counselling for you. If you at least go away for a couple of weeks in good company, then we'll see. After a chat with Bett I think you can be trusted to do what you need to do.'

Ana steadied herself against the bed. She had already spoken to the hospital counsellor, Bett an old trusted friend, who had offered support. Support was a telephone call away. 'All right,' she agreed with reluctance.

Chapter 19

That afternoon Ana telephoned the prison from home. She wanted to speak to John about her leave.

She sat in her favourite chair overlooking Boston Bay. The sea glinted where a cats-paw of breeze clawed stripes across the blue waters and the ship, she'd heard being loaded overnight, was leaving. Attended by the pilot boat, it left a silver twisted streamer of wake in farewell, as it headed towards the horizon. The two puller tugs had already butted their way back to their berths.

'Thank you,' she struggled through a faltering teary voice to Gus who had answered the phone. 'Thank you helping me...'

'That's OK, lassie,' his own voice reflected the guilt and still shock at the attack. 'I just wish we'd been quicker...'

There was a silence as both sought words.

'No! No! Thank goodness you were there. You and the dogs...' She paused. 'We're off to Renmark on a houseboat for a week or two...later this week. That'll get me back on my feet. Fishing and all the rest...' Again she choked up, couldn't talk any more. The silence lengthened before she managed. 'Would you put me through to John, please?'

'Yes, lassie...just a moment.'

John Fellows was his usual bluff self.

Caring and spoke in a loud voice into the phone. From memory she could smell his cologne. The coffee that pervaded his office.

'Feeling better? Great! Going to the Murray? Renmark? Great!'

There was a silence as John listened. 'You've got six weeks compassionate sick leave. More if you need it. Just get better. Don't worry about the paperwork, it's all fixed.' There was a pause. 'Sue Childs will come over from Yatala to fill in. Your job will be here when you want to come back. There'll be an inquiry but that'll be a formality. Not a problem.' He skirted around the question she wanted to ask, suddenly declaring, 'I'm not telling you anything but I think you'll be all right. Quite all right.'

So, she thought, he's checked the medical records and her attacker was HIV negative at last testing before he had been released from Yatala Prison. Probably Hepatitis negative too... He couldn't say so, it was against regulations and even if she got a court order she could not find out, officially.

'You're all right,' John repeated with emphasis.

'Thank you, John,' she breathed but doubts would remain in her mind until after her own test results came back negative.

She couldn't ask about the man's lifestyle.

Drugs? Sexual activity? Medical negativity was often a transient thing in a prison population and an ex-prisoner's life.

'So, Ana, go and relax.' John's voice got more enthusiastic. 'House-boating at Renmark... I've heard of the Liba group. Wish I was going too. Be nice on the river at this time of year, especially if you go up river.'

The call ended leaving Ana with the distinct impression that John was finding it difficult to talk to her. All the accusations that Peter had flung at him would have stuck and made sleep difficult. Impossible even given their friendship.

He'd have worried about her and the consequences of the attack on the prison protocols. The Adelaide hierarchy would be demanded reports and answers, unions the same. Most of the staff who liked her and even the prisoners would have mixed reactions. With the latter it depended on whether she had provided a challenge or a comfort to them.

Demetrius Quinn sat, guarded, on a chair outside the Prison Manager's office waiting to hear what would happen to him next. He suspected that he would be shipped back to Adelaide as soon as there was a van going. They wouldn't risk flying him after the fight he'd put up. He didn't want to go to the Remand Centre, it was tough there. He'd argue for Yatala and his mates but the system probably couldn't be bucked, not this time. Not with murder charges hanging over his head.

It had only just sunk in properly.

The bastards were pinging him for the murders of the women! He'd need a lawyer and soon.

Quinn overheard parts of the telephone conversation through the door. Renmark. Liba...houseboat.

That fucking counsellor!

His anger rose again. She was no help, keeping information about his son away from him. She had to know where they were going but the bitch wouldn't tell him. 'Whores! They're all bastards and whores,' he muttered as he heard the Manager's phone replaced in the cradle.

The officer standing next to him frowned, shifted his position, and Quinn shut up

Constable Angela Epps was on her first day back after a month's leave. It had taken a while to get her head around all the murder information she'd received at the morning's briefing. After coffee, she was sent to the airport to collect some papers, menial stuff, and she was a bit miffed that she'd missed all the excitement and drama of the investigation and arrest the day before. On an impulse, she pulled her car into the lay-by at the entrance of the airport twenty kilometres north of Port Lincoln

'I've got the stuff for the Major Crime boys off the police plane,' she said into her radio. 'Is anything urgent?'

'They've already received most of it by fax. Have you got a problem?'

'No ...but would it be OK if I followed up on something I saw yesterday when I was showing some friends over the new land release at Point Boston? It's just a hunch but...it could be connected with the current enquiries.'

'As long as you do it quickly and there's no possibility of personal danger,' the dispatcher said. 'You're on your own.'

'Nah. This should only take an extra half hour or so.'

'OK. Keep in touch. Out.'

Angela swung the patrol vehicle north to drive off the highway and along the road beside the airport. Big land release advertisement signs beckoned visitors and, ironically, the road also led to the Port Lincoln gun club. She passed the gun bunkers on her right and noted that a red flag was flying. Someone was there and she heard the crack of a rifle shot. Maybe a pistol, she thought. There were further bangs again as the shooter lined up the targets as often she and the police did in practice.

Onwards the road was paved for a while for five kilometres then it reverted to a good bush track with thick stubby mallee on each side. Ahead the blue sea was flat, calm, with a speckle of islands making dark bumps on the horizon.

Yesterday something blue way off in the scrub had caught her eye. It was just where the track changed direction and the sea was suddenly visible as the land opened out into the surveyed house blocks. Her Adelaide visitor friends had been enthralled and chattered on about selling up to come to live in such an area. Getting transfers. Being envious of Angela and her stationing.

Then her eyes had followed the track to the fabulous seaside panorama; just as the developers wanted visitors to see.

She remembered another flash of blue. A blue car was mentioned this morning's briefing as missing and Angela thought, there were many shades of blue in the sea, but this tone was different.

The blue was as in a dark blue car duco colour.

Different. Just that bit different from washed sea blue.

The car topped the rise and instead of looking towards the land blocks she levelled her gaze into the bush. 'Nothing,' she muttered aloud as the breeze swept fine blonde hair out of her pony-tail and into her eyes. Cripes that wind was cold. Straight out of the east. She shivered. Moved back a pace.

There! There was the flash of blue!

Angela pushed her way towards the colour. It was little more than one hundred metres through the tough mallee scrub.

'It's a blue Honda. Covered in tree branches.' Angela struggled to keep the excitement out of her voice as she reported back to the Port Lincoln base. 'I only went close enough to verify that it was a dumped car.'

The phone crackled in her ear. She was close to being out of range. 'You didn't touch...'

'Course I didn't touch anything...I'm not a novice and I know it's the car mentioned at this morning's briefing. Has to be.' Angela listened as the registration plate numbers were read to her. 'Yes, that's it!'

'Well done, Constable! We've made the arrest but this could give up more evidence. Stay where you are and I'll alert the technical wizards.'

'Yes Sarg, there's dried blood everywhere...enough to keep them happy.'

A short laugh came over the radio.

'I'll put the 'Crime Scene' tapes up and wait then. Pity I didn't bring my bathers. I'd have time for a swim.'

Another laugh. 'You could always skinny dip. That'd please...'

Breaking all etiquette and rules Angela snorted a rude reply and snapped shut her phone.

She got out of the car and went to the boot to get the yellow crime scene markers to secure the area.

Chapter 20

The van veered wildly.

For an instant it righted itself as the driver fought to correct the swerve of the skid. He failed and over corrected. The van rolled once, twice before it slid down a steep embankment on its side. As the sound of screeching metal diminished a big red kangaroo, with the van's headlights no longer blinding it on the highway, thump, thump, thumped away into the darkness. Headlights blazed twin cones lighting the saltbush and mallee scrub before they widened out to diminish into the vast nothingness.

The van's engine coughed, spluttered and huffed into silence. The head lights dimmed out. Momentarily all was quiet except for the tick of the hot engine mount as it cooled in the cool desert air.

A beat of time passed.

Demetrius Quinn kicked at the metal a jagged tear that split open one side of the van. It separated and he pulled himself through the rent. He moved forward, climbed onto the vehicle and flung high the cabin door. The prison driver lay crumpled and wedged under the weight of the guard. He was obviously dead; his neck bent into an impossible angle. The other guard struggled to free himself as he hung from his seatbelt. Quinn reached in and punched him hard in the throat. The man slumped unconscious. Or dead. Quinn didn't care as he slammed the door shut.

Bangs and shouts thundered from the prisoner lock up

section.

'Shut the hell up!' Quinn screamed at them. 'Wait!'

His white bandaged head and arms stood out against the pitch darkness and the broken handcuff that remained on one wrist jangled as he moved. He heaved open the cabin door again and fumbled in the guard's pockets looking for keys. As he got the back door of the prisoners' compartment open another prisoner pulled himself through the same hole Quinn has escaped through.

Jahan Omar stood dark, almost invisible, against the night. 'I'm OK,' he said, 'but old Jarvis is hurt.'

The fourth prisoner, Victor Jones, another who'd been picked up on rotation at the Port Augusta Prison at midnight, pushed his way clear out of the rear doors as Quinn opened them. He held his head and staggered as his feet touched the rough ground. 'Cripes! What happened?' he asked.

'I said Shut up! Let me think,' Quinn said. 'We're got to get out of here. Now!' He stood still then pulled the bandages and dressings off his wounds. 'I'm going up onto the road. Flag down a car.'

'What about Jarvis?' Jahan said. 'The guards?'

'Don't worry about the guards, they're dead. You,' Quinn directed Victor, 'help me get the clothes off the bastards. I'll need them. Keep out of sight. If the old man is OK then get him out, otherwise leave the bastard. We're not carrying no deadwood. Just keep quiet until I get back. Noise travels a long way at night.'

Quinn and Victor moved off towards the front cabin.

Jahan fumbled back into the prison compartment. The last prisoner lay still, his left leg twisted and obviously broken. He muttered to himself and rubbed his chest.

'C'mon Craig,' the younger man said, 'gotta get you out of here. Someone's going to get help.' He pulled Craig's leg free and the injured man screamed in pain.

There was a thump on the side of the van.

'I said to shut the fuck up!' Quinn's voice threatened. There was another thump.

Jahan clamped his hand over Craig's mouth and got his shoulder under the older man and lifted him out of the van. He lay him down onto the ground.

'Hang on. Keep it quiet. I'll look after you,' he said.

Quinn, pulled on the guard's jacket and torn trousers over his own clothes, and scrambled up the embankment onto the highway.

The highway was deserted.

The moon, slung low in the west, provided just enough light to see the road close by and away in the distance he could see the glow of lights from a township. After ten minutes of shivering in the cold air he saw headlights that dipped and shone again on the undulating road. The lights came from the north. Surely the guards had no time to get out a mobile message as the van rolled. It had to be civilians. Still better be sure. Quinn crouched back onto the verge. If it was the police coming he could drop. As the light got nearer her could see that it was a four-wheel drive. He hesitated. Possible police out here in the semi bush? In a four by four?

He stood. Chanced it.

The vehicle slowed as Quinn stepped forward. One person. Good. The driver saw the uniform in his headlights and braked.

'What's up?' the man said.

'We rolled. Bloody roo on the road,' Quinn said with an accuracy he could only have guessed at. 'Have you got a first aid kit? I've already phoned for help, an ambulance and a backup crew are on their way, but my mate's been hurt. Could use anything you've got.'

'Sure,' the farmer stepped out of the car. 'It's in the back.' He went to the back double doors. Quinn followed. There was a hunting cross bow and a sling of arrows, or bolts, lying beside the kit.

'What do you hunt with those?'

'Feral goats, deer sometimes too.'

'Yeah? Never heard of that. Where? Near Here?' Quinn kept the conversation going as the man was turned towards him.

'At my sheep station in the Flinders Ranges. These arrows'll stop anything. You should try it sometime.' The man warmed to his passion. 'Great sport and the goat and deer meat is good to eat too. I'm on my way to get a few at first light...'

As the farmer turned, still talking, and reached into the back compartment for the first aid kit Quinn slammed the double doors against his back stunning him. He dragged the man's head back, and his next blow, again using one door as a weapon broke the farmer's scull. The man crumpled into a dead heap behind the vehicle.

Quinn smiled. 'I just might try the cross bow sometime...' he said.

He heaved the corpse to the off side of the vehicle, away from the road and the immediate vision of the next motorist who might come along then he stripped the top clothing off the dead man. He pocketed the wallet before dragging the body further into the saltbush right off the verge of the road.

'Quinn,' Jahan said. 'It's not worth me going with you. I've only got a couple of years to go before my sentence is finished. I don't want more time when this is over.' He hesitated aware that he was speaking to a hard man. 'Someone should stay with Craig...get him to a hospital.'

'Bugger that,' Quinn thrust his face into Jahan's dark one. His adrenalin was up. He waved a hand towards the road. 'You dip shit! You'll come with me or you'll both stay here...with the bastard up there.'

Jahan reconsidered his options.

Ten minutes later the prisoners were in the captured vehicle and continued south towards Adelaide. Coming to a major intersection off Highway 1 Quinn turned the car south-south-east on a road heading away from Adelaide.

Four hours later when van hadn't responded to phone checks and a wait ensued in case their mobiles were in a blind spot, the prison authorities realised that something was wrong in the routine prison transfer trip that usually took ten to twelve hours to Adelaide. The police were called in and they started to look for the transit vehicle.

It took longer than necessary because the van wreck was not easily visible from the road where it had skidded down the embankment into the tall mallee scrub.

A patrol officer, spotting yet another wheel skid loss of tyre rubber on the road, pulled up. Nothing. Rubber skids on the road were usual with the number of kangaroos about, and there were also always numerous black rubber strips thrown from the huge truck tyres carrying freight north to Darwin from Adelaide. The Perth to Sydney traffic ran on this stretch of highway too. He radioed back to Port Augusta and was told to come back as another car from Port Pirie would do the check from there. A police plane was now in the air following the road. They were not expecting to find the van there as they thought that somehow it would be found in Adelaide. The manhunt was being concentrated there.

The patrolman was making the turn to retrace his path back towards Port Augusta when he glanced into the rear view mirror. Something metal caught the sun and flashed. A conscientious officer, he stopped and looked, and then he scrambled down the embankment to the carnage below.

Already enough time had passed in the bush for the cloud of early morning flies to have been attracted to and discovered the blood. They crowded the wound made entrances into the bodies of two dead prison officers slumped in and near the prison van.

It took the police an extra two hours to stumble over the partly clad dead civilian lying off the other side of the road in the saltbush. The flies had found him too, and they signalled the presence before they led the crime scene officers to the corpse.

They weren't looking for that body.

Chapter 21

News travels fast when there's a prison escape.

At first Ana thought that the escape was from Port Lincoln Prison itself but, as the newscaster reported the crime as from a prison van, Ana felt herself go tense as if her insides were tight knots. She knew in an instant who had escaped, she could feel it, was sure despite Peter's protests and assurances.

Perspiration gathered at her temples as she telephoned John Fellows who, with reluctance, confirmed her fears. Quinn was one of the escapees.

Ana found the Senior Sergeant's card. She phoned him in panic.

'Don't worry,' the Sergeant insisted. 'We'll get them soon.'

'But what if...they...he comes back...'

'He won't. They're probably out wandering around in the bush still.'

'Could he have stolen a car?'

'Yeah, maybe...But they almost always go for the city. The Adelaide boys have put up roadblocks.'

'But the news said that he could already be in Adelaide...or gone somewhere else?'

'Don't worry. We'll get them.'

'He wanted to find his son, that's what I remember from before he attacked me. He was fixated on the boy...he may come after me. He was sure that I knew where the boy and his mother are. I've no idea why, but... '

'Well...we'll cover that. I've gotta go. As I said before stop worrying.'

The phone clicked off in her ear.

Rick swung around in his chair. Tipped it back as he stretched.

'That was Ana Foster, the counsellor who was bashed.' He said to Mark. 'She thinks that Quinn who assaulted her could be after her. Not likely, I reckon, he's got connections in Adelaide and people there he'd likely have a go at. Settle a few old scores – he's got nothing to lose. That's where his woman and the boy went.'

'Quinn's a nasty piece of work, you said that he's violent against women. ' Mark commented.

'But I wonder why she thinks she's so important to him...'

'I'd be unhappy if I were her, Sarg, she's lucky to have survived that attack. Maybe he thinks she knows where they were going after they got off the bus in the city?'

'That's what she said, but I don't think so. Told her that.'

'I reckon you're right but I can understand her worry.'

'Well, I think he's to hell and gone. They'll get them in Adelaide. Quinn's the main concern...he's the hard one.'

'The others? What Jahan Omah isn't? He's in for manslaughter?' Mark asked.

'Yeah, but the stupid type. King hit someone in a drunken brawl, got a poor mouth piece and he gets manslaughter. He's not got long to serve. Victor Jones, another idiot! Growing a crop in a national park for God's sake! Someone has a go at pinching it and he takes a drugged out pot shot with a .22. Straight through the back of a car seat into the back of the vic's neck. The judge took a poor view on account of his army sniper training. And previous Break and Enters. Got life.'

'And the other man? The old man?'

'Too long in the tooth to be a problem. Recidivist burglary. A crim of the old school serving out his life. He wouldn't want to be out.'

'Are these their given names? No a.k.a.'s?'

'Who knows? Identity theft's easy these days. Especially if anyone wants a change, make a new start.'

Mark swivelled back on his chair. Clicked through his screens. 'Hey…Sarg! This's convenient. Correction's got the prisoner mug shots on line.'

'Give me a look.'

Mark turned his screen and Rick could see the four photographs lined up down the screen, with the prisoner's main statistics. 'Quinn looks as if he could blend into anywhere. He's got looks although the fair hair could be a problem to him,' he said.

'A head shave it'd fix it.' Rick looked towards the younger man's too long for regulation curly locks. 'Some others could take notice and get a haircut.' He grinned at Mark. It was an ongoing joke between the two men. 'We'd better add to the description sheets that Quinn could change his hair.'

Mark laughed. 'Get a load of Jones! He's been advised and done the blow-out-cheeks-and-shut-eyes trick for the photographer. Got some mutilations and scars, it says, but they're not detailed.'

'How in the hell are we supposed to work with this photo?' Rick reached over and stabbed at Mark's screen with his pen. 'Get the computer boffins to fix us a decent mug shot, and get all his details.'

'The other two look pretty ordinary.'

Jahan's dark hair and face stared out at them from the screen and Jarvis looked like anyone's shrunken and balding grandfather, who couldn't help smiling for the camera.

'Well get these printed off for the local boys. Not that I'm expecting them to go anywhere but Adelaide, despite Ana Foster's fears.'

'Hope you've packed your luck,' Lauren Bell-Scott chortled down the phone line to Ana. 'We haven't played cards since last year and there's not much else to do at night without having the generator roaring in our ears. I'm feeling lucky...'

Ana smiled. Same old Lauren, she was always trying to portray herself as the blonde airhead. She wasn't. And she was the great organiser. Already, after briefly inquiring how Ana was, she had launched forth into the provisions they were planning to take to the houseboat. It mainly consisted of diverting things; chocolate, wine, the latest magazines and 'Don't worry about food,' she said, 'we'll go shopping at Renmark.'

'OK,' Ana agreed. She didn't want any of this but felt it was the best to get away.

Lauren continued, 'But you must bring your own fishing gear. I'm certainly not going to have anything to do with that sort of mucky stuff. No worms on hooks for me either.'

'Not a problem,' Ana said. Her responses were mechanical.

'We'll bring our canoe and we'll hire one for you and Peter. Such fun to paddle through the old channels.'

Ana raised a smile.

Lauren, with her society ideas, would have little knowledge of the river conditions. In drought times the Murray water was diverted to the main channels only. It was fortunate that they would probably be going upstream through at least Lock 6 into the deeper water sections.

'We'll take turns cooking if you feel up to it. And remember how much Tom loves his barbecue bacon and eggs each morning. You can sleep in until the smell drags you out of bed, then you can go fishing and catch fish for dinner. Or maybe catch yabbies like last time. You could make your famous chocolate mousse too, everyone loves that. I'll add liquors to my list...'

Her voice prattled on in a forced good humour and Ana briefly wondered if she could take, and survive, the total organisation she knew would come from their good friends. She sat back in her chair. Maybe that was just what she did need, someone to take away the need to think, to take the entire decision making away from her for a week.

Ana played the role set out by Lauren. 'Of course I'll bring my fishing gear...not that we'll catch many fish but it will be fun trying and I have a couple of new recipes to try on you,' she said.

Yes it might be good to let the water and sky, the birds and the company do a magician's trick to escape those terrible words that continued to drum into her head through her waking and sleeping moments.

'I promise to look after you, Ana,' Lauren reached out to her. 'Peter's told us what happened and I think I remember what I need to do to look after your hand. I'll Google what I need and we'll manage it together.'

My doctor has given me dressing kits,' Ana said.

Suddenly the old Lauren came through again, 'Great...and we'll drink lots of lovely local wine and bubbly to help drown our sorrows. You and I've always celebrated life and we'll do that again. And have campfires at night under the stars. It'll be like old times.' In true Lauren fashion she abruptly changed the subject again. 'I'd better go now. I'm off to a fairy party.'

'A what?' Ana asked.

'A fairy party in a Fairy Shop,' Lauren said. 'My niece, Chloe, is seven years old today and I'm taking her and Marie to the party this afternoon. I'm to be the Fairy Godmother.'

Ana chortled. The movement hurt her neck. 'How?'

'I have to dress up in a silver and pink costume and touch everyone with my magic wand so that they'll receive a little present. The costume's so elaborate I'll feel like a drag queen! Everyone gets sprinkled with fairy dust too…It'll be fun…but why everyone receives presents as well as the birthday girl is beyond me…' Lauren paused her prattle. 'I'll tell you all about it when I see you. Bring some photos too.'

'Does the Fairy Godmother get to drink champagne while she does the magic?'

'But of course, darling! It needs buckets of champagne to survive one of these parties with a dozen little fairies and their little brother elf brats. Lots of bubbly. It will get me ready for the houseboat…' Lauren laughed. 'I'm dropping the children off at Tom's parents tonight and we'll leave Adelaide after that. We'll still beat you to Renmark. When will you get going?'

Ana felt the brief stab at the mention of other people's children but it passed, as usual.

'Peter says we'll leave in the morning too. We'll cross on the ferry and stay overnight in the Morgan pub. We should be in Renmark by lunchtime. I'm looking forward to it now. See you Friday then?'

'For lunch at our little place before we go shopping and we send the men off to the winery?'

'Done.'

Ana replaced the phone and ran her hands through her hair. Done, she thought, and then she winced. The wound on her scalp hurt. She wandered to the bathroom mirror to inspect it. A small tuft of hair was gone near the midway; it didn't show much, but as the nurse noticed, the antiseptics that she had used to cleanse the wound had removed most of the colour that her hairdresser had applied. Her own natural colour was coming through the dark tresses.

Chapter 22

'Maps!' Quinn snarled. 'Look for maps. Bloody useless bastards! Look again. Do I have to do everything?'

As dawn broke Quinn pulled the stolen Range Rover onto the side of the road and down into a small wooded gully. A dry creek-bed lay ahead. He was very aware that the police could have their search underway and their methods would be state of the art. He'd learned more and more about police ways from other crims in prison and was careful. With luck the filth were chasing their tails around Adelaide.

They had travelled through the Flinders Ranges since turning off Highway 1. The roads rose, fell and folded back on themselves like layers of folded pastry. Now they were in the foothills on the eastern side of the ancient mountains. Only a couple of cars, and none of them police cars, had passed them on the dark roads. The tension as each set of bright headlights beamed towards them had lessened as the night wore on.

Quinn's current curses were aimed at the farmer he'd killed. The only thing that the dead man had got right, as far as he was concerned, was that the car was more than half filled with fuel. He was tired, let down after the adrenalin rush of the escape, and the killings, and he was irritable.

'No bloody maps,' Victor said. 'Where're we going anyway? You said Adelaide. This's not the road to Adelaide.' He was wary. Quinn had established himself as leader and he'd seen him kill.

'We're going to Melbourne. Or Sydney I haven't decided yet. They'll be expecting us in Adelaide. Road blocks'll make it too bloody hot to go there. I've got contacts in Victoria.' Quinn swung around in his seat. 'Just find me a map, you pisser?' he said.

'There's no maps. Damn it! I've looked. The man was a local farmer, you said. Why'd he have maps in the car?'

Craig groaned in the back seat. He was propped up against the door and his broken leg was being supported on Jahan's lap. Quinn reached around from the driver's seat again and swiped a fist at the old man. 'I told you to shut up!' he yelled. 'I'll tip you out if I have to.' He glared at Jahan, 'I said no dead wood.'

'Leave him alone. I said I'll look after him. When we get where we're going I'll get him to a doctor.'

Jahan had found the first aid kit in the back of the vehicle. Despite jeers from Quinn, he had used a roll of bandage to stabilise Craig's fractured leg a little. It wasn't a pretty job but it did give the leg some support. Jahan knew from experience that if the broken leg wasn't held in place, the bone could poke through the skin, and then Craig's pain would increase as would the probability of infection. He liked the older man. They had become friends of sorts over the years of imprisonment. He saw, as the early morning light lit the old man's craggy features, that Craig was already pale and sweating with shock. He moaned again as Quinn jolted the car forward pushing into the creek-bed. He had not driven a geared four wheel drive car before and was having some problems. No-one was willing to contest him for the wheel. Not yet any way.

'Shut the old bastard up, that's all you have to do. Shut him up.' Quinn insisted. The threat was obvious. 'And give me that cap from the back there. I want a hat.'

Victor commented as he passed the black and white cap through to the front seat, 'The last signpost said Burra. Maybe we can ask for directions, or check for other sign posts. They may not be looking for us yet.'

'The shits'll be looking alright but maybe not for this car. Not yet, but we'll have to get something else as soon as we can.'

Craig moaned again as Quinn shifted, jolted, the car into reverse to clear the gully. He gripped the wheel and gritted his teeth. Damn the old man, he thought.

'The Murray Highway'll go towards Victoria.' Quinn said aloud. 'Keep an eye out for that. At least it'll be going in the right bloody direction.' Maybe through Renmark, he thought.   I've some unfinished business there...

They stopped at Burra for fuel and food at a service station come general store.

Quinn went in and did the shopping, wearing the hat. He browsed the shelves and saw a packet of dark hair dye. Nearby was a pack of disposable razors. On impulse he turned his back to the counter area, crushed the dye packet and slipped it and the razors into his back pocket. They might be useful if the hat wasn't sufficient to hide his blond hair. The police would be on the lookout for someone with fair hair. He turned to grin at the girls at the checkout desk who cast appreciative glances his way. Quinn knew how his good looks affected women and he ran his hand down his chest to emphasise his physique.

He gathered the purchases together and eyed the girls. If he'd had time he could have had little fun with these females. They looked like whores. Make it a double whammy; fast sex then a couple more bodies. No witnesses. As he talked to the lithe country girls he could feel his body quicken.

But he was in a world of desperation, whatever he did could end up badly. If he didn't get away he'd be dead or banged up for life. Only two things really mattered – his boy and this woman who knew where the boy was. She had to know. He'd never get another chance and chasing her to Renmark was on the way to freedom.

'See you, girls?' he flirted. 'What time do you finish? Got time for a walk down to the mines? Show me the sights…' and smiled as he eyed the spelling and signature on the stolen credit card before he signed for the purchases. They didn't check Quinn's forged signature against the card. Too busy looking at his face and hard body. They giggled, flushed pink and flipped sweet smelling hair.

Too easy.

Too easy to bother.

His smile vanished as he left the store. He got back into the car and took a side-track off the road east and drove to park under a dense patch of trees in a bush thicket. He needed to sleep and eat before they went on and he didn't trust anyone, other than himself, to drive.

That night they crossed the river on the Morgan ferry.

With one person less in the car.

They holed up again to pass the daylight hours under cover of willow trees by the Murray River outside Renmark. Jahan slipped away and came back with sweet and juicy oranges taken from overloaded trees. Fruit unpicked because drought had made the fruit smaller and unattractive for exacting supermarket shelves. Even Quinn slurped into the sweet fruit with the others.

Chapter 23

Ana logged onto the Internet and read the Adelaide 'Advertiser' newspaper early next morning. She scanned screen after screen to check whether the escaped prisoners had been captured.

She didn't want to telephone the police again, not after Rick's condescending attitude. The on line paper reports consisted of the latest celebrity scandals, political squabbles and global financial problems. Ana drew in a breath, paused as she read a smaller headline. "Prisoners seen in Adelaide." Unconfirmed sightings were seen in the eastern suburbs and at some night spots often frequented by bikies.

Reassured for the moment Ana started packing for the trip. As an afterthought she put the most recent 'Port Lincoln Times' paper into her suitcase. She hadn't had time to read it and it was full of detail about the investigation and the arrest of Quinn for the murders.

They left Port Lincoln just after eight in the morning for Renmark on the road north.

Ana put the car radio on to the ABC station to curb Peter's need to continue his reassurance of her. It was hard to listen to and she just wasn't up to responding. The program was interesting and they listened with few comments.

In this way they reached Cowell in two hours. They stopped and bought live oysters beside the jetty before driving on to board the car ferry, at Lucky Bay. The trip was to be another two hour trip across the gulf to Wallaroo and as they left the harbour a bottlenose dolphin surfed the ship's bow-wave. Long slow waves coming up from a recent ocean storm gave the ferry a rolling motion although the day was sunny with patchy clouds that decorated the southern horizon.

Ana relaxed but was aware that she looked battle scarred. She wore sun glasses to hide her bruised eye and she had covered the more severe marks on her neck with a blue silk scarf. Feeling vulnerable, and to avoid the stares she felt she was getting from other passengers; she sat back and closed her eyes pretending to sleep.

Maybe she did drift off for a moment but she awoke feeling nauseous. She could feel every wave movement, slight that it was.

'Hey, sleepyhead,' Peter said as he slid into the seat beside her. 'I've brought coffee and a couple of doughnuts from the cafeteria.' He stopped as he saw her pale face. 'You OK?' his concern was evident.

'I think I'm a bit sea sick,' Ana confessed; she hated to admit it. The smell of the doughnuts pulsed another sick spasm. She pushed the plate away and reached for the coffee. 'It's unusual though, I've never been sick before. It must be the boat's slow roll today.'

'Are you sure that you're not pregnant?' Peter was hopeful. 'Not a little bit preggers?' he joked.

Ana shrugged. Annoyed.

Damn his jokes. Always the little edge to them. 'No, I'm sea sick,' she said and crossed her arms in front of her body. 'And don't you start making jokes about it. Go eat your doughnut somewhere else. The smell is making me worse. Please, please leave me to suffer in peace.' She smiled as she tried to lighten up her response.

'Come up onto the top deck. You'll feel better in the fresh air…'

'No, please leave me to try to sleep again and I'll be better after the coffee.'

'Sure about the preggers?' he tried again. 'Or are you worrying again…?'

Ana closed her eyes to shut him out and after a moment he went away.

She felt bad, almost unfaithful to his wishes but now wasn't the time for baby talk. After what had happened he could still talk babies! Besides they had a mortgage and they needed her extra salary. She thought of her prison office. Of returning to that room.

She started, jerking upright. The horror of a baby now with an HIV threat hanging over her head! The queasiness returned. She pushed what was left of her coffee away and slumped down further into the seat.

The memories of the past days whirled around in her head. She hadn't wanted to talk, not even to Peter. Dear Peter, he was very caring but his anger at the assault, at his irrational feelings of inadequacy to have protected her even in a work situation. So male, so endearing, yet his anger was oppressive. Feelings of guilt at being attacked surfaced. It wasn't her fault but his attitude was hard to manage.

He'd always questioned her choice of Corrections and prisons for her work. 'Why there?' he challenged. 'Why with that type of person? Criminals? Why not other areas, or go private.' She'd never really answered him or let him know that there were few areas, if any, where a counsellor was completely safe. Just as she'd never said much about her childhood, except that she had been fostered by some wonderful people after coming to Australia. Always, and she'd been happy and encouraged his interest in his personal story, his family and the fun he had had as a child. Peter had a need to start his own family, to replicate a similar family. He was so fixated that, since the assault he hadn't thought through the possible disease aspect of a pregnancy at this time. He was probably in denial himself.

She couldn't cope with it.

Not now.

It was no good she couldn't sit there pretending to sleep. Maybe the queasiness would improve if she did get some air. She went up onto the top deck where the wind was sweet and tangy with salt. It helped and she joined Peter. His smile was glowing in its protectiveness. See I was right, it said, although he didn't say the words.

Together they looked for fishing boats, prawn boats that worked out of Wallaroo just as they worked from Port Lincoln. They watched seagulls ride the air currents and terns splash dive behind the ferry looking for titbits the propellers churned up. The crew were readying the boat for berthing. Ahead the coastline of the sand dunes below the farming land, the marina and the township of Wallaroo firmed into sight. She found it easier to talk of the things they were doing and seeing rather than the insecurities of the past and future. She felt Peter's need also for safe topics.

As the ferry moved into its berth, a pair of cormorants spread crucifix wings to dry on the rocky breakwater after their morning's fishing. They went down to their car on the lower deck and as the car bumped up the ramp off the ferry, Peter, with a gleam in his eye, headed to the pastry shop for his favourite Cornish pasty for lunch. Only in the Copper Triangle could they get traditional meat and vegetable pasties like these. Peter loved them.

'I'll get a few extra to have for lunch tomorrow, or Sunday, on the houseboat,' he insisted as he headed into the shop.

'Yes, if they last that long,' Ana smiled. It was good to have these diversions. To stop her mind wandering. Maybe this holiday was going to help.

Peter arrived back to the car carrying the bulging bag of pasties and another with a gooey creamy chocolate confection for them to share.

'I hope you've got your land-legs back now, he asked. His smile was wide as he sniffed the aroma of the pasties. 'These are good.'

'Sure. I'm OK now. Let's go to that children's' playground up on the hill to eat before we head off,' Ana suggested.

'The one with the old boats made into swings and things?'

'Yes. It's very clever and I like it. Then we'd better get going if we want to book into Morgan tonight.'

'Or we could go on to Renmark,' Peter said. He eyed the purple half-moon shadows under his wife's eyes. 'No, let's not. It would make too long a day and maybe a stopover at Morgan would be better.'

'Yes, Morgan...and we can walk down by the river after dinner.'

They bit into the pasties sitting on benches in the shade of a tall gum tree. Corellas picked at gum flowers overhead and sparrows waited for crumbs at their feet. The pasties were as good as ever and Ana laughed that if the holiday was going to be as it started, one of food and relaxation, then she'd better watch her weight. Walks along the river would be a definite necessity.

Chapter 24

'I've been called back to Adelaide' Rick announced as he thrust the phone back into the cradle. 'Damn!'

Mark put his hand over his own phone mouth piece and looked across the squad room to his boss. 'Why?'

'This prison escape has been gazetted as a major crime and the lads are leaderless. Hugh Crighton's had a heart attack, poor sod. Banged up his car and a local patrolman was trying to write him a ticket when he realised that Hugh was sick. Ambulance, hospital, tests and now a triple bypass. He'll be off for months. Anyway, now they need an extra person with rank.'

'And it's you...'

'Yeah. Another of the boys is away on US FBI study jaunt,' a raised eyebrow smirk was aimed at Mark. That would be for the profiling course, he surmised. 'Jack's picking up an Interpol arrest from Paris, and now with old Hugh down I'm it for chasing up these escapees,' Rick said.

'From the office?'

'Yes. Probably at first, then who knows if the bastards aren't rounded up. You're to hang on here and complete the Quinn investigation. Get the attempted murder on Ana Foster sewn up tight.' Rick gathered up a couple of papers and his mobile. 'Run me out to the airport, will you? They've booked me on the next flight. I'm keeping my hotel room here as I think that we'll get these prisoners quickly. There's been plenty of public sightings reported but none have gone anywhere.'

Rick had shifted gears and was thinking himself into the Adelaide pursuit, Mark noted.

He hung up from his call. 'Finally we know who the poor sod farmer was, and the rego for his 4x4, that should make things easier. They've given out the plate numbers to the media?' The younger detective reached down and pulled at one of the thick red socks he wore with his boots. He'd picked at something that itched. He found the offending grass prickle and dropped it into the waste paper bin. Country policing had minor irritabilities, Mark thought.

Rick watched as Mark inspected the other sock. It was unusual for him not to make a scathing comment.

'Yes,' Rick said, 'but the fact that the farmer was going hunting has caused a furore at headquarters. The thought of Quinn with guns scared the shit out of the Adelaide mob. The family reassured them that it was a cross bow and arrows that he was hunting with and everyone felt better.' Rick laughed. 'Cross bows and arrows? Bloody archaic!'

'Ever had a look at the modern archery equipment, boss? They're not wood but Teflon and steel now. The bolts especially hit hard.'

Rick grunted. 'Having them may be one thing but I'd guess that they'd take a bit of practice to use. Better that he's not got guns... They haven't told the media about the cross bow.'

'Why do you reckon?'

'I don't know. Sometimes decisions are made higher up not to tell everything.' Rick chuckled. 'Maybe they think the public'll pin a Robin Hood tag on these killers. Quinn especially. Handsome bastard and bloody bows and arrows. Public bloody hero! But if the archery stuff turns up somewhere we'll know that the bastards have been that way. I'll let you know more when I'm with the squad.'

'Do you think that they've got to Adelaide then?' Mark asked. 'I've had a look at Quinn's previous record on line. He has a definite hatred of counsellors. One of his victims was a psychologist who was treating him as part of an early parole release condition. His prison history goes back to juvenile and there's something there about women workers that he hates.'

'Got a reason worked out yet?' The little profiler jab again from Rick.

'Maybe they understood him more than he wants? Maybe one of them has challenged him in the past. Got past his charm and good looks and got closer to his core. From reports I got from Ana Foster's co-worker friends at the prison she was just the person to do that. Maybe he sensed it,' Mark insisted.

'Yeah. That angle's a possible motive for the assault but I still say that they're headed for Adelaide.'

Mark shrugged his doubts.

'Look, I reckon, they've managed to lay low or get underground. One of them will surface. There was blood in the prisoner section of the van so one of the bastards's hurt.'

'They're working who's been hurt by testing the blood DNA?'

'Sure. But someone hurt'll flush them out. It's my guess they're already in with the bikie gangs.'

Mark raised a questioning eyebrow. 'Bikie gangs?' he said.

'Quinn was arrested with them before. Look at the report. He hadn't got his colours so he was only an associate then. They'll remember and it'll take court orders or breaking in to get them out of those bloody fortress strongholds.'

'Well I've got a hunch that they're not in Adelaide. Even with the bikie connection. Bet you a beer...' Mark swivelled his chair.

'You're on. Now off your butt. Get your keys and get me to the airport.'

Chapter 25

Morgan is a sleepy little country town set on a large bend of the Murray River.

Once, in the heyday of river traffic, its wharves had handled huge bales of wool and dray loads of bagged wheat. For many kilometres around the town trees had been cut for wood to burn in the hungry boilers of the large paddle wheelers. Now only the passing car trade ventured into the hotels that once filled the throats of the river men with beer and cheap brands of Irish whisky.

The pub menu offered more than the usual schnitzels and roasts. Ana had a Caesar salad with sun-dried tomatoes, herbs and chicken strips but Peter succumbed to a pub schnitzel smothered in mushroom gravy. His stomach had obviously forgotten the number of pasties he'd eaten for lunch, Ana thought, as she watched him demolish his meal with a pint of beer.

Later they found a little antique shop and they browsed the musty shelves. Peter bought Ana a book, that identified the various Murray River water birds, and afterwards they wandered among the remnants of the old wharves that stood high above the levels of the modern river's water channel.

Ana and Peter stayed the night in the hotel, and in the morning went for an easy morning walk down towards the green parks to where the ferry crossed the slow brown Murray River.

A free ferry ran twenty four hours a day. Nearby one small park catered for people who wanted, and needed, to let children have a run after being confined in the car for hours from Adelaide. A fenced off section of the river, perhaps ten metres by four, allowed children to swim in the shallow waters in safety on hot days. Usually wild ducks with teal blue necks and curly tail feathers swam nearby, the children paddled, and the parents could sit watching in the shade of river gums.

But this morning no families waited for the ferry in the pretty little park.

Instead there were two police cars and an ambulance, all with red and blue flashing lights, parked there. Uniformed people crowded down towards the reeds beside the river and police tape formed a fluttering yellow barrier.

Ana drew back and crossed the road towards the larger upstream park. With a shiver she pulled her jacket about her as she continued to walk up the hill then sat on a wooden bench. It felt better to watch from a distance. The remembrance of ambulances and police cars were too recent for her.

Peter, ever curious, went down to the river to check it out. The police ignored his questioning look so he ambled onto the ferry.

'What's going on?' Peter asked the ferryman.

'They've got a body. Looks like someone's fallen in. Last night or the night before. A body's caught in the reeds.'

The ferryman scratched at a red mosquito bite on the white strip on his neck. A white strip, where the sun hadn't touched the skin, normally protected by his hat and collar. The mozzie had found the softer place.

'A body,' Peter echoed, 'that must be unusual?'

'Nah! Happens here often enough.'

Peter raised questioning eyebrows. 'Often?'

143

'Yeah. At night, late, the young idiots stumble out of their cars to have a pee while they wait for the ferry. Next thing they've fallen into the river. And it's harder to stay afloat in fresh water. Not like the sea. And in summer, when they're full of booze and meat pies, they think they can swim across.' The ferryman swung an arm back towards the lazy river. 'The river doesn't look wide but it is when you're drunk, or stupid. Don't know why they do it. Too drunk to wait for the ferry. It's the young men usually. All raging testosterone and they think they'll live forever.'

'Must be hard when you find them,' Peter said.

The ferryman scratched again at the mosquito bite. He shrugged. 'This floater looks like an old guy though...'

A uniformed policeman came up to the ferryman, pen and pad in hand.

The ferryman did not want to become involved. 'I didn't see nothing happen. The body was just there when I started my shift at seven this morning. Dave Higgins was on last night, and the night before. You'd better speak to him.' He started to move back towards the wheel house.

'Wait, Sir,' the officer instructed. He noted the ferryman's photo ID; got his address and phone number then the man gave him the night worker's name and address. 'The boss has given you the OK to let those cars on. Get the ferry moving.'

'About time too.'

The ferryman waved the traffic forward, car engines were started, puffs of smoke erupted from high truck exhausts, and the first in the line rattled down the gang plank to board. The line lessened by a dozen vehicles as Peter walked back to Ana who still sat, well away, in the shade by the old wharf.

A mobile ice-cream van was parked near her and the metallic tinkle of 'Greensleeves' was somehow out of place, incongruous to the activity of the drowning incident nearby.

Two small girls, pink butterfly clips bobbing in their hair, were lined up buying icecream cones with their parents. The smaller of the girls swung around and dropped her cone into the dirt, the woman scolded at her and the girl cried. The man turned back and bought another cone and the child wiped her tears away with her cotton T-shirt. The woman walked with a brisk pace ahead while the girls danced around the man as they made their way back to their car apparently oblivious to the drama at the river below.

Ana watched the family tableau as it unfolded before her, not making professional judgements, just diverted by it. She wondered if she would always relate the sound of an icecream van now with this place, with the ambulance and the police cars. With flashing lights.

Things were out of place.

Out of time and sync.

The psychologist within her knew that, linking irrational and unrelated happenings was a sure indication of post-traumatic stress. She thrust the thought away. She'd telephone Bett last night, for support, and arranged for further consultations if she felt she needed them. With that she put the thoughts aside as she watched Peter come towards her. He'd have all the news about the happenings beside the ferry. Be busting with it...

By the time he'd climbed the hill to her the ferry was half way across the river. He sat down on the bench beside her and stretched his long legs.

'And...?' she said.

'Someone drowned. They found him floating down there. Ferryman said that it happens often enough. Usually it's idiots who get drunk and fall in. This time it's an old man. He probably slipped into the water when he went to have a pee.'

Ana wrapped her arms tight about her slim body. She shivered. A thread of doubt ran down her neck to her back, and the vulnerability she felt before squeezed back into her thoughts. She could feel the swollen and bruised flesh on her neck begin to throb.

Was Quinn anywhere near?

'Are you sure it's not the escaped prisoners?' she asked.

'No. It doesn't look like that,' Peter responded a little too fast. 'But it's too soon to know who it is. And we'll probably never know because we'll be too busy having a good time on the houseboat. ' He shifted closer and put his arm about her. 'I'm sure it's OK. Just an accident. A floater.' He smiled to make a joke of the macabre scene below.

Ana let herself relax.

It was no use being upset. Or uneasy. Get real, she admonished herself, this was just a normal reaction in response to my attack. She had counselled many people after trauma telling them that their fears, while they seemed real and even irrational, filled still with horror, were normal. The fears would fade in time.

'Would you like an icecream from that van?' Peter asked. His tongue flicked along his lips.

'No, but you get one if you want,' Ana found a tired smile. Peter loved ice cream. It was one of the endearing things about him.

'I'll wait for a glass of wine with lunch,' he grinned back.

'Let's get going then,' she said. But somehow she didn't want to have to pass by the drowning scene or to go on the ferry. 'We don't have to cross the river here, do we?'

'No need. We'll go back on the main road and be in Renmark by lunch time.'

'Good. In time to meet Lauren and Tom at that little restaurant we went to last time.'

'The Liba houseboat'll be ready at the Lady Alice Wharf. We should be able to shop and pack our gear aboard this afternoon,' he said.

He looked over at Ana. She looked tired. Her scarf covered most of the bruising around her neck but shadows were still dark under her eyes. The sooner they got going and away the better, he thought. Maybe she'd snatch a nap on the way to Renmark. He stood, put out his hands to her and pulled her gently to her feet. 'Come on, my love. Let's get going again.'

Ana smiled a wan smile at him and rummaged for her phone in her bag. 'I'll give them a call,' she said. 'See where they are. I'll bet Lauren has made a restaurant booking. It'd be nice to have a table overlooking the river. Last time we could see the town lights on the water at dinner that last night, do you remember? Lauren'll have asked for the best table even for lunch.' There was a chuckle in her voice.

Peter smiled with relief at that chuckle, the first he'd heard since the attack. 'Yes, and it'll be good to see the river now fuller. Plenty of water. Last summer's floods in the upstream rivers have got down into South Australia. Well, the papers said so, and I reckon the river'll be great. Soon we'll be away, up river. Away from people, away from all problems and we can relax.

Chapter 26

The long lunch was finally over.

It was strained at first as Lauren and Tom tried not to comment on Ana's obvious injuries, nor her quiet manner. While they waited for their meal shopping lists were written, a winery selected for the men to go to visit, all yet without their usual gaiety or anticipation for the houseboat week ahead.

Ana seemed to snap out of her withdrawn status. 'How was the fairy party?' she remembered to ask Lauren.

'Darling...What a party! Fabulous!' Lauren's eyes lit up. 'The fairy was sick and an elf turned up. He was called Jason, the Elf of the Forest.'

'They have Elves of the Forest? New one on me.' Peter quipped.

'You would have loved him,' Lauren laughed at Ana, ignoring Peter's comment. 'He was gorgeous. Tall, dark and handsome and in tight elf greens he looked amazing. The children adored him. The mothers too! He was apologetic because he wasn't the Forest Fairy Fiona everyone was expecting and poured champers for us and all the while flung fairy dust at the children. He charmed everyone.'

Tom rolled his eyes. 'I've heard nothing else but Jason this and Jason that since the party. I said he was camp but Lauren'll have none of it. Straight as they come she says. I'll bet!' He laughed at his wife. 'She wishes...'

Lauren smiled. 'Well, he was amazing. And he can come to my party any time he wants to.' She curled a strand of blonde hair around her be-ringed fingers and flirted across the table at her husband. As usual she was Country Road smart in oatmeal linen slacks and a flowered shirt that brought out the colour of her deep blue eyes.

The Jason debate continued through antipasto and white wine for the women and robust pasta courses for the men. As they sat back, food contented, Lauren kept looking at her watch, and the door of the restaurant. She smiled hugely as another couple hurried in.

'Kari! Blair! At last!' she exclaimed.

Ana sat stunned, hardly believing her eyes, as her younger sister and her husband stood in the doorway.

Kari rushed forward and threw her arms about Ana.

'Our surprise,' Lauren continued. 'We contacted them and they were free for the week. It was so hard not to tell you. They've never been on a houseboat so this was a great opportunity. We've ordered a ten berth so there'll be plenty of room.'

Ana remained with a smile on her face as Lauren rattled on and Tom sat with a huge contented grin stretched across is open face.

Free for a week, she thought. Summoned by Lauren all the way from Sydney to help me is more likely. She sat and stroked her sister's hand and then she reached over to brush back her hair. Tears glistened in Kari's revealed dark eyes. Blair Raymond, a quiet gentle giant of a man, stooped to buzz-kiss Ana's cheek. His strength poured into Ana and she leaned into the embrace of her only family.

'Thank you,' she said simply. 'I don't know what to say to you all...'

'Don't say anything. Just be prepared to have a great time,' Lauren declared. 'And I've already done the shopping. The lists were a bluff to hide the fact that we needed to buy extra for Kari and Blair. You did remember the Cowell oysters?' Lauren interrupted herself. Peter nodded yes. 'Great...and we've got steaks, an amazing pork roast, eggs and bacon, all the bad stuff. Got everything we'll need and Tom has bought heaps of wine and beer for the men. Let's go! Our Liba paddle wheel houseboat No 26 will be ready and waiting at the landing.'

Ana sat beside Kari as the three women drove down the main street of Renmark. They had come back into the town to collect insect repellent that Lauren had forgotten, but insisted that she couldn't do without. 'Mosquitoes can give you the Ross River Fever virus,' she said. 'And I didn't pack any sunburn cream.'

The men were left at the landing to do the business, pay the bills and pick up the canoes, the paddles, the yabby nets and worms for bait that had been arranged. It was all waiting and just needed checking. Even with a short time to plan this trip Tom was meticulous in every detail.

The women found a chemist, then at Ana's suggestion a deli for her to buy an extra tub of Golden North vanilla icecream, the one Peter liked best.

'Let's get back to the boat. I'll bet the men have already cracked a coldie. A white wine will be good' Lauren said.

'Stop! Pull over!' Kari suddenly instructed Lauren who was driving. 'Look! There's a Mystic Exhibition in that hall. I can get some charkas healing stones for Ana. I didn't have time to get any before we left home.'

Lauren found a park almost in front of the old Institutional Hall, but she made small clicking noises with her tongue and shook her head in disbelief. 'You've got to be kidding,' she had to say as she followed the two sisters into the building. Her nose wrinkled as she smelled incense and other sweet and exotic smells she could not identify.

Kari was in her element. She glanced around the long line of tables, the banners, mystic statues, the bright Asian colours: the vivid reds, the orange and green tones.

Scarves caught Lauren's eye and she ran some through her fingers. 'These are nice,' she said. Out came her purse and she put a multi blue scrap of silk around her neck. It matched her clothing today. Considering Ana and Kari for colouring she bought three scarves from a pretty young stallholder dressed in florid gypsy clothing. 'But no,' she said, 'I don't want my palm read, thank you.' A satisfied look came into her eyes as she looked for the sisters. Gift buying was fun. Silk scarves she knew about and the one she had chosen would cover Ana's bruises rather well, she thought.

'I'm going to find you something,' Kari told her sister. 'Something to help you heal.'

Ana looked sceptical. 'You think these things can make a change in anything?'

Kari grinned. 'Well you've made changes,' she said. 'You've changed in lots of ways over the years. You do Tai Chi and you have a different hair colour. You wear slacks and blouses when before you only ever wore long skirts. Don't you think that life and your surroundings initiate change? You do that in your work, you've told me so.'

'Yes, but...'

'Now believe that these can influence and help too. It might be a placebo effect,' she said, 'but everything helps. Just believe a little...'

Kari wandered from stall to stall looking for the required realignment of Ana's charka in the goods on sale. She enthused over a range of small pyramids of rose quartz which she said would heal and protect her sister.

'You must choose,' Kari said. 'They can only work if you choose the stone yourself.'

At her sister's insistence Ana selected as delicate pyramid with light and dark pink layers within the shape. After Kari paid Ana tucked it into her handbag and her fingers stayed holding the shape as they wandered through the stalls of fortune telling, reiki healings, patterning, glass crystals, wind catchers and many others that only Kari had any ideas about. Her sister bought calming lavender, other oils for massage and a candle warmer with scented oils for burning in the evenings and after they did their Tai Chi on the deck.

Lauren muttered, 'I'd rather be sitting around a campfire with a good glass of red at night...'

There was a sudden loud scream.

Ana started.

She shied back against a stall loaded with herbs.

Before them a huge woman, with flowing grey hair and a patterned purple caftan, had fallen, collapsed into a sprawling heap on the floor. She twitched slightly.

Lauren, ever the practical person, and Kari, the helper, moved forward to assist her.

Ana cringed back at the scene unfolding before her. Any drama was too soon for her.

'Stay back! She's all right,' a man's voice insisted. 'She'll heal herself.'

The woman lay prone on the floor but after a few moments, still lying there, she sang one huge vocal note. It was an operatic mid to high range note from a voice that was full and compelling. The tone lasted for almost a minute. No one moved. As the sound died away to silence the woman got shakily to her feet amid the circle of curious onlookers and those still trying to help. She smiled wanly and grabbed for the arm of the man who had commanded them to stay back.

'What happened?' he asked. 'You haven't had a reaction like that in a long time.'

"I had to re-align my charka,' the woman's voice trembled.

'But why?'

'Something, someone terribly, terribly wicked passed by,' the woman's fingers dug into his forearm. 'On the road outside,' she said quietly, trying to whisper for his ears only.

Ana heard.

Her bandaged fingers sought and wrapped firmly around the little rose quartz pyramid. The cold hard edges cut into the palm of her undamaged hand.

Quinn and the two prisoners, in a stolen blue Mazda car, had passed the hall at that moment on their way through Renmark on their journey east. They had broken into a farm house where they got food and clothing and Quinn had shaved his head of hair. Victor and Jahan kept their opinions of Quinn's streaky razor grazed scalp and remaining pale eyebrows to themselves.

Rick and a local police officer pulled into a parking spot opposite the Institute Hall next to the Renmark Police Station.

The Major Crime Squad had been divided into two units after a decision was made in Headquarters that the escaped prisoners had probably not gone to Adelaide. In replacing Hugh Crighton Rick found himself transferring the pursuit to the Riverland. Renmark was the obvious choice given the central position and with the largest contingent of officers.

'Do we have to set up a command post in that old building?' Rick grunted.

'The place'll be empty tonight. Be all cleaned out and ready for us by morning.'

'Well it's going to be inconvenient working from there. Getting all the phone links, the computers and all the rest in on time for us for an early start. Are you sure that the local office isn't big enough? Surely there's a...'

'It's the station redevelopment, Sir. With all the extra staff and you Major Crime people... the Conference Room's not even ready yet...'

'So this old place will have to do then?' Rick grunted his annoyance as he answered his own question.

Chapter 27

The Liba houseboat was ready to go.

Ecotourism ready.

It sat, a house on twin pontoon hulls, squat and stable at the Lady Alice wharf, linked by the narrow gang plank to the shore. A gaggle of moor hens and paddling ducks glided around as though checking on the boarding.

The first time they had gone on the Liba houseboats, Lauren had been appalled; they were old-ish, not modern and where was the spa bath that she had visualised relaxing in on the top deck? There wasn't even a top deck. They certainly weren't the five star accommodations she was used to.

Tom was adamant – these boats were as he remembered them from his youth and he wasn't going on any other. They were comfortable, more than adequately equipped, and they're very age meant less 'housework' and daily maintenance. It was a done deal and even Lauren agreed that slumming it every year or so was fun.

'Slumming it, indeed!' Tom would mutter.

The houseboat, had two bedrooms each side of a passage way that led aft. Lauren quickly designated the rooms before she and Kari unpacked the foodstuffs away into the fridges and freezers in the central kitchen adjoining the dining and lounge area. The men iced down the beer in the big deck esky on the front deck and moved easily along the side gangways as they stowed and secured fishing gear, worms for bait, and yabby nets on the back deck. The rear deck housed the large paddle wheel that pushed the craft through the water. They checked with the owners that the petrol tank was full for the paddle and for the latest river news.

Lauren and Kari insisted that Ana was to sit on the front deck, to relax in her big coat against the afternoon autumn chill. Exhausted and upset from the incident at the Renmark Institute, she was glad yet felt a bit guilty letting them do all the work.

With an owner aboard the men cast off the heavy rope lines fore and aft, and the gangplank was hauled aboard. The owner's presence would confirm they could handle of the craft. There was no doubt of that, given that they had hired the houseboat before, and they knew the waterway laws. However protocol had to be followed. Tom, the skipper that evening, hooted the whistle three times to warn other craft that they were going astern. The huge paddle began to gather momentum and the strong beat took them out of the moorings. Within a hundred or so metres, they swung alongside the river bank again and dropped off their guide.

'You'll be fine,' he said. 'Have a good time and remember our radio schedule. It could be useful.'

As the late afternoon sun glinted off the brown waters, the houseboat's turning wheel foamed a wide vee wake that spread out to the willowed shore. They chugged past the swamp where a ghost of gum tree trunks stood sentinel. Black swans, speckled wood ducks, and pied cormorants swam there or presented up-ended tails as they put their heads down to snaffle in the mud for their food.

The houseboat turned into the main channel of the Murray River and headed up river to a landing spot half an hour away at survey mark 572, marked as Whirlpool Corner on the river charts, for the night.

'Oysters and pasties for dinner,' from Peter. 'That'll do me.'

'Champagne first night out. It's tradition,' Lauren said.

Mark reached for another crime scene photograph but turned away as the phone rang.

'How's it going?' Rick questioned. 'We've had a bit of a breakthrough here,' his voice was jubilant. 'The body in the river at Morgan was Craig Jarvis. The old lag from the Port Augusta prison. Initial autopsy reports that he'd a broken leg, probably in the accident. He'd had heart troubles but cause of death was strangulation. No water in the lungs. Manually strangled before he was dumped in the river. Looks like Quinn's work.'

'So they've not gone to Adelaide then. What, are they heading for Melbourne or Sydney?'

'Looks like it. I've brought the gang up here to the river. I think Quinn and the others are in the area.'

'Come again, boss. You're not in Adelaide? Thought you were going to the city.'

'Keep up with things laddie. I don't know how you can be a dee if you're so slow.' It was obvious that Rick was in his element. 'As soon as the body was found at Morgan I sussed that it was old Jarvis. Got the gang transferred up here. The body confirmation proved me right.'

Mark grunted. Rick was ahead of everyone else, as usual. 'Have they split up, do you think?'

'Nah. Still together but I reckon that they got off the main Adelaide road fast, turned east at Crystal Brook, then they've decided to head on towards the eastern states. More chance to hide there.'

'Yeah, Quinn's bikie lot are in all states,' Mark said. He looked about the quiet squad room. Twirled a stray thread from his jacket in his fingers.

'We've got all the details out on the car.'

Mark sat up. His usually controlled voice was sharp. 'You don't think that Quinn's after Ana Foster still, do you? She's gone to Renmark.'

'No! Pure coincidence. They just decided to go where we wouldn't expect them to go. Places to hide in the Finders and along the Murray Valley Highway when they had that much of a head start. Quinn's a smart one. But how'd he know she's going there?'

'I hope that you're right and they'd be well away from her by now.'

'Sure to be. Anyway I rang to find out if there have been any developments,' Rick asked. 'Anything more to link Quinn with all the murders. I want to get that bastard; nail him good.'

'Tim, the knife expert has arrived from Adelaide and he and Myers are going over everything again. Including the blue Honda belonging to Elizabeth Woods.

'Too much has been happening here. My minds full...she was the boat victim, wasn't she?

'Yes, boss. Her car had blood everywhere. They're going over it carefully again. Just in case Quinn left a sample. Could have got scratched. They've found it inside and spots on the outside of the car. Hard to tell where the swine killed her.'

Rick grunted. 'Well keep at it, but remember there's a budget...'

'Sure...Adelaide's already reminding me that pathology costs money. Then they go on to insist that we're to get enough to convince the courts.' Mark yawned. 'Sorry, I'm just about to call it quits for the evening. What's it like at Renmark? Cloudy and overcast here today.'

The small talk was unusual between them rather indicating their tiredness and the long hours working and travelling both were doing.

Rick echoed the yawn. 'Well, it's clear here. A full moon. I can see it over the river. Dark already. I've got things to organise for tomorrow's search before I can go to the pub for a late dinner. Keep me up to date with the investigation.'

'Sure Sarg. Have a good one.'

After a scratch meal of reheated Cornish pasties, oysters, champagne and broaching two bottles of excellent red wine, the houseboat group relaxed around the table and talked about the coming days.

But as the yawns started, the financial 'wizard' and workaholic Tom had turned to the news on his radio to catch the latest stock market reports. In the early news, before the weather and Tom's reports, they had heard that a convict, Craig Jarvis, had been identified as the body in the river at Morgan. The escaped prisoners were now believed to be heading eastward along the Murray Valley Highway.

'So that was the body all the excitement was about at Morgan,' Peter said to Ana.

He went on to describe what they had seen to the others.

'They're here...' Ana blurted.

'No, darling, they'd be long gone with the police after them. Remember it was yesterday they found the body. They would have gone through Morgan the night before that. They'd be in Melbourne or Sydney by now.'

'But...'

'Relax...' Peter took her hand. 'It's OK. They're gone.'

Soon eye lids began the droop and each couple had filed off to bed.

It was still mid-evening but, after the long day of travelling, all but Ana were soon asleep. But when she closed her eyes she was thrust back in her office; she could feel Quinn's hands around her neck. She was gasping for breath sure she was going to die. The waking nightmares terrorised her sleep. She crept out of their room, and down the passage to the back deck.

Ana leaned on the rail trying to banish the relentless disturbing thoughts.

A gentle waft of cool air moved her long silken nightgown against her legs as she faced the full moon as it rippled a silver pathway across the river from high in the mid-eastern sky. Cool moonlight pooled at her feet like milk. She listened to the waters lapping against the low lying houseboat and the feathery rustling of the reeds along the unseen bank. The river noises were complimented by bouts of snoring she could hear from the bedrooms behind her. Far off a boobook owl hooted, once then twice, and she listened as it was answered by another closer pair of calls. The comparison of male snores and bird enticements was delicious and she relaxed enough to decide she would tease the others about them in the morning. Peace wrapped itself about her as the smell of the old river, and the ever flowering citrus blossoms from the orchards nearby, breezed into her senses.

She was idly marvelling that fruit and flowers could exist together on one orange tree when the realisation struck that the houseboat was still within the local precincts of Renmark.

The Demetrius Quinn threat she felt enveloped her again. She shivered. Her nightdress wasn't enough to contain the goose-bump chills that ran down her neck and spread down her back. Again she could almost feel him, his presence, and his stinking sweaty hate.

Peter's voice made her jump. 'Ana, darling, what are you doing out of bed? It's too cold out here.'

The back door bumped softly as Peter came towards her and wrapped the woollen jacket he was wearing around their bodies. She could feel his pyjama clad warmth. For propriety he wore pyjamas when they were away and this clad body newness was nice, she thought. She pushed back into him as he stroked a strand of hair from her face. 'You'll catch your death of cold out here like this,' he admonished as his arms followed the jacket about her body.

'I couldn't sleep and I followed the moonlight outside,' she said trying to give a softer reason for leaving their bed.

'I thought you had just gone to the bathroom to pee, but you were a long time away so I came out here looking for you,' there was humour in his voice. 'Wow, the moon is beautiful,' he said softly. 'And you are too...' His lips found the special spot at her temple that sent shivers through her body.

She leaned closer and felt his body begin to respond. His intensity was wonderful but immediately the weight of worry she felt in her head jolted her.

'No Peter!' she said too strongly and pulled away to stand clear of him. His warmth. His love. His desire.

'What's the matter?'

'We can't! We can't make love. No sex. Nothing!' Her hissed cry was a plea. She was now standing clear of him and as he moved towards her she put up her hands against his chest to brace him away. The bandaged hand stood out white in the moonlight.

'Is it something I've done...or not done?'

'Of course not! You've been wonderful.' She brought the bandaged hand up thrusting it into his line of vision. 'It's this. Remember I've been bitten by a man who might be HIV or hepatitis positive. I'm not safe until the tests come back. Not safe for anything.'

A sob started in her throat and she turned away.

'But...?'

She wasn't going to cry. Not again. Not even in front of Peter.

'I'm going back to bed. I need to try to sleep.'

She went back into their room and lay on the farthest side of the bed away from him. Denying them both even a cuddle. She was isolating herself. Through the door glass she watched the moonlight mark the ripples until the moon moved higher and the river became a dark pool.

Peter had returned and his body was stiff beside her. Later soft slow muffled sounds from Peter's side of the bed told her when he was asleep again.

And finally she slept too.

Chapter 28

'God, you're useless!' Quinn struck out at Jahan. 'There's got to be grog on this bloody boat. Fucking find it!'

The escapees were on a moored houseboat they found amongst willows outside Renmark. An old boat, it was easy to jemmy open the door. Somewhere to hide. Somewhere to rest.

'I've looked. You broke open the cupboards. There's none. You'll just have to go without.' Jahan, a Muslim, had no overpowering need for alcohol.

'Don't look at me,' Victor said. 'I'm not going back to that town to raid a pub. Shit Quinn, I'd go a drink but the car's out of bloody gas and we're stuck here. At least we can eat.'

Victor and Jahan exchanged glances.

If Quinn hadn't killed old Jarvis at Morgan, two nights ago, the cops wouldn't be looking for them in the Riverland area. They'd still be looking in Adelaide.

But old Jarvis had cried out on pain. Pain so bad he screamed when he was awake and moaned in his sleep.

It had been enough for Quinn.

He thrust open the car door, glared at Jahan, then put a hand over the old man's mouth and hefted the old man's thin body out of the car. It was done in a second. Jahan heard nothing, then a splash, as he unclamped his seat belt ready to go into the dark to Jarvis's assistance.

'Don't say a word!' Quinn gritted as he got back into the car.

Then he seemed to slump. 'It's better this way. The old bastard was gone...dead meat. Even I couldn't stand to hear him scream.'

They had stopped the car by the river while Victor did a recce. The ferry was on the other side of the river but on both sides there were interstate trucks waiting to cross. It would obviously be back. They could use the ferry in amongst the large vehicles. Victor said nothing about Jarvis when he came back. 'No problem with the ferry,' was all he said.

Quinn's psychotic tendencies were becoming more obvious and the other two escapees were very wary of him. If they could stay low on the moored houseboat they had broken into just out of Renmark then they could perhaps wait until the police dragnet had moved on. There was a battery operated radio, plenty of tinned food and they listened to keep up to date with what was reported about their escape. Quinn laughed when they were reportedly seen in Mildura, Hay in New South Wales and as far away as Sydney and Melbourne.

'Stupid bastards!' he crowed.

But he was paranoid that they would be sighted by the people in power boats on the river and threatened to kill either of them if they were seen. They believed he would. They shut up and kept out of his way, as they had when he decided that they were staying near Renmark. 'Tomorrow,' he said, 'we'll get another car.'

They had found a river map on the houseboat that also marked the roads adjacent to it. Ahead lay a road above the river and they could follow that into the National Parks. There they could be virtually invisible. Tomorrow lapsed into another day with only cold tinned foods allowed and Quinn's continual griping about wanting a drink.

Quinn, however, demanded that they keep prison rules. Keep the place tidy. Make the beds and clean the kitchen, so when they moved on a quick check by the cops nothing would excite their interest. Nothing was said about the broken cupboard locks and naturally it wasn't his job to do this tidying up. Victor pulled his bed up in an acceptable manner. An ex-army man he was competent, though disinterested. Jahan wore Quinn's anger and kept out of his way after he was ticked off for the mess he lived in. The kitchen mess was Quinn's but Jahan cleaned up as ordered.

Later next morning they went up to the road. Quinn tucked a hammer he'd found on the houseboat, into his belt. He flagged down a truck.

'Your off side tyre looks a bit down, he said to the driver.

The driver swung the door wide and jumped down from the cabin. 'Nah,' he said and kicked at the wheel. 'I've got a heavy load on. It's OK'

'Where you going with all that stuff, mate?' Quinn asked looking at the laden vehicle.

'We're working on Lock 6, dredging and rebuilding the weir,' the driver pushed his wide hat back on a head of greasy hair. His face sported more than a week's growth of grey and brown whiskers. 'Up river from here,' he said in response to Quinn's raised eyebrows question. 'I'm done after this load, going home to the missus.'

Quinn gave a half salute.

He'd found out what he wanted to know and his impatience began to show in the tapping of fingers against his thigh. He waited his opportunity which came as the man turned to climb back into his truck. Then Quinn pulled hammer, and hit the truckie hard. There was a dull crack as the man's skull fractured. He crumpled at the knees and it was all over.

Victor and Jahan looked on in horror.

Quinn, nostrils flared. 'Don't just stand there, you pricks, give me a hand,' he shouted.

They rolled the body down the bank and splashed it into the river. Jahan yelled as two pelicans were disturbed. Large black and white birds with wingspans wider than a man's outstretched arms, took off in flight. Jahan stumbled back and fell. He'd never seen such creatures before. Quinn laughed at him and marched back up to the truck he'd just killed for.

Victor shrugged. 'He'll kill us just as easily. Like old Jarvis.'

'Yeah, and when we're caught we'll be up for the same killings as he is. We should try to get clear of him...' Jahan agreed.

Morosely, they climbed aboard the truck. Quinn started on the bumpy winding track that followed the river.

'The bastard police won't be looking for a truck that is travelling as it's supposed to be along the river,' he said with his own perceived logic.

'Yeah, but won't they miss the truck and driver when he doesn't get to the work site,' Victor said.

'That'll be their worry not ours,' Quinn snapped.

'But...' Victor shut up as Quinn scowled at him.

They passed a side track that looked like it might lead to the Lock 6 work site and around another bend the truck veered. Quinn stopped the vehicle.

'Shit!' he swore. 'Get out and see what's the bloody matter.' He told Victor.

'The off side tyre's blown,' Victor said with a little irony in his voice. 'We'll have to change it.'

'Not here, we don't. Get in and we'll go as far as we can.'

Quinn started the engine again and they lurched along the rocky track. By late afternoon the tyre was shredded and they were forced to stop. By a stroke of luck they had found another empty weekender houseboat moored two kilometres further on upstream and by necessity they set themselves up there. Victor was allowed to drive the truck under some willow trees and change the tyre. He and Jahan covered it with branches and fronds to disguise the truck from view.

By the time the truck repairs were done Quinn had broken into the houseboat. This time, there were bottles of wine from local wineries, good wine, stored in a locked cupboard. After he'd smashed the lock they settled in for a binge.

'You'll drink with us,' Quinn told Jahan.

'I'm Muslim, I don't drink...' Jahan started to say.

'You'll drink!' Quinn said, 'or bloody else...'

Although disgusting and drunk Quinn slept with one eye open and any thoughts the other two had for leaving on their own were abandoned. Soon they were as drunk, as he was, on a very small amount of wine - usual for men who had not drunk alcohol for years. They slept and surfaced to eat, and drink again, for the next twenty four hours.

Quinn woke, hung-over and nasty, and sat concealed but watching every houseboat that passed.

It was a stroke of luck that he'd overheard a conversation at the Port Lincoln Prison. The whore was going to Renmark and onto a Liba houseboat. There seemed to be dozens of boats on the river, many of them carrying the Liba brand. His mood was intensified and he was frustrated by the fact that he didn't know which boat Ana was on.

In the late afternoon Liba Houseboat 26 rounded the bend and chugged past the prisoner's vantage point. Ana was out of sight in the kitchen helping Kari prepare a beef curry for dinner.

Quinn didn't see her.

To Ana his hiding place was just another weekender houseboat moored waiting its absent owners.

Nothing unusual, many houseboats were left like that.

Dawn spread an early mist over the river as though the night was reluctant to retreat. It left fog to lie on the water, to hang on the willows, like blinds, and to shroud the sun until the day could waken properly.

Jahan woke with the first glimmer of light and went to the back of the boat to pee. His stream arched out towards a pair of musk ducks that fussed the morning and he grinned and changed the direction away from the birds

Victor stepped out of the shadows.

'Quinn's gone,' he said.

'Where?'

'How the hell would I know? The bastard's not on board the boat, that's all. I've checked.' Victor paused and then said. 'I thought I heard something but didn't get up to look. Thought it was Quinn prowling and I've seen enough of him without running into that shit in the dark.'

'Do we clear out? Before the he gets back?'

'Well he's deserted us. What do you think? Can we get away now? They've found old Jarvis, but has the search moved on? Maybe we've got a chance.'

There was a scuffle in the bush, a splash, and then footsteps on the back deck. Jones and Omah froze into the lee of the wheelhouse as the back door opened.

'Up early boys?' Quinn said.

'Where have you been?' Victor demanded. 'You don't let us loose but you go off when you please.'

'I went to dump the truck. You two were too drunk to hear me go? Pissed as farts and passed out. I found there was a town quite close to us. Too close...we'll have to move on today.' His voice was unusually matter of fact. Quinn had taken a fancy to a light overcoat; he'd taken from the forward bedroom, and wore it each night as the evening chill set in. Now it was missing, and just he and his rumpled clothing stood there before them.

'Lost your coat?' Jahan let Quinn know he'd noticed.

'None of your business...' Quinn said. 'Pack this place up and we'll move out after we've eaten.'

'Did you get another car?' Jahan asked.

'No, I didn't. We walk. We're on the edge of a national park.'

'Yeah, I saw that from the river charts in the front locker,' Victor agreed. 'Thought you'd want to get another car.'

'It's always me that does the dirty work...'

'You seem to enjoy it...'

'Well it's too dangerous now,' Quinn said. 'If we pinch another car then it will give the pigs a think that we're still around.'

'What about where you went in the night? Will the cops be interested in anything you did?'

'None of your business what I did. Leave it!'

'So we walk?' Jahan was a city man. Walking in the bush wasn't something he'd done before.

'We walk or you can stay here. It doesn't bloody bother me.' As his eyes narrowed Quinn let his exasperation show.

Jahan bothered.

Quinn's definition of someone staying had so far been lethal. He didn't want to become one of the body count. 'I'm with you,' he said as he followed the two men back into the main houseboat room.

Victor spread the river chart. 'The river winds back and forth through the park so there'll be tracks, OK even for those soft city feet. Thought prison gardens would've toughened you up,' he said to Jahan.

Victor's jab at Jahan was unusual. They'd never shared a cell at Port Augusta Prison, or any other institution, but they'd been civil to each other enough in the Mess. But now Victor was tired and sick of it all. Nothing was going right ever since the escape. Given the chance, he'd be in Adelaide. Not hanging out with a psycho and a soft man.

'I'm tough enough...' Jahan said.

'Shut up. Get this place cleaned up a bit and we move. Carry only what you need. We should find another boat along the river without any problem. There's boats everywhere, even in the parks.' Quinn started back outside. 'And cover the tracks where the truck was...we don't need to advertise if any dip shit comes checking,' Quinn yelled back down the passage.

Victor stuffed some emergency rations into a backpack he'd found on board. He slung it over his shoulder, ready to move.

Jahan paused a moment, while shoving food into another backpack, to look through the window. Down the river it was quiet, flat calm and the sun was showing through the trees on the other bank making the water's surface gleam. There was a tall white bird wading in the shallows nearby and in the trees behind the boat many birds called in different voices. A man could get to like a place like this, he thought. Even with pelicans around.

An hour later they left the boat and walked upstream into the Murtho Forest Reserve, looking for their third houseboat.

Chapter 29

Timing is everything and luck is supposed to assist the worthy. In this case it favoured the unworthy.

As they stepped ashore, a fast motor boat roared around the bend two hundred metres downstream.

The prisoners melted into the scrub.

Aboard, they could see a uniformed policeman and a boat handler. The boat swung in and tied up to the stern of the houseboat they had just vacated. The men went along the decks peering into the windows. They tried the door, which Victor had jammed shut, and appeared not to see the wedges or the slight damage he'd done forcing the door.

Victor was a pro at that sort of thing. He'd many years of break and enter to get at dope crops before he'd thought of using another national park to grow his own marijuana. It was also a useful skill in prisons when he wanted to move about without the screws being aware. He'd learned lots of trades in prison and still he couldn't see how many of the legitimate ones were going to make him the money he wanted in the future. Despite the abstinent years inside, he craved a snort, and the alcohol binge they'd had wasn't enough to satisfy him. He smiled to himself, as Quinn struggled to push aside a mallee branch and muttered oaths. Victor liked parks. Maybe someone else was growing a bit of dope. He'd keep an eye out.

'Bastards!' Quinn's furious whisper curled around their ears.

'Buzz off! There's nothing to see.'

'Gawd, some people leave their boats in a mess,' they heard the driver shout to the policeman as he climbed back into speed boat. 'There's charts and stuff everywhere. You'd think that even city weekenders who owned a smart boat like this would leave it in better nick.'

Quinn growled. 'I bloody told you to leave the place as we found it. Now they'll be suspicious.'

Both men were silent. Quinn did nothing to clean up any place although both had to admit that, other than messing up a kitchen, he was an innately tidy man. Perhaps it was a sign of his many psychoses. This wasn't the time to comment.

They stayed until the power boat and the police departed. Then they set off.

Quinn slung the cross bow he'd stolen from the farmer across his shoulders and pushed a handful of the steel bolts through his belt at his back. He couldn't go anywhere unarmed even if it was this archery set. Over the days that they had been holed up on the river boats Quinn had worked with the cross bow and bolts. He worked out how to draw back the steel string and to cock it. He'd sent one bolt across a cabin to punch deep into a chair. A satisfied grunt was followed by hours of practice. He'd line up something through the sights then either fire the arrow or imitate firing. He collected all the arrow bolts for future use.

The two other men eyed his weaponry but said nothing.

The policeman wasn't sure about that last houseboat.

He'd contact the owners. Maybe even suggest to his seniors that they get the forensic boys in to have a look.

After dinner that night Blair built a campfire on the river bank.

The pearly moonlight was punctured by the blaze of red

flames and the cluster of the men's figures sitting around it.

'One match! I got that fire going with only one match! Pretty good hey? Deserves another red.' Tom, the city man, was pleased; he'd never been a boy scout. He poured glass of red wine for himself.

'You are hereby designated as the official fire lighter.' Blair decreed, a lazy smile crossing his face.

'Beginner's luck. But it's a good thing we've got plenty of matches.' Peter joined the banter although he had been as quiet as Ana all day. The evening's good dinner and several bottles of good wine were starting to loosen them up.

'OK I'll accept the challenge.' Tom laughed, stood and dragged another dry branch towards the fire.

Lauren crossed the gangplank to the men. 'What's this I hear? A challenge?' She asked as she raised an elegant eyebrow. 'Or is this a men only thing?'

'Maybe. Have you bought nibbles,' Tom said. He set up chairs for the women.

'I have brought cheese, dry biscuits and cashews,' she tossed her head. 'Surely you're not hungry after the huge dinner we've just eaten...'

Ana and Kari joined the men.

Tom sniffed as Ana went past him. 'God, woman you smell good. Peter how do you survive this woman's perfume? It takes my breath away.' He made a show of bending and sniffing Ana's hand. She was forced to laugh.

'Perfume is my only vice, Sir. How could I declare any other vices with you lot?' she said.

'I wish perfume was my woman's only expense,' Tom teased as Lauren sat down beside him.

Kari exchanged a look with Ana. 'Thank your stars that we don't have more exotic tastes after our beginnings. Our start in life...' she said in the general direction of the group.

'Yes, well...' Tom was silenced.

'And Ana's our only leap into the future...Hey Peter,' Kari raised her glass of red wine and grinned towards her brother in law's face across the flames, 'When are you and Ana going to have that baby you're always talking about?'

Ana gasped and leaned back in her chair, into the shadows, and physically excluded herself from the group.

'Shit! I'm sorry.' Kari said. 'I wasn't thinking...'

Conversation floundered.

The group sat in an awkward silence looking into the flames that curled and eddied. They crackled and hissed as sap in a cross branch ignited. Smoke rose in a silver stream like a lazy genie filtering out of the hollows of the logs and soft firelight flickered across their faces. Slowly the atmosphere relaxed again as they sipped wine and crunched the snacks.

Ana suddenly stood. 'I need to check on something,' she said. 'It's early. I may need to see if I can get a mobile contact out. I think we're still close enough to Renmark to get a signal.'

'Do you want me to come with you,' Peter offered, guessing why she wanted to make a call.

'No. It's OK,' she said to the group. 'I'm OK.' She saw his pained look. 'I may give Bett, my counsellor friend, a call too.'

The latter wasn't true, Ana had never lied before, and it satisfied them.

Ana sat on the edge of her bed.

Before her was the Port Lincoln Times newspaper she had brought from home, although she didn't have the latest edition which reported Quinn's arrest for the murders in full.

Murder, except occasionally domestic violence that led to a killing, was rare, thankfully, she thought. A long time ago someone was killed over drugs but this was almost unheard of in the country town. City, she corrected herself, Port Lincoln was a city.

But two murders of young women close together. Were they tied to the earlier killing that had been reported?

No wonder the Major Crime Squad had come to town.

One thing that struck her when she first saw the articles was the physical descriptions of the victims. It's a good thing I'm older, she mused, 'they both look much like me. I could have been a victim if I were their age.

Ana sat up suddenly, aware that she was sounding paranoid, even to herself. 'It's post-traumatic stress syndrome kicking in. I should speak to Bett again,' she said aloud.

She could keep up the pretence of trying to get over the attack when they were with the others but if she was just with Peter, she was on her guard. The more he tried to be close to her, to give her support, the more she needed to withdraw from him. It was transference, she knew that. But clinical analysis couldn't stop her reacting. Peter hadn't assaulted her, but every time he came near her, her defences went up, as though his overtures of gentleness were really Quinn's hands reaching for her throat. Knowing how desperately Peter wanted a child, his gentleness signalled his desire for sex. It only made her more defensive, more afraid, as if Quinn's assault had somehow been sexual.

Ana was exhausted, too tired to think, and the very fact of her exhaustion worried her. She worried for herself and she worried for Peter.

Had her body been poisoned by the bite?

Had Quinn ruined everything?

She looked at her watch. Bett would be long gone from the hospital and she didn't want to speak to her at home. Didn't want to disturb her at home. She knew this was a denial of Bett's professional assistance, but she was almost afraid of sharing her fears in case there was a confirmation of them from her. Bett was not above stating the obvious.

Instead she decided to telephone the Detective Charlton. She had the number of the Port Lincoln Police Station on the card he'd given her. Maybe he would still be at work. She didn't like the man, his attitude was bad, but she needed information and he was probably the only one who could give it to her.

She sat on the edge of her bed, took a deep breath and dialled the number.

Mark answered the phone.

It was relief, she remembered his quiet kindness.

'Rick's gone to the Murray Regional office to head up the group there...' Mark hesitated as he heard an intake of breath over the phone.

'Why's he up here in the Murray area?' Ana asked.

'It's really an unrelated matter,' he said, keeping to the police policy that details of personnel whereabouts and investigations stayed confidential. But Mark hesitated long enough for her to guess.

Ana persisted. 'Is it?' she said.

There was another pause from Mark.

From Ana's perspective Mark, the approachable and considerate detective, was being evasive. 'Is there another reason that Detective Charlton, Rick, is here?'

'OK. We are operating on the belief that Quinn and the others are heading to Sydney or Melbourne via the Murray Region. Now we think they've passed through already. Gone on to confederates there.' This wasn't quite true but he hoped that it would reassure Ana.

'Was there a reason for that belief? It can't have been just a guess...'

'There was the body of an old man found in the river...'

Ana gasped. 'At Morgan! We were there when they found a body by the ferry...'

'Well, it looked suspicious, and Rick has the expertise for the investigation.'

'That was days ago, wasn't it? They'd have gone on, surely...' Ana was beginning to feel foolish. With luck her fears were groundless. Quinn and the prisoners would be interstate by now. 'I feared that Quinn was after me...' she said.

'I know that,' he said. 'You suffered a serious assault and he certainly threatened you, but I think you can relax.'

'Yes, I'll try to do that.'

Ana's fingers moved over the photograph of the face of one of the murder victims in the newspaper beside her. 'I've been looking at the newspaper reports of the awful killings in Port Lincoln. I feel so bad about them.' She smoothed the photograph again. 'I knew Tara Henson a bit. Knew her more by sight...and I've heard that the other women were much like her. You arrested Quinn for one murder but could the killings be linked? He did them all?'

'We've thought of that,' Mark said without a trace of impatience or condescension.

'Of course you have...I'm sorry to be a nuisance. But I guess with the assault and all, and the fact that I look a lot like the women...older of course...I'm a bit stressed still.' Ana was beginning to feel a fool. Here was this young man - it was late - taking a call from her when he was busy. 'I'm sorry to take up your time...' she faltered.

'It's fine you called and you're not a nuisance,' his reassurance was gentle.

'Thanks. You're sure they've gone on?' Ana attempted to replicate his relaxed tone. 'It's some coincidence that they've travelled this way...'

'I'm sure it's just that...and we believe that they're a long way away now. So don't worry.'

'Do you think Detective Charlton would mind if I rang him?'

'He wouldn't mind at all. You can contact him at the Renmark station if you need.' Mark recited the local telephone number as Ana scrabbled to find a biro. 'Got that?' He repeated it as she finally was able to scribble the number onto the margin of the newspaper.

'Thank you,' Ana said softly.

'Feel free to speak to me again. Enjoy your holiday, but keep your head down.' Mark's voice was warm.

'Do I need to do that?'

There was a moment's hesitation. 'Until we catch Quinn and the others it is always a good idea.' Mark said.

'I'll do that. Thank you.' Ana clicked the mobile shut. Despite the shiver of apprehension that crawled at the nape of her neck she was feeling more at ease. Mark's words had that effect.

Peter stood in the doorway. 'Who was that?' he asked. The call sounded cosy. He turned away and went back into the main cabin where the others were now seated.

Ana's shoulders tensed again as she felt his disapproval.

Chapter 30

The next day, after barbequed bacon and eggs breakfast on the deck, the houseboat group continued on up the river.

They were half way to Lock 6 and planned to be there by opening time the next day, at ten o'clock, and to be waiting ready in line. Early to pass through in time to find a good mooring spot on the banks where the upstream water was deeper.

Fishing hadn't been good for any of the enthusiasts; Ana, Tom or Blair. Well, not very good, although they had caught one legal sized callop after returning a couple of undersized ones back to the water. One callop wasn't going to make a meal, not even an entrée for six people. Blair filleted the fish, and it rested on ice waiting, as he said, for them to catch more.

Ana had caught yabbies in her nets. They all loved the little crustaceans and netting them was her special job. This year she was proving to be very successful. She managed to flip the small ones out into a bucket but the large ones waved huge snapping claws at her. 'Help!' she'd call to the men and held up her bandaged hand as an excuse for the asking. 'Please can you grab them for me?' From the bucket they went into ice bags, to go to sleep, until they were plunged into boiling water to cook.

The previous night they fished as dusk wove reflections of the sky onto the still river. Tom fought and reeled in a large carp. It flopped about on the deck. "I hate these things,' he said. 'How some idiots let them go into our rivers. They've killed off many of the native fish.'

'I agree but did you know that European carp are considered a delicacy over there?' Blair said.

'Where?' Tom asked.

'In Europe. In England and Italy especially but elsewhere too.'

'You're kidding. Those slimy things?'

Blair insisted. 'They're prized fish in Europe. They have big fishing competitions for them.'

'You're just saying that because that's all you've caught so far.'

'They eat them at Christmas. Put them in the bath to keep them fresh, and clean them out, before they kill them for the big festive dinner.'

Tom walloped the fish with the shaft of his big fishing knife. It kicked and he hit it again. The yellowish fish lay still. 'Well, not this one.'

'I'm tempted to have a go at cooking some. There's so many of the things. They must be good for something,' Blair said. 'Maybe a fish curry...'

'You'll eat it first...the rotten things are full of bones!'

Ana listened to the men's conversation with amusement.

In Australia European carp are vermin. These caught were not legally allowed to be returned alive to the river. Not considered a good eating fish, they had always killed the carp outright and thrown them to the whistling kites. The ever resourceful Blair was a good cook, and Ana knew that on his and Kari's cooking day now there'd be a fish dish. Maybe a bony fish dish.

Ana was happier fishing from the back deck when they were moored each day for lunch and then stayed for the night. She wasn't catching much but it gave her time to just drink in the sights, the smells and the sounds of the river with enough happening around her to not have time to think too much. The days were shortening into early autumn sunsets that spread colour like paint across the sky to leak down as reflection into the river. Then dragon flies hovered and fish splashes broke the water into rings. Sometimes she joined in to the men's banter, and the fishing competition between them, but tonight she just listened.

Next morning Ana settled on the front deck as the houseboat moved along at a respectable five or six knots. They passed the tall red cliffs that hunched over the river at Headings Lookout, then Warwilla Homestead and on to the beautiful gardens of Chowilla Woolshed.

She had her new bird book and identified three different types of cormorants, the sea bird she was used to and two other smaller birds that were more common on the river. The pelicans she expected to see were very few and far between and she surmised that they had flown inland to the waters of Lake Eyre to breed. It was unusual, she thought, the Murray was so drought stricken last year but flood waters had surged down from Queensland on the Diamantina to the Lake Eyre. How did the huge birds know there was water there and would it remain long enough for them to breed successfully, she wondered? And this year, with plenty of water in the Murray, why hadn't they come back?

She saw families of wrens flitting in amongst the reeds and listened to the sharp call that belied their tiny size. The cobalt blue magnificence of the males was in sharp contrast to the brown wren hens but all danced and fluttered on legs like stiffened threads. Waders, spoon bills, ibis and egrets were often too far away to distinguish, even with her new book, other than by guessing and the myriads of duck varieties were also too numerous to identify properly. It didn't matter just seeing them was enough. Watching the birds relaxed her and gave her other things to think about.

Things, other than Peter's quizzing of her about the phone call the previous evening, before they had even got out of bed.

'Did you speak to Bett?' he asked.

'No…'

'Who then?'

'I was just checking with the police.'

'For goodness sake! Why? You're supposed to be putting all that stuff behind you now.'

Ana didn't want to tell him that she'd spoken of her doubts and fears to Mark. She shrugged.

Peter frowned, and then his face eased to one of concern again. 'You should've spoken to Beth, Ana. Don't you want to get better?' he said.

He gathered her into his arms and she sat there very still, almost rigid. There it was again, the feeling that she was partly to blame for her situation.

Later Peter came to join her on the deck. It was cool there, and he shivered, but she knew that he was trying to spend time with her. She pointed out the Welcome Swallows picture in the bird book to him.

They're stowaways,' he said, of the half a dozen small birds that dazzled with their aerial acrobatic displays as the houseboat moved along.

Ana smiled. 'You're right!'

The birds lived on the pontoon ledges under the houseboat and flew about for most of the day. As they grew tired after feasting on insects on the wing, they perched on the side rails, like black and blue pegs on a washing line.

After a quick lunch of ham sandwiches they continued onwards with Peter at the wheel.

His soft jazz music fanned out in gentle timing with the thump of the paddle wheel and the sound of waters.

Ana had gone onto the deck again with her book and the others, claiming it was too cold for them in the breezes outside, stayed inside. Kari had cooked a batch of biscuits in the gas oven, they cooled on a rack, and the warm and spicy cinnamon smell enticed their interest in afternoon tea.

Peter was following the directions on the river maps and was quietly content for the first time. Ana was where he could see her and she seemed at ease turning to point out birds and other things to him as they motored passed.

Suddenly there was a tremendous jolt.

A thump followed the jolt and the boat rocked to a standstill. They all lurched. Peter thrust the levers to cut the motor to neutral.

'What the hell happened?' Tom yelled. He raced out to the deck and peered over the side.

They were on a very wide section of the river with Lock 6 only a kilometre or so up stream. Twin lines of old wooden poles jutted out from the bank and red square danger signs warned of huge sandbank nearby.

'We're well clear of that bank,' Peter said. 'The chart says that we have plenty of room. Look it should be more than a metre deep. That's all we need isn't it?'

'You should've been further over to the right bank,' Tom said. 'Plenty of water there... Rev up the motor and see if we can pull clear.'

Peter did that and a huge plume of very muddy water erupted from below the paddle wheel spokes.

'Stop, it's not working! We're not moving,' Tom yelled from amidships.

Blair grabbed an oar from the dingy on the back of the boat to test the depth of the water. The blade came up less than a metre wet. He went all around the boat testing. 'It's shallow everywhere,' he said. 'Shallower than what the chart says.'

The women decided that the best policy was just to let the men work it out, although Lauren added teasing and amused comments, until Tom frowned at her. They could be in trouble stuck out in the middle of the river. When in doubt check the paperwork and Ana quietly found the houseboat instruction booklet and gave it to Peter. He smiled; his brow creased in worry at her, checked an index and found what he needed amid the pages. The other men still moved about talking loud in loud voices and trying to make a plan for getting off the sandbar.

'OK, all hands on deck,' Peter said after reading the notation. 'Apparently many people get stuck here and it's no use just pushing the engine as we are now, just going forward then reversing. We have to try to get the wheel paddles lower in the water. Make them dig into the mud. It says to fill the dingy on the back deck with water to make the back heavier then everyone to stand there on the back deck, holding on, while we gun the engine.'

It took twenty minutes to fill the dingy with water drawn from the river.

Twenty minutes while they all sweated heaving the buckets and the men got testier.

They tried to move the houseboat again.

Tom started the motor and gunned the engine as instructed. The boat moved a little then ground to a stop again. They were going in the wrong direction to get out, and the boat just seemed to rock back and forth pushing any way except towards the deeper channel they could see off to the right bank.

'It's not working,' Tom stated the obvious. 'What else does

the book suggest?'

'Nothing. Contact the Jane Eliza Landing Headquarters.'

Tom looked at Peter. 'You ran us aground so you can speak to them.'

Peter shrugged. 'OK. Tell me when you want me to call them up.'

'Better do it now... we're stuck and we can't stay here overnight, can we?'

They contacted the Liba management. No problems. Hang about and they'd get back. There was humour in the radio voice.

Ten minutes later they were called up.

'The Lock Master at Lock 6 will be along in his boat and he'll tow you off when he finished work at 4.30. You'll like Sam,' the voice continued, 'he's a great friend to us. Rescues people all the time. You'd better empty the water out of the dingy, it won't be needed,' the radio voice instructed. There was a chuckle – 'It's in the instruction book but filling the dingy has only worked once before. Maybe we weren't told when other houseboats got themselves aground. Maybe they'd used the dingy method and they'd got themselves off,' he said. 'Let us know when you're free.'

The men emptied the dingy.

It was just after three. They knew they would have a wait.

'Might as well have afternoon tea,' Blair said. 'Biscuits ready Kari?'

Ana went back to fishing and Lauren started dinner preparation while the men alternatively grumbled blame, or teased each other, likewise.

Kari came to sit with Ana, bringing afternoon tea with her. 'We haven't had much time together, Sis,' she said as she settled on the deck and dangled her toes above the disturbed weedy water. 'You've managed to keep a bit of an exclusion zone about yourself.' She nodded towards the remains of an old jetty almost alongside. 'You're a bit like those wooden stumps. Sharp and prickly...'

'I know and I'm sorry. I just seem to need space. Not from you...'

Kari shaded her face against the sun light reflecting off the water. 'Dare I say that I've seen some tension between you and Peter?'

Ana gave a rueful laugh. 'You can...we don't seem to be on the same wavelength.'

'That's understandable given what you've been through.'

There was a pause as they watched a small flotilla of pelicans sail out from a wrecked jetty to see if there were any fishy pickings. Kari threw cake crumbs and the ducks, arriving with the bigger birds, scrabbled for the floating bits.

Ana sighed. 'Yes, it is, but he's in denial about the possible consequences of what's happened.'

'Give it time. He loves you to bits, always has, and he'll get his head around things.' Kari stood and brushed the crumbs from her pants. 'I'm here for you, Ana. We all are.'

Chapter 31

At 4.45 in the afternoon a huge powerful motor boat roared down the river towards them.

It spun in a wide arc, making a metre high peacock crest of water fly, before it pulled up next to the houseboat. It was a showman display and a prelude to the professional boat handling to come.

'I'm Sam, Lock 6 keeper at your service,' the man grinned from under a wide black Akubra hat.

'Hrrrummmph!' muttered Lauren to the women. 'He's hunky.'

Aged in his late twenties, dressed in black jeans and driving a powerful silver boat, Sam looked very good. The women sat back and enjoyed the scenery and the experience.

'Have you tried the water in the dingy trick?' Sam asked. 'Waste of time. So who managed this grounding?' The men pointed accusing fingers at Peter. 'You should have kept the boat further over to the right bank. The river's still a lot lower than the chart says and, although the deeper channel looks narrow, it's the only way to pass here. Never mind. It gives me something to do and you're the third lot this season...so don't feel too bad.'

Lauren cut in. 'Doesn't your wife get annoyed when you get called away after work?'

'Nah! No wife. I was just going yabbying this afternoon. That can wait until tomorrow. OK' he turned his attention back to the men. 'Let's get this show on the road.'

After giving instructions to Tom, Sam's silver boat roared into life. He used the boat as a ram, not bashing against the side of the houseboat but coming in fast to drop the nose of the powerboat under steel railings that ran the perimeter of the houseboat.

Then he gunned the motor again.

Water sprayed high as his boat pushed and shoved at the houseboat. Their own paddle wheel churned and the houseboat shuddered. For a long while nothing happened, except the water around the houseboat got churned up. Dirty and brown and full of weed. Ana thought that the stumps of the old jetty appeared to be getting closer. She watched but decided it was perhaps not the right time to comment.

'Hmmm, a tough bastard!' Sam shouted as again he brought his boat in and butted under the railings first from the port side and then from the starboard. 'We're moving it,' he shouted above the shriek of his motors. The houseboat shuddered one last time and they could feel the mud release them. 'Keep going! Keep going! I'll push you around,' Sam yelled as the houseboat broke free and its blunt nose eased and turned until they were safe in the deep water.

'Thank you! What do we owe you?' Peter called.

'Nothing. It's on the house.' But Sam accepted a bottle of good wine. 'Thanks,' he said. 'I'll see you tomorrow at the Lock?' With a wave he was gone in a great plume of spray.

'We'll look forward to that,' quipped Lauren.

Kari nudged Lauren. 'So who's it to be? Jason the Elf or Sam at Lock 6?'

There was a chortle from Ana and the men grinned towards Lauren.

'I rather think Sam,' Lauren said after a flick of her blonde hair and a flirty smile at her husband. 'Rather the hero today. Yes, Sam. He's a man of dreams.'

'And I almost expected a Hi Ho Silver!' Tom muttered.

At 7.15am next morning an early morning jogger tripped over a near naked body of a young woman.

She was sprawled face up half in and half out of the riverside reeds at Loxton, 20kms from Renmark.

As per procedure, the young Loxton detective taped off the area and treated it as a crime scene.

The path was close to a road and he figured that it wasn't unheard of some of the local youths in the town to get drunk then try to hitch a lift home. He thought that she'd been struck by a car and then her body had tumbled into the reeds. Only such a scenario could account for her injuries being so severe. He knew better than to touch a body, but his closer inspection revealed that her hands were missing. Both of them. He was horrified to see also that her throat may have been cut and her face disfigured.

'I think it's a drug related crime because of the missing hands. She must have a police record and whoever killed her is using her as a warning to other druggies or suppliers,' he said to the first patrolman in understandably total misreading of the situation. 'Of course it could be a sex crime,' he commented further to cover all bases considering her nakedness. In fact his only correct notation was that the body appeared youngish and she had long dark hair. There was no trace of a handbag or other belongings although the area was scoured with great care.

The body was duly placed into a black plastic mortuary bag and sent on to Adelaide, by road, for forensic examination and autopsy.

A brief radio item, with the policeman's summation, was reported as a gristly find. The news subject matter turned to more football team games for the following weekend and these were discussed in detail. The radio station had learned that floaters, or drug related deaths were less interesting to the football public than the last hard fought local game. After that there were the Australian Football League teams to talk about. The semi-finals were already being talked about even this early in the season.

In Port Lincoln Mark Llewellyn turned on his computer on his cluttered desk and took a sip of his first cup of station coffee for the day. It was an awful office instant coffee brew. When would they get some decent coffee? It was too early for getting coffee from a shop but a bakery was near, hmm maybe, he thought. They made a mean coffee... Later someone would be going out and he'd ask them to get a cup for him. He needed to get on with things now...

He added his password and sat forward. The opening screen always gave a previous twenty four hour major incident message array and the board would be updated this morning. There were other reports that he could turn to depending on rank and security status. He had access to most reports; all he needed.

A brief description of the Loxton murder was there and the first detective's initial opinions. The one thing Mark did notice was that the victim was listed as young and dark haired. He took another sip of the instant coffee. Gave up on it and put the cup aside.

Is everyone killing dark haired women, he wondered. He mentally added a murder pin, like those on the board near him, to place the state wide position of this latest murder.

Was Quinn killing again if he was in the Murray vicinity?

On the houseboat Ana woke to a morning so calm that the sun cast a soft shimmering light into their bedroom. The light bounced about the cabin and cast patterns on the pale green walls.

It was seven am, probably time to think about getting up, she thought.

Peter was already gone from the bed and she could hear the pump for the shower going in the aft bathroom. Lauren and Tom, as the main contributors of the houseboat had the one ensuite, and the two other couples had no problems with sharing the one other bathroom. It was quite good to lie there waiting for her turn to shower as the pump could only cope with one shower at a time. It gave her reason to linger before getting up. She smiled and snuggled back into the folds of the quilt for her turn.

She moved in bed and the pain and stiff discomfort of her neck reminded her again of everything she was trying to put behind her.

She could hear a radio and raised herself on one elbow to listen. Tom, as usual, wanted to hear the overnight stock-market listings had turned the main room radio on half way through the news. He'd never admit that his hearing was not perfect and consequently the radio was turned full up. The birds on the opposite bank could have heard it. This morning any reports of the escaped prisoners' whereabouts she'd missed but a local news station reported the Loxton murder.

Ana had a moment of panic, but the detective interviewed said it was drug related. Nothing more; and she relaxed.

Whoever was there, Tom as she'd surmised, turned the radio off quickly after the news, the stock reports and the weather and before the football news began to drone on and on. They were on holiday, as Peter tried to decree. Let them just enjoy themselves. Make the world go and stay away.

Soft schmaltzy music, Lauren's usual choice, began to wend in from the CD deck. Soon she would be calling everyone to breakfast, couldn't help herself organising everyone, and soon Tom would be firing up the BBQ impatiently to cook his bacon and eggs.

Tom's breakfasts were legend on any holiday they had shared together and despite, or because of, the background of this trip nothing was going to alter that.

Usually he was assisted by another male, with females to the galley to prepare and set the table only.

The smell always coaxed the latecomers from beds, their books or to put down fishing rods. Mounds of bacon were fried, eggs nestled in the rings until their edges crisped and tomatoes sizzled ruby red. Toast was burned to a variety of colours.

Everyone then gathered on the front deck to demolish the feast, followed by toast and jam with coffee and tea. On occasion the mist lingered past dawn, but by the time this monumental breakfast feast was consumed, the sun had risen like a slice of orange fire to burn off the damp. They would turn their faces or backs to the warmth and wrap hands around the heat of their cups.

Ana lay back into the cosy bed and the sunny room. She feigned sleep when Peter came back from his shower and felt bad about it when she could feel him standing and looking at her.

Yes, let the world stay away...all of it, she thought.

The world, the past and everything.

Maybe not Peter...just his needs.

But she knew she wouldn't be allowed to skip breakfast.

Chapter 32

Ana's group planned to journey on up the Murray River all that day and, after casting off the mooring ropes, they left their snug overnight spot.

Rounding yet another bend in the river, Lock 6 lay ahead of them.

They all came onto the fore-deck to watch.

The lock lay to the extreme port side of the river with a weir barrier that stretched to the opposite bank. Tall cranes were stooping and lifting like puppet birds on a glass and other building activities evidence of the construction being done on the existing weir gates. The 'on board Liba News' paperwork stated that fish traps were also being built to try to limit the passage of European carp down the river. A constriction of yellow floating buoys was strung across the waters looked like a welcoming festoon.

Two shags dived and reappeared as they approached. A lone pelican swam within the area obviously waiting for any fish that was stunned in the water that cascaded over two of the lowered weirs on the starboard side. The bird appeared fat and well fed and turned to gaze in the direction of the approaching houseboat.

On the river bank leading to the lock area were a couple of houses, to house the lock keepers and their families and down beside the lock was a small building that looked like the Lock Office. Ahead on the river they could see the great lock doors were open and dark marks on the lock's wall showed how high the water was up river.

As required they gave the three long blasts on their whistle to advise the Lock Keeper, Sam, that they required passage through his lock. They waited until the lock light flashed green in response. At the signal Blair steered the large and unwieldy houseboat into the high walled and vast lock enclosure.

Slowly they were dwarfed by the enormous walls. 'Built in 1926' was branded on the far wall above the sludge of green grey water growths. Machinery gave a deep throated growl and the heavy lock gates slowly closed behind the craft until they were hemmed in between the walls.

Sam appeared with a wave. 'We meet again,' he grinned. Then, all business, he commanded, 'Put her in neutral, steady...'

Peter gave a rueful smile and grabbed for the heavy rope that the lock keeper dropped to him, 'Tie it forward,' Sam said. He passed a second rope to Tom who tied it secure knots onto the aft railings.

Lauren, true to form, was making asides about Sam's cute appearance and how she it would be fun to 'meet him in a bar somewhere' as the women stood together on the fore deck.

Ana raised her eyebrows with amusement at Kari.

Lauren corrected in a side mouthed mutter, 'Or a bedroom...'

She'd run a mile before she would do anything she'd hinted at, Ana thought. Lauren would never change and they loved her for it.

'Here we go,' Sam said looking down at them as he pressed a button on a hand control. 'Don't touch the water, it's electrified,' he warned.

There was a feeling of power under the deck, under their feet, as brown water boiled and surged upwards making small spirals and visible mounds of air and fluid turbulence. The pumps hummed and the men shortened the connecting ropes as the houseboat rose higher. The process stopped as the water reached the dark green water sludge marks that indicated just how high the water was above the lock and weir system. They could now talk to Sam almost at the same level.

Sam took in his ropes and signalled to Blair at wait. The heavy doors upriver swung back to reveal a river that looked fuller.

'Hey, Sam,' Lauren said. 'How much water does the lock hold?'

'More than a million litres.'

'Can we go back and forth a couple of times and let the lower reaches and the lakes have some more water?' Ana asked. 'It's still drier down there compared with the upriver mark.'

'All you South Aussie's ask that. Wish I could do it. Would be worth my job not that it would make much difference. The river's flowing again. Plenty of water'll be going downstream soon.' Sam grinned again. 'I sound like one of the old river men.' His mock salute waved them away. 'Take her out slowly and I'll see you when you come back.'

'That'll be by the end of the week,' Tom said.

'I've pulled the ten day shift so I'll be here.'

Sam waved his Akubra hat at them and Tom, now standing next to Blair at the inside wheel, mumbled 'Hi Ho Silver!'

The river did look fuller above the lock.

Maybe it was an illusion.

There were less dead trees standing tall like stubbed out cigarettes and also fewer shallow areas where wading birds could walk to thrust their beaks into the marshy mud and water slurry. The higher banks were willow lined. Onward they passed Bunyip Reach and Bunyip Homestead before the river bank rose to become high red cliffs again.

Thousands of white sulphur crested cockatoos inhabited

nesting holes in the crumbling cliff faces. They flew in and out shrieking in decibels that pierced the eardrums. Kari standing on the back deck watched the beautiful birds. She smiled; they were funny to watch as, like galahs, it seemed impossible for them to fly straight without interacting together. They moved like rampaging school boys screaming and yelling at each other. As the houseboat passed the white cockatoos whistled and screeched in annoyance at being disturbed.

As before whistling kites hung and circled in the air above the river guarding apparent territorial zones of sky. Disturbed by the boat, with the sight of a predator seen high above, had the cockatoos rising and forming a cloud of hysterical circling birds.

'Queen's Reach is just up ahead,' Tom said. He pushed his hat to the back of his head and scratched a sunburned spot. 'Looks like a good place for lunch. Maybe a bit of fishing to see if there's anything this side of the lock.'

'No sandbars there?' Blair said.

'OK - so that's how it's going to be is it?' Peter groaned. 'I'm not going to be allowed to forget my running us aground this trip at all?'

'Not a chance!' said Tom. 'I was never allowed to forget that I lost an outboard motor over the side one time in off Outer Harbour and we had to row back to shore. That was a misdemeanour. Yesterday's effort was a real cock-up!'

Peter looked to Ana and the others for support.

Ana smiled and pursed her lips. She shook her head. 'Not a chance,' she said.

'OK then. So be it,' Peter accepted his fall guy position.

'It's a full day's travel to the Old Custom's House.' After lunch Tom had the charts spread out in front of him. 'We should go there for a look as usual. It's called the Border Cliffs Homestead now it says here. Apparently all the masters of river boats were required to present their clearance papers before they could go either up or down stream.' He read the notation mainly for Kari and Blair, the newcomers to the river. 'That was well before the locks when the old paddle steamers carried merchandise of wool and wheat. It was even before there were good roads between the states. We'll have to visit there – it's historical.'

'I'll bet the store'll have newspapers and beer too,' Lauren commented. 'You boys can't run out of beer,' she grinned.

'You like a beer too,' Tom fired back.

'Yes, but...'

'A newspaper would be good,' Tom retaliated. 'I'll check the stock reports. Pity there's no fashion sales out here, Lauri-girl.'

As the banter went on Ana thought that she could find out more about the escaped prisoners and about the Loxton murder. Maybe there was even something about the Lincoln killings. There had to be an excuse to go where she could get information. She couldn't shake off the need to know as much as possible.

'Yes, can we make the next overnight stay close to the Old Custom's House? It should be fun to restock. Maybe they will have a few souvenirs as well. Maybe a tea towel,' Ana said.

Lauren rolled her eyes. 'I'd want something more exotic than a tea towel. I'd love a nice chocolate covered icecream. Not tub icecream but a Magnum.'

The strain of 'Greensleeves' threaded into Ana's thoughts.

'Greensleeves', ice-cream vans and Morgan led back to the prison and the attack. Suddenly the chatter and good spirits, her own and the others, receded into her black dog void. She closed her eyes and leaned back into her chair.

How long would it be before she could think of other things?

How long would it be before she could be normal again?

Would it be never? She raised the bandaged hand to her

forehead.

Peter saw her movement and despaired for her. And himself. She wouldn't let him reach her – he didn't have a clue what to say to her anymore.

Chapter 33

Mark Llewellyn hunched forward in his chair.

He was alone in the Port Lincoln detective's office. Everyone else had gone home; even those who sought to curry a little bit of favour with the Dee from Major Crime.

He held his mobile clenched tight in his hand and the computer screen glowed into his eyes. Eyes, so tired, they felt rimmed with pepper. He knew he should wrap it for the night but first he wanted to speak to Rick.

'Busy. Get off your bloody phone he implored. I don't want the message bank; just get off so that I can speak to you.'

He hit the re-dial button again.

Rick answered with a grunt.

'Finally, boss. You can't be that busy with all those squaddies around you to do your bidding.'

Again the grunt. 'What? Can't I leave you do a job on your own? You're like a kid who needs his mother's tits to suck on...' there was Rick's chuckle and the usual off colour humour.

'One day, Rick, some female senior is going to hear you and then you'll get done,' Mark said not without a little concern. In these days of political correctness Rick's many such comments could be misconstrued.

'Tough! What do you want then?'

'Have you seen the Loxton medical report?' Mark asked.

'When in the hell would I've had the time to see that report? I'm working hard enough here chasing these escaped crims to follow up on other bodies.'

'What's going on Rick? You're usually all over me keeping you up to speed.'

'OK, tell me.'

'There's still no ID on the latest victim. But she was stabbed, bashed and then stabbed again with a large knife. The doc says that there were no drugs in her system. She was small, young about twenty five, and had long dark hair. Sounds familiar?'

'If you are hinting, as I think you are, that this could be another like Lincoln's, that Quinn's killing here too. You'd think the bastard wouldn't be that brazen to be starting again — already?'

'Anything's possible, Boss. He's got nothing to lose.'

'No. Nothing to lose.'

'There's one disparity from the killings here. Her hands were cut off.'

'Possible maybe…. but I think that the Loxton Dee may be right. She probably has a record and they've cut off her hands to slow down the ID process.'

'You haven't seen the last find. Are you on line? Have a look.' Mark's voice was insistent.

'Tell me.'

'A woman made a hysterical call to the Loxton station. Her dog'd come in to her house with a severed hand. She reckoned it'd got it from the river, probably been floating. Her dog's a Labrador, swims and eats anything. It was a left hand, pretty well chewed, but the little finger looked like it has been cut off…not bitten off. There's the suspicion that the mutt had already eaten the other hand. Maybe we were lucky that it'd saved the left hand for later… '

There was a pause. A grunt. 'I guess that makes a difference then. But it could be just a coincidence this time. Or maybe that finger is missing again. We've never given that possible missing finger evidence out to the media mob. Hmmm...a probable link to Quinn.'

'Probable, boss? The pathologists are doing their bit to make sure that it was from the same body, but... '

'You're right. But heaven help us if could it be a copy-cat!'

'Nah...The press haven't got onto the missing fingers info. It's not public knowledge.'

'And they'd better not...'

'Sarg...It's got to be him at it again. He's in the area...but how in the hell is he managing to kill and be on the run too?'

'I think the bastards are holed up somewhere and he's making forays into the towns and farms for what he wants. I still think he's on the river but we've got the net as wide as we can. Never enough people...'

'I saw that there was a big fire in a wine distillery out of Renmark. Lots of casualties. Bad?'

'Yeah, bad enough to take most of the local boys off the escapees for the whole day. Now there's a hint that the fire might've been deliberately lit. Adelaide asked me to have a look...needs us Majors for this one too.' His tone became incredulous and impatient. 'Cripes Mark, I'm thinner than butter on a dieter's toast now...how much more do they want for their dollar?'

Mark heard the sound of a female voice. Rick grunted 'Thanks.' A pause then a slurp. 'Ah...a good strong cappuccino. I think the boys at the top've given the order keep me filled up with strong coffee. Chain me to my desk for twenty four seven.'

'More likely they don't want you making that muck you call coffee. You might insist that they drink it,' Mark retorted. 'Boss, I'm only waiting on any other evidence the new pathologist from Adelaide can add to what we've got. He's supposed to be a whiz on knives wounds that'll surely help if we can be sure of the knife that Quinn used. He can't have it with him but I'll bet he'll have got another knife somewhere. We know he has the cross bow and arrows.'

There was a snort from Rick. He still didn't give much credence of the archery notion.

'Things are quiet otherwise and the Lincoln people are continuing on the jobs I've given them. But what I want to ask is can I come to Renmark to have a closer look at the Loxton investigation?' Mark continued.

'Do you think this one is really connected then? One of your profiling hunches, is it?'

'Yes, boss, I'm working on a hunch. But I have to admit I wasn't impressed with the local Loxton Dee's initial summations, and cripes, his comments to the press!'

'The idiot was a bit much wasn't he? Green as gangrene. So you reckon you can come over and assist without putting your great big feet onto somebody else's local investigation then?'

'Yes, boss. I think it's necessary. Before any other evidence or link is overlooked … and we are Major Crime.'

'OK book your flight to Adelaide and get a car. I'll fix it.'
'Done already!' Mark's voice was tiredly triumphant in Rick's ear.

'I don't know why Mark spent so much time convincing me,' Rick muttered aloud as closed his phone. 'I was going to call him in on the escapees anyway.' Especially after that report of a suspect houseboat break and enter.

Amid the chatter and other's revelry the stop-off at the Old Customs House Ana remained feeling an outsider.

'The three B's,' Lauren said with a laugh to the men. 'That's what you always want here. Beer, Bait and Bacon! How I'm supposed to keep Tom's cholesterol count under control I don't know.'

'It's just this one week a year,' Tom protested.

'And you'll be back on muesli for breakfast when we get home.' There was a hint of sternness yet amusement in Lauren's voice. She loved her executive husband but battled continually with the formula of business lunches and after work drinks that was a part of the creed of financial management. The cutting of tax concessions stymied some of the corporate practices but she watched his waistline when she could, even if he didn't. She turned aside to look for one of the local tea towels that she'd scoffed about. There they were; bright and cheerful pictures of the Murray and the Old Customs house. She bought three.

'Double the bacon order,' Tom said under his breath to Peter.

Ana found a local Murray Valley newspaper.

It was exactly as she feared.

The Loxton murder was featured there with the description of the young dark haired woman. The paper even hinted that maybe the escaped prisoners, who may be still in the area, could be responsible. Almost, with an editorial reluctance, the paper stated they were probably in Sydney by now. In graphic prose Demetrius Quinn's and the others' criminal records were dwelt upon although there was no mention of Quinn's assault on her.

For that she was grateful. But the similarities between the victims of the Lincoln murders, this local one and herself, fuelled the paranoia that welled up in her. She almost choked on the ice-cream that Lauren insisted she eat and fled back to the boat and to her bedroom before the others came clomping down the metal gang plank and back aboard.

Peter seemed immune from the gloom that surrounded Ana after the Customs House stop-off. He let her be. On a whim he'd fossicked about the shelves and made a purchase of his own. After buying it he hid it away in his pocket but was ready to share some dark chocolate he'd bought. They'd all enjoy that.

That evening, after travelling another kilometre up stream before mooring for the night, the group sat relaxed around their camp fire.

Ana had slept for a while and no one had mentioned her previous absence. With resolution she had eaten her dinner although the food felt like a hard, hot bloating ball in her stomach. Two glasses of red wine helped but she suddenly had a fear that she could become addicted if she used alcohol to get through this hard time. Sense came back as she made herself realise that the others had drunk the same amount as she had, or more and they weren't alcoholics. Maybe not, but more bottles of red wine, or port as it was tonight, were drunk around the fire. Houseboat trips were that – a reason to eat, drink a bit too much on holiday, and to relax.

Ana toughened her thinking. Her years of study and practice strengthened her resolve.

She could act a part. Put up a front and she decided to become the fire keeper. The official fire poker.

If Tom was challenging to light the fire with one match she claimed the right to poke the fire to keep the embers flaming and not just smouldering so that smoke got into everyone's eyes.

Ana took over Tom's stout stick he'd cut and which was returned to the deck after use each night. 'I'm attending the fire too,' she insisted.

'What! Listen women, fire is men's business,' Tom parried.

'Rot', she said with a fierce stare.

And that was that.

With a soft wind blowing and the smoke rolling hither and thither her fire poker expertise was questioned but she stuck to her guns to keep the position. It was something she could do; an act, physically and mentally, to keep her mind on pleasant things.

To keep her demons at bay.

As the night wore on there was a rustle and then a thump on the boat. Ana started and threw a handful of dry leaves on the fire to make it brighter. To give them light. It flared and there was relieved laughter as a ring tailed possum scampered up the gang plank with what looked like a grape in its mouth. It scooted up the tree that held the guy ropes.

They had a little thief.

Kari went back on board and gathered more grapes and some apple pieces and put them at the base of the huge tree. Her eyes flickered to her sister, and with a small smile, she said, 'Can't let the little thing starve.'

'You'd never let anything starve, darling girl,' Blair said as he passed the port bottle around again and topped up their glasses.

There was a moment of quiet reflection as they all sat watching the flames. A waft of cool air flickered around Ana's neck. She shivered and leaned forward to rearrange the fire stumps. 'I'm going to have to rotate myself to keep all of me warm,' she said.

Peter grinned. He pulled a woollen scarf from the pocket of his coat and passed it to his wife. 'This might help,' he said and ran a gentle finger down Ana's cheek as he tucked it around her neck. She smiled at her husband. Eased her face against his hand. 'Better?' he said.

'Yes. It smells a bit of fish bait,' she protested giving the scarf a noisy sniff.

'Can't have everything,' Peter shrugged to the others. His eyes looked skywards in a mock shrug. 'I thought a bit of a worm smell would make you think of all the fishing you and Tom are doing...'

'We're not catching much,' Ana said.

'Look who's talking? I'm getting lots of carp,' Tom protested.

'They're not fish. Can't eat the horrible things,' Lauren said. 'It's a good thing that Ana's getting yabbies in her nets. Otherwise we'd starve.'

Kari protested a laugh in her voice. 'There's enough food and grog on board to keep us here for another week...'

'No! Definitely not! We'd run out of bacon then where would we be?' Tom's comment brought an immediate laugh.

Ana smiled as the banter went back and forth; but she was the last to relax.

She felt eyes watching.

A little while later there was a heavier sound of movement. Peter had his powerful torch on the bank beside his chair. He switched it on and caught the brief sight of a kangaroo in the darkness.

'It's only a roo,' Peter tried to reassure her. 'There's plenty about.'

But Ana wasn't totally convinced. Now any sound that they heard would be classified as an animal. Another roo. Or an emu, they'd seen the huge birds along the bank.

What if it isn't?

Ana didn't give voice to her fears.

Ana still had a strong feeling she was being watched. Her rational self said no she was letting her imagination get the better of her; but irrationally she wished she could sense evil like that strange woman at the psychic fair. Then she could voice herself healed and the feeling would go away. If she had a little of Kari's psychic beliefs she may feel better. To perhaps 'know things.' She'd questioned her sister's so called ability with her own psychology training, but she had learned to just accept. Some people had insights that even psychology didn't understand.

Regardless she secreted her fishing knife beside her side of the bed that night.

Chapter 34

The prisoners found their third vacant houseboat tied up to dead trees and willows near a group of many trees and saplings near Marker 630 at a spot called Queen's Reach, above Lock 6. The boat was an older one, with a shabbier look that less wealthy people actually lived on it more permanently rather than just used it as a weekender or hired it out. What pleased Quinn was that it was well hidden and a boat approaching had to be almost abeam of it to see the craft. Especially if the boat was travelling upstream.

It was getting dark and Jahan had fallen behind, yet again, when they found the houseboat.

'It's a bloody good thing we've here. I was getting sick and fucking tired of you moaning about your feet. Sore feet? Bloody soft shit!' Quinn was tired too but not about to admit it. 'See if you can find food and this time we'll drink less grog. Someone has to stay sober and be on watch. I've got a feeling that the pigs are still keeping an eye on the river,' he instructed Victor.

They hadn't put out the gang plank that would be a giveaway that someone was in occupation. Jahan struggled to board the boat. His shoes sank into the mud and his trousers legs flapped wet. Quinn laughed as Victor broke open the locked door.

'You've got first watch tonight,' Quinn informed Jahan. There was no humour in the depths of his dead flat eyes.

The old river began to speak again to Ana as, alone at night; she again sought the sanctuary of the back deck.

The evenings were so still. The moon rose, reaching for the full, half an hour later each night and somehow she managed to be there as it crept above the willows and trees of the eastern bank to light the night. She breathed in the smells of the old waters; still a drift of orange blossom from unseen orchards and the scent of musty reeds that whispered secrets to the wind. There it was tonight full and golden. It lit a path across the dancing ripples, that Ana felt, looked almost firm enough to tread. The moon rose higher and slowly bleached to white. It encouraged the magpies, on high branches, to fill their throats and to scat their melodies down the river into memory.

Ana's many aches and bruise stiffness were beginning to slacken and their reminder message of trauma to recede with this time away and the river. She was starting to abandon the responsibilities of the prison; the police questioning that she still felt hinted that she was to blame for what had happened, and to leave behind the distractions of a busy life.

That dawn, when she went to the back deck, she saw river fog laying feather fingers of mist upon the water, pelicans sailed like small galleys out of the white. On another glorious morning the sky was echoed so completely on the mirrored waters that the red and gold of the sunrise seemed to come right up to her feet. There came a moment of silence before the birds began their morning song and she left her footprints in the overnight dew on the deck.

She was beginning to feel good, reborn as the slow old river called to her.

Three days had passed on Houseboat 26 and it was time to start back towards Renmark.

Ana's bruised eye was almost back to a more normal colour and she didn't wear her dark concealing glasses all the time. Lauren had also dressed and treated her hand each day and the big white bandage had been replaced by smaller skin coloured adhesive dressings. The hand was healing well. With these reminders lessened the friends started to tease Ana and each other as they usually did when they got together.

They saw an emu swimming in the river, unusual to all of them, and suggested to Ana that it was watching her.

She began to relax further and the competitive aspect of playing cards together at night re-emerged, after the embers of the campfire have been quenched - by the men. Putting the fire out was men's business they decreed.

There was laughter and banter, 'Women get to your stoves' the men suggested although Blair demurred and took over the kitchen one night to produce particularly sumptuous beef curry. Not European Carp they were thankful for, but all the trimmings were there. He'd hand ground spices of coriander and cumin seeds, onions fried and beef seasoned and sealed. Tomatoes chopped and added, and everything slow bubbling on the stove. Rice had boiled over but the remainder was white and fluffy. He'd used every pot and pan available and as a consequence after dinner he was made to wash up.

'Can't I use the dishwasher?' he begged. Washing up wasn't his scene at all.

'No!' an emphatic chorus rewarded him. 'We'd have to run the generator and it's too noisy on a night like this. Get on with the dishes.'

Kari, responding to his plaintive looks, wiped up for him.

'Come on,' Kari pulled Ana to her feet as the boat chugged midstream next morning on the way back down the river. Peter was again allowed to steer although he was teased and chiacked by the men yet again for his one sand bar moment of poor driving. 'Let's do Tai Chi on the front deck. There's enough room there and it's a lovely day,' Kari suggested.

'Sure, why not.' Ana followed her towards the door. The others were engrossed in what they were doing. Lauren was intently reading a house and garden magazine although she had a house cleaner and a gardener. Tom was using his computer, off line, to work out financial matters and Blair had fishing gear spread out on newspaper covering the large dining table and was sorting fish hooks.

Blair looked up. 'I've been losing too many traces to the snags in the river. Got to make up some more,' he said. 'How's your stuff going, Ana? Need some too.'

Ana smiled. 'Please...then I might catch up with your quota of fish caught.' It was the most relaxing of all fishing quietly with Blair on the back of the boat. He let her be, just commented on things fishy, the weather or the birds on the river and in the sky. 'Soon we'll have enough callop and yabbies on ice to make a meal,' she said.

'You're ahead of me with yabbies,' he responded. 'That last one I pulled out of the net for you was a beauty.'

The two women stood on the front deck. 'Ready, we'll warm up,' Kari took the lead. She was the most proficient at Tai Chi, always had been. Ana's Port Lincoln group was more relaxed in their practice. More laughs and chatter. Kari meant business and followed the moves and the ideology closely.

'All right,' Ana obeyed. 'Wait!' she suddenly called. 'Look!'

Above the river bank a whistling kite hung motionless hovering in the air. Its black and grey wings barely moved; its attention was intent on something below it. It dipped one wingtip feathers sideways and sliced the air as it silently dropped lower to hang now just metres over the water. The houseboat moved towards it. The hawk glanced towards the boat then swooped, dropped into the water, feet and talons outstretched. The bird rose, a large fish tucked under its body, and flapped strongly to the top branches of a tree.

Ana opened the doorway into the main cabin. 'Did you see that? That's one callop we won't get,' she called to Blair. 'A big one too.'

'Pity it wasn't a carp,' he said. 'Bloody birds...'

'Are we going to do Tai Chi or you going to rabbit on about fish,' Kari interjected. She grinned. 'OK,' she said to Ana. 'That eagle was something to see.'

As Peter watched from his driving point the women lined up and began a warm up. They flowed into the rhythmic movements.

Kari chanted softly. 'Begin...catching sparrow's tail left....right...forward ward off...scoop up sand...release...single whip...flying hands...catching hands...white crane...brush knee left...play pipa...brush knee left...right...play pipa...brush knee left...forward parry and punch...bring tiger back to mountain.' Ana silently breathed the moves with her. It felt good. The pattern repeated and continued, 'Ward off...monkey retreat...needle on the seabed...waving hands in cloud...'

Something whizzed past Ana's head.

On instinct she ducked.

There was the sound of a splash.

'What was that?' Ana exclaimed. 'Another bird? That eagle?'

Kari came out of her dreamlike trance. 'What's the matter?' she asked, her voice sounded annoyed at the break in her concentration.

Ana moved to the side of the deck and peered into the waters. The swallows were gone, not flitting about as usual. 'The whistling kite must have attacked the swallows,' she suggested. 'It swooped past my head.'

'Let's get back to...Whoa! Look out! What's that?' Kari yelled as what looked like a heavy stick thudded against the front rail and clattered onto the deck.

It was an arrow.

'Peter!' Ana yelled through the window to him at the wheel. 'Did you see that...? Come, come quickly!' She drew back to stand with her back against the cabin windows.

Peter put the engine into neutral and came out onto the deck followed by the others, curious at the women's urgent calls.

Blair picked up the short arrow. It had a strong shaft tipped with a steel point. 'Cripes a metal arrow...It looks like a hunting arrow to me,' he said.

The houseboat was midstream on a narrow section of the river. They could see no-one on the either bank.

'Hoy! Is anyone there?' Tom yelled towards both banks.

There was no reply.

No movement on the tree lined banks.

Nothing.

There was an old houseboat moored about two hundred metres upstream from their present position. Tom peered back at it. It looked deserted but maybe there was a family with children living on it. There was still no movement. 'It's got to be an accident. Kids mucking about.' he said. 'Pretty serious for kids though... Peter, c'mon get this boat moving.'

'Yeah, don't ground us again,' Lauren dared to say.

Peter frowned. 'We'll get past here OK. We're well away from the bank...'

'I'm sure it was kids.' Tom said. 'It's probably scared the shit out of them that their arrow went this far. And then I yelled at them. A pot shot at something that they actually hit.'

Peter looked at Ana as he started back into the cabin to take the wheel again.

She was pale. Her injured eye had sunk back looking darker as she stood still hard up against the back windows. Her gaze hadn't left the arrow in Blair's hand as the talk flowed about her.

'You take over, Tom. OK?' Peter suggested. He drew Ana back into the confines of the cabin area then on towards their bedroom. 'Come on,' he said quietly to her. 'Come and sit with me for a while. I'll ask Kari to make you a calming tea. I know she's got peppermint amongst her teas. Would you like that?'

Ana nodded.

Was it an accident? She dared to hope that it was.

Or was someone trying to kill her? Or them?

Or Kari? That didn't make sense. Not Kari.

Her? Demetrius Quinn? Why hadn't they caught him yet? Where was he if he was still on the loose? She could feel the tensions returning. At the same time she was angry with herself for allowing herself to be weak. Weak and intimidated.

She sat with Peter and drank the tea that Kari passed in to the bedroom with a smile. The day was bright. Peter was being quiet, supportive and as she leaned against him she decided that she had to be strong. We're on holiday, dammit! Pull yourself together woman, she urged herself.

'I'm OK now. Thank you.' Ana hugged Peter, wanted to kiss him but was disease wary and she pulled back. 'I'm OK. Tom's right – it was an accident. Let's go and join the others.'

Peter, almost grateful that Ana had come to be comforted by him, cringed at her need to actually thank him for supporting her. He was hurt that her hug had stopped before he could kiss her. He remained a moment, elbows on knees, to compose himself before he went out into the main cabin area. He ached with indecision the first time ever in their relationship. Startled, Ana sat down beside him again. She slid the door shut cocooning themselves into the room. 'Peter..? She asked. 'What's the matter?'

'It's not good. I can't go on like this,' he took her by the shoulders and pulling her towards him and attempted to kiss her again. She pulled away but his grip held her firm.

'No! We can't...' she said loudly into the face that was now so close.

'Bugger it! We need each other. Bugger everything... I don't care - we're in this together.' He slid across the bed and pulled the curtains to the side deck door-way closed. 'Come here, woman...please.' Then he was back and he grabbed at her.

'No!' she pleaded pulling away. 'If you go ahead now... force it ...it will be ... like a rape!'

He gasped as the blood drained out of his face and he paled. He stopped mid movement, any other ideas he had lost and stared at her. He felt violated by her rape statement.

'I mean it! There's nothing in this world that'd make me willingly put you in the position to get infected with the HIV virus. Nothing! It's bloody HIV we're talking about...not measles!' Her voice was a tear-stained hiss through clenched teeth.

'Ana...'

She took his face in her hands. 'Darling, we can still be together. We can be intimate without sex. Without kissing.' She wiped a stress tear away from Peter's face and smeared it onto her own cheek. Her fingers began a slow stroking and massage of his face, his neck and shoulders. The dressing on her hand was no impediment. 'Without the exchange of bodily fluids.' She attempted a laugh. 'It can be done.'

A low moan escaped his lips. 'I love you, Ana,' he said as his mouth nestled into the folds of her blouse to kiss the valley between her breasts. It was enough for now.

She shivered. 'It can be done,' she repeated.

Quinn, hidden on the bank, swore. Finally he'd seen that whore woman and he'd missed when he fired at her. Now they were gone.

He flung the cross bow and an arrow against a nearby tree. 'Useless pieces of shit!' he yelled.

The cross bow skidded into the river.

'Bloody Hell!' His anger increased as he had to lie down on the bank to reach into the water to retrieve the weapon. His jacket became sodden. 'Whore-woman! It's your fault. Everything's your fault. I'll bloody get you yet. Wring the truth out of you!'

Peter and Ana returned to the main cabin hand in hand. After the heated words that all had heard a while earlier, they were greeted with smiles; somewhat worried smiles.

No-one said anything.

No comments. No recriminations and no 'what ifs'.'

Tom, the amicable smoother, he had to be married to the volatile Lauren, left the steering. In triumphant he placed an empty Banrock Station wine bottle, a wine they had enjoyed the night before, on the table.

The arrow stood up in a jaunty angle.

'That's great,' Tom said and hang his hat on the end of the short shaft. 'We have a holiday trophy,' he exclaimed.

Chapter 35

As they progressed downstream next afternoon they became aware that there was a lot of motor boat traffic on the river.

More traffic than the usual tinnies with fishermen aboard going out after work to try their luck along the reed beds or near the willows. They watched as a boat called into a moored houseboat and two uniformed men slowed their crafts run past to say hello to the Liba houseboat crew.

'Can we come aboard and see any fish you've caught?' As the boat got close they could see that the men had NSW Fisheries insignia on their shirts.

'Sure.' Tom said and took the rope offered. He tied it to the back fishing deck. The two men stepped aboard Liba 26.

'There's many boats about. Anything the matter?' Blair asked.

One man pushed his cap higher on his head. His eyes seemed to be checking more than the fish on the houseboat. 'Nah! We've got a blitz on. Just checking that everyone's got legal sized fish. With the river higher people will be starting to catch more fish. You're not returning carp to the river, are you?'

'No, we know the rules, Tom said.

'All OK then.'

The other officer went forward to the ice locker where Blair bought out the callop they'd caught to show them. The fish were already filleted. He nodded appreciably. 'The fish look fine, good size.'

'Anything else?' Blair said his eyes on the curious man.

'That's all. See you later, maybe.'

The men returned aft and climbed back into their boat. Blair looked towards the arrow partially hidden by his cap. Maybe he should have said something about kids mucking about. He started for the rear of the houseboat but Tom had already pushed them off. 'Good luck' they called and the craft sped away up river.

'That was strange. We've never been checked before. I suppose it's normal.' Lauren as usual had arrived on deck in time to see the brief encounter.

'It would be more normal if we were in New South Wales. You need a licence to fish there. Curious that they were still down the South Australian side of the border where a licence isn't required.' Blair said. Something's up, he thought, but he kept his opinion of the brief visit to himself.

That afternoon they spent a long time trying to find a suitable mooring site before darkness fell. That could make a serious problem.

The problems were physical.

At one point they couldn't get the boat close enough to the river bank because of tree snags in the deep water that impeded their way. Blair drove the boat in until the houseboat scraped against the snags.

'Whoa – you'll ground us. Just like Peter!' Tom laughed as he went forward to push against an old heavy branch that marked an underwater fallen tree. Blair backed up, the paddle wheel at full power and the sounds of scratching against the hull shuddering through the hull as the boat pulled clear. They swung downstream again.

Two hundred meters further on a river bank spot looked perfect. But, as Tom jumped ashore with the mooring rope in hand to tie the first rope around a tree, a huge colony of big black ants surged out of the ground. He scuttled back on board.

'No way,' he said stomping ants off his boots. 'We'd never be able to put a gang plank down there or think about a camp fire.'

Backing out again, this time sounding the obligatory three short toots on the horn, they rounded the next bend to find they were approaching high red cliffs again as noted on the charts. They didn't want to go as far as the Bunyip Reach Homestead at the other end of the cliff line and they had already decided to stay two nights at whatever mooring site they found.

'This'll do,' Peter suggested as they brought the boat in close. 'Better check again for more ants though.'

Tom leapt ashore. 'It looks OK. There's been a campfire here before.' He stamped his feet about raising dust. No ants responded to his challenge.

'Rain dancing, Tom?' Blair enquired as he came forward with the other stern rope. 'Not bad. But we'd prefer the same great weather for the rest of the trip.'

'No ants.' Tom continued his dance as he accepted the thrown rope and circled a huge tree. 'Looks a good spot. Might even be a good fishing place.'

'I hope so. D'you know we've caught less fish since we've been above the lock in deeper water. Ana says that the flow is better downstream and there's more bird life. More waders...'

'That so? Maybe then we'll only stay here for one night and head back through the lock earlier than we've planned. Something to discuss around the fire tonight. Are we still on for cards later?'

Blair and Kari had been taught the card game that the others played and were having a good dose of beginner's luck.

'You're getting more and more competitive, Blair. Thought you weren't like Tom, the money man.' Peter thumped the gang plank ashore and settled the heavy beam into place. 'You and Kari are winning. Must be cheating...what do you reckon Tom?'

Ana called from the kitchen. 'Darling, the steaks are ready for the barbeque. Will you light it please?'

'It's good to hear you're back in the good books to 'darling' again,' Blair chided his brother in law. 'Feeling better is she?'

Peter remembered coming back into the room into their bedroom early that morning, damp clean and smelling a soapy man smell. He'd dropped his damp towels and naked he'd moved to her window side of the bed, bent and kissed her forehead. She ran her fingers up his smooth thigh. No invitation, now, just appreciation. He knew he looked good naked.

'Come on, rise and shine. There'll be coffee with breakfast and some of those yabbies will be waiting for you to pull the nets in. That's your job.' He'd grinned to Ana. 'You catch 'em, you cook 'em and we'll eat 'em.'

It was like being with an out of bounds virgin, enticing but frustrating, he thought. He'd kept their pact and, surprisingly there was a new romantic feeling between them. Like they were starting all over again.

It was good. It held promise.

Chapter 36

But Ana wasn't feeling better about everything.

She could see the holiday arrow trophy, from every part of the cabin section, and every time she looked at it her fears returned.

The men's reassurances just didn't make sense. No child could shoot an arrow that far out into the river. Not even a naughty child. Maybe a teenager had the strength... she thought. Now she was certain that the first thing that had whizzed past her on the deck was another arrow. Not a bird as they had suggested. A hunter wouldn't shoot two arrows so indiscriminately out into the water.

There was a smidgen of doubt in Ana's mind that the arrows had been loosed at the eagle. Surely not. She thought. The arrows looked expensive. No, she decided those arrows had been shot at them. As she tossed a bowl full of salad greens she could feel herself cringe into her clothing.

Her thought went to Quinn, always to him. I am neurotic, hardly professional, she thought. Everything that happens I attribute to Demetrius Quinn.

Ana went into the bedroom looking for her mobile phone. 'I'll call Mark Llewellyn', she decided. 'Get some reassurance. They must have got the prisoners...and Quinn.

Damn, there was no signal from the river level.

She looked outside.

The red cliffs loomed high beside the boat, between them and where she thought a river tower might be.

She could see a track to the cliff top. Perhaps if she went ashore and climbed higher up?

A motor bike hammered the silence of the late afternoon along a road above the river. A road was marked on their charts. The nearness of it above the river was scary, but there had to be the chance of getting a signal up there. She could keep away from the road, and from any danger travelling along it, but she needed to call Mark.

'I'm going to see if I can get a signal up there,' she called to Peter as she went ashore. 'I feel I want to report to the police about the arrow.'

'Do you want me to come with you?' he asked.

'No thanks. I won't be long and it's your turn to cook the barbeque. I'll be OK.'

Ana found the path that led from the mooring site to higher ground. She stood beside the road and without trouble made the call.

'Hello, Ana Foster here. You sound close. Must be good signal from Lincoln,' Ana commented as an opener.

'I'm actually in Renmark. I came over to help the boss on a few matters.'

'Oh?'

'Routine...' he filled a gap knowing her concern about the prisoners. 'There's been a winery fire...' It wasn't a lie but evasive to the truth.

Ana's voice was hesitant. 'I don't want to sound a stupid woman but something happened today that got me a bit worried.'

Mark sensed more than a bit. 'Tell me,' he said. 'Maybe we can help. That's what we're here for.' The quiet concerned tone was back.

'Someone took a pot shot at us on the houseboat. An arrow landed on the deck...'

'An arrow, you're sure about that?'

'Of course I'm sure! We got one of them and I think there were actually two arrows fired. The first one missed.'

'Describe the arrow. Was it a child's arrow?'

'No, it wasn't a child's arrow!' Frustration threaded into her voice. 'It was a steel shafted thing with a very sharp point. Blair, my brother in law, said it was a hunting arrow.'

'No one was hurt?' Mark asked.

'No, but it was odd.'

'Ana, where exactly were you when that happened?'

'In midstream down from...I think it was called Queen's Reach on the charts.'

'Where are you now?'

Ana's voice was louder over the phone as though she had pressed the phone harder into her ear. 'Are you not telling me something, Mark?'

'First, where are you moored now?' he said.

'By some red cliffs. I had to climb up to get a signal to speak to you. Why? You've got to tell me. It's Quinn? Isn't it? He's still here?'

'Ana, you've got to go back to the boat immediately. Quinn is still at large, and the others too. The others, they're not the problem, but get back to the boat and we'll try to send someone to meet you as soon as we can.'

'How do you know this? Why are we in danger as you say?'

'It wasn't released to the press but the prisoners stole a hunting cross bow and arrows when they escaped. Quinn has it. He's the dangerous one.'

As Ana stood up on the road high above the river Quinn appeared next to the houseboat.

He walked like a man hiking. He swung a stout stick and his stolen boots stomped the rutted track beside the river, Quinn even whistled an off key tune. He made no attempt at silence and he scared a flock of river ducks to flight. As they wheeled away he appeared to stop to watch them go but in reality his eyes were centred on the houseboat. His friendly demeanour belied his thoughts.

He called a greeting to the men he could see as he came alongside.

This was Liba 26. The bitch's boat.

Where was she? He could wait and it would be worth anything if he could get her. An inner voice told him that this was not the time. He could see one man on the foredeck and two others at the back of the houseboat.

No women to be seen. Three men against one. No contest.

He'd play it cool.

'Hello,' he called.

Blair answered. His voice was cautious but he was a trusting person and could not imagine that this man could be an escaped prisoner if they were still at large.

He checked the area before answering.

The man appeared alone. Everything looked clear and the stranger's appearance was relaxed and friendly. The open river bank was close by and it couldn't hide others.

'Hello?' the reply was a query. 'You out here on your own?'

'Sure. Why?' Quinn answered.

'There's a few problems in the area,' Blair was circumspect as Tom came to stand alongside him.

'Oh, I've been hiking in the National Park...upstream. What's going on?'

'Escaped prisoners. Three of them are supposed to be in the

area. Have you seen anything?' Tom asked.

'Nothing. I've been on my own. Haven't seen anyone.' Quinn smiled. 'The prisoners from the local prison at Cadell?'

'No. Escaped from elsewhere.' Blair said. 'Haven't you heard? It's all over the radio.'

'No. Not carrying one but thanks for the warning I'll keep a look out.'

Blair noticed the small hiker's pack. 'Where're you camped?'

'This side of the river from Queen's Reach,' Quinn lied. He remembered the name on the charts they'd stolen. 'It was a bit of a hike to here across a big loop in the river, but my camp's there. You been up that way? It's very beautiful.'

'Yes, we've come past there earlier. Keep a watch out for the prisoners and give them a wide berth. You're obviously a more experienced bushman but they are reported as dangerous.' Blair glanced up at the sky, the sun was shining and it was warm. 'Can I offer you a drink?'

'Thanks... but no thanks.' Quinn remembered the odds and he couldn't be sure of his reaction if he saw her. 'I'll be heading back upstream away from here...so I should be OK from any problems. Thanks again for the warning.'

Quinn turned to go.

He was fuming. Where was that woman? That whore...? He turned back. 'You guys on your own? Fishing trip away from the women?'

'Nah,' from Blair, 'our wives are in the galley cooking. Well, two of them are, one's ...' He stopped, brought up short by a frown from Peter. 'Oh,' he covered his slip. 'She's somewhere, probably reading a book in her cabin.'

Quinn left, swinging his stick hard against the reeds along the path.

Ana, with panic in her feet, skidded and slid down the cliff path from the road towards the houseboat. She arrived; less than ten minutes after Quinn hiked on, to tell them about her call to Mark.

She listened as the men described the hiker. They were as worried about him being in the same line of Quinn's fire as they were.

'He was bald and had a couple of days beard growth.'

'Are you sure that the man was a hiker?' Ana asked. 'Describe him again...'

Tom was insistent. The man looked, talked, was clothed and had a backpack like a hiker – ergo he was a hiker.

'Are you sure?'

Chapter 37

'God, I'm spending too much time in this chair. I've got to get out. Mark, are you there?'

Rick put his hands behind his neck, shook his shoulders and stretched as he waited for a response from across the large temporary muster room in the Renmark Institute. The same institute that had held the Psychic Exhibition and the smell of incense and oils could not quite overlay the bad coffee and the stale take-away boxes. The cloying smells lingered in the under ventilated room.

Most of Rick's time was spent there and he was getting restless.

'I'm going for a walk. Find something to eat.' Still stretching Rick sauntered out of the room.

The couple of other officers hardly looked up from their paper reports. Their desk computers that were strung with macramé knots of cords that fed off the few power points in the old building.

Mark turned towards the retreating figure. 'Hang on, boss...' he began as he clicked his mobile shut, then he frowned as another call buzzed demanding attention.

Rick didn't hear him, or didn't turn back.

Boss's privilege.

'Yes...' Mark was brisker than usual. 'What?' He listened, then his voice was frustrated, 'That came out in this morning's briefing.

We think the prisoners are still together. There's no evidence to the contrary.' He listened again. 'Sounds unlikely but follow it up then, but keep your distance and don't do anything on your own.'

A head raised in enquiry from another desk.

He clicked his mobile shut and stretched in relief as the phone stayed quiet without the eternal buzz that demanded his attention.

'That was that Loxton Dee' he said to the open room. 'Got a report that three men in a fishing dingy went past the border point into the other states. They didn't look like our escaped lot but he thought that maybe they were in disguise.'

There was a sigh from the other end of the room. 'Same dee who was first on the crime scene for the Loxton woman vic? Cripes he's young...Keen! He'd investigate an empty envelope.'

'Or a used condom,' the response from another voice caused a ripple of chuckles.

Mark grinned then said. 'Well he's going to take his own boat and go as far as the borders. In the dark, mind you. We've got the Victoria and New South Wales boys keeping their eyes open but I still think they're in this state. And I think they are definitely after the Foster woman, well Quinn is anyway. Demented bastard. Maybe we'll get him because of it.'

'Mark?' a young female police officer called.

'What!' again he gave an irritated, tired response. 'Sorry...'

'This Loxton victim...' the officer hesitated then pointed at a white board.

Everywhere Mark looked there were white boards. He raised an eyebrow.

The officer moved closer to the board, tapped it. 'Have you noticed that this vic has blonde streaks in her hair? Two of the Lincoln women had them too...a coincidence? A copycat killer? Or has Quinn targeted women with blonde streaks?'

Mark sat upright in his chair. Another link: it had to be another link between all the killings. Like the missing fingers. Maybe not a coincidence.

He grinned at the officer. 'Takes a woman to see other women's hairstyles. I hadn't noticed past the long dark hair. Well ...show me. It may be significant.'

'You probably haven't noticed but I've got streaks...see blonde and red.' She bent her head and pointed to her hair.

Mark moved close and touched the young constable's hair. It was pulled back tightly in regulation manner but he could see that her mid brown hair was highlighted with the streaks she was talking about. A pale golden, a whitish colour and a deep auburn.

'Yes.'

They both moved to the photograph on the board.

'See,' she said. 'There... you can see the different colour tones in this Loxton crime scene photo. Even with the wet hair. I noticed them when the 'before' photos of the Port Lincoln victims came on line last week. Both Tara Henson and Elizabeth Woods had coloured streak accents in their hair. The contrasts weren't so noticeable in the crime scene shots but then the hair was often badly contaminated.'

Mark smiled at the constable. 'What's your first name "J. Taylor"?' he read off her ID badge.

'Jessica, sir. We were introduced yesterday but with all the staff here you probably don't remember...' She blushed aware that she had put him on the spot. 'Sorry Mark...Sir,' she fumbled for words.

'OK Jessica. Keep looking for things that appear odd to you. That's what makes a good detective and don't be ever be hesitant to speak up.' He grinned, 'and don't let me, my boss, or anyone not listen to you either.'

'Thanks Mark.' She didn't add that she had already tried to

talk to Rick about her observations but the senior man hadn't been interested. Too caught up in the prisoner escape perhaps, she'd thought.

'Give me that observation in a brief email and I'll add it to the files. You'll get the credit if it comes to anything. A good clue... to add to the long lists. Every bit counts.'

Mark paused in front of the photographs then looked around the room. Everyone seemed listless staring at computer screens or hunched in their chairs over piles of written reports. Most had hardly noted the young woman's enthusiastic comments nor their movement to the boards.

Everyone looked whacked.

'OK, listen up,' Mark said aloud to the room in general. 'Enough for tonight! Finish what you're doing and take a couple of hours off for dinner. Keep your mobiles on and only come back tonight if you have something absolutely vital that must be done. Or you get called in. Some of you have families and I don't want the job to be the cause of divorces. OK?'

He didn't add that the long hours, and often being away working, was the reason for the breakdown of Rick's marriage. His own fiancé got more than a bit miffed at times.

The room cleared with alacrity after the slump. Mark caught up with Jessica as she started out the door. 'You going home or getting a bite to eat somewhere?' he asked. 'I don't know what's good or what's not in Renmark. So far I've only eaten takeaway or from the motel's kitchen. Both were OK but...'

Jessica flushed as another young constable caught up with them. 'David and I are going to get Chinese,' she said. 'You can join us if you'd like.' Jessica grinned as her husband pecked her on the cheek, 'This's the second extra ask out I've got tonight. Is it possible that tired men want company more? Nice to be asked of course.'

Mark hesitated. Discomforted. His invitation was from pure boredom at again eating a meal alone without someone on the other side of the table.

Why hadn't he been detective enough to see the ring on Jessica's finger. Now he felt an idiot. Not the only idiot from what the young woman had said.

The young policeman smiled. 'I'm David Taylor,' he said. 'Come with us. We're both interested in Major Crime...' he saw the hesitation on Mark's face. 'But not so much that you'll have to talk all night about it. Maybe we can talk fishing, wine or something else ...my family owns a winery here.'

'Sounds a good exchange,' Mark relaxed. 'Done, let's go then. It'll be good to have a night off, and a bit of company.'

Chapter 38

'Describe him, that hiker. Tell me again,' Ana insisted next morning at the breakfast table. The usual breakfast of bacon and eggs she'd moved around the plate rather than touched. 'So far you've only told me he had a bald head under a cap?' She sat opposite Tom, Peter and Blair. 'Come on…Everything you remember. How old was he? What colour were his eyes? How tall was he?'

Not much more information was forthcoming. Yes he had blue eyes. They eyed each other over and said that he probably was as tall as Tom.

To Ana it sounded that it could be Quinn. 'Are you sure about the lack of hair?' she demanded.

'Yes, I'm sure. He must've been bald if he had a few days growth of beard. He wasn't going to shave his head if he didn't shave his face, would he? Not when he was out in the bush.' Blair statement was emphatic for him.

'And he looked like an experienced bushman. Told us he'd hiked for days and I think he said he was going back upstream. And yes, he was on his own,' Tom said.

'He wasn't a bad looking fellow,' Peter conceded.

'He might've had tattoos on his hands.' Tom said. He frowned as if he wasn't sure.

Every instinct in Ana fired.

Quinn had been truly handsome.

And the tattoos. It was him… she could feel a tightening in her throat.

She moved inside to the main cabin and sat down on a lounge chair where she could see every area. Kari went inside and sat with her. Lauren packed up the dishes and went into the galley to wash them.

Kari had caught her sister's fears and phobias and Blair was mildly cross with Ana for infecting his wife. Both of them were watching for ghosts. This trip was supposed to be a healing holiday away from phantoms. He'd been sure that the escaped prisoners were well away but Ana's call to the police last night seemed to have raised the anxiety levels again.

'I think we should cut this trip short. I want to go home. Today,' Ana bit into her lower lip to stop a tremble. 'I just want to go home.' Peter came and sat beside her, and silently he rubbed the back of her tense neck.

Tom, who had paid most for the houseboat holiday, interjected. 'But we've got another four days paid for…shouldn't we put things behind us and relax. The police will get them. The coppers, Rick and Mark, you've got to know them well. They'll call us …'

'No! I want to go as soon as possible.'

Lauren, as practical as ever, said, 'I'll make coffee all round and let's make plans to go back.' She touched Ana's shoulder as she past her chair.

The men exchanged glances. Peter brought out the river charts and they spread them out on the table.

'We're here,' he said pointing at the marker 624 under the red cliffs. He looked at his watch. 'It's already too late to get back in time to go through the lock today. It closes at 4pm.' He smiled. 'Even the gorgeous Sam won't open for us after four. How about we start early in the morning and be ready to go through when it opens at 10am the day after tomorrow? There's really no other alternative,' he said gently to Ana. 'Let's enjoy these last nights together and go back as soon as we can cover the distance.'

'If that's what we have to do, alright. I'm sorry but I feel so vulnerable. I feel that I'm in a room where I can't lock the doors and there are monsters outside. Monsters with gigantic teeth and sharp knives. Or at least huge cross bows and a million arrows...' Ana strained to smile.

'Agreed,' Tom caved in to the inevitable. 'And I have one very good bottle of bubbly saved for the last night. I'll put it on ice and we'll drink it with Lauren's pork roast at dinner. How does that sound?'

Outside a small bird swooped down onto a brown falcon trying to divert it from its own nest. The falcon turned to claw at the defending bird then gave up. It flew on.

'Thank you,' Ana said to Peter as they undressed for bed that night.

'For what?' Peter's tone was cautious.

'For backing me today when I said wanted to go home.'

'Ana, for goodness sake you don't have to thank me for anything.' Peter was on the defensive. 'Shit...I've let you down. In everything.'

'Not everything...just,' Ana's face crumbled. 'I'm no real use to you now. Not until we get the results of the blood tests.'

Peter stretched his naked body across the bed and took a small packet from the chest of drawers on his side of the bed. 'I found these at the Customs House...' his voice was a query. 'Do you think these will give you something else to think about for a while?'

'Oh yes...and what is that?' Ana's voice softened. She reached over and took the packet. 'Oh…' she murmured. 'We've never used these before…I'm not sure I know how.'

'Stop talking woman and see what you can do with one.' Peter rolled over from his stomach and his intentions with what could be done with a condom were immediately obvious.

'Hmmm…' Ana said approvingly. With hushed giggles, like teenagers on the lounge room sofa with parents in the nearby bedroom, she managed to fit the appliance. 'Now,' she said as she lay next to him. 'I need you now. I can't wait…'

'Neither can I…'

Ana groaned softly as Peter's fullness entered her.

Her arms and legs closed about him and as gently he was able he kissed her breast and ears. She bucked and jerked under him and despite his best efforts he found that he had to ride the wild storm with her.

It would be over quickly.

Their release came together.

Chapter 39

Rick slammed down the phone. 'Mark, my office...now!'

Rick's scowl belied the fact that his 'office' in the large open space of the Institute Hall was the Men's Room. One of the few places where they could lock the doors, and talk tactics or policy business, without being overheard.

Sometimes it was necessary.

From Rick's face Mark knew that it was necessary now. He met Rick at his office door. They went in to interrupt a junior constable zipping up his fly, the man quickly splashed water over his hands and left.

Rick stood with his back against the wooden door jamb. 'Adelaide is hammering at me,' he grumbled. 'Why haven't we got them yet? I don't know. They're not bloody realistic.'

'Situation usual,' Mark said.

'They're not willing to take any men off the local winery fire investigation. It's been confirmed as arson. One of the casualties died today, so it's murder as well. Big, too in local politics. As if escaped murderers aren't big!'

Mark nodded in agreement.

'What a time to be understaffed!'

'The Star Force, boss?'

They can be here stat but they need four to five hours to react, to get here and to ammo up. They can't just wait around doing nothing until we have a positive sighting. It's not the way with them.'

'Pity. They'd be just what we need in a showdown.'

'Well, we might not get them. They're not even going to take bodies off Traffic Detail to send here – the government might miss out on some fine revenue,' Rick moved to the urinal. 'Might as well take a piss while I'm here,' he growled. 'They'd probably want to know why I was taking time off for that, if they knew!'

As usual Rick could underplay what was bothering him.

Mark headed for the urinal one down from him. Give the man a little privacy. 'We've got everyone here on this almost 24 hours a day. I sent them home early last night, well at 9 pm, after you'd gone. Everyone was bushed and sick of eating fast food.'

'Right on too,' Rick responded.

He was good at looking after his officers, Mark thought. 'Does Adelaide want our blood as well as our sweat?' This was a usual thing. Get the job done without costing extra money.

'I've got them to make a couple of concessions. We can keep the police plane in the air looking for another day. Not that the spotters can see much from it. Too much bush near the river, but better than relying on boats or trying to follow them in cars.'

'This's the first time we've not been able just to get in a car and follow crims. Frustrating, isn't it. But the plane may spot them yet...' Mark conceded.

'They're also considering sending the dogs here. Just considering! Bloody Hell!' Rick paused from his rant and took a breath. 'The dogs could be useful when we do corner the bastards. They can do something if we can pick up a scent. We just need that location – where the hell on this confounded river are they?'

'We'll get it and soon I hope... you know I'm still getting stuff in from Lincoln on the murders there, but most of my hours are on the three escapees here. I'm to continue to keep tabs on the original murders, aren't I?'

'That's more than OK. As I've said before, get the Quinn murders tied up so tight that some bloody court system can't let him go again.'

'Sure boss.' Mark said. He zipped.

'We're narrowing the bastards here down, though. From the call you reported last night with the Foster woman, I think they're not too far away.' Rick finished washing his hands and threw a paper towel towards a bin. It missed.

Mark picked up the paper towel and put it in the bin.

Rick raised an eyebrow at him. 'Maybe I was a wrong thinking of her as fixated on Quinn. She's a target. Why?'

Mark washed his hands, pushed them wet down his face. 'It's the boy. He thinks she knows where his son is. I'm sure that's at the core of him being here.'

'You've told her group to come back to Renmark, haven't you? Get them back through the Lock then if the mongrels follow we can put a concentration of manpower this side of it. I reckon then we'll have this wrapped up in the next 24 hours. Want a bet?'

'I wish...' Mark said.

Victor and Jahan were very drunk when Quinn arrived back at the houseboat they had purloined.

Initially he was angry but, he reasoned, if he could keep them drunk and hung-over they would do what he wanted.

Just as soon as he found out what he needed he'd kill that woman whore, psychologist, or whatever she was. After that not much mattered. They'd got him on the murder charges already so one more made no difference. He was banged up for life now anyway. It would be her fault if he didn't see the boy ever again. Her fault if he spent the rest of his life inside. Her fault that he'd killed so many on the run.

His look was hard as he sat down opposite his slumped and drunk companions. It was her fault that he was saddled with these two fucking losers now. Her fault, and if she'd told him where the boy was before the escape he'd be safe from the cops and somewhere else.

Her fault…everything.

'Hey, you stinking bastards!' he shouted across the table in the large cabin. It was a mess but this afternoon who cared. 'Who wants to arm wrestle?'

Jahan leaned forward and offered his arm. In a moment Quinn grabbed the arm and pinned it to the table. 'Hey, I wasn't ready,' Jahan argued. They set up again and Quinn dealt the same winning thrust.

'Next?' Quinn lined up across the table against Victor who raised his left arm. 'Not that disgusting hand,' Quinn cuffed the arm aside. 'You use your right arm, like you're supposed to, idiot!'

Victor was beaten just as Jahan had been and neither man was willing to go against Quinn again. He knew he was the winner and sloshed their glasses full of a very good cab sav they had taken from a locker.

'Tomorrow we go back to Lock 6 to finish a job,' he said. They peered at him but neither man said anything. 'We go back and afterwards we can pinch another car and get away. We'll go to Adelaide this time. After being here they'll expect us to go on to Sydney. We'll double back and confuse them.'

'Sure,' Victor slurred. 'Hey Quinn, we've been talking while you were away. We haven't got any kids…you got any?

'I got one I know of… a boy. Eight years old.'

Victor with enough drink in him to state an obvious said. 'Thought you were inside for ten years.' He smirked an aside to Jahan. 'Got a kid palmed off as his. He's not all that good. At least we'd know if we've got kids.'

'You know nothing, you bloody mongrel. I had one of those prisoner loving girlfriends visit me while I was in Yatala. I like my women commando and we did a quick lap dance before the bastard wardens could stop us. I passed on more than a fucking mouthful of rollies that day,' Quinn laughed.

He leered at the memory of the event.

He sat back hands clasped over his crutch. Good one, he remembered. His face went dark. Now he wouldn't get a chance to see his son again. The boy's mother was out of the control of his threats and she'd disappeared already.

That hurt. Not her going, but the boy... Nothing else ever would ever hurt like that. Just to see again the boy who looked so like him.

He knew that the counsellor bitch had helped her. Like the others had done before. He hated them, always had always would. Whores all. He could see it in the woman he'd attacked. Worth it, he thought. And he did know her from somewhere and he wasn't finished with her yet. Not by a long chalk.

Quinn filled his own glass this time before slopping what was left in the bottle between the other two men, and then drank the tumbler-full straight down. He pushed the empty bottle off the table. It hit the wooden deck hard and skidded away into a corner.

Get another bloody bottle,' he commanded. 'I need more booze.'

Chapter 40

'I reckon we can confirm the hiker that Ana's group saw, was Quinn,' Mark said as he stopped at Rick's desk.

'Eh?' Rick looked away from his screen to butt his chin at Mark. 'How so?'

'A call came in from the shop girl at Morgan. She said that she had something to add to her statement of the night when old Jarvis was killed. She'd been taken with Quinn's face but when they did a stock-take they found a packet of black hair dye missing plus disposable razors. Dye's not the usual stuff that gets nicked. She thought it could've been used to change someone's appearance. A good think… She also now remembers the tats on Quinn's hands. Usual prison ones – HATE and LOVE. It fits with Ana's description of the hiker.'

'So Quinn is dark haired or bald now. Maybe the others too. No need for Jahan but Quinn and Jones. Get it out to the squads.'

'Done it already, Sarg. Or they could have all shaved up. But what is it with hair colouring lately? It seems to come up with everything…'

'Them's the breaks. You'll learn when you get as old as I am in the job. Usually coincidences are just that, coincidences.'

Mark grabbed his chin in anguish as he stared into his computer screen at a Major Crime notation there.

'Hey, Rick!' he called over his shoulder.

He looked around but Rick was out of his station, probably getting another coffee. He'd refused another cappuccino from the local people and he was probably waiting for the thick muck he called coffee to brew, Mark thought with a wry grin. It was coffee so strong that it tasted foul. Rick revelled in his 'proper brew' as he insisted on calling it.

His eyes returned to the screen and his brain resisted the information. It detailed a body found in the bush in the Coffin Bay National Park.

Another one.

Another one in the Port Lincoln area.

Mark's breath whistled through his teeth as he read the report under the Major Crime heading.

A Coffin Bay Park Ranger had found the scattered, almost skeletal remains, in the area where he was to clear scrub to put in a fence inland from the beach at Point Longnose. Kangaroos were eating the new trees he'd planted out last winter and he'd finally got official permission to put up a fence. An older man, he'd seen most things including dead humans, and he was very matter of fact as he radioed back to his base.

'Wait there! We'll send someone as soon as we can.'

'Yeah.' He checked the GPS on his phone and gave his exact co-ordinates.

'Don't go near the remains again.' The instruction was sharp, emphatic.

'Cripes I know that! Haven't come down with the last bloody shower of rain,' he muttered as he signed off.

He'd gathered up his fencing tools and went back to his Land Rover. There he cleared a safe area, gathered twigs and wood, lit them and made himself a cuppa. Sitting back in the bird interrupted silence of the bush he wondered on the state of a world when bodies could be dumped in his beautiful park.

Patience could have been his middle name as he was waiting there, his billycan still on the boil, when Detective Hank Arnold, the younger pathologist Tim Hayden, and the local Coroner finally arrived. It was a good hour from Port Lincoln by car.

They were clad in boiler suits and masked, the ranger noted. He pointed out the site and the team began their investigations. The Ranger put more water on to boil and rummaged in his bag to see if he had enough cups to give them tea. He lined an odd assortment of enamel mugs up and waited.

'The remains are older than the ones before,' Hank said.

Older, but not by much,' Tim agreed. He scanned the area. 'They're very exposed. Been here since the end of last year. It's a guess but I think that they would have been completely dried out otherwise. Four to six months you reckon?' He raised eyebrows at Hank.

'Can be attributed to the current serial killer?' Hank asked.

Tim squatted down by the torso remains. 'There,' he said pointing to what appeared to be marks on rib bones. I don't think they are markings from feral animal teeth. They're knife cuts. Lots of them. I'll be positive when I get her back to the lab. It looks the same MO.'

'Her?'

'Definitely female. See the hip structure. She's smallish but I don't think she's a child.'

'Enough flesh for DNA?'

'Plenty with the latest techniques but I think that we'll have enough from the teeth for a positive ID before we'd need to go that way.'

'Sexual crime?'

'Fair go Hank! It's too skeletal. There's not enough here to state that.'

The more detailed first pathological report followed.

Evidence of knife gouges across the frontal spine at the neck indicated she'd had her throat cut. Her sternum was punctured and some rib bones had thrust cuts again more than suggestive of a frenzied attack. With no possibility of blood remaining, the pathologist couldn't say which of the knife blows were struck first, hence if she'd had her throat slashed first or last. The final comment was that the murder was very like the others. Just older.

'It's got to be Petra Cullen.' Mark said. 'Please let it be her. She's already been missing for a long time and don't let it be other young woman we don't know about yet.'

He read on.

Not all remains were there because, as usual, they had been scattered by animals. The main culprits, foxes and feral cats, even in a national park.

The hands were gone although there were a few metacarpal bones and phalanges scattered yet to be finally assembled into their exact position when the skeleton was placed on the autopsy table. The right tibia, fibula, most of the feet bones, left ulna, radius, and some of the ribs were gone. What hair was still there appeared to be mid to darkish brown. There were bits of clothing still adhered to the underside of the remains which could again assist with the ID.

Mark reread the paragraph. Was the little finger of the left hand there? Possibly not.

As an aside, the pathologist noted that this woman had extensive rheumatoid arthritic nodes on her joints and she was also probably being treated for that condition. This was a different aspect of the MO, and with this condition the identification was going to be easier through the local GPs. Still, it was noted, the woman was probably in her early twenties from the overall evidence.

Mark sat back.

So Petra Cullen. His guess was looking correct. He flipped his screen to Petra's the original Missing Person report. Yes, there it was. Rheumatoid arthritis.

He ran his hands through his longer than normal regulation hair. Diverted, he admitted that he did need a haircut soon. He stared up into the expanse of the old building's high ceiling feeling the weight of another senseless and cruel death. One they may never be able to attribute to Quinn. Each case had to have linking evidence. Something concrete before they could lay charges.

He flipped the screen back to the pathologist's report. He almost felt guilty wishing it was Petra. At least when they confirmed her fully, the family would have an ending. He wouldn't be knocking on someone else's door. People who weren't expecting terrible news.

He brought his thoughts back to the immediate business of what they could surmise even if they could never prove it. Mark's profiling training suggested that the killer may have been less selective with what seemed to be the first killing than with of the later crimes. Was she easier prey because she was sick? Maybe slower? He may have been hurried in the pick up or murderously excited because of some other factor.

There was just the time frame to be reviewed.

It didn't quite jell with the other murders.

Half an hour later Rick was back with his coffee.

'Check your Major Crime screen,' Mark advised and waited while his boss clicked onto the screens. Rick took a sip of his hot coffee brew then raised his cup with a 'want one' enquiry.

Rick's coffee smelt good, as always, but Mark'd been caught

before. He shook his head and waited.

'Shit!' Rick's expletive was quiet and exasperated. 'The pathologist is pretty sure that it's Quinn again. What do you think?'

'It appears victim specific and method specific – text book stuff. Like all the others there's overkill involved.'

'You've got any inkling on the ID?'

'It looks like Petra Cullen.'

'No knife found at the scene I suppose? That would help.' Rick looked hopeful.

'Getting the knife would be a bonus. But no, the perp's too controlled for that. The pathologist's an expert on knives so I guess we'll get word when the more detailed autopsy report comes in. He was very definite with his observations already though. Must've spent a lot of time at the scene.'

'He sounds OK.'

'A bit of doubt about the time frame though?' Mark commented.

'Yeah, but with old ones it's not always easy to tell. Even for experts.'

Mark got to his feet. The lingering smell of Rick's coffee reminded him that he did want one, even if it was just an instant He paused, standing by Rick's desk. 'So what's next, Boss? Do you or I go back to Lincoln or do we wait until this mess is cleared up here?'

'We wait and get these animals first.'

'I hope that they get a positive timeframe on this one...tie it in completely with Quinn's release from his last stretch,' Mark said.

Chapter 41

With the decision made to leave early next morning Ana felt the world lift off her shoulders. Making love with Peter had helped. Suddenly the Quinn threat was gone or, at least, he was gone. Moved on. She wanted to believe what he had told the men. He was going upriver.

The decision to go faded the warning from Mark too. She felt they were doing something positive by going back, away from the threat.

As the late afternoon wove sunset patterns across the river she hurried, from her fishing spot on the back deck, to help with dinner.

Lauren had promised her special dinner of roast pork.

As chief cook for the night, Lauren sliced the rind on the pork roast to make the crackling. They argued and laughed over the fineness of her scoring until it was just right to everyone's satisfaction.

Kari came out to check but was waved away to set the table. She could find the apple sauce and a dish to present it in.

With the gas oven set at its highest temperature they waited until the intense heat was achieved before they put the huge leg, rubbed now with olive oil and sea salt, into the oven. Potatoes were boiled, smashed in then roasted to be crisp and crunchy. Chatting like teenagers they prepared more vegetables ready to slide into the pan later - carrots and sweet potatoes, onions and roasted whole garlic bulbs. There were frozen beans to be steamed in butter and served with nutmeg. When half an hour later the rind had crackled to Lauren's satisfaction, she turned the oven down to let the roast cook - slow now, topped with its scrumptious topping.

Peter and Blair had remained out the back fishing and Peter came in with a fat callop, large enough to add to the fish that still lay on ice.

'Are we to have these fillets as an entrée tonight?' he said. 'Or do we have them for breakfast tomorrow?'

'Not on your life...' Tom appeared in the kitchen, drawn by the smell of the pork and by the overheard conversation. 'I'm cooking bacon and eggs as usual.'

'Will there be time if we're to leave early?' Ana asked.

Tom cast an accusing glance at Lauren. 'I'm not allowed bacon and eggs at home and these breakfasts are the only reason I come on these houseboat trips. OK I'm joking. We can't change now...for whatever reason,' he pleaded.

'It's for your health. Don't blame me if your cholesterol is up again...' Lauren bit as she always did.

'So it's to be as an entrée tonight,' Tom said with a grin. 'That's decided then.'

'No, hang on,' Lauren said sniffing the aroma coming from the oven. 'We'll never eat all this tonight.'

'So all this fine fish is to go to waste?' Peter said.

'We can't do that,' Kari insisted. Waste wasn't in her vocabulary. She and Blair's specialist stained glass business just made ends meet. She paused. 'I've have remembered a great recipe for fresh water fish, with soy and garlic. I can do that for lunch tomorrow, just with a little bit of salad. We'll have it after we've gone through the lock.'

Ana looked at the women as they worked and chatted.

This was how the holiday should have been all along, not the way that she'd let it become. Quinn had made it horrible, she corrected herself. The attack and the escape was the nightmare. She knew that her bruises were fading, her neck was no longer swollen and the pale sticking plaster dressing on her hand was the only thing still showing from it all.

She dragged her thoughts away from Quinn to try to laugh as Lauren, deciding something else was delicious, started on again about Jason the Elf of the Forrest. He was delicious. Sam wasn't bad either... This elicited moans from the men, chuckles from Kari, and suddenly Ana's laugh was real.

It's over; tomorrow it will be over... she thought. Back to Renmark and then home as soon as possible.

Tom came back from the front deck icebox with a bottle wrapped in a napkin. 'This is my special treat,' he said, 'and today is the first day I've felt like opening it.'

With a flourish he unwrapped the covering napkin to display a bottle of champagne. The label was new to them. "Lauren's Dream" it read. 'This's a new brand...' he began.

'My new brand! My dream!' Lauren was triumphant. 'Tom has bought us part ownership in a winery, a very good winery and they've bottled this wonderful bubbly under my label.'

'Wonderful! What a dream?'

'Lucky you!'

'Taste it first. The label's just the beginning.'

Lauren was triumphant. 'Here's the new crystal flutes I've been hiding for this moment. I hope that you like it?'

'They'd better - or they won't get the cases we've had sent to their homes.' Tom preened in the fun and extravagance of it all. Before they'd left the city he'd phoned his wine partners and ordered the wine sent. It was good being rich and sharing with friends sometimes.

'There's no Elf on the label, Lauren...maybe you could have put an Elf on it,' Blair quipped.

Peter pretended to groan. 'This trip will be remembered for the Lauren's Elf and me running the houseboat aground,' he instructed them all.

No-one mentioned Ana's problems. Or the arrow that still held a hat as trophy, or Quinn and the escaped prisoners – still at large.

'We'll drink to that,' Tom said.

The champagne was good, fruity, dry, and the wine sparkle tickled their noses as it should.

Ana felt tears escaping with the bubbles. 'I'm sorry...' she started to say. 'Sorry I've ruined this holiday...'

Tom would have none of it. 'Come on old girl,' he said, 'we'll as have another glass and we'll all feel much better.'

Chapter 42

In the Loxton Police Incident Room Mark had finally received the dive student list from Port Lincoln.

He couldn't complain, he thought, he had changed the investigation scope to go back a year since the body at Coffin Bay was found. There was no hunch involved, just a feeling that a smart defence council could cause problems with time lines and dates in court.

Quinn's release date and the estimated murder dates.

The dive boat courses were just another angle that had to be completed. Anyway who said that Quinn had ever attended a dive course, he thought, he could just be a proficient swimmer who'd used or stolen a boat. The wreck wasn't that deep, and although Elizabeth's body was found wedged into the wheelhouse roof, maybe it could have been settled there by the tides if she'd just been taken out to sea and dumped.

The fax list was endless. Name after name, some of them repeats as the students had either failed in their first attempts or gone on to complete a second more extensive training course.

The names were varied. Among them he recognised Anglo Saxon, Australian, Croatian, German, French, Greek and Italian. Even Korean and other Asian names. None meant anything at first reading and he knew that he would have to get the Lincoln police to trace each one to question them, just to parry any defence questions.

A couple of names came up as having past police history. All minor offences, traffic, nothing serious. But they would have to be checked. One name had a slight ring to it, a similarity. Then on a wild hunch he typed in another similar name in another section.

Interesting, he thought.

Unlikely but interesting.

Finally on the houseboat the evening had fizzled to silence.

It was the last night. A good meal, more champagne, they'd played cards - with Tom and Lauren triumphant in winning overall, and then after port and brandy everything seemed over. That slump that said that the holiday was done. They'd locked all the outside doors and everyone but Ana and Peter had wandered off to bed. She wasn't ready to go yet.

'Leave the dishes,' the others said as they left. 'We'll have the engine going in the morning and the dishwasher can be put on.'

Ana began to wash the crystal glasses. They were too good for the dishwasher, and with hot water already in the sink, she continued onto the plates and cutlery. Peter was looking over the charts ready for the trip back to Lock 6 in the morning. Washing dishes was therapeutic, stopped her thinking thoughts that she didn't want. Peter wandered over and dried the last pots. In half an hour they'd finished and Ana wiped down the sink.

'I have been thinking about a baby,' Ana said quietly. 'Not just for us, but near death things make one think a bit differently.'

She paused, cloth in hand.

Peter said nothing, waited.

He knew Ana. She would debate aloud and he could feel the gentle surge, a quietly ecstatic surge of hope. He'd always known that he wanted to be a father and with this beautiful woman the mother of his child. He'd also never thought that she would take such a long time to consider having a baby. Ana going off to study at uni, that changed things... was passing through his mind when he was aware that she was speaking quietly again.

'Kari has commented too. When I said something about testing DNA, can't remember when, she said that I was the only one of us who could pass on our own DNA to another generation. I'm not saying that she put a guilt trip on me, just that she had a point. And it's made me think...am I being selfish? To you and me? To Kari?'

Peter stayed silent. He reached over and gently drew back a wisp of hair from her neck. 'No, darling. You have to be ready. I am willing to wait...but...'

'If everything's clear then soon,' she promised. 'I have always dreamed of a child too, you know...'

'I'm sorry if I've been insistent...'

'You have but it's OK. Just maybe it's happened already...before...'

There was a bump at the front of the craft and a scuffling sound. 'What's that?' Ana started.

'Probably more possums...they're everywhere. Kari's been putting out the vegetable peelings for them. You jump at everything, woman,' Peter teased gently. He yawned. 'We've finished here. I'm off to clean my teeth and bed. Coming?'

'I'm going out to pull in the yabby nets first,' Ana said. 'Won't be long. I'll chuck out the remaining meat bait too. We won't need it after tonight. It's getting pretty smelly.'

'Ripe's the word,' Peter chuckled.

There were two nets, simple nets like crab nets that they had been using with baits tied in the centre with light strong string.

Ana mainly attended to the two nets. She dropped one near the front of the houseboat, close into the shore reeds and the other on the opposite side half way along the deck. She pulled them in morning and night and any time that they moved the houseboat. More often if the yabbies were crawling to the baits. She mused that this trip they had produced some good yabbies and she'd cooked them for lunch one day with garlic and white wine. Treated the fresh crustaceans like Belgium muscles. They were delicious. So good and it was another thing that helped her think of other things than Quinn.

Sometimes the nets caught a little on the tangle of reeds and snags but always they came free without too much trouble.

Ana pulled and tugged at the first rope near the gangplank. It didn't budge. Maybe it's caught again, she thought. It shouldn't be as there were no problems earlier when she'd lifted it.

'You there, Peter? Will you give me a hand with this, please?' she called quietly, not wishing to wake everyone.

Peter came to help. He teased her that she'd got it tangled. Together they struggled and they pulled the net free. It was very heavy as they lifted it onto the deck.

There was something large in the net. Surely not a fish, Ana thought, or maybe a fresh water crayfish. That would be exciting but they were protected and would have to go back into the river.

'Get a torch quick,' Peter instructed.

Ana ran back into the main cabin and grabbed a touch from near the driver's panel. She flicked on the beam as she returned.

There was a huge stone in the net. A stone that was so heavy that the net webbing only just held it. Peter lifted the stone out and Ana drew in her breath. There was a small crushed yabby caught under the stone. Obviously the stone had been put there after she had thrown the nets out before dinner.

'Let's check the other one,' Ana said in a strained voice.

The other net also contained a stone, a large irregular stone that could only have come from the river bank.

Peter shone the torch along the bank.

No-one was visible but as the torch light moved they could see where a stone had been pulled from the earth.

In her imagination Ana could see a man pulling in the nets in the darkness of the deck. It had to be while they were celebrating. While they were laughing and eating and before she and Peter had done the dishes. They might have heard something otherwise. But it might also have been while they were talking afterwards. After the dishes.

That bump?

Someone had been on the deck!

Quinn! It had to be him!

He'd been on the houseboat! In their territory... He could have grabbed any one of them. Kari when she put out the apple peelings! Perhaps he hadn't been alone. The other prisoners with him. The three of them could easily kill them in their beds!

Ana felt sick. She leaned against the cabin wall as her internal whole being screamed. She had to clench her teeth against the bile that rose up from her stomach. Burned her throat.

Peter went to check the mobile phone. Maybe they could contact the police even if seemed they were the object of a prank. Mark or Rick would believe them.

There was no signal.

No signal. He shook the mobile. Shit the battery was low! He hadn't charged it when the generator was running. 'I'll wake Tom and borrow his mobile. I'll call the police. But I think whoever was here has gone now. I'm sure of that ...'

'Don't wake the others,' Ana insisted.

'All we can do is lock up and go to bed,' Peter said as Ana shivered. Her face was white and drawn. I'll take in the gang plank that should keep the bastards off if they return.'

It was a futile gesture and they both knew it.

'We'll keep a guard,' Ana said.

It was well after midnight but both also knew that they would have to sit in the dark of the cabin on guard until the dawn. Tomorrow they would leave but they couldn't do anything until then.

It was impossible to drive the houseboat in the blackness of the night on the river without running aground. Although there may be safety if the houseboat was midstream it was physically impossible, with no anchors, for the boat to hang untethered away from the bank. Again what little current there was could run them aground.

They had to stay where they were.

Ana, with Quinn's assault in mind, picked out the biggest sharpest knife from the galley, and sat at the table with the knife beside her ready for anything that may come. Peter crept around the boat locking all doors before he armed himself with his fishing knife and a stout fishing rod and prepared to sit across the cabin. This way they could see both ways along the dark bank. They could both see the back deck area if someone were to try swim in to cross it.

'Just don't go for me in the night,' he warned her as he wrapped a rug around her against the coldness rising from the river. It with no real attempt at a joke but Ana smiled a tight smile.

'If we survive this night I'm never coming back,' Ana muttered. 'Never...ever!'

An hour later Blair joined them.

He'd stumbled half asleep out to pee over the stern. He found the door locked and barred and seen the dim light in the cabin. He paused in the doorway and whispered. 'The back door's locked. What's the problem?'

They both jumped!

Two pairs of startled yet bleary eyes looked at him. When he insisted he'd stay with them they sent him to get his own choice of weapons. Big gentle Blair came back with another knife and the oar from the dingy. He sat resolutely by the doorway.

They settled again to wait it out until the new day.

At three am Peter tried to call Mark Llewellyn's number from the houseboat deck with Blair's phone. Again there was no signal. Was it just because they were below the cliffs on the river? Was it because Blair's phone was a city phone without a country capacity?

Ana was beside herself with fear and worry when Peter decided to go up to the cliff top to try to get the call done in the dark. Blair, still with them on guard, would provide protection for her and the others.

With Blair's help Peter pushed the gangplank back out linking the houseboat again with the river bank. Ashore he started the climb up the steep track to the top of the cliff in the darkness lit only by the thin beam of a pencil torch. The small rocks slipped under his feet and cascaded back down behind him an avalanche of bouncing noises. He used the rough scrub as hand holds to steady him and to facilitate the climb. Despite his personal physical fitness from gym work and jogging most days, Peter had never felt so exposed and vulnerable in his life. In that climb he understood better how Ana was feeling and why she seemed so paranoid.

With feelings of slight panic Peter reached the top to stand above the river. Below the houseboat, with one small light burning in the cabin, looked small and deserted. Again that feeling of personal vulnerability swept over him and he moved back to be out of the possible vision of anyone on the bank below. There was a clear spot beside the ongoing track and he went there.

Quickly he punched in Mark's number again. No response. Damn, he thought. 'Leave a message' the number instructed.

'It's Peter Foster, Ana's husband,' he said. Damn again, he thought, I didn't need to say that. 'We know Quinn has been on the boat. We're by the red cliffs upstream from the lock...' Mark's message bank beeped. Full.

In frustration Peter tried 000. It rang. The short wait seemed interminable.

Finally an answer. 'Put me on to the police at Renmark, please,' he said then he tried to explain why he wanted the police. The operator, wherever he was in Australia, stated he was not convinced that this was a 000 matter.

'Stones in yabby nets? That's not an emergency,' the voice said sternly. 'Is this a joke or are you just wasting my time?' Peter's annoyance and frustration began to get through to the operator. 'I'll give you the Renmark Police Station number,' he said. He did so and rang off.

Blair's mobile was now showing 'low power'. Shit! Peter thought, didn't anyone keep their phones charged? He tried Mark again. No answer. Peter decided to text but he was slow and he only got some of the message through before the power indicated he should send immediately. Wanting to shout and throw the mobile over the cliff and into the river, Peter hit the send button.

Chapter 43

'Bugger off, Quinn!'

A second vicious slap was delivered to the back of Victor's head as he lay sprawled out on his belly across the cabin divan in the latest houseboat they had broken into.

'Get up!' Quinn snarled.

'And I said... Bugger Off!' the voice was muffled into a cushion. A blue nautical patterned cushion. 'Let me sleep!'

'And I said...Get up! Get up now! We're moving.'

The small night lights of the cabin were switched on. Footsteps, a clatter of feet in the kitchen and another slap.

'Shit! Quinn...?'

'We're moving out.'

Something hard and metallic pressed into Victor's neck. He thrust an arm back and slapped back. A sharp steak table knife was sent flying across the cabin.

'You shit! What'd you do that for?' His tone became menacing. 'You ever touch me again and you'll get yours.' To show his distain Victor flopped his head back onto the cushion.

'We're moving. Now!' Quinn said. 'We've got a job to finish.'

'No...not this time.' Victor raised his head again. 'I'm tired of you giving the orders. No one put you in fucking charge. We've followed you and look where we are now.'

'We're OK.'

'OK?'

'Yeah, the coppers checked this boat out yesterday. Bastards found nothing. They'll leave us alone.'

'You are kidding, aren't you? Leave us alone?'

'They will. They'll think we've gone on to Victoria or New South Wales. The borders are close.'

'In your bloody dreams...' Quinn sneered.

'Look out the window...it's still bloody dark! I'm not stumbling about going anywhere in the bloody dark.' Victor slumped back face down again with an exaggerated sigh.

Quinn moved quickly. He rammed a knee into Victor's back and somehow the arrow shaft was in his hand. The metal point of it arrow head touched the base of Victor's scull where the spine met his head. The point pushed in none to gently.

'I could easily kill you...' he said in a conversational tone. A menacing tone. 'You'll do as I say. We're moving.'

Victor moved with a speed that completely stunned his assailant. He reached back and, grasping the arrow hand, he twisted and threw Quinn across the cabin from his supine position. Quinn had no time to even shout before he crashed into another sofa under the window on the far wall.

'Shit! You bastard!' Victor yelled. He sprang to his feet and advanced towards Quinn hands circling in a defending position. His hung-over reserve, his hesitation to cross the ten metres between them to finish the fighting manoeuvre, gave Quinn time to recover.

'Where'd you learn that? A shitty soldier-boy were you?' Quinn snatched up the cross bow and an arrow from the table and strung the shaft onto the cross bow string. With a fluid movement he brought the cross bow up into a firing position aimed at Victor's chest. There was an ominous click as Quinn cocked the weapon.

Victor's head cleared from the alcohol binge they had

consumed the previous night. He attempted a laugh. 'You think you can hit me with that? You think you can control me, and Jahan?'

'Want to try me soldier boy? C'mon try it! Have a go!'

The manic look that Victor had seen at the escape was back on Quinn's face.

Victor shrugged. 'Your time will come...I'll be waiting. Then I'll give the orders and we'll be a long way from here. Not following your idiotic plans... your vendettas.'

'But until then...I said we're moving.' Quinn cut him off with a sneer. 'Get Jahan and we're going. Right bloody now!

Roger Snow, the Loxton junior detective, was on his day off and awoke very early. Most days he went for a five kilometre run in the mornings before work but today he had other ideas.

His embarrassment and the ticking off he'd got from his sergeant earlier in the week rankled.

He'd never seen a body so mutilated as the slain woman's was, even at a vehicle accident scene. Then the mashed remains had sent him off the road bush to vomit his hamburger and chips breakfast into the irrigation ditch beside an orange plantation. He knew he was a laughing stock at the station because of his reactive, wild statement to that damned reporter. He felt a fool and the amused glances, snide references, and being excluded from drinks after work confirmed he was on the outer.

Now he had a plan and maybe he could make amends without damaging his reputation further, he thought.

Responsibly he made a four thirty am call to the Renmark police station. The night operator decided that this was regarding the escaped prisoners and the local police had enough to handle, transferred his call to the Institute phones. Major Crime voice mail greeted him.

Roger identified himself quietly, trying to sound efficient.

'I've got a hunch that the prisoners are still about and are going back to Lock 6. Maybe they'll steal another car or truck and take off. I'm going to drive to Lock 6. I've got a fast boat there I use for fishing. I'm leaving now and I'll start going upstream and I reckon I can do it without the buggers becoming suspicious of me.'

He paused. This next bit was probably nothing to do with the escaped prisoners. They'd had a report at the Loxton station. He wasn't sure but maybe it tied in with his hunch.

'I don't know if you have been told that there's a truck and driver missing from the construction work going on at the Lock. His foreman said that the bloke was having a few marital problems. Had a row with his wife on the phone the night before he disappeared. With the winery fire the possible disappearance it hasn't got a high priority listing, but I thought that maybe it could have something to do with the escaped crims. Not sure why but I'll also keep an eye out for the truck.'

Well he'd done the message, he'd better get going. 'I'll report asap. Better be off then...' he finished.

Mark's alarm clock bleeped with an insistence that jarred into his dead sleep.

'Damn it!' he mumbled at it and reached over to hit the offending noise before it could get louder as it was set to do. He couldn't trust himself to react when it first went off.

It was five forty-five am and just getting light.

He raised one eyelid and looked through the open blue and purple striped curtains. Overcast. A willy wag tail was bashing what looked like a moth to bits on the window sill. It separated the wings off the morsel and downed its breakfast. Mark grunted. He felt as tatty as those discarded wings. Got to get some more sleep, he thought as he pushed his brain to surface out of the deep sleep valley. He swung his naked form out of bed and, looking around yet another motel room, he orientated himself towards the shower.

Thank God for a good piss and long hot shower, he thought. He ceased towelling himself to recognise that the shower water smelt different here. Get on with it, get yourself going, he thought, of course the shower water smells like the Murray River here. It is river water here. Doesn't need a dee to work that one out.

He rummaged around in his suitcase for a clean shirt. Nothing remotely business like or formal was left. Doc Martin's as usual. A tee shirt then today with jeans. Maybe the motel would push a load through the washing machine and dryer if he asked them nicely. He'd ask them nicely.

Mark flicked open his phone. Messages galore. Mostly sign offs from the squad last night. A call from his fiancée Erica Marryat, sounding annoyed that she hadn't been able to contact him over the last few days. 'Pick up, occasionally,' she said. He'd need to call her soon or she'd be less susceptible to the sent flowers that had helped before. Their relationship was fragile as workloads and distance kept them apart. Their opinions differed on their client lists.

He stopped the sleepy reproachful thoughts as the next call came through.

A fading in and out message from Peter Foster. What? He replayed it as he sat down at the table to re-listen.

What in the hell was the man saying? … Something about yabbies? Were they promising yabbies? Crazy!

But the note of Peter's voice sounded urgent.

Mark switched to text messages and there was Peter again. The words 'Quinn' and 'on the boat' were there before the message ended. Did it end because Peter was out of power or because he'd been stopped, Mark worried? He checked the message time. Early hours of the morning. Well after he'd left the car to pick up something to eat from the truck stop out of Renmark. It was the only thing open at that late hour. His mind wandered as his stomach acid made itself felt. He groaned. Who ever said that truck stops had to serve good tucker had their heads on backwards. Bloody greasy spoon! He'd resorted to Mylanta before he could sleep. He reached into his bag and got another antacid tablet.

With dirty washing was still piled on the end of his bed, Mark left for the Renmark Institute a quarter of an hour later. He was the first in.

No Rick. Nothing stopped his morning jogging, or finding that first coffee, save an earthquake.

Mark had earthquake news this morning.

Quinn was still in the area.

Confirmed by Peter Foster's call.

The message bank light was flashing, and with no other detective in the room, Mark opened the voice mail.

Bloody hell, that Loxton dee again! He listened and had to concede that just maybe Snow would see something that other pairs of police in boats had missed.

But was Quinn was there still? And where? He went to the end of the room and switched on the kettle. Instant coffee and biscuits would have to do for breakfast.

He tried Rick's mobile. No answer. He was probably in the shower or still on the run. He left a verbal and a text message to please come in as soon as possible. Like 'sirs' Rick didn't mind a 'please' on a message from a junior man.

'Yo!' Rick's voice was a decibel above the clatter of his boots on the Institute's stone steps. He came bustling in smelling of coffee and bacon.

Mark quickly relayed the messages he'd got.

Rick seemed more concerned about Detective's Snow's call. 'You're kidding. That young idiot going up river on his own?' he griped. 'What the hell is he thinking of with the chance that he could run into the likes of Quinn? It's too late to get him back I suppose.' He took a deep breath then his mouth lines deepened as he stared at a spot over Mark's head. 'Not again...' he muttered. Rick seemed to shake himself into the now. 'So the bastard Quinn's still close! We'll get him this time. But where the hell's he going?' Rick eyed his subordinate. 'Maybe you weren't too far wrong saying he was chasing that Foster skirt.'

This was the closest he would get to acknowledging Mark's statements, or Ana's ongoing fears. But that was OK. When everything was over Rick's reports always accredited others with the work they had done. The ideas that paid off.

It was Mark's turn to grunt a non-reply.

'But beats the shit out of me why...OK there's the boy but... ' Rick said.

'He's a psychopath ... they don't always need logical reasons. Or they make them up,' Mark said.

Rick turned his attention again to the Loxton detective. 'So he's starting at Lock 6 and going up river...Nothing we can do. Hope the idiot's OK and not on a wild goose chase.'

'His Loxton Boss said Snow knows the river well. He should be OK,' Mark said. He paused unsure why Rick was so concerned about the young detective's initiative action.

Rick picked up an empty coffee cup, swirled the dregs then put it down again. He was back to his decisive self as he instructed. 'You'd better get someone on to the missing truck and driver. See if anyone's checked if he got to Adelaide. It's probably nothing but it could mean the prisoners have got a vehicle stashed somewhere.'

'I've jotted a note to one of the boys to do that. Will you hold a briefing early or will you wait a while? We've got nothing concrete as to which way they're going.'

'We've got enough to get that plane back to buzz the area again. See where that Liba boat is and get a general spin on where Quinn and company might be.'

'I'm not sure about that, boss. What if the plane spooks the crims? Quinn's so out of control it could be enough to make him act. The Fosters are civilians remember.'

Rick scowled. 'OK, then contact the Liba people and get them to find out where their boat is. They do have radio don't they? Tell the Foster party to get out into the middle of the river and stay there.'

'That didn't help before when Quinn fired arrows at them.'

'Tell them to keep out of range of the shore...' there was a note of exasperation in Rick's voice. 'Get people in here asap. I want everyone in the know and up to date.'

'There's probably nothing I can do here until things begin to happen. I'll stay with the Quinn murders? They're still working on them in Lincoln.'

'Do it, but be ready to roll...' There was buoyancy in Rick's voice. Again he could smell a successful ending to the case. Dead or alive he wanted Quinn. The other prisoners were collateral as far as he was concerned.

Chapter 44

The Institute was buzzing.

While officers were preparing for action; checking arms, shaking out Kevlar vests or answering phones, Mark logged in to the Port Lincoln investigation.

First the Elizabeth Woods killing and her car found at Mariner Point. Blood tests showed mainly hers, of course, but there'd been a note that there were another spots of blood found that may not be the victims. There it was. DNA, fast tracked again, had found markers from Elizabeth and Quinn. Gotcha! Mark thought. Prosecution material. Also traces from others who'd worked the case, and one that he didn't expect. Surely a mistake but a mistake like that could be bad in a defence's hands.

On an impulse Mark went to the Past Evidence Bank. Shit, he thought. Many of Quinn's original hard evidence items were missing. Been booked out without a name attached six months ago.

He telephoned immediately down to Adelaide Headquarters.

Bill Tape in the Evidence Room answered. 'We've been putting all the old evidence on line...'

'Yes, I know that, Worm, but does that mean you're getting all the evidence boxes out and checking that they are still complete and intact?'

The use of the name 'Worm', as in tape worm, elicited a chuckle from the older man who working out his 'injured in the line of duty' work days in the exacting evidence area. One shoulder with no muscle left, his useless arm flopped, was a drug punk's ticket to a very long stretch in prison.

'I looked up Demetrius Quinn's evidence list on line. There's no details. Have a gander will you please.'

'Sure, be a tick.' There was the clatter of keyboard keys. Conversationally, 'That's that bloke they're chasing up on the Murray?'

'The same.'

'The box is here. Not much in it. Notation it was signed out by one of your mob - the Majors. Lee Thomson eleven months ago.'

Mark knew Lee.

Lee was just about to retire when Mark had joined the squad, about the time that Rick's marriage went on the rocks and things were tense all round. He was another like Rick, saw things in black and white, and after an impossible to prove case Lee said he'd had enough. He'd left to run a plant nursery. Or some such venture. Mark remembered that at his boozy send-off they'd joked that he was still into dirt and Lee had responded, 'Yeah, but no bodies are going to be buried there.' An oft used laughing comment was made that there'd be no bodies because any old cop knew too much for people to find his corpses.

'Do you know if Lee was in on Quinn's original case?' There was a hands-in-a-chocolate-box type thump and rustling sound.

'Yeah he was.'

'Who booked it back in?'

'Don't give me a laugh... is you getting thick? You did!' Worm laughed. He read off Mark's service number. 'That's you isn't it?'

'Yeah, that's my number but I didn't sign it out or in. Isn't there a space for initials on the box ticket?'

Again another thump as the box lid was turned over. 'M.D.L. Your initials.'

'When was it booked back in?'

'A week after it was booked out.'

'Worm, this is important and urgent. On the quiet too. Would you send me an email of the contents of the box? All the listed evidence, what's there and what's missing. Down to the last hair and last bit of DNA.'

'Sure, Mark. I'll do it pronto. There's a fair bit but it won't take me long.'

'I owe you a beer. Thank you and remember, no matter who asks, this is on the quiet. OK?'

'OK. Maybe you'll owe me a whiskey instead... cheers.'

Mark sat back oblivious to the world as he tried to come up with a logical explanation to the morning's findings.

But Lee Thomson?

The evidence booked out and back before Lee retired.

'Something to eat, Mark?' He started as Jessica Taylor appeared at his side making a list to get from the nearby café.

'Yes, sure. A ham sandwich and a flat white'll do me.' He looked up at the young officer as he reached into his pocket for money. He flipped a ten to her. 'You're not just acting as the go-fer are you? You're better than that...'

She flushed. 'No sir, I'll be in at the final push.'

'Good', Mark said. He sat back ready to reengage his interrupted thoughts.

Jessica paused until he looked towards her again. 'I also checked on Ana Foster, just out of curiosity. You've met her in person haven't you? Coincidentally she's matches the description of all the victims. Slight build, dark hair and she's got a natural white blonde streak. I got it from the Corrections staff photo ID.'

'Have you noted this anywhere?' Mark kept the question casual.

'Not yet, been a bit busy,' she said. 'Was that OK?'

'Yes, Not a problem. Perhaps hold it with everything else going on. I'm hungry... looking forward to something to eat...'

Jessica took this as the signal to leave as it was.

Mark sat forward in his chair.

Classic thinker pose with his elbow on the desk. He needed to talk to Rick but wasn't sure what he should say to him, or ask him for that matter.

Lee Thomson was Rick's friend.

It would be difficult to find a reason for him having old evidence. This missing evidence. Also heaven help them if a defence counsel got onto the fact that Quinn's original case material was missing.

Deciding that he would wait for a complete response from Worm before he did anything more, Mark looked around the room for Rick. He wasn't visible. He stood from his chair and stretched. The tendons in his shoulders strained in protest.

Brain zapped like a mozzie he headed for the conference room john.

Rick wasn't there either.

Chapter 45

If an atmosphere could have got worse between the three convicts, it had.

It had deteriorated into a forced march. What Quinn decided they needed they carried from the houseboat they'd purloined overnight. The rough blankets, tied into rope parcels slung over their shoulders, slowed and hampered their movements.

Quinn, threatening with cross bow and arrow in hand, pushed down river with the two other escapees in front of him. A spoken word was hissed at; a trip or misstep brought curses and a nudge in the back with the cross bow.

Victor led. The better to be further away from Quinn but he bided his time and moment and waited.

They stumbled along the fallen rock strewn bank below the towering red cliffs. There was no way they could go except along the cliff top path, that was too easily seen. The pushed through clumps of reeds; through dead and alive mallee scrub, and tall gum trees that clung to the scraps of viable soil with gnarled roots. Above them an ancient geological division divided the red cliff face horizontally in two and scree, left since the last flood, was sharp and slippery underfoot.

Jahan in his stolen city shoes copped it both from the terrain and Quinn. Thwacks across his shoulders, and once he'd swung around to retaliate to meet a raised eyebrow; and a 'try me' look.

The two sullen men felt an inevitable roller coaster slip and slide under their feet, those same feet that ached from the day's march with the heavy packs.

Quinn was in charge, but even Victor had run out of steam. Questioning why had got nowhere it, whatever it was, would just happen as the day unfolded.

Both men had one idea, to try to survive, despite a man leading them into a hell where he stated he couldn't give a shit whether he lived or died. They were going with him...

The trekking was down river back towards Lock 6.

Below Queen's Reach, Quinn decided after looking again at the river chart, they would leave the base of the river cliffs to cross the isthmus of land. The river folded back on itself, he noted, as almost a billabong where the marking for Chowilla Dam was proposed then deferred in other drought years.

That's where they were seen.

Roger Snow cruised slowly along up river from Lock 6.

It was later than he'd intended because the outboard motor was cold and wouldn't start. After a quarter hour of flooding the engine, like a novice, he'd cleaned the plugs and distributor leads. On the next press of the starter button the infernal thing growled its powerful note.

His hot and flustered torso cooled and he put on his jacket rueing the moment of madness when he'd grabbed a red windcheater against the dawn cold before he set out from home. Now chilled by the movement on the cold river, he cursed, aware that the red probably acted like a beacon. Maybe that would help his disguise but he'd keep well clear of the river banks and trouble. He motored with the engine running as smooth and quiet as he could make it.

At each bend in the river he stopped, slowed to a halt and pretended to fish. Casting a bait-less hand line out he hunched under his hat and scanned the river banks for the escaped criminals.

Nothing.

On occasional there were other fishermen or a houseboat to acknowledge, with a wave. They weren't what he was looking for.

He moved on each time; now well past dawn, when continuing his tactic he pulled quietly in 100 metres below Queens Reach.

Movement on the bank caught his eye.

There they were!

Three men walking.

The prisoners were moving away from him across the river on the track below the high red cliffs. He pretended to fish for five minutes, watching them to be sure that it was them, and then gunned the motor to pass them by. He stopped again, still below his last sighting, where a bank of reeds thrust out into the river. If one of them knew anything about fishing they would expect him to stop there. Again his fishing was unsuccessful to anyone watching and he started the motor again. The convicts had disappeared into the bush by the time he drew level and he surmised that they could cut across the land to another line of cliffs above Bunyip Reach Homestead.

He was sure then that they had a river chart stolen from any of the houseboats they'd broken into. They had to have, he thought, they were showing a pretty good knowledge of the river and the land beside it.

After he rounded the next bend he tried to contact the Loxton station.

No signal. Again the high cliffs blocked a signal.

Another five hundred metres upstream he tried again.

'I've seen them!' he yelled into the mobile. The contact was faint and weak from the low position of the river.

'You're sure?' he heard back. 'W....?'

'Yes! What?'

Roger Snow's training kicked in. Where and how many people. 'Red cliffs by Queens'. Three men. It's them!' He said. 'Reckon they'll leave the river and come back on before the cliffs at Bunyip Reach Homestead.'

The phone emitted static and the only word he thought he heard was 'Renmark.'

Roger's boat was fast. By seven he made the Nelwood Gun Club upriver, secured his boat and borrowed a car from a surprised camper. Breaking every road rule in the book he reported to Renmark in person an hour later.

Rick bounded into the Institute, recalled there by Mark, as he'd recalled every officer. He tossed his motor bike helmet to the nearest officer. 'Park my brain bucket somewhere,' he said.

Despite the urgency Mark had to smile. Trust Rick, he'd knocked off work and had managed to find someone to lend him a motor bike. Gone for a spin and was now hyped up and ready to go. Ready for anything.

'OK Listen up everyone,' at Rick's nod Mark took the floor. 'Snowie here,' he indicated Roger Snow still in his red jacket 'has had our best sighting yet. Off his own bat and on his day off.'

Rick interjected. 'He'll be asking for overtime next...'

There were grins and an odd chuckle in the room. The young detective flushed under the thatch of tousled black hair. Nothing to do with the overtime – he was in again. Accepted.

'OK, Snowie, tell them what you saw... not the whole bleeding story... motor wouldn't start... fishing... bla bla bla. Just what you saw and where.' Rick had taken over the proceedings.

Again there was a mutter of chortles at his instruction to the young detective who had learned a great deal in the past twenty four hours. He realised he'd earned a nick name too.

Roger told them the who, the where and the when. Concisely.

'You're opinion?' Mark asked.

'They're off their heads. They're going back to Lock 6.'

'Why?'

'I don't know.'

'Hazard a guess?'

After his debacle with the press interview and the Loxton murder, not likely. He wasn't falling for that. 'No sir.'

'Maybe Quinn still has it in for the Foster woman,' Rick said. 'Mark seems to think so.'

'I reckon it goes back to Quinn's original killing,' Mark said. 'Been looking again at the old files. The victim got involved with him when he was ordered therapy by the courts for something or other. Anger management probably. She was a counsellor, like Ana Foster... From reading the records she was a red head but that was years ago.'

'Yeah, but the bitch got involved with him. Signed her own death warrant getting fixed up with that bastard...should have been murder. Got away with bloody manslaughter...' Rick sounded off.

Mark said. 'Now, as I understand, Quinn wanted Ana Foster to get his son back. Something she couldn't promise to do...it was enough for the assault at the prison and probably enough to keep him going after her. He thinks that she knows where the boy has been taken by his mother. The bastard is aware he's got nothing to lose with these current murder charges hanging over him. The Port Lincoln murders and the poor sods he's knocked off while he's been on the run.'

'We'll catch the bastard! That's what's next. Snow, get properly dressed. You're in. Everyone else stay here. Mark and I are going for a conference. Taylor, check on the whereabouts of the dogs. And the Star Force. We may need them here right now for the bust.' There was a general movement. 'Well, get on with it. By the time we get back I want a plan for the capture at Lock 6 organised and set up...' Rick said. 'You people, especially you Sarg, know the lay of the land there better than we can get from any maps.'

The local Sergeant nodded. It was good when the Adelaide boys recognised the local knowledge. He'd worked with many who didn't. 'Right,' he said. 'Taylor, grab the maps we were working on yesterday...'

As the Men's Room door closed behind them Rick said. 'God, you'd better be right about Lock 6. It has to be all out, no mistakes. We've got to get them, especially Quinn.'

'I'm sure Boss. They'll be there. Ready to strike when Liba houseboat 26 goes into or through the Lock. That's the only time that the boat'll be vulnerable.'

'A thought. Are there any other Libas upstream? Could we take over another one and fool them?' Rick headed for the urinal.

'I've checked. Only Eleven is close and it's obviously a much smaller vessel. Anyway we'd have to do a number change...but I suppose that wouldn't be a problem.' His voice trailed off...definitely not a problem.

'Can we swap the crew – put our people on board in time?'

'Thought of that too. It would be hard. It'd be a fussy manoeuvre, getting the civilians off and out men on and I'm not sure that we could hide the activity on the river. Quinn's street wise – got a nose for things happening. For trouble. Young Snow was lucky and canny himself.'

'What do you reckon the chances are of ambushing them before they get to the lock?'

This was Rick. He'd come up with a myriad of solutions; some wild and woolly then get Mark to bat at them. Often he'd then select something that had been an aside solution and pick at it until a plan would work was born. The plan could appear to be out of left field and usually baffled the criminals he was chasing.

'I don't think there'd be a hope even if we knew exactly where they are. So far they have evaded us seeing them. Sorry Boss, we're going to have to wait until they show themselves at the lock.'

'OK. So the houseboat people remain the target. I don't like it. Civilians as bait and they don't even know about it. The paperwork will be horrendous!' Rick sighed 'a that's better' sigh as he turned and headed for the hand basin.

Mark reached over and hit the flush tap, water gushed. He washed his hands at the basin.

'It's not going to be easy and we've got limited time. Can we fly down the dogs from Adelaide this morning rather than try to road them? It'll take a good couple of hours to do that even going flat out. They were effective against Quinn at the prison and just seeing them could slow him down. They'd help protect Ana Foster too and the other women,' he said.

Rick agreed. 'Order them! Now. Bugger the costs. They'll be useful against Quinn but, if necessary, shoot to kill,' he insisted. 'Save society a heap keeping those bastards alive.'

'You haven't told the boys here that the Star Force aren't likely to get here on time? They'll be on their way when they get reorganised after a big job they had overnight.'
Rick gave a shrug. 'A robbery and hostage operation. Reported sewn up a bit after dawn. They'll need down time and it'll take a while for them to tizzy themselves up for another job.'

Mark was never sure if his boss was slinging off at the Star Force's sometime late arrival. They could be on a job in minutes but were curtailed by their lack of numbers. More government budget dollar cuts, as Rick complained, usually more colourfully when he needed the Star Force expertise, their gun power, but they weren't available.

Mark opened the door for Rick to go back into the main room. The officers were clustered about a board.

Their plan was good with excellent local knowledge. As it was a Saturday the crew working on the weir would be off duty. A relief as that made fewer civilians to be concerned about. 'Less to get in the way' as Rick put it. A detail here and there questioned and he signed it off.

'Get ready, kitted up. We move in an hour...it's going to be one hell of a day.' Mark ordered.

'Where'd you put my bike helmet?' Rick demanded. He looked over at Mark. 'No, I'm not roaring up on the bike. It'd be fun but too noisy...' he said with a grin.

Chapter 46

Ana gazed through the forward window as overhead a jet led a finger of white trail against the sky and wished she were inside that aluminium cylinder being taken far away. Anywhere far away.

They'd slept fitfully after Peter got back from his telephone calls, then woken cramped and cold when the birds started their rowdy dawn chorus at first light. He was irritable and tired.

'Maybe we over reacted last night,' he said.

There was wariness in his voice that maybe also the police's opinion of them would be less. So much so they wouldn't take the situation seriously. When he looked at Ana's stricken face, he back tracked his assertions. He was in denial. What is the matter with me, he thought. Was he again reacting badly because the situation was out of his hands and he was unsure of what was going to happen next? After all the mending of the relationship between them he was again acting out his denial. On his irrational expectation that only he could keep Ana safe. He'd, in his own opinion, failed when she'd been assaulted at the prison and now that emasculating feeling returned.

'No!' Peter suddenly said. 'Let's get on with our plan to move. We need to get some help...'

Blair, had unwrapped himself slowly from his blanket and gave a groan. He shook his right knee that had cramped. It responded to the movement with an audible crack. He winced and after leaning down to kiss his sister in law on the cheek he shuffled off aft. They heard the water pump start a few moments later as he turned the shower on. The water warmth worked its magic for a long time.

Long enough for to rouse Lauren. With one shower only being able to run at the same time the group were used to the shower line up and Lauren was usually quick off the mark going into her en-suite first. It was a Lauren thing.

'What's going on,' she demanded as she came out into the cabin; her tone was peeved. 'I'm going to be late now getting breakfast ready for Tom to start the BBQ.'

She obviously still hadn't looked at her wrist watch. It was early even for her. Usually too early for Blair who could rouse himself out his bed to get a fishing line over the side as soon as he woke.

'No BBQ this morning!' Ana blurted out through a haze of lack of sleep and fear. 'We have to get going...now!'

'For heaven's sake why so early...?'

'We've been up most of the night on guard.' Peter yawned in emphasis.

'What on earth for...?'

'Someone put rocks in the yabby nets,' Ana cut her off. She pulled the doona tighter around her shoulders. 'So, who's been joking? You?' Lauren turned on Peter. 'You wouldn't tease her surely?'

'Give me a break!' Peter protested. 'Why in the hell would I do that? Ana's been through enough hasn't she?' His bite back was strong, an embarrassment of his lingering doubts.

Lauren's voice was businesslike. 'Tell me what happened last night.'

Peter told it from go to woe.

Lauren went to Ana and put her arms about her. They sat

together, dark hair against fair, for a moment. Then Lauren sat up, 'OK, she said looking at her watch. 'It's still before six, very early. I'll wake Tom and he can still have his BBQ breakfast. It's the last day with everything cut short, and he'll be very disappointed if we don't have his beloved bacon and eggs.'

'But...' Ana started.

'No, think about it. We can't go through the lock, until when? Ten o'clock? After breakfast we can leave here in plenty of time to get there when it opens. The trip's only short. Tom and I talked about it last night.' She cast a 'be reasonable' look at Ana. 'It will set us up for the day and make my old man happy... We've got to go back to work next week.'

That was a hint that the holiday was an extra for Ana; then it hadn't gone as planned and Tom and Lauren liked things to go as they'd planned. Ana felt a sharp pang of guilt and Lauren would have been horrified and indignant if she realised that her words had offended. Lauren drank a glass of water at the sink then, as Blair could be heard going back to his bedroom, she bustled off for her shower.

The forced happy BBQ breakfast and leave taking took longer than they thought.

The edge of apprehension brought forth a confusion of movement. Everything took longer.

Toast was burned and had to be recooked. Tom dropped the empty bacon dish and fat drippings went onto the deck. Lauren insisted it was cleared away immediately before fat set into the planking. He still managed to cook all the remaining bacon and eat more than his share. He caught Ana's eye and shrugged for, despite all his corporate expertise, Tom was a little boy where bacon was concerned.

Then the ropes securing the boat to the trees got tangled and flopped into the river with the possibility that they would foul the paddle wheel. Kari and Ana pulled the dirty wet ropes aboard and attempted to lay them into passable coils on the aft deck.

The very act of bringing in the gangplank was stalled when Blair, the strongest, somehow let the heavy wood fall into the river.

'Shit!' he yelled. 'Peter, give me a hand will you.'

Peter grunted a replying expletive as the women coping with the ropes got in his way. They dragged it back on board as Tom idled the engine.

The women stayed well clear careful not to interrupt proceedings again. Even Lauren kept her opinions to herself and Kari her supportive comments. The crankiness, from tiredness, apprehension to fear, reigned and the seasoned river voyagers acted like total amateurs.

The men finally got the houseboat under way and they moved downstream from the cliff berth. Ana sat alone on the forward deck as the other women retreated to the inside lounge. Last night the cliffs had glowed slightly with the moonlight; they represented black fear when Peter had climbed them but today they were just lumps of red rock with a scree of lighter stones forming the track he'd scrambled up and back upon in the dark.

A huge whistling kite, a bird that would usually delight her, dropped immediately in front of their path. It hit the water with its talons outstretched, missed the fish or whatever it was after and rose, to disappear above the cabin. Its call was harsh, jarring and harsh. Later a pelican fled before them its body just above the water; wingtips so low they left a parallel pattern of flick... flick...flick... making eddies on the still water.

Cumulous grey clouds, piled darkly high against the southern sky, predicted rain sometime in the day, were reflected cold silver on the water. The wind that would bring the change of weather to the river was sharp and doubled the gloom.

Ana waved at people in a houseboat moored, people obviously having breakfast on their deck, but was ignored.

No wave, no recognition.

Gone the river camaraderie.

An air of menace hung over the river.

Chapter 47

Quinn and his party prepared to cross the river at the Lock 6 construction site just before eight o'clock.

Quinn was cagey but surmised that the lack of workmen there this early was because most of the workmen lived in nearby towns. In this he was correct, but today was Saturday and any workmen on site would be police officers in workmen's clothing. They just had not 'clocked on' to the apparent eight o'clock shift yet.

'This way,' Quinn hissed.

He ran across the flat surface of the weir and onto the hard metal that was the top of closed lock gates. These were almost a metre wide and, although there was a drop away each side, it was easy to traverse the river this way as long as the runner didn't look down. With the prospect of being seen on this open run the three men crossed with speed.

They ran on to the concrete surrounds of the lock side getting the lay of the land before Victor and Jahan diverted their run and started towards a car parked behind the lock office. This would be their escape regardless of what Quinn wanted. He saw them from behind a building and yelled, 'Get back here!' at them.

Their run faltered to a walk.

Sam, on duty that morning, appeared in the doorway of the office. He had a coffee cup in his hand and took a sip as he came out to stand on a grassed garden area. 'Hey there!' he called to the two men he could see. He glanced down at his wrist watch. 'You're here a bit early the lock's not open for a couple of hours or more...'

Victor and Jahan stopped. It would be difficult to steal the car with the man there watching. He'd call the police.

'G'day,' Victor said.

Jahan was very aware of the person standing there. He knew that his picture, with the other escaped prisoners', would be in all the newspapers and on TV and his dark looks were of North African and not of Aboriginal origin. It could alert him to the fact that he was one of the escaped prisoners. He bent down as though tending to a shoelace.

'Are you waiting to get someone off a boat here? Or to go on one? That's not a problem. People do it all the time.' Sam indicated his coffee cup. 'Want a coffee? ... there's extra cups here if you'd like one... and I can find a tea bag if you'd prefer...'

'No, thanks anyway...' Victor couldn't think of an immediate answer. The lock man looked a bit put off by the hesitation. 'Maybe later.'

'Sure, any time.' Sam stood looking at the river as he sipped his coffee. 'The weather's about to change,' he said.

Quinn had sped around the small office building and appeared three metres behind Sam.

Without any warning he cocked the hunting cross bow and fired.

The steel point struck Sam's neck, thudding with a jarring whack into the cervical spine.

Sam lurched forward carried by the arrow's force, and then somehow he regained his feet and stood. Slowly gravity and death intervened and he crumpled to the handkerchief of lawn outside the office. His cup seemed to fall slowly and it spilled the coffee dregs in an arc as his arm swung. There was little blood on the back of Sam's shirt as he lay face down, but what there was echoed by the red Papa Mellion scarlet rose petals fallen already on the green morning dewed grass.

Victor and Jahan stood open mouthed as they stared back and forth between Quinn and the dead man.

Victor recovered. 'What in the fuck did you do that for?' He screamed at Quinn. 'He wasn't a problem. We could have just tied him up or something...'

Quinn barely glanced over at the fallen man. 'Lucky shot huh?' he boasted. He straightened up. His face took on the snarl they had come to know and fear as he fitted another arrow from those remaining he'd shoved through his belt. He raised the weapon. 'I can get lucky again so bloody well do as I say. Get rid of him.'

With no other option they dragged Sam's body away to behind the office and, directed always by Quinn, through a small gate to a patch of scrub. Quinn kicked the cup under the rose bush and the coffee arc of colour had already melded into the moisture on the lawn.

The action brought a feeling of shock and total resignation to Jahan and Victor. They were committed regardless of the outcomes.

When Victor went into the small office Quinn had already reached in and pulled out the telephone line and had crushed a mobile phone under his boot.

At the command centre Rick was adamant. 'We're not waiting for the dogs,' he thundered. 'Or the Star Force group. They're too bloody late!'

The K9 plane was delayed and had only just arrived at Loxton airport which was still a few kilometres away from Renmark. A paddy wagon was sent to pick them up.

'It would be better if we did wait, there's time.' Mark

remonstrated. His voice was quiet. 'The dogs got Quinn at the prison and protected Ana. They'll remember and they could be the difference between casualties or none. We don't know if the prisoners are armed. Could have got guns or knives off any of the boats.'

This was a statement that Rick would have preferred to have heard in private and not out in the main squad room. Now he couldn't brush it aside. He had to take notice of his second in command. Especially one who seemed ill at ease this morning.

'All right, we wait.' The words were flat. Annoyed. He gave Mark a sideways glance. 'Missing that bit of skirt you've been crazy enough to ask to marry you,' he tried. 'Got rocks in your head as well as your balls?'

There was no rejoinder.

Mark turned away. He had to be the worrying voice of reason. Not everything was going well. They had not been able to contact Peter on the houseboat by mobile phone.

Maybe his phone was not working or not recharged. Or they were too low on the river. There was still no signal.

The houseboat owners at Jane Eliza Landing hadn't come on duty so early on the Saturday morning and there could be no radio contact with Liba 26. Mark sent a Squad car and officer to their home but no one had been there. Perhaps the owners were taking their sons to play a football match shopping for booze, as Rick put it, and the message to beware had not gone out.

Even the phone at the Lock 6 office rang and rang with no answer. Again they could only surmise that the lock master there was attending to other matters.

Houseboat Liba 26 was on its own...

To make matters worse the plan to have police officers acting as workers on the weir project at the lock was adrift. No one could be spared from the Winery fire investigation. There'd been a minor traffic accident on the road between Renmark and Loxton that still needed police attendance while a load of oranges was cleared away. The only man Rick could get to pretend to be a worker was from the Loxton station and he promised to drive there in civvies and stop anyone going back across the river. It wasn't the force that he wanted.

At last the dogs arrived.

'Come on everyone!' Rick nagged. 'Short staffed again. Shit! Well, let's get on with it. Adelaide's on my tail.'

At nine forty they were able to leave for the lock, Rick, Mark, the police squad and the dogs.

Lock 6 was twenty three kilometres away from Renmark by road.

Chapter 48

Alone on the river, Liba 26 passed Bunyip Reach, to round the last bend to Lock 6 finally just before nine thirty.

Ahead they could see the lock and the line of buoys that stretched across the river at one hundred and fifty meters mark. From their position motoring towards the lock they were approaching from the starboard side of the river going down stream.

A crane on the port side of the construction work was in the lifted boom position and the hook hanging below swung in a slow pendulum arc in the strengthening breeze. The crane's control capsule was empty and there was no evidence of men at the worksite.

Tom said, trying to lighten the mood. 'It's a Saturday. Looks like they don't work at the weekends. Time and a half...it would cost the bosses too much.'

'They're all probably at the local footy. We've heard nothing else but footy news on the radio all week. Can't remember who's playing who though,' Blair said.

Three swans swimming line abreast looked back at the approaching houseboat and took off, still in formation. They rose, white underwings flagging and calling to each other. They disappeared over the weir to the lower river.

A red light was flashing beside the lock entrance gates.

'We'll signal as we get closer, Tom, again the helmsman, said. 'It won't be long until they're in business.'

Blair looked up from the chart he was checking. 'Opens at ten. We've got a bit of a wait,' he said.

They waited.

Quinn stood unseen by the lock gate.

He looked up stream as a houseboat slowly moved towards them, the paddle wheel making the distinctive signature wake behind it.

It was Liba number 26.

'Get back there and read up on the lock controls,' he instructed Victor as they ran back to the weir office.

The brick office was neat, institutional cream painted and orderly with a desk, a couple of wooden chairs, a filing cabinet, and few other items. No personal things except for fishing gear and a pile of yabby nets in a corner. A photograph of the lock in flood conditions with the gates open and a huge tide of water flowing downstream was above the desk. Another print showed the lock with a magnificent sunset behind it and a more recent photo showed a grinning Sam holding a huge callop.

None of this interested Quinn.

Victor and Jahan exchanged glances.

That was the man Quinn had killed.

Victor looked sick still after the murder of the lock man and Jahan's face was sweating. His dark skin a dull pasty colour.

Quinn pointed to a list of instructions above a control panel. 'You, Victor, an ex-soldier like you should be able to handle a few buttons. Get into that...' he pointed towards a coat hanger on the wall.

Victor took the neatly pressed Lock uniform shirt and put it on.

The Liba houseboat waited as the red light on the lock flashed.

Tom sounded the three long blasts to indicate that they wanted to pass down river. It was a bit early but worth a try.

The red continued flashing... no response.

After waiting a further five minutes Tom reached up and pulled the cord, signalling again that they wanted to go through Lock 6. The sound echoed back from the steel weir.

There was again no response.

'Wait!' Kari suddenly said. 'I feel something bad.' She turned to Ana and Lauren for support. 'Remember that woman who sounded that psychic singing note in the Renmark Institute the day we left. I get a feeling of that in the whistle blast. I feel a dread...'

'Oh come on...' Lauren interrupted.

'But you've heard that sound every time we reverse. How's it wrong now?' Tom asked.

'I don't know. I can't explain but it just is...there's something in the echo bouncing back from the lock gates perhaps...'

Ana's pale face turned towards them. Her clenched jaw pulled back into her hunched shoulders. 'I sense it too. Something's wrong...'

'For God's sake! Don't make things worse. We're all uptight. We don't need this stuff!' Peter nudged Ana's hand.

She pulled away. Then rethought her dismissive action and smiled a wan smile at him.

Kari left the cabin and came back with the small pyramid she'd bought at the Mystic Fair. She had Ana's handbag in the other hand. 'Get your own stone out of here and hold it. It's better that you do it. Put it somewhere on yourself, wherever, it will help to protect you.'

Ana found the small pink stone, held it until she could feel it take on the warmth of her hand and then put it into her pocket. Kari's gentle manner and concern soothed her.

Her face still tight Ana went outside onto the forward deck. A cold wind blew her hair around her face. Absently, looking forward towards the lock, she tucked the errant strands behind her ears. She shivered and went back into the cabin and retrieved a woollen cap and pulled it on.

Ana's usual position when they were travelling was on the front deck, today and bad feelings and the cold kept her inside.

The river was quiet and sullen brown.

No birds called.

Victor stood next to the lock side and pressed the button on the hand remote control. There was a clunk as the machinery engaged before it purred and the upstream gates began to open. He reached towards the signal light.

It was nine fifty one.

The light ahead flashed green and Tom opened the throttle. The paddle wheel at the rear answered and the houseboat began its rendezvous with Lock 6.

'Great,' he said from the corner wheel position. 'Sam's letting us through early before the official opening time.' He glanced a smile towards Peter. 'Remembers you grounding us.'

'Any reason's OK by me,' Peter rejoined.

Tom drove carefully into the lock space and brought the large craft alongside the shore side where Victor waited. The regulation Lock hat was pulled low on his brow.

The lock was now full of upstream water and the houseboat stood high, almost level with the shore railings when it had passed inside. The 1926 date and the 'keep out of the water' warnings were visible above the waterline.

Quinn remained out of sight.

Victor, again reading the instructions for the houseboat

passage on the big board beside him, was able to follow the next process needed. He got the gates slowly closing behind the houseboat.

Tom and Peter waited for the ropes to be passed to them and Victor, in no apparent hurry, dropped the shoring ropes onto the deck. The men tied them off fore and aft.

No words were said and the men didn't initiate the usual banter between themselves and the lock man.

Lauren had moved to the forward deck. She called to Victor. 'Where's Sam? He told us he was on duty all this week?'

Victor found a smile. 'Nah… he's taken his wife to hospital. Bit of an emergency with their baby.' The smile turned into a grin. 'I'm standing in and I'm new to the job. Just learning to operate the lock so things may be a bit bumpy.'

'Oh…' Lauren said. With puzzled brows she went into the cabin where Ana and Kari sat at the table. 'Sam's single. What's all this about a wife and baby? He told us...' she said.

'And I'm telling you…there's something very wrong. The place's heavy with bad vibrations,' Kari was terse and adamant.

Ana put her hand in her pocket and held her pyramid until the hard edges chiselled grooves into her palm.

With a toss of her head Kari looked hard through the window at Victor who, sensing the need to talk, stood chatting with the men. Ana followed her gaze to see the man Lauren said should have been Sam.

Kari's brow wrinkled in puzzlement.

That man in uniform?

Something?

A long time ago?

There was a clunk as the heavy gates closed shut behind the houseboat and in that instant Kari remembered.

The walls closed in around her.

Chapter 49

Kari shivered.

'Yes,' she said aloud. 'I know him! He's the young soldier. It's him! He's much older now but I know it's him.'

In her excitement at the recognition Kari overcame her dire predictions. She hurried out the doorway from the cabin and across the forward deck, to look up at the uniformed figure. She confidently called up to Victor. 'Hey there...I know you... Do you remember me?

Victor stared at her, then his eyes widened further as he peered through the windows into the lounge area towards Ana. Her mind reversed through the years as she gaped back at him.

'You were the soldier with the fruit...' Kari said.

'Yes...I was. You made it then,' Victor said. 'I thought you'd bought it.' He looked hard at Kari. 'I think I remember seeing you again in the hospital...you were cleaned up and gone before I was repatriated out. How about seeing you again...?' There was pleasure in his voice.

'Are we going through the lock or not?' Peter broke into the conversation aware that there may have been lies told and things were not quite right. But he decided to give the man on the dock a bit of lee way, as maybe he didn't know Sam that well, and was spinning a line. 'We need to get going.'

'What the shit is that idiot doing out there? He's bloody gas bagging with them!' Quinn stared through the office window then he turned to Jahan. 'Get the hell out there and tell him to get on with things...' He turned towards a backup control panel. 'Hang on, no. I can do what I want from here.'

The boat was tied to the lock, snug against the old car tyres protecting paint on both the boat and the lock.

Quinn jabbed at the bank of lock controls on the main office board and hit an Emergency Speed draining of the lock. With a thunderous roar the water level in the lock started to drop. The pitch of the machinery noise rose and the strong ropes that Tom and Peter had secured to the houseboat railings tightened. Tightened and strained.

The heavy house boat tilted.

The people aboard stumbled, grabbing whatever they could to stop themselves falling at the suddenness of it. There wasn't a huge tilt but the table and plastic chairs on the deck slid sideways. Bottles in the outside bin rattled and there was a loud smash as something fell to the floor in the cabin.

The tilt continued.

Peter shouted, 'Hang on! Don't get thrown into the water. It's electrified.'

One after the other, the two ropes tying the boat to the lock snapped, like cotton. The heavy boat lurched unevenly as it dropped and then righted itself on the draining water. The group were thrown about again. They managed to regain their balance, and stay aboard due to the warning from Peter.

The houseboat steadied but continued to fall. Both huge doors of the lock were closed and the pumps shrieked on as they drained the water almost to the bottom of the concrete floor.

There was another thud and a lurch, not unlike the moment when Peter ran it aground, as the houseboat keel bashed against the side then the bottom of the lock.

Lauren screamed as the group aboard clung to what they could.

'What the hell happened? You idiot! You could've have killed us!' Tom blazed up at Victor.

'I didn't do that...' Victor shouted back.

Inside the lock office Quinn yelled in fury.

He punched at the lock controls.

Victor and Jahan attempted to scuttle out of Quinn's way.

'Follow me!' Quinn shouted at them. 'Do as I bloody say! You're in this up to your ears and it's the only way you'll get away.'

Quinn grabbed his assortment of weapons he'd stolen from the last houseboat and ran from the office across the lawn to the top of the dock. He dropped all but the cross bow at his feet and cocked it ready to shoot an arrow down into the melee below.

Seeing Quinn above her, Ana choked back a scream.

She saw him aim something at her, froze for a beat, then dived and rolled hard against the cabin wall. His first loosed arrow missed. It thudded into the wooden deck next to her shoulder. In survival mode Ana scrambled around the corner of the huge ice chest where her body was protected by its bulk.

'Kari! Get out of the way!' Ana shouted. The instinct to protect her sister again hadn't diminished over the years.

Quinn shot off arrow after arrow, down onto the houseboat deck, trying to hit Ana through the ice box and the side of the cabin.

All arrows missed.

All... except one.

Peter had watched in alarm as he saw the man on the dock shooting arrows at Ana. He leapt onto the railing, hoisted himself up to the cabin roof, to the level of the dock to attack the man who was threatening his wife. For a beat he was out of Quinn's sight, shielded from view by the deck awning. Those below could not see Peter either.

Quinn thrust another bolt into the cross bow.

He took aim again at Ana - just as Peter threw himself at Quinn.

The arrow wasn't aimed at Peter.

He simply got in the way.

The toughened steel point tore through the fabric of his jacket and thudded deep into his chest.

Peter grabbed at the left side of his chest. By instinct, he pulled the arrow free. He gasped and, with not even time to register shock or pain, his life blood gushed.

He slid down onto the passageway between the sliding glass door of his and Ana's bedroom and the houseboat's side railing.

From the forward deck his body was invisible. His blood spread wider and wider before it trickled down into the water beside the dock wall.

Chapter 50

'One less,' Quinn muttered through clenched teeth.

He bent, picked up the knives. He thrust one knife at Victor and threw another to Jahan.

'Kill the bastards! Kill them all' he shouted, wielding a knife. He still held the bow and the last of his bolts.

Jahan, a basically non-violent man, stopped. He drew back reluctant to hurt the women.

Victor stood holding the torn rope with one hand and hefted the knife with his other. The knife felt comfortable in his hand. His gaze went from Kari to Ana as they huddled behind the ice box.

He hesitated.

He could see them as the girls, especially the girl with the streaked hair in the camp.

The girl who challenged him. Who'd toyed with his emotions, and who he respected in those moments because of her defiance. Her instinctive usage of the only power she had. Somehow he'd understood her.

'No!' he shouted. He resettled the knife in his hand into a throwing position and spun around towards Quinn.

Quinn saw his new opponent.

'Bastard!' he screamed.

He loosed his last hunting arrow at Victor. It hit him high in the shoulder and the force knocked him over the lock's low fence. His body crashed down onto Liba houseboat fore-deck.

Tom, responding to the uncertainty of the action, shoved

Victor overboard into what was left of the swirling water in the lock. He surfaced, struggling hard, and flailed towards the forward deck railing. Blood seeped from the imbedded arrow wound. The falling water dragged at him. With the 'Beware of Electrified Water' sign immediately above his head, his eyes glazed, maybe from the water peril or just from loss of blood. His hand gripped the railing and somehow he managed to keep his head above the water.

Quinn, obsessed, readied to leap the three meters down on board to finally confront Ana.

Kari scuttled off into the cabin area looking for anyone to help them. 'Blair!' she screamed.

Quinn's gaze closed in again on Ana.

She froze as she saw Quinn outlined against the sky above her. Stood with the fishing rod she'd grabbed as a weapon.

Unable to move.

Feeling his hands about her neck. Again she was choking...

Fire came into her eyes. She sucked in a huge lungful of air and faced Quinn.

There was a flicker of the blue and red lights. A siren blared as the police procession of cars and vans burst through the perimeter wire gate and pushed fast through to the river bank and the massive lock structure.

Above the houseboat Quinn didn't hesitate. He leapt from the top of the dock directly at Ana, ignoring Tom and Blair now with her.

Car doors slammed two metres back from the dock edge.

The action was over in seconds.

Roger Snow, young and quick on his feet, followed ready to jump. Jahan, on the dock, defensively swung the tomahawk style axe; he'd grabbed, at him. Although hit only by the flat of the blade the uniformed policeman went down; poleaxed. He lay unconscious against the lock railings.

On the houseboat deck Blair and Tom struggled to keep Quinn away from the women. He was using the cross bow as a two handed weapon and had the knife in his grip as well.

'Jahan! Get down here!' Quinn shouted.

The prisoner obeyed. He jumped down onto the deck, stumbled to regain his footing, and then confronted the men. It was either fight the men below, and somehow escape, or be captured by the police he saw now arriving en mass.

Tom and Blair pushed Ana and Lauren behind them and dodged weapon blows as they grappled with the two prison hardened escapees.

'Peter! Where the heck are you? We need help!' Tom shouted. He took a blow to the head from Quinn and staggered. Blair pushed the canoe paddle against Jahan's axe.

Ana pushed the fishing rod into Quinn's face. He swore and pulled it out of her hands. 'You fucking whore!' he shouted.

Tom aimed a fist at Quinn.

Quinn ducked and looked up. A fleeting sight of police uniforms made him spin around and sent him running into the cabin. He pushed aside Kari and ran the length of the houseboat and burst out the back door. Still under cover, he climbed a wet and slimy ladder up onto the dock fifty metres away from the police cars and force.

Rick leapt from the second car and yelled for the dogs.

On the dock Shaun Richardson flicked a switch in the K9 cabin. The dogs were free. In a fury of barking they raced way towards the houseboat. As one they leapt down.

The huge German shepherd, Louis, lunged towards Ana.

It grabbed her again, as it had at the prison, and took her bodily down onto the deck. Like before, she curled into a ball as the snapping and barking dog stood over her. She gasped for breath.

The other dog shepherded a screaming Lauren from the melee, and held her guarded against the off side rail.

Quinn ran towards the down river lock gates.

Rick's head jerked towards the movement. He deliberately aimed and fired his revolver.

Quinn, now on the top of the lock gates, took the full force of the bullet in his belly. He clutched at air then, as the darkness came out to meet him, slowly his body went backwards.

Quinn fell off the gates into the river.

The water engulfed him.

Rick calmly holstered his weapon. 'You saw that?' he shouted to Mark. 'I got the bastard!'

'Yes boss, I saw him hit.'

Mark, Jessica Taylor and other police officers, somewhat more cautiously, dropped the three metres onto the boat.

Jessica landed close to Jahan, who was still confronting Tom and Blair, and was hit by a punch. She fell hard against the ice box. She stayed down, her arm at an odd angle.

Another pistol shot sounded and Jahan fell and lay still.

Mark lowered his pistol and above the shouts, yelled 'There's one more! Find him!'

'He's here!' an officer pointed into the water where Victor hung by one hand to the railing.

'I give up! Don't shoot! I'm not going anywhere...' Victor shouted.

With Quinn's arrow still embedded in his right shoulder Victor was hauled aboard and thrown down on the deck. Although he was covered in the sludge and mud from the lock bed he was rolled over, his legs splayed and his left hand held above his head.

Next to Victor, Jahan had not moved.

Chapter 51

Rick, puffing with excursion and adrenalin excitement, started as he slapped his hand against his holstered pistol.

He stared down at the captured man.

Victor's clothing was blood stained and his damaged hand was thrust towards him.

Rick looked at the chaos about him.

Blood everywhere!

Bodies!

Jessica, in uniform, lay on the deck injured. Snow unconscious or dead sprawled on the lock dock above. Now this man clutching his shoulder. Down and injured.

The hand...

His squad - dead and injured...

A bolt of white heat flashed though his mind. Flashback.

The refugee camp...

'No!' Rick yelled and dropped down onto the houseboat's front deck.

He stumbled - as his eyes stared.

Stared at the prisoner at his feet.

'Private...Pritchard...Private Keith Pritchard?' Rick said. His eyes widened further.

A statement more than a question.

A beat of time passed.

Victor thrust his body up to look at Rick. 'Sarg...You here? Last time I saw you was...' He attempted to sit up but a uniformed policeman pushed him down with a none too gentle boot. The prisoner struggled against the restraint. 'Sarg...did you see the girls? They're alive! They made it...never thought they had.'

There was amazement in his voice that transcended his own wretched situation.

Mark moved to stand by Rick.

He was ignored.

Rick's total vision was aimed at the prisoner.

Victor's hand was again thrust towards Rick.

A left hand with the little finger missing.

Rick blinked hard and his eyes became glassy.

'Pritchard,' he said. 'I've got lots of new fingers for you – I've collected them. Saved them for you. I've got a knife like the Toy too. Remember you always called your knife The Toy.' Rick look went from the prisoner at his feet to his raised hand. It curled as though clasping a knife.

'Boss...?' Mark moved in closer to Rick. 'Boss! Are you hurt?'

'No. I'm helping my man.'

Mark eyes widened at the bizarre statement.

The women had been released from the protection of the dogs. Ana and Kari came forward. Both women were distraught and Lauren pushed them away from the confrontation going on at the front of the deck. They huddled together.

Rick looked despairingly around. 'Finger cut off...finger cut off... all I can see was your finger cut off by your own knife.' He turned again to Victor – Keith Pritchard. 'I had to get more for fingers you, my boy...'

'Boss?'

Rick pushed aside Mark's restraining hand.

His eyes became clear again. 'You saw me get Quinn. The bastard ... my first professional murderer given manslaughter!

Wrong! Then my wife left me...wrong!'

Rick struggled against Marks hands. Pushed them aside again.

In a moment of disbelief Mark let his superior officer go.

Rick reached down and pulled a huge military knife from his boot. He crouched and his face changed again. 'Get me Quinn's body. I'll get you another finger, lad ... get the body out of the river.' He waved the knife in the direction where Quinn had fallen. 'It'll surface soon and you can have his finger...'

Mark stepped forward. 'Rick! Give me the knife,' he said.

A flicker.

A look of comprehension and reality came back into Rick's face and he drew his huge strong frame up into a military stance.

Mark tensed; ready to act if he had to against his own superior.

He felt the handler and the dogs go on alert behind him.

There was another beat of time when everyone was still. It seemed to go on forever.

Then reality flooded Rick's eyes and face again and his shoulders and his whole being slumped. 'Yes, you can have the Toy. I don't think I need it any more...' He paused. 'It's all over then, isn't it?'

'Yes Boss. It's over.' He took the knife from his hand then, pulled out Rick's gun from its holder. He passed both items to the local sergeant who had suddenly appeared at his shoulder.

Rick didn't seem to notice.

There was a stunned silence that seemed to shroud the two men and excluded all others.

'You planted the evidence against Quinn...?' Mark said to Rick.

'I had to. It was the only way to get him...'

'I was just getting it figured Boss. There was one piece of evidence, the hair, Boss. Getting it all figured...' Mark said. His voice croaked – he was high still on adrenalin from the fight but he was emotionally exhausted.

'You're going to arrest me?' Rick's voice was clear.

'Boss, I have to… there's no other way. I know you were in Port Lincoln and then Loxton when all the murders were done.'

'Well, you'd better get on with it … even I knew that someone had to stop me,' Rick said. The hushed and quiet officers strained to hear around them in a column of shock. 'It's best that it's you…'

'Charles Rick Charlton you are under arrest for the murders of…Tara Henson, Elizabeth Woods,' Mark said with precision then he halted. 'And …for the life of me I'm ashamed at this moment that I can't remember the other women's names. …And for the witnessed murder of Demetrius Quinn. Cuff him.' He said to an officer standing nearby. Mark sighed. 'Careful…he's a damaged man.'

As the police officer drew the senior detective's arms forward and snapped handcuffs onto his wrists, Rick looked towards Jessica Taylor standing clutching her arm. An air of bewilderment was coupled with the strain of pain on her face.

It's a good thing you refused to go out with me,' he said in a dull voice to her. 'You had the mark…I would have killed you too.'

From the side deck Ana screamed…

Chapter 52

Two hours later Rick Charlton slumped in the back seat of the police car with his eyes closed. He had been rushed there after his arrest and was under guard.

Ambulances had taken Victor, also under guard, Jessica and a now conscious Detective Snow to the Renmark hospital. The houseboat civilians, as Mark had to think of them with everything else demanding his attention, were gently but firmly confined to the houseboat lounge area and the back deck. A police woman was with them and provided cups of tea and coffee from the galley to everyone. The crime scene was confined to the front and side decks and keeping them away was all he could do until the next contingent of more senior police, plus the forensics team arrived.

When Ana had screamed at the sight of Peter's body all Mark could do was hold her against his chest. Envelope her in the safety of his arms until her stunned sister and the other woman arrived to help.

For some reason he couldn't fathom Mark could still feel the shape of her rigid body against him.

See the tangle of dark hair with the stunning white streak. See a pulse leaping in the hollow of her neck and smell the exotic essence of her. Perhaps it was because he'd been involved with her for so long to try to keep her safe, from a distance, without knowing her. Without knowing her face properly. It was something he'd have to think about later, he decided, but her imprint was there. In his mind and on his body.

The local sergeant accompanied him as Mark went towards the car. He carried Rick's weapons wrapped in one of Lauren's new tea towels and opened the boot to find an official evidence bag to put everything in.

'I've got to get...' he couldn't say Rick 'the arrested man back to Renmark. He can't remain here.'

'Yes, Sir. It'd be better.'

'Do what you can for the civilians.

'Yes, Sir.'

'I've got to get them off the houseboat as soon as I can.'

'Sir.'

'For Christ sake – cut the Sir. Can't handle it today. You know my name. Been using it all week.

'OK Mark. It seemed necessary given all that's happened here today.' The Sergeant was an old hand. He knew when a hint of deference to a person's rank could help steady that person during or after an emergency. This young detective had done well given the circumstances that had thrown everyone.

Any action caused ripples but the arrest of a senior serving police officer...

'Thanks - but it's no longer needed.' Mark touched the older man's arm. 'You've been a rock today and thank you... I'll talk to everyone later. Thank them too. They did a good job. You know of a good place then for the civilians?'

'Sure. There's an excellent local pub. Good secluded suites with a private sitting room. I know the owners and they'll look after them well. I'll give them a call.'

'Good.'

'Do you want the police doc to see them before they're moved? Just to clear them as uninjured.'

'Do it, if they'll agree. I'll be back as soon as I've got the prisoner secured.' He gestured towards the lock, the houseboat and the whole area. 'You'd better do a check of the whole area. See if you can locate Quinn's body... and I've got a feeling there's another body.'

'Sir?' slipped out.

'One of the women mentioned a man named Sam.'

'Shit! One of the lock keepers is Sam Reynolds...'

'Find him. God I hope he's not here...and please try to keep this as my crime scene not matter who turns up from Adelaide.'

'Do my best, Mark.' The older man turned away to issue orders to his men. Not much chance of Mark being able to retain this scene. Everyone would go for the glory; or the cover up.

Mark got into the car next to Rick.

Rick looked so weary that his face seemed to have fallen in on itself, like someone caught without their dentures. For the first time ever Mark thought he looked his age. And then some.

Rick'd asked that Mark travel back with him to Renmark. It seemed a reasonable request and was going to be the only time that the two men could speak before all the formalities that had to follow. Not only that but everything would be taken out of his hands when the headquarter heavies, and the Internal Investigation Branch, got involved.

With Rick anyway.

Mark knew his own every action, his every breath, would have a please explain tacked onto it. He would be questioned again and again. The stack of looming paperwork could topple under its weight and sheer volume.

A driver and another uniformed man sat in the front and both seemed to have their ears ramped backwards. The men in the back seat ignored them.

Rick opened one eye. 'The prisoner?' he said as Mark got into the car.

'Yes,' the younger man was closed faced. Angry. 'You've bloody earned the title with all the blood spilled on the deck down there. The women you killed.'

There was a long pause. 'I'm glad it's over,' Rick said. 'I was totally out of control.'

'Hell, Boss...' Mark said as emotions of, rage, disgust and betrayal beat down into his head. He wanted to punch out at the lights of manacled man beside him but only professionalism and training clamped his clenched hands beside his thighs.

'It's time you dropped the 'boss', Mark. It's over.' Rick repeated. The rain started as the car pulled past the broken gateway and turned onto the highway. They gained speed and the low scrubby mallee bush seemed to flash past like tufts of dirty broken green glass. Rick looked sideways at it for a moment before turning towards Mark again. 'Yes, it's done. All done.'

Mark had a hundred questions and he was very aware that he should not be questioning Rick at this stage. Everything had to be by the book.

'We should wait until we get into the interview room,' he said. 'It's all got to go on tape,'

'Nah...I just want to talk. I need some answers too. I'll say it all again for the record. Chapter and verse.' There was a hint of the old humour. 'I'll be the perfect criminal interviewee...confess it all.'

'Alright...but we do have witnesses.' Mark indicated the men in the front. 'Witnesses I'll call if I have to.'

The two police men shuffled in embarrassment in their seats. Ears went pink. Mark noted that the passenger was active with pen and his notebook.

'That's OK. You'll do what you need to.' Rick looked hard at Mark. 'What did I miss? I was sure that I'd covered all my tracks.'

'You almost did.'

'Thought I was doing what I had to do and I'd never be caught.' There was a sideways look towards Mark's side of the car. One that didn't meet his eyes. 'Not unless I was ready to be caught, or I'd topped myself. I left the letters I've already written for you. They're in the Port Lincoln motel room.'

Mark had no answer to this egotistical statement.

'What tipped you?'

'OK. My first hint of oddity was that Lee Thomson did the advanced dive course. Maybe he'd taken up diving after retirement. I was about to check on that when I came over here.'

'I realised that I had to use a different name. I told the dive mob when I arrived that Rick Charlton was sick... They didn't even check that Lee'd done the beginners course. Just let me do it. Must have been my honest face.'

'But when I chased up plane bookings and car hire I found that you were there at that time, and of the first murder.'

Rick grunted. 'Don't miss much do you? With the new travel regs I had to book plane and hire cars in my own name. Show ID.'

Mark pushed on. 'The hair in Naomi Simpson's mouth. She was killed so quickly so how did Quinn's hair get so conveniently there? It didn't quite add up.'

'Wasn't easy. Took planning.'

'We'll get to that. But it was all so pat and you reacted so fast. It was almost as though you'd seen Quinn in Port Lincoln. Or knew that he was there. Did you?'

'I saw the bastard when I came over for the dive course. That set me off...that and the missus clearing out while I was away two years ago. Never understood her going.' The total lucidity that marked Rick's detective work was gone as he rambled on. 'Should've taken her on the Pacific cruise… a holiday I'd promised her instead of going off to do something I wanted to do. I've always been a selfish prick. Maybe none of this would've happened if she hadn't left me about then.' He paused. A long silence.

'I'd kept the vision of the chopped off finger in check all these years. Everything exploded in my head. I was a loser again.'

There was a rattle as Rick tried to poke Mark in the ribs, an old comradely movement. Mark pulled away. One of the police officers looked back into the rear seat.

Rick rattled the cuffs again. 'What else?' he said.

'Then you had a ring they'd found at the dive scene. At first I just passed it off as nothing important as you suggested. But your comment was just too off hand, not like you at all.'

Rick laughed. A mirthless hollow sound. 'The ring was marked A & Q. Didn't you see that? White gold and I'd dirtied it up. Angela and Quinn – Quinn's first victim gave it to him…and I had to be sure that he'd be linked to the killings.'

'Well, I didn't see it. But it was so out of character you playing with a piece of potential evidence. Sure, you'd always had something found in the vicinity of a body – the smelly shells this time - something that connected you in with a victim, but not something so vital.'

'So you saw the initials?'

'No, but the Lincoln man I passed the ring to made out them out. He told me and I followed up the A & Q. Got a connection when I checked the old evidence on the computer. But it was never there. Later I checked with Worm and found that Quinn's hair & other DNA markers were missing. I considered the Lee Thomson notation first. He'd checked it out. Why would he steal the old evidence? Didn't add up at all.'

'Had to use a name. Lee's retirement was useful. Like the dive course.'

'But that ring; it was only mentioned at Quinn's trial. They didn't have it. They'd never had it. I got the old trial transcript and a witness said that Angela gave him it to him. I wondered why it was missing. It wasn't mentioned ever in Quinn's prison possessions lists.'

'Clever little detective, weren't you? Someone must have taught you well.'

Mark frowned at his former boss. 'Couldn't help yourself, could you? What if it'd come out in court and some clever lawyer'd made a connection with his first trial?' he said.

'Stupid in hindsight.'

'But I was too bloody late to stop the Loxton killing! You were pointing the ring out to me before. Did you intend that? You were taking souvenirs like any serial killer...and some of it did you in.'

'Always the clever profiler.' The old sneer surfaced. 'When I saw Quinn out of prison I had to get him. Fixed up for ever, not like the first time, when he got off.'

'Ten years for manslaughter isn't really getting off.'

'It bloody well was to me. When he escaped I went off my head. I'd actually stopped killing. The rage came back and the Loxton woman ... she had to go. I stumbled on her running along the road while I was out on the bike. Killing her was instinct. Tried to make it look like a drug execution by the hands off. I kept the finger. Young Snow wasn't far off when he rattled on about that one. I nearly laughed.'

'I thought you said something to Jessica the night before last?'

'Can't remember...that police woman? Yeah! I asked her out. I would've killed her too.'

'Why?'

'I had to keep the pressure on getting Quinn convicted for

sure this time. Even though he was killing himself on the run. I couldn't be sure that it was him and not one of the other bastards. He might've got off still...' Rick's harsh voice ground almost to a tired halt. 'But I had to keep killing the women. I didn't know how to stop.'

There was a pause as the car tyres ate up the kilometres towards the end of their interaction.

Their partnership. It was over too.

'But the one damming evidence,' Mark said, 'was the small smear of your blood found on the blue Mazda back in Port Lincoln. You were never officially on the scene and there was no way that you could have explained it there. I was the only one who picked that up when the pathologist listed the police and people on site. Your DNA showed up when you were in Adelaide? Impossible!'

'I scratched myself on the bloody prickly bush getting Elizabeth Woods out of the car. Thought it wouldn't be discovered. It was such a little scratch on my ankle I only found it later in the shower. Didn't give it another thought.'

'There's always a slip up. You taught me that...'

There was another moment of silence.

The silence lingered. 'I killed a man today,' Mark said as he stared out of the car window. 'First time...'

'You'll get used to it. Part of the job.'

Mark turned back to face Rick. 'Maybe for you...'

But Rick wasn't interested. He gave a hollow chuckle. 'Private Keith Pritchard,' he said. 'I didn't recognise him as Victor Jones not from the mug shots. Maybe if I'd known ... Nah! It was always Quinn. But life can throw coincidences at you, can't it? Never underestimate the coincidence,' He said in final advice.

Rick closed his eyes and leaned back into the car seat as the first houses, grouped together in clumps to form the outskirts of the township of Renmark, were passed.

Finally Mark had to ask. 'Why did you kill women? And then only dark haired women?'

Without opening his eyes Rick said. 'My wife was dark haired. Like them. Maybe I was killing her for leaving me.'

The excuse sounded lame, especially to Mark from his profiling background. He made no comment.

'Bloody women. Never trust them. They make you have thoughts you shouldn't have.' Rick now turned to look at Mark. 'I never told you my father was a preacher, did I?'

Did that make any difference, Mark wondered, to the madness that had obviously gone on inside Rick's head?

'Did you know that Ana's husband, Peter Foster, was killed today?' Mark asked.

'Eh? Civilian casualty. That'll be an increase the paperwork for you.' It obviously hadn't been a fact that Rick had noticed with his own arrest. 'Always hated the paperwork ... and it was probably his own fault,' he said

Mark looked sharply at Rick. This was irrational. 'He had nothing to do with anything other than trying to protect his wife,' he said.

'Well, she was a pain in the arse. Dead set that Quinn was after her. I suppose he was. I got him because of her, though, so I guess she was useful.'

'Useful! But her husband died...'

'Nothing to do with me.' The older man sighed. 'Gawd... I could do a beer,' he said.

Mark sat looking straight ahead. He felt sick to his stomach and acid rose burning into his throat like a cancer.

It would take time and more than beer to clear it.

Chapter 53

'You're not going to be able to stay on the boat,' the Renmark Sergeant said.

Tom was nursing a blackening eye. He had ice wrapped in another Customs House tea towel pressed against it as he came from the cabin and out onto the back deck by the paddle wheel. They were allowed there, not the front deck where the evidence of bloody carnage lay.

The huge walls of the lock towered still above them and the shallow water in the lock smelt foul.

It was an hour later.

They were all in a state of shock at what had happened. And Peter's death.

God, Tom thought, Peter's dead.

It hadn't sunk in. It was still an abstract with the confusion going on around them. Organised police confusion, but definitely that to the houseboat group.

The two dead bodies still were aboard and Tom grieved further for the indignity of Peter's body still lying there.

'No?' he said. 'We can't stay? Why?'

'This is a crime scene now and it's going to be swarming with our lab people soon. Sorry. And we've still got to get Quinn's body out of the river. Haven't got that yet.'

The Sergeant seemed genuine in his concern for them. He'd been around by the side deck where Peter Foster's body was and seen the man's wife in what he assumed was their bedroom. The curtains were closed but through a gap he could see her lying hunched gripping a pillow and sheets to her face. He knew what she was doing; he'd seen it a couple of times before after a sudden death. Smelling her man's scent maybe for the last time.

'It's going to be hard on Ana...'

'Yes Sir, I know it will.'

'Do you want me to tell the others?'

'It would help but I'll make it official as well. The Liba people have offered you another houseboat. Free of charge. But I thought you'd probably want to be off the river...'

'Yes, somewhere else would be better.'

'I thought so too,' the Sergeant said, 'and I've booked you into a pub in Renmark.'

'A pub. Something quiet I hope.'

'Yes, it's OK. Decent too. You'll be needed for a day or so to make statements. Gotta be done, sir.'

Tom grunted.

'And it's going to be a bit of a climb to get back onto the lock. The bastards jammed the mechanism and we're waiting for someone who knows what they're doing to come and free it up.'

There was no answer to that. No way they could stay and no where they could go on the houseboat if they did.

Catch 22, Tom thought.

Tom shrugged in resignation. He went back inside and the Sergeant walked down the side of the boat. Towels were hanging there and he saw that they were getting wet, not drying, from the rain that had set in.

He quickened his steps. Time to find something to cover the crime area. Rain could contaminate evidence and the Adelaide detectives probably wouldn't want to work in the rain. Get their suits wet.

'Bob, find a tarp or something as quick as you can', he said to one of his officers.

'On it, boss, saw the rain coming. What really happened here, Sir? The senior major crime man arrested by the younger one? It all happened so fast. The men are talking. They want to know...'

'Well, stop them talking. Just get them getting on with their own jobs without chattering. It will all come out eventually.' He stopped. 'I hope it will... I'm not even sure what happened.'

'There'll be a cover up. Always is with the brass.'

'Not this time, Bob, I think it's all too big.'

By eleven thirty the first police procession from Adelaide started.

The houseboat group were still on board Liba 26.

The young officer Mark Llewellyn had come back and taken over the whole scene again. They group had not met him face to face before but they felt a connection from Ana's interaction with him. He came into the lounge area, where they were seated still in stunned silence.

'Do you mind if I leave my stuff here?' he said 'It's easier here than getting back up to the cars again.' In the exposed tee shirt, jeans and scruffy hair he didn't look like the detective he was.

Tired brown eyes looked them over as he went to sit beside Ana. To take her hand. 'I'm so sorry,' he said simply. He offered no platitudes. No, I'm sorry for your loss.

'Thank you,' she said as he released her hand and stood.

'I'll do what I can to get you away from here as soon as I can. The photographers have to have photos, showing the people on board for the trial. There will eventually be one. The senior detectives from Adelaide will also want to interview each of you but I'll try to hold them off until tomorrow.'

'A uniformed copper said that we're to be moved into

Renmark. That's it – we have to go,' Lauren demanded.

'Definitely. For your own good and safety. The press will be here soon and I'd like to get you away before then.'

Outside from the cabin they watched as the two dead men, Peter and Jahan were placed in body bags ready for departure to Adelaide and post mortems.

'Don't make Peter travel with the killer', Ana begged. 'Don't let that happen, please.'

'No I won't,' Mark reassured her.

Lauren and Kira enveloped her in their arms as Mark hesitated. 'I can tell you one thing though. When they get Quinn's body from the river they'll know within twenty four hours what his HIV status was. Your boss at the prison, John, told me that he thought that all was OK from Quinn's records. Nothing makes things better but I can find out for you. No matter what I'll tell you and at least then you'll know.'

'Yes,' she repeated. Comprehension was far away from her eyes. 'At least I'll know...'

'I'll stay in touch with you all the way.' They never doubted him as he shook hands with them all before he left.

Upstream and downstream a procession of craft, houseboats and motor boats waited for Lock 6 to clear so they could pass through.

They were going to have a long wait.

Finally with almost everyone gone, a police car stood sentry duty above on the dock, the silence was almost as bad as the noise.

Blair came to stand beside Tom. 'They've got accommodation set up for us. We can go now. The cars are waiting.'

'I hope that it's OK.' Tom tried a small joke. 'Lauren's used to five-star at least...'

'I doubt she'll get it this time.'

The Renmark Hotel set across the road from the Murray River had a three and a half star rating.

Old, more than a hundred years old, elegant and had quiet areas.

Lauren took one look at the soft lounge suite; the occasional tables topped with a bowl of early pansies, and forgave the lack of the extra stars. A dining table was set and there was a drinks cabinet – full she saw. She was mentally and physically exhausted and would slum it this time. She led Ana to the deepest chair and pushed her unceremoniously into it.

'I need a stiff brandy and dry,' she said. 'How about you?'

Ana rolled her eyes. Sighed. 'Yes please.'

'Tom, you be barman please. Anyone else?'

He poured without the usual pre drinks banter. Brandy for the women and he and Blair had whiskey. The brands were acceptable.

They opened the curtains to reveal the river. Lights made pale patches in the waters along the shore and the willows ruffled their fronds like water birds ruffling feathers.

The next morning left no weather reminders of the gloom of yesterday.

Huge white cumulous clouds pushed easterly under the bluest of skies. Higher up streaks of thin white cirrus stayed motionless. A flock of homing pigeons seemed to have the hotel as a fulcrum as they flashed past in a pirouette of whirling wings. Kari stood at the window watched as they settled into a loft. Someone had an old fashioned hobby.

She'd heard the gentle sniffle of crying over night and had stopped Lauren from going in to Ana. The first grieving was better done alone and in private. Ana had held it all together well and Kari knew that her sister would want it that way. If it became obvious that they were needed they would not let her be on her own. Kari drew her fingers against her eyes. That was not to say that she hadn't shed tears overnight and Blair had held her until, finally, she'd slept for a while.

Today was going to be hard, she thought.

'Mark has called,' Blair said as he snapped shut his phone. 'The cop cars will pick us up at nine.'

Ana came to breakfast but as they left to go to the police station Lauren saw that her croissant had just two tiny half-moon bites taken out of it.

Chapter 54

There were three interview rooms at the Renmark Police Station.

One door was firmly shut and Mark ushered Tom and Lauren into the second and two officers started the taped interview with them. Kari and Blair were asked to wait.

'You can have someone with you if you'd prefer,' Mark said to Ana referring to her sister. 'Your interview will be longer obviously though and it may hold you up if she and Blair have to wait.'

'I'll be alright,' Ana said. She was dressed immaculately in blue slacks and a white blouse. Her hair was loose and the white signature strands framed her face.

He shook hands formally with her noting her cold hand in his warm ones. Blue eyes met brown and his genuine compassion and care flowed to her. Her face looked thinner even overnight.

Death was a bastard! He thought.

It took no prisoners.

Ana, Mark and a female uniformed officer went into the interview room.

It was about the size of her office at the prison. Utilitarian cream and had a small slot of a window high on one wall. Glass bricks filtered the light and, irrationally, she saw that there was a tiny rainbow of refracted sun light bending around the corner wall. A mirror was fitted into the opposite wall.

Mark clicked the recorder on the table. The interview progressed in the same manner as when Mark had interviewed her at the hospital after the prison assault. The content started from the when she left hospital in Port Lincoln and covered just about every moment of her time that was concerned with either Quinn or her interaction with the police. All police.

After about three quarters of an hour he clicked off the tape, stretched and asked the officer to please get coffee for them all.

As the constable left the room he said. 'You're doing a great job and I'm sorry this has to be totally formal and concise. Everyone and everything is under scrutiny – me too.'

'I hope that I've remembered everything as it happened. It's a blur now but I'm doing my best.' During the interview Ana had looked either at her hands on the table or into Mark's eyes. They were direct and kind, but terribly tired. Eyes, so bleak, that looked as though he'd been looking against searing sunlight for days or inwards to dark places.

The sun had moved higher and the rainbow had gone from the wall.

The female officer returned with coffee in paper cups and the tape started again, but this time she faltered. Her narration had got to where Peter had climbed the red cliffs to contact Mark and finally the police 000 number to tell them about the shock and fear when they found stones in the yabby nets. 'Peter came back and told me about it but I guess that's only hearsay when I tell it,' she said. After reading enough of prisoner's court reports she knew that hearsay evidence wasn't admissible in a court of law.

Her hands clenched on the table. He reached and covered one hand. 'It's OK,' he said. 'Relax. I have Peter's call and text on my mobile phone and all 000's are recorded. The message that Quinn was in the area was a turning point for us. Peter's, and your bravery, got him.'

'Thank you,' she said. 'Peter did an amazing thing to go up there in the dark.'

The interview continued.

Every nuance of the day he wanted. What she saw, what she heard said, everything. How had they known about the Lock Master supposedly being on duty at the lock yesterday? Mark smiled slightly, 'Oh, the grounding and Sam coming to the rescue,' he said. 'Was that the first indication that something was wrong?'

'It made us wary. And that's maybe why we were so suspicious when Sam wasn't there when he said he would be. He'd told us he was single...and the man on the lock said he'd gone somewhere with his wife.'

'Did you know the other man on the lock? I caught a mention that you and Kari did?'

'I don't really know. Kari was sure she recognised that he was a soldier we knew from a long time ago. She came to tell me before it all started happening.'

'So you weren't sure?'

'No. Not then.'

You've discussed the prisoner since then?'

Ana nodded. 'A bit. Not much.'

'Did you see Quinn shot?'

'Yes, he was shot and fell backwards out of sight. I looked and saw Rick pointing a gun towards the gates where Quinn had been. Then your Sergeant Rick...?' She paused.

'Charlton' Mark supplied for the recording.

'I only know him as Rick, started shouting a name, and something about fingers. I didn't know what he was talking about and I was trying to see where Peter was...'

She broke down into tears. She hunched into herself.

'You were the one who found your husband.'

'Yes...he was just lying there. And there was blood dripping along the deck and into the water. I can see him...' She looked up at him. 'And I screamed and screamed. I knew he was dead. Alone there and dead.'

Her throat was working as if she wanted to scream again as Mark terminated the interview. 'That's more than enough for now', he said.

Ana left the interview room followed by the two police officers.

Kari came towards her and put a comforting arm about her shoulders. She glared a look at Mark. 'That took a long time,' she said. Blair and I are done already.

'It's alright, Ana said.

The door to the first interview room opened and Rick, with two burly detectives in suits, stepped into the hallway.

Ana looked towards Rick and brushed her hair away from her face.

Rick stopped dead and the two detectives with him closed each side of him. 'Move on,' one of them said.

To Rick or Ana - neither of them moved.

This was the first time that Rick had seen Ana's face and hair without bandages. His face crumbled. Reformed into the bulging eyes and glare of pure hate.

'You!' he said in a cold whisper. 'You're to blame!' He jerked his hands forward. No handcuffs this time. Not needed in the precincts of the police station, they'd thought, given his so far quiet demeanour.

Mark pushed in front of Ana.

Rick's voice broke in a tirade that was directed into Mark's face. 'The camp...she diverted my attention...the fruit...the attack. She was the one! She did it.'   Rick swung again towards Ana. His hands made to upholster a pistol, realised there wasn't one there and instead thrust his pointing hand towards her. Like a knife. He shouted. 'She finished me in the army! Everything's gone! I killed because of her!'

'Boss?' Instinctively Mark reverted to the rank name in shock.

Rick lunged towards Ana.

He was restrained by Mark and the two suits got rumpled.

Ana was pushed back against the wall.

'Miss, you'd better stay of the way,' one of the detectives said.

'No!' Ana said. 'He said he killed because of me? I have a right to know what he means.' She looked desperately at Mark. 'I have a right after all I've been through. A right because of Peter.'

'No!' One of the detectives insisted. 'This isn't the time.'

'You'll never find out the full reasons unless you let me talk now.' Rick's voice had almost returned to normal. Taken on his detective everyday timbre and ways.

Mark looked at him. 'Yes, let him talk. She deserves some explanation.'

'As long as it goes on tape...' the obviously more senior man said and they trooped back into the first larger interview room. The prisoner was put into a chair, the four police officers; Ana, Kari and Blair were left standing.

'So what her husband died yesterday. Collateral damage and serves her right...' Even with the recording going Rick started to flare again.

'You keep this up and it'll end right here and now,' one of the senior police threatened.

'And you'll never know then will you...' Rick said. There was spite in his voice.

Mark wanted to shout – stop the manipulation. Get on with it.

'So...maybe there's justice. It was because of her that my men were killed in that refugee camp. The bastards attacked during the bloody fruit dispersal. If she hadn't acted the way she did we wouldn't have been there to watch her, every day.'

'So you blamed her for your own lack of leadership…?' from the senior man.

'She was the bitch. Defeated Keith Pritchard. Every day. She flaunted herself to get the fruit for herself and her sister!'

'What!' Ana broke in. 'I was what ten, eleven years old?'

'Pritchard wanted you. We all wanted you.'

'That's disgusting,' Ana lifted her chin. Straightened to her body to her full height.

'Yes. There! Just like that….she did it every day. And we came to watch. Then there was the ambush. They killed my men. That's why I've been killing her all the time.'

'It'd nothing to do with me…or Kari.'

Rick's voice faded. 'My father was a good man. A preacher and I was ashamed. Of my thoughts and for letting myself be diverted. Got the blame. That was right.'

'And the fingers?'

'That's all I saw after the ambush. The bloody knife Pritchard called the Toy cut off his finger. It lay there next to her in the dirt. Like a bloody penis. She'd got his penis…'

Chapter 55

Half an hour later five shaken people trooped up the hotel stairs.

Ana went straight to bed but they could hear her dry retching and sobbing in the adjoining toilet. This time the two women went to her and shepherded her into her bed. They sat holding her until her shivering body relaxed and she slept exhausted.

In the afternoon Mark came to the hotel.

'I've news', he said looking for Ana.

'Can it wait? She's finally sleeping properly,' Lauren suggested.

'I'm here.' Ana came into the room. 'Whatever news you have is for all of us.'

Mark hesitated. 'One piece is tough – the other better. Which first?' He tried a smile.

'The tough one first,' Ana said.

'The post mortems have been done. I'm not supposed to tell you but it's not worth my sanity or the respect I've developed for you all not to tell you the results.' He took a deep breathe. 'Peter died instantly. The post mortem showed that the arrow went through his heart and he fell not knowing what hit him.' He reached over and took Ana's hand. 'I wouldn't lie to you. That's exactly what happened.'

Ana sat gripping the hand that held hers. No-one made the inane statement that he wouldn't have suffered as was usually said after such news like that, but each thought that.

'You said you had some better news too. That would be good.' Ana held her breath.

'The prison reports are through and it's official. Demetrius Quinn had clean blood. No HIV – no hepatitis. Nothing.'

'You're sure?'

'Totally. And he broke a toe a month ago. Probably kicking something he shouldn't have at the Port Lincoln house. The local doctor did a blood test. Nothing unusual.'

'God, that's a relief,' from Tom.

'All his stinking badness was in his head. We'll find his body for the final proof but you can be sure.'

'You haven't found him yet?'

'No, but it's only a matter of time. The river is flowing quite fast past Lock 6 from the water that's come down from upstream. He'll surface soon.'

'You're sure?' Ana's voice had a hint of worry.

'Yeah, we're sure. Two of us saw him hit hard and he fell into the river. He's gone. The yabbies'll have him.'

Slowly she exhaled. 'Well, that's something at least,' she said. 'Thank you.' She looked to Lauren and peeled back the large Band-Aid that still covered the bite marks on her hand. 'You said the wounds looked good. You're right and you looked after them well for me. Now I can take this off and let the clean air do the final healing.'

'Those sutures can come out too. I'll do it now…'

The women left the sitting room.

Tom let out the breath they had all been holding. 'Are you still on duty Mark? It's bloody near beer o'clock', he said.

'I can have a beer with you. They've let me off the leash for the day…'

Dinner that evening was much as it had been the night before.

Excellent repast but, although Anna sat with them, she just rearranged the food on her plate and ate virtually nothing. She left the table and went to her room. The men settled for some diverting TV and after a few moments both Lauren and Kari followed Ana.

She sat on her bed. Still, tearless and she held Peter's hair brush. She put it away behind her body.

'We're here...' Kari said as they sat one on each side of her.

Lauren took her injured hand, turned it over and looked at the healing wounds. 'I don't know how you are coping,' she said.

Kari shook her head. No don't go there, she thought. Bull at a gate Lauren. Not now.

'I've never lost anyone really close to me,' Lauren said. 'How are you putting one foot in front of the other? I don't think I could get out of bed if something happened to Tom like this.'

Ana squeezed Lauren's hand. Almost comforting her friend. 'Nothing else I can do...'

Kari started to say something but Lauren went on. 'He wasn't there was he? Peter wasn't there in that terrible body bag, was he?'

'No he wasn't. He was gone.'

'Tell me about Peter, Ana. Not the big things but the little things. Where will you see him?'

Ana broke hand contact and palmed her eyes. 'I see him in the garden. He liked digging. Planting flowers. Watching them grow sitting on an old chair he'd pulled out from the shed. He'd put herbs in with the flowers.' The faintest of smiles came.

'So he'll be in the garden then?'

'Yes.' A pause. 'And in the kitchen. He'd sit on a breakfast stool and watch me cook. We'd have a glass of wine. He'd always mash the potatoes. Put onion and herbs in with them. Too much butter. Mash them so long they'd be getting cold. Peter thought he was a good cook because of it.'

'He'll be with you. Always.'

'Yes, always.' She laid her head on Lauren's shoulder. 'Thank you,' she said. Kari cuddled in on the other side. Over the top of Ana's head Kari mouthed, 'Thank you.'

There comes a moment that most woman would never forget. Ana's came next morning.

She woke tired and pasty still.

Kari met her before breakfast and said. 'I think you're pregnant.'

'No?' Ana said. 'It's possible but I don't think so. It's that psychic nose of yours isn't it?'

'I got a pregnancy test from the chemist yesterday on the off chance.'

'You didn't. You never fail to amaze me.'

Ana disappeared. She was away a long time. Finally, when Kari was just about to go to look for her Ana returned. She seemed to stand taller.

There was a wavering smile on her face. 'Peter and I are going to have a baby. To become parents.'

Kari whooped and the rest of them, taking their cue from her, enfolded Ana in their arms amid congratulations.

'The rabbit died...that's what they used to say isn't it?' Blair said in his clumsy big man way.

'Well - at least the test bars turned pink!' Ana was serious for a minute. 'I'm not sure about things. So much to do...But this means that I have to go forward... and Peter does too.'

Chapter 56

72 hours previously...

A shadow moved across the Murray River under the lee of Lock 6.

It hesitated then allowed itself to be drawn into the torrent of spill water that flowed through the weir. It reached the bank and huddled into a clump of reeds.

As night finally came and the river gave up a soft mirrored sunset, it floated two kilometres downstream to an old deserted houseboat.

A shadow of pain, hate and avowed revenge...

The End

ABOUT THE AUTHOR

Rendezvous at Lock 6 is my first full-length novel after many years of writing short stories and poetry. Mystery, thriller and Sci-Fi are my favoured genres with the main interaction between people. I have been successful in winning many competition over the years. A short animated film *The Long Beach* was made from my story of the same name and was short at Short Film Festivals including in the USA, Europe, South America and within Australia. I also wrote the script for that production. Currently my short story *Walking with Granddad* is about to be read nationally as part of the ABC Open Program.

A follow-up thriller to *Rendezvous at Lock 6* – *Rendezvous in the Red Centre*, is in production.

On the personal level, I am a retired Social Worker / Counsellor who has had the 'writing bug' my whole life. Retirement has finally given me the time to write to novel length given I've studied, raised a family and worked until now. My storytelling landscape is Australian as 'that's me' and I love the vast diversity… although I have ventured overseas.

Helen van Rooijen
helenvr@southernphone.com.au